SCATTERED SOULS TRILOGY

Die Alive

By ASHBORN RAVEN

Cover design by Ashborn Raven

For everyone who has ever loved someone back from the edge—and for those who needed it and never said so.

CONTENT WARNING

This book contains themes that may be distressing to some readers, including:

Mentions of rape

Mentions of sexual assault

Forced proximity

Accidental pregnancy

Pregnancy loss

Psychological abuse

Trauma responses, including panic attacks, dissociation, and nightmares

Medical trauma

Stalking

Obsessive behavior

Power imbalance in relationships

Violence

Unethical hacking

Captivity

Mentions of self-harm

Explicit sexual content

Voyeurism

Bondage

Reader discretion is advised.

Listen along while reading:

"One Way or Another" — Giorgio Moroder

"Hands on Me" — RHYXA

"Dirty Mind" — Boy Epic

"Nothing's Gonna Stop Us Now" — Starship

"This Year's Love" — David Gray

"Bad Angel" — Nikki Idol

"Inhale Me" — 88DS

"Triggered" — Chase Atlantic

"Say Yea" — Niykee Heaton

"Lady, Touch Yourself" — Nikki Idol

"Seven Devils" — Florence and the Machine

"My Way" — Crucifix

ABOUT THE AUTHOR

Ashborn Raven writes dark, emotionally driven stories that explore the edges of control, trauma, and obsession.

Drawing from a background shaped by discipline and high-stakes environments, her work delves into the complexities of power, survival, and human connection.

Die Alive is the first installment in the Scattered Souls Trilogy.

PROLOGUE

"You don't need all that," Michael calls over his shoulder as I reach for my full riding gear.

It's ironic, he's the one who never rides without armor, yet tonight he wants nothing between him and the wind but hope and a leather jacket.

I hesitate. Six months on tour has turned me into a machine: rehearsals, flights, soundchecks, interviews. My body aches with fatigue, and perhaps a bit of daring is just the ticket.

So, I toss the gear on the bed and give him a small nod.

"Remember, we have an early start tomorrow," I remind him, pressing a gentle kiss to the back of his hand.

He smiles like a man who grew up with mountains in his lungs. Michael has always talked about these rides, the summit runs, the hidden overlooks, the way the sky feels bigger up here.

He's been riding longer than I've even known him, and when he taught me, something just... clicked. I never expected to love it.

But God, I do. The freedom. The thrill. The way the world blurs into something that finally feels quiet.

If it were up to me, I'd travel to every city strapped to my blacked-out Ducati Panigale V4, a second-anniversary gift from Michael that still makes me blush.

We link arms as we head down to the parking garage, my boots clicking on the concrete. I can't help smiling. I rarely pause long enough to appreciate my life, but right now, wrapped against his side, I feel it.

Two number 1 albums. A handful of awards. A career I built from nothing. And a man who loves me with the same fire I love him so, I really can't complain.

"Ms. Delvine, we leave early for Las Vegas," Jaxon calls out as we pass by.

"I remember, Jaxon. Thank you."

The moment we hit the road, I understand why Michael didn't want me covered head-to-toe. The wind bites at my skin—sharp, cold, alive. I've never felt anything like it.

I'm usually the one choosing safety over thrill, but Michael insisted I try this once. Just once. The only thing I refuse to compromise on is my helmet. Different states, different laws—but I kind of need my brain to function.

Michael motions ahead. Whispering Crest is close.

He's talked about these mountains for as long as I've known him, even before he ever dared to kiss me.

When we finally park and cut the engines, the silence is unreal. I slide off the bike and peel off my helmet. I freeze.

The sky is drowning in stars. A billion of them, maybe more, spread across the universe like someone shattered a galaxy just for us.

"It's beautiful," I breathe. "I don't think I want to leave."

Michael just chuckles, low, knowing, like he's been waiting years to prove his point.

He grabs me by the waist and kisses me hard and fast, the kind of kiss that steals the cold straight from the air.

Up here, above the noise and the spotlight and the endless demands, something shifts inside me. I could live on this summit. Forget fame. Forget business. Forget everything. This feels like home.

"Come here," Michael says, tugging my hand and drawing me toward the edge of the overlook. "I told you I wanted to show you what living is really about. You can't get this in the city."

He's right. The stars spill across the sky like someone shattered glass over velvet, and the distant skyline glows faintly below us. It's impossible to look away. And I can feel him watching me, too.

Not in that intrusive, heavy way when strangers stare. I'm used to that. But Michael watches me like he's afraid this moment will disappear.

He usually hides it well, careful not to make me uncomfortable, but he doesn't know that I love it... the way his eyes travel over me, reverent instead of hungry.

He guides me to a huge boulder, and we sit, legs brushing lightly. "Would you live here, if you could?"

I laugh softly, still staring at the sky. "Not now, but someday I could. With you."

A streak of light arcs overhead, then another. It feels like the universe is performing just for us. He doesn't respond out loud, but he doesn't need to. I know he misses this place.

The simplicity. The normalcy he gave up when he became the drummer... and fell for the rock star.

We sit for what feels like minutes, but when I glance at my watch, hours have slipped by. Time bends differently up here.

"You ready?" I ask, standing to take in the view one last time.

The air is colder now, sharper, like the mountain is reminding me we don't belong here forever.

But when I turn, Michael isn't beside me.

"Michael?"

He steps out from behind a cluster of trees, shaking one leg like he's trying to get a wrapper off his boot.

"Had to take a leak," he says casually.

I blink at him. Why do guys always shake their legs afterward? Dominance? Reflex? Ritual? I'll never know.

"Let me take a good look at you," Michael murmurs, spinning me lightly by the shoulders.

Two years together and his affection still hits me in unexpected waves, soft and steady reminders of how deeply he loves.

I grab my helmet and swing a leg over the bike, but before I can settle, he steps in front of me. His hands frame my face, warm and sure, like he's memorizing me all over again.

His mouth meets mine in a kiss that steals my balance more than the bike ever could. It's deep, deliberate, full of everything he never says out loud. When he parts my lips, I melt into him without hesitation.

I always do.

There's something about the way he kisses, like every time is the first, like he's relearning me, like he never plans to stop.

When he finally pulls back, I'm breathless... and he's still looking at me like I'm the only thing in his entire world worth seeing.

Easing out onto the winding road, and I feel shaking in the engine's hum, something that wasn't there before. And Michael is nowhere in sight, only his taillight a faint red dot down the mountain.

But Something's wrong, very wrong. The handlebars start to tremble beneath my palms, a subtle shake that turns violent in seconds. The whole bike vibrates like it's coming apart under me.

"What the hell...?" My voice is swallowed by the helmet, the wind, the engine screaming louder than I can. Up ahead, Michael rides steady, oblivious, just far enough that he can't hear me. I try anyway.

"Michael!" It comes out strangled, useless.

The front wheel wobbles harder. So, I ease off the throttle, but nothing. No control. No response. It's like the bike isn't listening to me anymore, like someone else has taken over.

Panic claws up my spine. I try to steady the line. I fail. The curve is coming too fast. My stomach drops and my mind flashes white. I'm not going to make it. This is it. I know it before the tires even leave the pavement.

CHAPTER 1

ELLIA

“I am not sure I am ready for this,” I say as I am motioning towards all the clothes and makeup that are set up in the penthouse.

I know I agreed, but it doesn’t seem right.

“But you are. Where is that spitfire, ambitious teen I knew all those years ago? You are one of the strongest people I know, and I know many.”

Abby, my agent, has been with me since I was a wild teen giving my dad shit. She has seen me through the laughs and tears, and not once has she given up on me. Whether she can tell I am starting to give up or not, she will understand whichever move I make, maybe.

“I am not the same person I was all those years ago; hell, I am not that person I was a little over a year ago. She died on that mountain, Abby.”

“I will not have you talk of all that nonsense. You hear me? I will not stand for that,” Abby voiced while watching me turn my nose up at all the clothes laid before me.

“Fine, but we need to do something about these clothes. I cannot wear what I used to, not even close.”

Abby has been a stone’s throw away since that day I woke in the hospital. If there is anyone I could count on, it would be Abby. And maybe a few others.

Abby waved her hand at Cole and Hunter, signaling them to collect the rejected outfits. "We'll salvage what we can," she said, her voice tight with concern. "But with the press tour just weeks away, the Grammys around the corner, and the album release..."

She paused, choosing her words carefully.

"Are you absolutely certain about scrapping everything?" Her eyes searched mine, waiting for confirmation that I wasn't making a mistake.

“Yep,” I murmur over my shoulder as I walk away.

“Okay then,” Jason says enthusiastically.

Gathering everything, “we will be back in a few days with a fresh start.”

My signature wardrobe lately has been oversized hoodies, loose shirts, and sweats. Armor disguised as comfort. Clothes that hide the scars I still can't face in the mirror. And if I can't stand the sight of them, why would the rest of the world?

I watch the team roll out with the clothing racks, metal hangers clinking softly as they disappear toward the private elevator. It fills quickly, a jumble of fabric, garment bags, and bodies. I can barely see Hunter wedged in the back, and the man is massive.

As the elevator descends, I head toward the kitchen, where I know my lead security is taking up space.

This penthouse has been my sanctuary since I returned from the hospital. With floor-to-wall glass windows overlooking Lake Coeur d'Alene, the distant mountains, and the kind of sky you could fall into if you stared too long.

During the day, the light spills across the polished white marble floors, and at night, the stars reflect, as if the universe is leaning in to watch me breathe.

The living room stretches before me, silent and pristine, like a museum exhibit where I happen to live.

At its center sits my oversized black U-shaped couch, a dark island where I can disappear when the world's gaze becomes too much.

Across from it hangs a flat-screen TV, my window to fictional troubles that make mine seem both enormous and insignificant at once.

A partial glass divider separates the master bedroom from the rest of the space. Inside, my bed hugs the floor, sheets twisted from restless nights, the sole evidence that these pristine rooms aren't just for show.

Beyond that, the ensuite bathroom gleams with polished stone surfaces, its elegance a cruel joke against the woman who can barely meet her own eyes in its mirrors.

The kitchen, to the left. Stainless steel, matte black cabinets, a table I rarely sit at unless Jaxon either forces me to eat or him catching up on life events on the small TV tucked in the back corner.

Two rooms branch off from the main area: my office, a chaotic island in this sea of minimalism, where lyric notebooks, contracts, and sheet music pile up beside pens that inevitably fail me when inspiration strikes. My team delivered these supplies months ago, believing I'd start writing again. I wasn't ready.

Now Jaxon runs his operations from there instead.

The second room is a spare bedroom that sits pristine and untouched, its perfect emptiness somehow louder than any mess could be.

The circular staircase coils up from the open hallway like a ribbon of iron and glass. I've lost count of how many nights I've stood at the bottom of those steps, wondering if I'd make it up them, wondering whom I'd have to become once I did. Because the second floor is quite different from the first.

Downstairs is who I really am. Up here is who the world thinks I should be.

At the top of the staircase, the glam room waits like a spotlight I never asked for. Vanity mirrors lined with soft bulbs, makeup cases stacked neatly, rolling racks of clothes arranged by color and style.

The air always smells faintly of hairspray and perfume, and sometimes, if I am honest, of exhaustion. This is where stylists could transform me into Ellia Mae, the performer. The product. The brand.

A short hallway leads toward the gym. And the two spare rooms sit on the opposite side of the floor, identical in layout but empty in different ways. One of them hasn't held more than dust and silence.

The other... Jaxon has unofficially claimed it as his own. He never said it outright, but the folded blankets, the neatly lined boots, the hum of his late-night phone calls. I haven't said it, but his presence here gives me a sense of security.

He stays because he worries. He stays because he refuses to leave me alone. And I should be grateful. Maybe I am. But after a year in this house, he's seen me in moments no one should witness, when the mask slips, when the shaking starts, when I'm too shattered to pretend I'm fine.

He's seen me beyond broken, and even though his presence is meant to protect me, sometimes it feels like a mirror I can't escape.

When I step into the kitchen, the first thing I see is Jaxon at the table, a mug of coffee cupped in his hands, the morning news flickering across the small screen.

He glances up long enough to give me a nod, and I answer with a faint smile before sliding into the chair beside him.

Morning after morning, I find him already there, eyes fixed on the television screen, scanning headlines and scrolling text as if searching for ghosts among the living.

He never says it aloud, but I know he hasn't forgiven himself for that night. The guilt sits on him like a shadow he can't shake, tightening his jaw, sharpening the lines around his eyes. He thinks he should've stopped it, should've known, should've done something more. But he did do something. He found me.

I don't know the details, not the ones that matter. I've never asked. I'm not sure I could survive hearing them. But pieces slip through anyway, in the way he watches me, in the way his hand tightens around his mug, in the way his eyes soften every time they meet mine.

There's a hurt there he'll never name, and I carry my own version of it. We are just two ghosts sitting at a kitchen table, pretending coffee can fix anything.

"Any word?" I finally ask, my voice barely more than a breath.

The silence between us cracks like thin ice.

Jaxon doesn't look away from the screen. "No."

He exhales, slow and controlled, the way he does when he's trying not to scare me. "But the fact they haven't turned up on the news doesn't mean a damn thing. Don't read into it."

His jaw flexes, finally turning to me, eyes steady, voice low. "I still have my sources pushing nonstop. We will find them, Miss. Delvine."

He says it like a promise. But underneath, I hear the fear he won't admit, the fear that maybe this time, even he is already too late.

Jaxon used to be just another part of my security detail, one more set of sharp eyes in a black suit. That changed when David decided to retire and spend more time with his family, and suddenly, I needed a new personal bodyguard.

I was more than ecstatic when he broke the news to my manager, Faith. Dave had been with me since before I even had a name anyone recognized, but the idea of Jaxon stepping into that role... it felt right in a way I couldn't quite explain.

When Jaxon took over three years ago, he added more personnel, vetted anyone who came near me, and stayed close.

I don't know if he has a family; he has never mentioned anyone, well, except August, his best friend, the rugby player from down under.

I have to crane my neck to look at Jaxon when he stands this close. Even at my 5'11, he makes me feel small.

When he turns back to me, those eyes catch the light, not just green, but something deeper, like lake water where the depth suddenly drops away.

His black hair falls across his forehead when he leans down, and the tattoos climbing up his neck disappear beneath his collar, hinting at a canvas that continues unseen. I've caught myself wondering where those patterns end. When he smiles, something inside me goes liquid, unstable, and I have to press my knees together to stay steady.

There's a bottled-up anger simmering beneath his skin, radiating from him so intensely it makes the air feel charged. Before the accident, he would study me and keep his distance, well, as much as this job would allow. Now, he doesn't exactly hide, even though he tries.

I nod in agreement, hoping he doesn't feel the agitation radiating from me.

I don't say much to him throughout the day, but having him near keeps some of me at ease. The rest, I am furious. I want to murder someone, well, a couple. I want justice.

CHAPTER 2

JAXON

Three hundred and sixty-five days. Three hundred and sixty-five fucking days. And now this thing I can't name is taking root, this cold weight settling in my chest.

What if they're gone for good? What if there's no trail left to follow?

I push the thought away the moment it forms, but it leaves its fingerprints behind. A stain spreading wider with each sunset. But I'll be damned if Ellia catches even a glimpse of it.

If she catches worry in my eyes, if she senses even a crack in my confidence, then whatever hope she's holding onto will shatter. And I can't have that. I will not let that be the thing that breaks her. There's too little of her left to lose.

I've seen this woman in every version of herself— at her brightest, laughing like the world couldn't touch her, at her lowest, curled into a silence no one else could reach, and once... the version I still can't talk about, the night I found her on that mountain.

There were signs before that night, tiny shifts most people would miss, but not me. I'm her head of security, her shadow. Watching her is my job. But somewhere along the way, it became more than that. I knew her patterns, her rhythms, and her tells. Ellia never stayed out late without checking in.

Never disappeared for hours. And when Michael didn't bring her home, when he didn't come back at all, something in me snapped.

I didn't tell her the whole story. Not about August, not about what he saw, not about how fast he showed up when I called. And what Ellia doesn't know, what I'll probably take to my grave, is that months earlier, I put trackers on all her vehicles.

A security precaution, that's what I told myself.

But deep down, I knew it wasn't just that. There was something about Michael that never sat right with me. And I was right.

Michael had wondering eyes, but Ellia never noticed, which probably would have saved her from his deception if she had. In the pit of my stomach, I knew he was another piece of shit. But he was her "soul mate".

I came close to telling her a few times, but each time that fucker popped out of nowhere, like he was lying and waiting in the shadows, like a fly waiting to pounce on a new pile of shit. I shake my head to push that memory down.

The moment her tracker flatlined on that mountain slope, everything around me ceased to exist. In my bones, I felt it. Christ, I knew what we'd find.

When we got there, she lay still as death. Her skin held a chill that had no business existing on such a warm summer evening. No rise and fall of breath.

The impact had shredded most of her clothes, leaving them hanging in tatters. The state of her jeans—no, I can't let myself go there again, but I felt something inside me snap when I saw her lying there, stripped of fight, stripped of breath.

I don't know how long I stayed on my knees beside her that night, trying to pull her back, begging her to breathe, to stay, not to leave me, not now, not like this.

She couldn't hear me, not a damn word, but I said it anyway. Over and over.

I get up to refill my coffee, fully aware her amber eyes are glued to me. Always looking for guidance, for support. She has it, but I can't fix this.

It has been a year, and nothing. Like the fucker disappeared into thin air. Along with that bitch of a so-called best friend.

According to the stories I'd overheard, Ellia and Robyn had been joined at the hip since high school. Some best friend. She was Ellia's personal assistant, standing 5'6" with those wide blue eyes and that strawberry blonde hair.

Robyn knew exactly what weapons she carried, and she aimed them straight at Michael. She didn't hesitate to betray fifteen years of friendship for a night in his bed. I know she had a hand in tampering with her bike.

When August saw her lying there hurt, bleeding, so still, he mistook her for gone, and something snapped in him just as hard.

August isn't built for the kind of brutal world Ellia and I have been dragged through. Not the way I am.

He'd never seen her like that. Hell, I wish I had never had. But that night didn't care about what any of us were ready for.

All I know is that when she finally gasped, a tiny, ragged sound that barely counted as life, and I nearly broke with it. She came back. Barely. But she came back.

And that's why I can't doubt out loud. Not to her. Not ever. Because if she loses faith, then they win. And I refuse to let that happen. Not after what they took. Not after what I saw.

I shake my head to push the memories away.

"How are you holding up with the whole comeback?" I murmur, taking a slow sip of my coffee, like it'll hide the fact that I'm watching every flicker in her expression.

Ellia stares into her mug for a long moment before answering. "I'm not sure yet." Her voice is soft, thin around the edges.

"I know I should be ecstatic, excited to be back on the road, to see my fans again, but my body still wants to hide. It's like... It's like I want to crawl into a corner and never see the world again."

She looks up, her amber eyes catching mine before sliding away like water over stone. "What if there's nothing left to bring back?" The question settles between us with the weight of confession. "What if Ellia Delvine died on that mountain, and everyone's just too afraid to admit it?"

I recognize the abyss opening beneath her words and not just fear, but a terrible clarity. She's not asking for reassurance. She's asking if I see it too.

"I wonder sometimes," I admit, leaning forward, my voice a shelter built between us, "if we're all just ghosts pretending we survived our worst moments."

The honesty costs me, but I offer it anyway. "Maybe the trick isn't coming back. Maybe it's learning to haunt yourself differently."

She hangs her head as if defeated. But she is far from defeated. Even if I have to show her how far from being broken she really is. I will stitch and piece every little part of her until she is whole again.

She is mine, and she will realize that one day. Every scar, every broken piece. She thinks it is a burden, every tear that she has yet to shed. Mine.

Ellia wasn't always this fragile. Before that night, courage ran through her veins like wildfire. One trauma at her lover's hands stole what came to her as naturally as breathing.

I remember how she'd enter rooms, commanding attention without trying, that signature white streak flashing behind her left ear against midnight-black hair. Though she barely reached my shoulder, she moved with such certainty that everyone looked up to her, not down. That's the woman I'm fighting to bring back.

I search her amber eyes for that old fire, that spark that used to make stadiums full of people hold their breath. It may be buried now, like embers under ash, but I know every part of the star she was is still there, just waiting for enough oxygen to catch flame again.

The silence between us grows thick, almost palpable, pressing against the room like it has something to say, then, barely above a whisper, she murmurs, “Jaxon... I don’t think I’m as strong as I keep telling everyone. Maybe I should delay the comeback, just... a little longer.”

Her voice doesn’t crack, but something inside it does. Something small. Something she’s been holding together with sheer force of will. And hearing it, hearing her say it, cuts deeper than I’m prepared for.

CHAPTER 3

ELLIA

The silence in the room pressed against my eardrums like damp fabric until my phone vibrated against the slick surface of the table. I lifted it and saw Faith's name lighting up the screen.

The video connects, and there sit both Faith and Jo. "This ought to be good," I say as I thumb the phone screen.

Meeting Faith for the first time is like being hit by a freight train painted hot pink: immediate, unavoidable. She's the living, breathing reincarnation of Estelle from Friends, the gravel-voiced, chain-smoking matriarch of blunt pronouncements, ash-stained fingertips forever tapping against her coffee cup.

Opinions tumble out of her mouth in jagged shards; you never asked, you never wanted them, but you end up swallowing every last one.

But unlike Estelle from Friends, Faith is the gayest lesbian I've ever known. She's wed to Josephine, my publicist, and together they're a two-headed chaos machine.

Faith's swagger could fluster half my security detail, and whenever those two tag-team me, it's always "for my own good," of course.

I brace myself. With a sharp inhale, Faith asks, "Ellia, how are you holding up?"

I want to scream that I'm alive and breathing is all the report anyone needs. Michael isn't dead yet. I'm still here, still breathing.

"Breathing," I murmur. "What do you need?"

Everyone tiptoes around me now, like I'm made of glass that might shatter if they breathe wrong.

Since that night, since I crawled out of hell with my skin still smoking. And sure, I understand, they witnessed me unravel in real time. But they've got it all wrong. I'm not some delicate thing that needs protecting. I'm scorched earth, still smoldering.

Faith makes a soft clack, leaning forward to tap the ash from her cigarette into an overflowing tray. "We need you to approve some changes to your upcoming press tour."

"Not a problem," I murmur, pinning my gaze on the flecked marble floor. "When can we meet?"

Her exhale rattles the ashtray. Faith and Jo exchange a look. Jo's dressed in a crisp pencil skirt and a pastel blouse that makes her seem almost chirpy, as if she floats on a cloud of scented candles. But there's a rehearsed edge to her brightness, like sugar-coated poison.

"Well..." She falters, fumbling for the words.

I raise an eyebrow. "Jo."

"Sorry." She clears her throat. "Faith and I were thinking, you should make your comeback on The View."

My gut twists. The View: where strangers dissect each other's lives over drinking glasses of hot coffee and manufactured outrage.

"I think the fuck not. You've lost your ever-loving minds." I hear Jaxon snicker behind me.

Faith's voice dips an octave as she jumps in, her tone practiced.

"They're offering... a lot, Ellia."

I press my thumb against the bridge of my nose. "Define a lot."

Faith takes a sharp drag, the ember glowing red in the dim light. "Six figures."

I close my eyes against the glare of that number.

"They want to claim they 'brought Ellia Delvine back from the ashes.' Their words." Jo's bright inflection makes my skin crawl.

I turn to Jaxon, my head of security, meeting his stormy gaze. His jaw is clenched, tattooed arms crossed as though daring anyone to argue. He doesn't need to speak; his expression says it all.

"Faith," I say slowly, letting each syllable land. "I hate The View and everything they stand for."

"We know," Jo chirps. "We told them. They don't care."

Faith snorts. "Honestly, I respect their desperation."

I rake a hand through my tangled hair, irritation prickling at my temples. "Why the hell would they offer that?"

There's a pause. Faith's voice turns gravelly, serious. "Because you vanished, Ellia. Because you survived. And because they want you to recount that night, in your own words."

My stomach twists into knots. Jaxon's glare sharpens, a silent promise of retribution.

"No," I say, firm as stone. "I'm not letting five camera-ready strangers tear apart my trauma over morning coffee."

Faith clicks her tongue. "We figured you'd say that. They'll send a revised offer, probably with more glitter."

I groan, sinking back into the chair.

"I'd rather go skydiving with a faulty parachute."

Jaxon mutters under his breath, so low I can barely hear: "Over my dead body."

Faith perks up. "See? Even the guard dog agrees."

I huff. "You two play nice."

"Mm-hm," Faith replies, voice dripping sarcasm. "When I'm the queen of England."

I can almost feel them whispering behind my back, but I force myself to look away.

"No," I say flatly, letting the single word hang like a gauntlet.

"Understood. We'll be in touch," Faith replies, and then the line clicks dead.

At least they've stopped pushing, temporarily. Now I just hope everyone else will.

"Ms. Delvine." Jaxon's voice cuts in; smooth, steel-edged.

I let out a tired exhale, not bothering to mask my annoyance. "Jaxon, for the millionth time, call me Ellia. Mrs. Delvine is my mother."

He doesn't answer right away, but when he does, his voice resonates in that gravelly way that can pull you back to earth even when your mind's careening into space. "Would you like to take a walk down to the lake?"

He must sense the storm roiling inside me, the fight I'm losing, and I finally released the breath I didn't know I'd been holding. "Take me somewhere," I whisper, voice cracking. "Anywhere."

"Ms. Delv..." He stops himself, jaw tightening for a fraction of a second.

“Ellia.” He says it carefully, like he’s afraid of breaking something fragile. Or crossing a line he knows he’s already too close to.

“You’ve only just started down this path for your comeback. Do you really think taking a trip right now is a good idea?”

Jaxon pauses and settles into his usual seat, his eyes drinking me in like he’s memorizing me, like he’s afraid I might disappear again. And he’s not wrong to worry.

When the world feels too loud, I retreat to my own room for days. Or when I know I am on the verge of breaking completely. When breathing starts to feel like a performance.

I’m not strong enough to deliver. I don’t mean to shut people out, but I can’t seem to help it. Solitude has become easier than navigating the sharp edges of uncomfortable tension. So, I choose the quiet. I chose the walls of my room to disappear.

I stay hidden most days, like when the thoughts and scattered memories take over.

The fears don’t just show up anymore; they control my whole life. Coming in waves is my only salvation these days. But when they hit, it’s the kind that knocks you down even when you thought you were standing steady.

And every time I finally step back out, Jaxon looks at me like this, like he’s counting the seconds, measuring the distance, making sure I haven’t slipped away again.

Jaxon's gaze lingers, and I feel myself fracture along invisible fault lines. The break is silent, imperceptible to anyone watching, but his eyes narrow slightly, catching the tremor before I can mask it. He always does.

“I’m fine,” I say, out of habit more than truth, rubbing my temples, in hopes he believes me.

His eyebrow arches upward in a half challenge, half question, silently informing me that my words might fool others, but never him.

My fingers tighten around my mug. I look down, then up, then finally meet his eyes.

“I just...”

The words snag in my throat, sharp and unfamiliar. “It still feels like I’m... coming apart. Even when I look put together.”

A silence settles between us, softer than before, almost careful, and Jaxon leans forward, forearms braced on the table, voice low.

"Elli..."

It's the way he says it so quietly, reverent, like the nickname is a promise instead of a word, that does me in.

My chest tightens, and the air shifts. And suddenly, hiding feels harder than admitting the truth.

"Some days I feel like I'm drowning in my skin," I whisper.

The confession slips out before I can reel it back in.

I blink, startled that I even said it. "I didn't mean to..."

"Ellia," he cuts in, soft but certain. His gaze doesn't waver. "You don't have to explain the parts you're not ready to face."

I swallow hard. Because that right there is more comfort than anyone's managed to give me in a year.

CHAPTER 4

ELLIA

Stepping onto my jet feels like crossing into another world, one I built long before everything fell apart, one that still doesn't quite feel like it belongs to me anymore.

The Gulfstream G650 is a sleek shadow against the tarmac, all polished black metal and quiet power.

Inside, the cabin opens up with smooth lines of matte black leather and soft lighting, spacious enough to hold my entire team when we're touring.

Today, though, the space echoes with absence. This plane used to buzz with my entourage, their voices filling every corner.

The leather seats are spacious, made to fold into beds when needed.

Toward the rear is a furnished bedroom, and a bathroom finished in matte black stone and soft amber light; warm, quiet, and crafted entirely for me. It feels like stepping into my private retreat, not a jet meant for touring.

Behind me, I hear Jaxon step inside with heavy boots and his controlled stride, that ever-present awareness rolling off him like a second skin.

Our steward straightens immediately. "Good afternoon, Ms. Delv..."

Jaxon cuts him off before the sentence has a chance to breathe. "How long is the flight time?" His tone is crisp, all business.

The steward blinks, thrown for half a second. "Uh, eighteen hours, sir."

"Crew count?"

"Just the three of us today."

Jaxon nods once. Efficient. "Meals?"

"Prepared and ready whenever you are," the steward replies, posture tightening as if he's suddenly standing inspection.

Jaxon's eyes flick around the cabin, assessing every detail in seconds—the exits, the spacing, the staff, the distance between every object and me. His presence fills the jet long before he even glances in my direction.

I don't know whether to roll my eyes or breathe easier. Maybe both. This man knows how to control a room, or a jet, for that matter. No nonsense, straight to the point, commanding without even trying.

And God help me, the way he does it... the butterflies he gives me are ridiculous.

The first time I saw him, my breath caught in my throat, well before that night on the mountain. While I stand tall at 5'11", Jaxon makes me feel almost delicate, his frame easily clearing 6'5".

I've never admitted aloud how completely he is Michael's opposite. Michael, with platinum blonde hair where Jaxon was dark, blue-eyed where Jaxon's shifted between emerald and wolf green, and standing several inches shorter than my 5'11" frame.

Robyn found him when my previous drummer wrapped his car around a tree three weeks before our tour. I needed someone who could keep the beat without missing a note, and Michael delivered. But I never truly understood the gulf between these two men until that night I watched Jaxon pin Michael against the wall. His forearm pressed against his throat, all because he'd invited groupies to his room.

The tattoos that climb from his knuckles to his jawline tell stories in ink and bone with skull motifs that seem born from his skin rather than etched into it.

His hair, midnight-dark like mine but without my signature streak of white, always looks like he's just run frustrated fingers through it.

I sink into the leather seat at the back of the cabin, my territory.

From here, I command a view of everyone while the bedroom waits just steps away, a silent promise of escape when the weight of eyes and expectations becomes too much. No one can approach unseen; no one can hover at my back. This is my sanctuary in the sky.

I don't like people behind me. Maybe it's the fear of someone sneaking up on me, or the idea of eyes peering over my shoulder while I'm working. Maybe it's just one more thing the mountain took from me. Either way, this seat feels the safest.

Not all of my work is for my singing career. Most of what really matters happens in the shadows, a quiet, deliberate move only a handful of people in my life know about.

I always use a pseudonym when I invest. No face. No name. Just leverage.

The only time anyone ever sees me in person is when I decide to buy the entire company outright. And by the time the previous owner finally pieces together who their "shadow investor" really was, it's already too late for them to brag about knowing Ellia Delvine personally.

"Elli, are you comfortable?" Jaxon's voice cuts through my thoughts.

I blink out of my head and glance up at him. "Yes."

But the way his eyes linger on me, always assessing, unconvinced, tells me he doesn't believe that for a second.

He called me Elli again. Twice now, if I'm keeping score. I wonder if he's noticed the way I smile to myself every time he says it instead of Ms. Delvine or Ellia.

It took him long enough to figure out which name I actually prefer.

It must have felt like hours before I finally broke the silence.

Jaxon hadn't said a word, giving me space the way he always does, but he stayed close, close enough to keep watch on the crew and on me. Close enough that I could feel his presence even when I wasn't looking at him.

"Jaxon..." My voice feels too thin in my throat. "Why didn't you walk away after that night?"

He turns slightly, just enough to show he's listening. I swallow, pulse stuttering. But he doesn't say anything.

"Do you look at me differently now? Because of what you saw?" The words spill out before I can stop them. And the silence that follows is thick enough to choke on.

I expected him to answer, but I wouldn't if I were him.

So, I sit there, staring out the window, pretending I don't care that the silence stretches on like a held breath. Pretending his lack of an answer doesn't sink its teeth into me.

Jaxon is quiet for so long, I think he won't answer. Then he huffs out a breath that almost sounds like a laugh.

CHAPTER 5

JAXON

Those questions cut me like a fucking sword, slicing me through and through. She just doesn't get it. The moment I saw her, not the stage persona but the real, raw Ellia.

I knew she was mine, but I couldn't have her because of some piece of shit I saw through. I waited for her to see the real Michael, but she never did, well, not until it was too late.

"Ellia," I say softly, because anything louder might break her. "I would never look at you differently."

She doesn't move. Doesn't breathe. Just stares out the window like she's bracing for impact.

I drag in a slow breath because she has no idea what she does to me.

"You're not just a job to me." The words scrape out of me quieter than I intend, but honestly. Probably too honest.

If she knew how fast I ran up that mountain, how my heart stopped when I saw her, broken, and still fading. If she knew the nights I would stay awake outside her door just to make sure she was still breathing. She wouldn't ask why I didn't walk away. She'd already know. But she doesn't. She still thinks what happened made her less.

"What I saw that night... the shape you were in..." I pause, because even in my head the memory is a blade. "It didn't change how I feel about you. Or about this."

My voice drops, rougher than before.

"But it did confirm something I've never said out loud: I failed you in ways I should never have allowed."

Her breath stutters. She's listening, every muscle in her body tight. I lean forward, elbows on my knees, hands clasped to keep from reaching for her.

"And I swear to you, Ellia... those two will answer for what they did. I don't care how long it takes. I don't care what it costs me. They will not walk away from this."

She still doesn't move. Not a word. Just her breathing, faster now, sharp around the edges, like she's holding back every question she's kept buried for a year. I can feel them pressing against her ribs, clawing their way up her throat.

I'm not prepared for those questions. My throat closes. If she asks directly, I'll answer. I'll have to.

My hands clench until my knuckles whiten, remembering the photos spread across my desk at 2 AM, her bike's brake line with the precise cut, too clean for an accident.

The pattern of bruises on her inner thighs. The ligature marks on her wrists were too delicate for such violence.

Last night, I paced the hallway outside her room again, listening for her breathing through the door.

Three hours, back and forth, while she finally slept. The carpet's wearing thin in that spot now.

I still see it when I close my eyes, her body at the bottom of that ravine, positioned like she'd been arranged.

The medical report sits locked in my safe: "injuries inconsistent with impact trauma alone."

All the signs point to someone who wanted that crash to be fatal. Someone who didn't plan on her living long enough to crawl out of the dark again.

Was it because of the affair he didn't know I'd already figured out? Or the money he and her so-called best friend siphoned off behind her back?

It had to be close to $30 million by the time they were gone. Whatever the reason, he didn't expect her to survive. He didn't expect me to find her. And until she's strong enough to hear the truth...I'll carry it for her.

Every single piece of it. Even if it fucking destroys me every time I relive that night. My chest tightens at the thought, the memories clawing up where I keep them buried, and before I can pull my walls back up, I feel her eyes on me.

She watches the way my breath turns shallow. The way my hands tremble, just barely, against my knees.

"What are you not telling me, Jaxon?" Her voice is steady, but her eyes, her eyes cut straight through me.

"I..." The word barely forms before she turns away, heading toward the bedroom at the back of the jet.

Fuck. Great job, Jaxon. Just give her the truth. But I can't. If I tell her everything now, here, like this, she will break in a way I'm not sure either of us can fix.

So, I sit there, jaw locked, fists tight in my lap, watching the door close behind her. Every instinct in me screams to go after her, to pull her back, to say something, anything, that doesn't make this worse.

But as soon as the door clicks shut behind her, I pull my laptop out from under the seat. The same laptop I've been using for a year to hunt Michael down. But the bastard has practically vanished off the face of the earth. Now and then, I catch a trace of him or her.

His little accomplice can't help herself. She shops like she's trying to get noticed. But by the time I get my guys on it, they've slipped away again like smoke.

And now, with Ellia stepping back into the spotlight, I know what's coming. He'll try again. He would finish what he started. Keeping her tucked away in Idaho was the only reason he hadn't found her. That distance bought us time, but nothing more.

I performed background checks, cleared, and monitored everyone around her. The doctors, physical therapists, stylists, managers, and anyone with proximity to her. Trust isn't a luxury I can afford.

When I finally vetted her lawyer, John Bishop, the first thing I had him do was draft airtight NDAs for every person in her orbit. Anyone who steps into her life now is bound to silence so tight they couldn't whisper her name without permission.

It's extreme. It's excessive. But it's the only way I sleep at night. Because until Michael is found, until he's stopped. I'm the only line between Ellia and the darkness still hunting her.

And I'll burn the fucking world down if I have to. Drain every resource, call in every favor—before I ever let him get close to her again.

CHAPTER 6

ELLIA

I couldn't fall asleep, but that's no surprise. I never really do anymore. If I'm not lying awake, staring at the ceiling until dawn, then I'm waking up drenched in fear from nightmares I can't outrun.

There's no middle ground for me. No soft drift into sleep, no peaceful in-between. Just silence or screaming, nothing else.

When I finally drift into a restless slumber, the nightmares come fast; they always do. Flooding in like a broken dam, I can't stop.

I'm back on the summit, overlooking the city lights far below. Everything is too still, too quiet. Michael sits beside me, expression blank, like he's listening to a conversation I can't hear.

I'm talking to him. I know I am, but the words vanish before they ever reach my ears. It's as if my voice has been stolen, ripped right out of my throat.

A cold prickle crawls up my spine. I turn, and there she is. Robyn. My ex–best friend. My assistant. Smiling like she's enjoying a private joke as she crouches beside my bike. Her hands move quickly, purposefully. Wires. Bolts. Pieces she should never touch.

I try to scream for her to stop, but nothing comes out, just silent panic vibrating in my chest. She laughs like she can hear my terror, anyway.

Michael rises from where he sat and walks toward her. He doesn't hesitate. Doesn't look back at me. Just joins her, like they've done this before.

"She'll never survive this," Robyn says, voice warped and echoing through the dream.

Michael doesn't even flinch. "I know."

Then he glances at her, a greedy smile twisting the dream-version of his face.

"Soon we'll have everything we want. No more of her rules. No more of her." He leans closer to Robyn, voice dripping with satisfaction. "And rich. Did I mention rich?"

"What the fuck, Michael?" I try to scream it, force the words out hard enough to shake the mountain beneath us. But nothing comes out.

My voice disappears the second it leaves my throat, swallowed whole by the dream. It's like shouting underwater. Like the air itself refuses to carry my words.

I can't believe what I'm seeing. They wouldn't hurt me. They said they loved me. My mind refuses to accept it, even inside this nightmare.

I straddle the motorcycle, my pulse hammering against my ribs, each breath shallow and insufficient. None of this is happening. It can't be happening.

When I blink, the summit is empty. Robyn is gone. Michael is gone. No laughter. No voices. No shadows. Just me. And my bike... exactly how I left it when I parked. Sleek, matte black. No wires cut. Bolts intact. Perfect. Untouched.

The hotel isn't far. Jaxon will check everything and fix whatever's wrong. That's what he does—solves problems I can't.

I inhale deeply, find my balance, and launch myself downhill. Then, as I lean into the first curve, everything vanishes. Darkness swallows me whole.

Pain tears through me, contorting my limbs into impossible angles. I try to move my arms, but they might as well be concrete, pinned beneath the weight of what's happening.

My leg, I don't understand why it won't move. My body hurts. I feel a warm liquid trickling down my body. My back, why does my back hurt?

As if I were a witness to an accident, I see myself. Bloody, broken, lying on my stomach. Am I breathing... No, no, I am not.

I try to scream at myself to wake up. It's not real, it's not real, none of this is real. But the nightmare doesn't care.

It keeps dragging me deeper. I'm kneeling beside myself, a version of me crumpled on the mountainside, still and silent, like I've slipped out of my own body.

I'm screaming, but no sound comes out. My mouth moves, my throat strains, but it's all swallowed by the darkness around us.

'Wake up.' I shout the words inside my head so loudly it feels like something should break.

'Elli, get up. Please get up.' The wind shifts, chilling, wrong.

They're coming back. The warning tears through me, frantic and raw. I don't know who "they" are in the dream—Michael, Robyn, shadows, ghosts, memories, but the fear is real. Real enough to make the world tilt and pulse around me.

I reach for my other self, grabbing at her shoulders, shaking her, but my hands pass straight through.

"Elli." Jaxon's voice cuts faintly through the darkness, distant and distorted. But I can't see him.

"Elli, wake up!" I shout it in my head, my mind echoing the words my mouth can't form.

Wake up, wake up, wake up!

"Elli... Elli."

Hands close around me. Firm. Warm. Real. Panic detonates in my chest. Oh God, it has to be Michael. I can't move. I can't turn around. The nightmare holds me in place, trapping me in that impossible, suffocating dark.

"Ellia. I got you."

The voice shifts to a lower, steadier, more familiar tone in a way that cracks through the dream. Is it real? Am I imagining him? Jaxon.

I strain to make out his figure through the murk, but blackness weighs on my eyelids like wet sand. The darkness tugs me deeper until, gasp, consciousness breaks through.

I surface to reality, eyes wide, finding Jaxon above me. He balances on one knee that dimples the mattress, his hands steady on my shoulders, firm but gentle, as if I might shatter beneath his fingertips.

His eyes, wide, worried, fiercely present, lock onto mine. "Elli," he murmurs, breath warm against my forehead, "wake up. It's a nightmare. I've got you."

"Don't touch me!" I scream, the words ripping out of me before I can stop them.

I yank the covers up to my face, scrambling backward until my spine hits the headboard hard. I can't move any farther, and I can't breathe. Everything in me shakes.

Sweat clings to my clothes, soaking through. My hair sticks to my cheeks. My eyes burn, tears threatening to fall no matter how hard I fight them.

I blink—once, twice, again and again—trying to force the room into focus. Trying to drag myself out of the darkness, still clinging to me.

And slowly... painfully... I recognize the dim cabin lights. The hum of the engines. The smooth walls. I'm safe. I'm on the jet, not on the mountain.

Jaxon hasn't moved. He's still kneeling in front of me, hands lifted now, off my shoulders, palms open, showing he won't touch me unless I ask. His voice lowers to a whisper meant only for me.

"You're safe, songbird. You're here. I'm right in front of you."

CHAPTER 7

JAXON

Working on a lead, I start following the trail Robyn's been leaving, careless, messy, and exactly her style. Store-to-store, purchase-to-purchase. Then one transaction makes my jaw lock.

A Bentley? Are you kidding me? She just bought a Bentley Bentayga V8. Good God! The woman has to be stupid or arrogant to draw that kind of attention while she's supposed to be in hiding.

I don't even need to check twice. There's no universe where she could afford that on her own. Not without Michael and not without what they took from Ellia.

I trace the registration, force the database to cough up its location, and if I don't get someone on the ground right now, they'll vanish again. They always do. Like smoke between fingers.

I grab my phone, already dialing. "I've got a location. Bentley Bentayga, black, new plates. Los Angeles. Move now. Don't lose them this time."

Before my guy can confirm, I catch it, movement from Ellia's room. That familiar rustle of sheets being kicked away. I don't need to see her face to know what's happening.

The nightmares found her again, right on schedule.

It's a cruel ritual—the moment sleep claims her, the terror begins. Her muffled cries penetrate these walls like they're made of gauze instead of drywall.

Most nights, I barely make it to the couch before it starts. When I rush in to wake her, she lashes out with such raw fear in her eyes, as if the ghosts from her past have materialized right beside me.

I start to hear the quiet whimpers through the closed door; she doesn't remember the ragged breaths she'd deny if I ever mentioned them. And most nights, I end up crashing in the massive living room, close enough to get to her door in seconds, far enough that she doesn't accuse me of hovering. But I am hovering. I always am.

Her nightmares have a rhythm now. I can feel it. The way her breathing changes. The way her fingers twitch like she's trying to fight something she can't see.

The phone dangles from my fingers, forgotten, as my body tenses toward her bedroom door. Then I hear it: her scream. The kind that rips straight through the walls, through bone and nerve, through anyone with a heartbeat. A sound dragged up from the deepest place inside her, fighting to claw its way to the surface.

I don't think. I end the call without a single word, already moving, already sprinting. I'm through her door in less than a second. Ellia is thrashing across the bed; caught in a nightmare she can't escape.

Sheets twisted around her like she'd been wrestling shadows. Her skin was damp with sweat, her breath coming in sharp, fractured pulls.

Her black hair clings to her face, and that white patch, the one I've always thought made her look fierce and untouchable, stands out starkly.

Tonight, it's dulled to a slate gray from sweat, but somehow it still looks beautiful on her. Only she could pull off something like that without even trying.

My chest tightens. This woman fights in her sleep harder than most people fight in daylight.

"Elli," I say, careful, measured. I keep my voice low, the kind of quiet that doesn't startle, doesn't corner. Because I've learned the hard way that waking her too fast, touching her too suddenly, only scares her more.

Too many times, I've rushed in without thinking, grabbed her shoulders, shaken her awake, desperate to pull her out of whatever hell her mind trapped her in. And every single time, she's fought me. Not because she knew it was me, but because in that moment, she couldn't tell the difference.

"Elli... It's me. You're safe." My hands hover inches above her, ready if she needs me, distant if she doesn't.

Her legs kick at the sheets, her arms flail as if fending off something only she can see. Her breath breaks in uneven gasps. Every ragged inhale twists something in my chest, makes me want to tear apart whatever haunts her sleep with my bare hands.

"Come on, songbird." My voice softens even further. "Find me. Follow my voice."

Her eyes snap open; wild, unfocused, drowning in whatever nightmare she hasn't fully escaped from.

"Don't touch me!" The words tear out of her as she scrambles backward, dragging the sheets with her until the headboard stops her escape cold.

Her body trembles like a plucked wire, lungs fighting for air, gaze fixed somewhere beyond me, somewhere I can't follow. It's a knife to the gut, watching her recoil at my silhouette. Every damn time.

Then recognition flickers across those amber irises, and the terror loosens its grip on her face. Not completely. Nowhere close to completely. But her breathing steadies, one ragged inhale after another.

If she fucking knew how much I ache watching her unravel like this... how it feels to sit there and do nothing but wait while she battles demons I can't reach. She'd understand why I hover. Why I stay too close, and why I refuse to leave her alone at night.

"Jaxon." Her voice is thin, still trembling around the edges, but there's a calmness trying to form underneath it. The same quiet steadiness she reaches for whenever she's fighting to pull herself back together.

I swallow hard, keeping my tone even, controlled. "I'm here, Elli."

I shift just enough that she can see my hands are still open, still gentle, still hers to accept or refuse. "You're safe. I'm not going anywhere."

Settling back in my seat, it feels like an eternity, a stretch of silence so long it could break a weaker man.

She finally returns to the cabin and must have taken a shower. Her hair is pulled back into a tight, low bun, that stark white patch standing out against the jet-black strands she tries so hard to pretend she doesn't care about.

She hates the attention her poliosis brings. Says it ruins any chance of blending in, of pretending to be anyone other than herself. She always claims she'll dye it, yet I've never once seen her without that natural streak.

She's changed into another matching sweatshirt and pants, soft and loose, the kind she wears when she needs comfort more than glamor.

Deep jasper tone, rich and subtle, and it brings out her eyes in a way that makes my chest tighten, a quiet kind of beautiful.

She doesn't speak for a while. And I can tell she's still trying to calm herself, still pulling pieces of her mind back from whatever nightmare dragged her under.

Her shoulders stay tight, her head lowered, like she's trying to hide her face... or the storm still flickering behind her eyes.

I expect her to drift back to her usual seat, to put distance between us the way she always does when she's shaken. But she doesn't.

Instead, she moves toward me... and slides into the seat right next to mine. Her scent reaches me instantly: sweet lavender with a hint of warm vanilla, and it wraps around me before I can brace myself. It's familiar. It's grounding. And it drives me absolutely, quietly insane in all the ways I'll never admit out loud.

"We're almost there," I say, finally breaking the silence stretched thin between us.

Her head lifts just enough for her eyes to find mine.

"Where is there?" she asks, voice softer than before, steadier but still fragile around the edges.

"Australia," I answer, letting a slow smirk pull at the corner of my mouth.

And she knows exactly why. Exactly who. And the small flicker of recognition in her eyes tells me I made the right call.

Out of everywhere in the world we could've gone, this is the one place that might coax her back toward living again.

"August," she whispers, barely there, but I hear it.

Of course I do, and then she smiles.

Not a full one, not the bright grin she used to throw around like confetti, but a small tug at her pouty lips. The kind of smile she only ever gives when a memory hits her in the right spot.

It suits her. God, it suits her more than she knows. And for a moment, I just let myself look at her, really look at her, because seeing her smile at all feels like witnessing something rare, something fragile.

Something I'd trade blood for if it meant keeping it a little longer.

CHAPTER 8

AUGUST

Jaxon called me yesterday, voice tight, clipped, like he was barely keeping himself from jumping out of his own damn skin, to tell me he and Ellia were on their way to Sydney. He didn't give me much else, but I guess he doesn't have to.

When Jaxon calls, it's either life-or-death... or Ellia. And since she's not dead, thank bloody God, I figured it had to be the latter.

Practice has had me in a chokehold the last couple of months. Between drills, scrimmages, and coach riding my ass like he thinks I'm still nineteen, I haven't had time to breathe, let alone see Ellia... or Jaxon.

The last time I saw her, she was walking without assistance, slow and careful, but walking. Both arms finally healed from the breaks. Still stiff, still fragile-looking, but she held herself like she was trying to pretend none of it hurt anymore.

Jaxon and I spent weeks hunting for the most off-the-beaten-path place we could stash her. No paparazzi, no wandering fans, no spotlight. Just another "wealthy recluse" renting a quiet penthouse where no one looks twice at a closed door.

For three months, she lived in that sterile hospital room while a rotating cast of medical professionals poked and prodded her broken body back toward something that resembled living.

She stayed silent for three weeks of those days, as if somewhere between the first impact and the last, her voice had been left scattered across that mountainside. And when words finally did come, they emerged from a stranger wearing Ellia's face.

Michael may have left her beaten down and barely holding on, but her will to survive outmatched anything any of us expected.

Her injuries ran deep, the kind that take time and grit to come back from. There were days she looked exhausted to her bones, and days I could see that flicker in her eyes, the one that said she was tired, hurting, maybe wondering if fighting was worth it.

Jaxon may have put the fear of God into every single person involved in her recovery, making it brutally clear that nothing, not a word, not a whisper, not a single detail about what happened to her was ever to leave that hospital. And not until she was ready. Until we were ready to tell her about the assault.

I was right there beside him when he started handing out NDAs like they were discharge papers. The looks on some of their faces, shock, guilt, and a few who suddenly remembered they had somewhere urgent to be, told me everything I needed to know.

Let's just say the ones who hesitated, the ones who blinked like they were reconsidering their entire moral compass, didn't show up for their next shift.

She spent three days, three long, agonizing damn days in a medically induced coma. The doctor tried to explain it in the simplest terms he could, though none of it made it any easier to hear.

The way she went down that mountainside... her brain had been rattled around inside her skull, like a ping-pong ball hitting the walls of a table.

The helmet saved her face, thank God. But it couldn't stop the internal chaos, the way her brain jolted with every impact.

Hearing it laid out like that, slow, clinical, matter-of-fact- made my stomach twist. Because all I could picture was her body hitting the ground again and again, while we had no idea where she was.

Three days of machines breathing for her. Three days of waiting for her eyes to open. Three days of praying, she'd still be Ellia when she did.

Jaxon didn't sleep a single damn minute until she woke up. Sat there like a statue beside her bed, eyes red, jaw clenched, refusing to blink in case she opened her eyes while he wasn't looking.

The nurses tried to make him rest, but good luck with that. Man didn't budge. And that was the moment I knew. Knew exactly how much he loved her.

He still hasn't said it outright; as a matter of fact, he probably never will. Not his style. Not with everything they've survived.

I take a slow, steady breath and try to choke down my protein shake, but who am I kidding? I'm buzzing. Excited, restless, and completely useless.

By the time their jet lands, I'll be at practice, and I have no fucking clue how I'm supposed to focus. Coach already thinks my attention span is questionable on a good day. Wait until he sees me today. But just like Ellia, my team is counting on me.

And I can't exactly tell them, "Sorry, lads, my friend, the one I'd cross oceans for, is flying in and I'm losing my damn mind about it."

Last year, when I was in town visiting Jaxon for a week, that's when I met her. I knew of her, of course. You can't step foot in a pub in this country without hearing at least one of her songs blaring over the speakers, or drunk women butchering her songs on karaoke.

My teammates had her on their playlists long before I ever shook her hand. Everyone does. Hell, the rookies practically worship her, though they'd sooner die than admit it.

And look, if she isn't as big as that one global pop icon, we're apparently not allowed to name without summoning an army of lawyers...she's close enough that the comparison still makes people sweat. But her voice, God, her voice, something out of this universe.

Ellia Delvine wasn't just a celebrity when I met her, knowing her name and seeing her in person? Two completely different things. And yet somehow, she's also the kind of woman who laughs at her own clumsiness and forgets she's famous half the time.

Quiet in a way that makes you lean in, but fierce enough that you know not to get too close unless she lets you. And she let me. God knows why.

"Mate, what's got you bouncing off the walls?" Reed calls out the second I step onto the field, giving me that look like he already knows I'm up to something.

"Nothing," I call over my shoulder, dropping into a stretch like I'm not vibrating out of my damn skin. "Just in a good mood."

All my mates spill onto the field, stretching, jogging, talking shit like usual.

"You must've gotten laid," Owen calls out, laughing at his own joke before the rest of the team even has time to pile on.

A chorus of idiots erupts behind him.

If they only knew, if they had even the faintest clue what had me this keyed up, they'd shut their mouths really quick.

CHAPTER 9

ELLIA

August is Jaxon's best friend. The story goes that they met during some late-night chaos, while August's team was visiting, whiskey spilled across a bar top, a stranger's insult, knuckles connecting with jawbones, and someone's body sliding across the room.

At least that's the version I've pieced together about their beginning.

I met August a little over a year ago, the same week as the accident, if I'm remembering right, and he definitely lives up to the rugby standard.

He is easily 6'4" tall. Olive skin people would absolutely kill for. Dark brown hair threaded with natural golden flecks. And eyes, deep, warm chocolate—that have no business being as soft as they are on a man built like a freight train.

August attended the New York show and the Colorado show. And Jaxon didn't exactly ask before getting his best friend backstage passes, but I never minded when my team showed off what they do for a living.

I have rules, of course, where people are allowed to go, what they're allowed to see, and how close they get to the parts of my life that aren't for public consumption, but I love it when someone genuinely loves what they do.

And August? He walked backstage like a kid seeing his first stadium. Didn't even try to hide it.

"We're here," Jaxon says, his voice low as he pulls into the gated driveway of what I can only assume is the most expensive house in all of Sydney.

The iron gates glide open like they've been expecting us. The kind of quiet, expensive welcome only old money or dangerous men ever get.

The lawn is perfectly manicured; every blade trimmed with the kind of precision that screams money. Vines climb the bright white exterior in soft, deliberate curls, artfully wild, the kind of wild that costs a fortune to maintain.

I should be used to places like this. Expensive things stopped impressing me a long time ago. But if I had the choice? I'd take a quiet villa in the middle of nowhere in the Caribbean over mansions like this any day. Less noise. Less pretending. Less of everything.

I spot movement to the far right of the house: two groundskeepers tending to the hedges, clipped uniforms, heads down.

My body reacts before my mind can catch up. I reach for Jaxon's sleeve, fingers locking around the fabric, gripping as if my life depended on it. My eyes squeezed shut.

I don't like this. I don't like any of this. Who are those people? Do they work for Michael? Did he find me already?

"No, no, no," I chanted over and over.

Jaxon stops the car before I unravel entirely. He doesn't shake me off. He lets me clutch his arm, lets me strain against it the way someone drowning grabs onto anything solid.

"I've vetted them," he says quietly, firmly. "I've vetted all of them."

Tears sting the backs of my eyes, hot and humiliating.

"I'm not going to let anything happen to you. Do you hear me?" he whispers.

I don't answer. I can't. When my eyes pop open, my gaze stays locked on the gardener. Every slight movement he makes feels like a threat waiting to happen.

"Elli," Jaxon murmurs, and this time he moves slowly, so slowly, lifting a hand to turn my face toward his. A gentle touch, as if I'm breakable. "Do you understand?"

He waits for the panic to loosen its grip on me, just a little, before he goes on.

"This is my house," he says softly. "I've owned it since August, and I became friends. This is his place to hide during the on or off-season. His fans have found every other place he's ever had, but not this one."

He doesn't look away from me. Not once. Not until he's sure I'm hearing him.

"No one here knows you're coming. No one here knows who you are. This place is ours, Elli. Safe."

His words land slowly, like pebbles dropping into deep water. I nod, barely. His hand is still cupping my chin, steady and warm, anchoring me.

He looks right into me, through me, and I know he understands that I understand. Only then does he let go. Slowly. Carefully.

He doesn't pull away from me completely. He still lets me keep hold of his sleeve, knuckles white from gripping it so tight. He gives me that much control, the little piece of security I need to breathe.

I keep my eyes trained on his hand, then the windshield, then the side mirrors, watching everything, while he eases the car forward toward the three-car garage.

When the engine shuts off, the silence in the car feels too loud. And I force myself to move. One shaky inhale. One hand braced against the door.

The warm Sydney air hits me first—humid, bright, too real after hours in the cabin. My legs wobble when I climb out, my combat boots hitting the garage floor with a soft crunch.

Before I can take another step, I see Jaxon rounding the front of the car. His stride is controlled, deliberate, like he's making sure not to approach too fast, like he remembers exactly what happens when people move toward me too suddenly.

He stops beside me, not touching, not crowding, just close enough that I can feel his presence at my side. I swallow hard, my fingers itching toward his sleeve again, but I keep them at my sides this time.

"Take your time," he murmurs. "No rush."

As I step forward, Jaxon shadows my movement quietly as breath, solid as stone. His hand floats an inch from the small of my back, maintaining that careful distance. He's memorized the map of my scars without ever seeing them, understands the territory that belongs only to me.

That deliberate space he keeps, not so far that I'd fall without him catching me, not so close that I'd feel the vulnerability of being touched, tells me more about his understanding than words ever could.

Inside, the house is just as elegant as the outside. High ceilings, clean lines, sunlight pouring through tall windows. Not at all what I pictured Jaxon owning. And definitely not the kind of place I imagined August living in.

CHAPTER 10

ELLIA

The tour Jaxon gave me lasted barely fifteen minutes, yet each room revealed something unexpected. I've seen wealth before; it lost its shine for me long ago, but something about the calculated elegance of this place caught me off guard. Or maybe it was just him, with those eyes that seemed to track my every reaction. My gaze kept returning to his profile against the tall windows, drawn there against my better judgment.

White and black marble floors stretch across the foyer in perfect geometric symmetry, glossy enough to catch distorted reflections of our steps. A grand staircase sits in the center, sweeping upward toward the second-floor bedrooms like something out of a mansion in a magazine.

And then there's the kitchen, large, polished, all white. Too clean, too perfect, untouched by real life. The kind of space people take photos of, and not cook in, but Jaxon assures me there is plenty of cooking in this house.

Everything about this place screams old money, power, and privacy. Jaxon had shown me all the bedrooms and which ones overlook the private beach. But that's the thing about him. He's full of quiet contradictions.

Gentle hands, lethal instincts.

A house like a fortress, but a voice soft enough to pull me back from nightmares. The more I see of this place, the more it feels like stepping into the parts of him he never talks about.

The last room on the tour is the primary bedroom. A four-post king-size bed dominates the space with massive, dark wood, the kind of bed that looks like it was built for a man who could bench-press a compact car. Which, given the size of August, actually makes perfect sense.

To the left, a large marble bathroom opens up like its own private sanctuary. A walk-in shower takes up nearly an entire wall, so big it looks like it could fit seven people without anyone bumping elbows. Ridiculous. Luxurious. Very... August.

A clawfoot tub sits in front of a massive glass window, positioned perfectly to overlook the beach below. The view is breathtaking, waves rolling in slow, steady curls, the horizon melting into shades of gold and blue.

"I'm digging August's taste," I say, letting my gaze drift across the room. Then I glance at him over my shoulder. "Well... yours."

Jaxon steps closer, close enough that the air changes, close enough that my pulse stutters. "This is where you'll be staying, songbird." His voice is low, right at my ear.

I shake my head, and I can smell the mint on his breath. The spice of his cologne. The faint leather undertone that somehow follows him everywhere, like it's stitched into his skin.

I can't control the tremor that races through me. It's not fear that makes my pulse scramble against my throat; it's worse. My body betrays me, relaxing into his presence like I've found shelter after years in a storm. Jaxon shouldn't feel safe, but he does.

Like I could lean into him and forget the world outside these walls. Like I could breathe for the first time without watching over my shoulder. And that terrifies me. I shouldn't want that. I shouldn't want him.

I swallow hard, trying to steady myself, trying to hide the shake in my hands. When I glance at him again, I catch the smallest flicker of something he didn't mean to show.

His jaw tightens, and his nostrils flare ever so slightly. His eyes drop from mine, just for a breath, like he's grounding himself. Control.

For the briefest moment, I wonder what would happen if he didn't. If he didn't hold himself together. If he didn't step back. If he let whatever he's fighting show, just once.

But he clears his throat and retreats half an inch, so small a movement that most people wouldn't notice, but I do. And I feel it like a loss. A slight whimper escapes my lips, wanting him to stay close.

Before I can process any of it, another throat clears. A deeper one. A familiar one. I turn toward the double doors of the bedroom.

August is leaning against the doorframe, arms crossed over his massive chest, wearing that cocky half-grin that usually makes people fall in love with him or run in the opposite direction.

His gaze flicks between Jaxon and me, amused… and maybe a little curious. "G'day, Elli," he says, voice warm and annoyingly charming.

A small smile tugs at my lips. "Hey, August."

My cheeks flush with heat before I can stop it. I take a few steps toward him, but he still doesn't move. Doesn't take his eyes off me for even a second.

"Yes," Jaxon says calmly as he passes me, moving to stand beside August. "Yes, you are, and you will."

For a split second, I just stare at them. Side by side, they're… ridiculous. I can't even tell who's taller or who takes up more space in the room. And even though I would never say this out loud, I'm pretty sure August has the slight edge.

I've seen the fan videos of him floating around. Locker room chaos. Teammates going wild. Shirtless and sweaty. Unfairly attractive. God, that man knows exactly what he's working with. Because one intimidating man in this room is enough.

I swallow and shove the thought away before my mouth can betray me. Heat rushes to my cheeks without permission. My hands fly up, covering my mouth like I'm bracing for impact, like holding on for dear life might somehow save me from my own thoughts.

God. Get it together, Elli. They will notice. Damn it, Elli.

The two of them exchange a look, one of those silent conversations that somehow says everything without a single word being spoken. I'm suddenly very aware that I am not part of whatever just passed between them.

"I've already moved my things down the hall," August says, firm as ever. "Your room is set up. That settles it."

His tone leaves no opening for argument. And honestly? I'm not in the mood to protest. Right now, I'd sleep in a closet if they told me to. Anywhere is fine. Anywhere that isn't loud.

Pushing off the doorframe, August takes a step closer, his voice softening just a bit. "You must be starving, baby girl," he says, eyes searching my face instead of my body this time.

I lift a brow, the corner of my mouth quirking despite myself. "Starving might be dramatic," I say lightly. "But I wouldn't say no to food that didn't come on a plastic tray."

August's grin widens like he just won something. "See? That's all I needed. Doctor's orders: actual food, immediately."

Jaxon exhales through his nose, already clocking the entire situation. "She hasn't eaten properly in hours," he says flatly, eyes cutting to August in warning. "Keep it light. Nothing heavy."

August holds up his hands in surrender, still smiling. "Easy, mate. Soup and toast. I'm not trying to knock her out."

I glance between the two of them, shaking my head faintly.

August chuckles. "Welcome to the care queue, love. You're terribly outnumbered."

"Thank you, August," I say as he leads me down to the kitchen.

CHAPTER 11

ELLIA

After a very much deserved lunch of homemade soup and buttery sourdough toast, just like August promised, I wander into the living room, still feeling warm and slightly unsteady in that post-meal way that makes your limbs heavy and your thoughts soft around the edges.

Just as I step inside, Jaxon presses a sleek black button embedded in the wall. From above, a massive TV, at least eighty-five inches of gleaming black glass, descends silently from a hidden compartment in the coffered ceiling.

The heavy charcoal curtains begin to slide shut on their own with a barely audible mechanical purr, sealing the outside world away in slow, deliberate motion.

The room dims to a twilight hush, golden recessed lights fading to a warm glow. The noise of birds, distant traffic, and the hum of everyday life disappears beneath the room's perfect acoustic insulation.

Just like that, the house turns inward, cocooning us in luxurious isolation. Yep, I could absolutely live here and not care about anything else for the rest of my natural life.

I drift over to the oversized, fluffy cream couch, the kind with cushions as deep as a twin mattress that looks like it was designed to hold all of August's hulking teammates at once without breaking a sweat.

It practically swallows me when I sink into it, the down-filled cushions conforming to my body, soft and ridiculous and perfect in every way that matters right now.

Not far behind me, August appears fresh from the shower, trailing the scent of expensive cedar and bergamot body wash.

His olive skin is still slick with water, droplets catching the low light as they trace down the hard lines of his chest, over the ridges of his abs, and disappearing beneath the waistband of his heather gray sweatpants.

His dark hair is messy in that careless way that says he didn't bother with a towel, just dragged his fingers through the wet strands and let the rest fall where it wanted, curling slightly at the nape of his neck.

The waistband of his sweatpants rides so low it's almost criminal, revealing that defined cut of muscle that angles down from his hips, the kind that makes my fingers twitch with the urge to trace it.

His skin is a canvas of intricate tribal patterns that sweep across his chest and spiral down his arms, the dark ink stark against his olive complexion, drawing my eyes exactly where they shouldn't go.

My breath catches before I can stop it, and it's instant. Heat floods my cheeks, burning all the way to the tips of my ears. My pulse kicks hard behind my ribs, a staccato rhythm I can feel in my throat. I don't look away fast enough, my eyes betraying me. He catches me looking.

Of course he does. One corner of August's full mouth lifts slowly into a knowing half-smile, like he's savoring the effect he has on me, storing it away for later.

"Careful, baby girl," he drawls, his accent thickening with each syllable. "You keep staring like that, and I'll start charging admission."

I choke on absolutely nothing, my dignity evaporating like water on hot pavement. And Jaxon doesn't miss a beat. Still calm. Still unreadable, though I swear I catch the faintest twitch at the corner of his mouth.

"Relax, she's medically cleared for mild cardio," he says dryly, not looking up from the tablet balanced on his knee. "Don't let it go to your head."

August barks out a laugh, deep and genuine. "Oi, you're meant to be on my side," he protests, running a hand through his damp hair, sending a few stray droplets flying.

"You don't have a side," Jaxon replies, finally looking up with one perfectly arched eyebrow. "You live shirtless. You forfeited dignity years ago."

I sink deeper into the couch, heat still in my face and between my thighs, mortified and wildly entertained. “Wow,” I mutter. “You two flirt worse than I do.”

“So, love,” August says easily as he drops down beside me, one long arm stretching along the back of the couch.

"What're you in the mood for, movie, show, dumb-ass reality TV like those stay-at-home parents or some shit?"

Before I can even answer, the cushion on my other side dips. Jaxon. Now they're both there. Both are too close, and both smell unfairly good.

August, all clean soap and heat. Jaxon is all leather, spice, and something darker beneath it. I physically cannot process this. My chest tightens and my skin prickles. The room feels smaller. Louder. Too aware of my body.

I spring to my feet like the couch just shocked me. "I need..." My breath stutters. "I just need to... go."

And then I'm gone.

Moving faster than my legs have any right to carry me, heart slamming as I might actually outrun the tension clawing up my spine.

Hell, at this rate, I might break another leg trying to escape whatever the hell is building between the three of us.

Jaxon and August? Together in my head like that? Absolutely not. Jaxon works for me. August is his best friend. That alone is a disaster waiting to happen.

And me? I'm not ready. Not even close. I can barely stand my skin some days, and the idea of being touched still feels like fire and panic all wrapped into one.

I catch a side glance of them both rising from the couch, their eyes tracking my every frantic step as I round the corner toward the stairs.

Please. Please stop looking at me like that.

"Ell..." one of them calls, but I don't slow down.

I take the stairs two at a time and slam the bedroom door behind me like it's the only thing standing between me and complete emotional combustion.

Pressing my back against it, chest heaving, breath coming in ragged pulls. Shaking. Wide awake in a body that doesn't know what it wants, but knows exactly what it can't have.

I slide down the door until I'm sitting on the floor, knees pulled tight to my chest like armor. My pulse is everywhere—ears, throat, wrists — too loud, too fast, too alive.

Am I actually going to survive this? The way the room shifted. The way the air changed when they sat on either side of me. The way my body reacted before my mind could shut it down.

Jaxon didn't even say how long we're staying here. A day? A week? Forever? The thought lands wrong in my chest.

Heavy. Unsettling. Dangerous.

My phone vibrates in my hand, and I nearly throw it across the room. Faith. Of course. I swipe to answer, trying to steady my breathing before she hears the wreck in it.

"Ellia Delvine," she says immediately, relief and irritation tangled together, "where the hell have you been? You vanished. You were supposed to be here three hours ago for the wardrobe fitting."

I squeeze my eyes shut, forehead dropping to my knees. "I...things changed."

"Changed how?" she presses. "Because I've got racks, designers, and one very angry stylist who flew in from Milan just for you."

I stare at the opposite wall, at the unfamiliar art, the unfamiliar luxury, the unfamiliar life I'm hiding inside.

"I'm... not in Idaho anymore," I whisper.

Another pause. Longer this time.

"Ell," Faith says softly now, all business gone, "are you okay?"

The question hits somewhere too close to the bone, and I don't answer right away. Because I can't tell her the truth when I don't even know it myself.

How could I explain that this mansion is closing in around me? Or the way Jaxon's steady silence and August's reckless smile have me stretched between them like I'm about to snap in two?

"I think so," I finally say.

"Okay, Ellia."

Uh-oh. Full name. She's pissed. And honestly, I deserve it. I disappeared without a word.

"How long will you be gone?" I hear Jo ask from in the distance. "I..." I hesitate; the truth is uncomfortable. "I'm not sure." There's a pause—tight, controlled.

"I'll cancel the fitting," she says at last, cool and collected but unmistakably irritated. "I'll keep the team on standby for whenever you decide to resurface."

Another beat.

"Oh, and Ell?" Her voice softens just enough to make my chest ache. "Be careful."

Before I can answer, the line goes dead. I stare at my phone. If I know Faith the way I think I do, I've got about two and a half seconds before she's on the phone with Jaxon, ripping him a fresh one.

God help him.

I must have stayed in that same position for hours, just staring at the wall like it might eventually give me answers.

At some point, the light outside faded completely. Night settled in long before I ever thought about moving.

My body protests when I finally shift, stiff, aching, unfamiliar with the way I've folded myself in on the floor. As I push up, every joint reminds me I'm not made of glass anymore, but I'm not exactly healed either.

A knock sounds at the door. I freeze. I wasn't expecting it. Jaxon never comes to me when I spiral like this; he knows better.

Slowly, cautiously, I reach for the handle and crack the door open. August stands there, fully clothed this time. No casual confidence. No teasing grin.

His face is torn. Like he's fighting something inside himself, the way men do when they don't quite know what to do with their hands. And for the first time since I bolted upstairs, I realize I might not be the only one unraveling.

CHAPTER 12

AUGUST

The door opens a sliver, revealing a slant of her face in the gap. It's Ellia, beautiful as ever, but with shadows beneath her eyes that weren't there before.

My voice sticks in my throat at the sight of her. "Elli..." Her name comes out rough, unplanned. My hand finds the back of my neck, rubbing awkwardly as heat crawls up my collar.

"I..." The rest dies somewhere between thought and speech.

She fills the doorway when she steps into the dim light, all long limbs and shadows, still every inch the woman who could command a stage without trying. 5'11 of fire and presence, only five inches shorter than me. And yet...she looks small.

It's like the walls upstairs pressed in on her so tight she had to shrink just to survive them. Her shoulders are slumped, as if she's been holding herself together with thread and stubbornness alone.

It hits me harder than I expected.

I clear my throat, trying again. "You... bolted earlier," I breathe. Not teasing this time. No charm. Just truth. "Wanted to check if you were alright."

She watches me like she's deciding whether to slam the door in my face or let me in. She's quiet. Too quiet. And I know I've completely fucked this up.

Her eyes flick past me, over my shoulder, and down the hall. Her weight shifts from one foot to the other, restless, on edge, like she's bracing for something to come at her from behind me. Like she expects danger to appear out of thin air.

It guts me. She's not looking at me the way she did earlier. Not flustered. Not surprised. She's scared. Suddenly that stupid, charged moment on the couch feels a lifetime ago, drowned under the reality of what she's still carrying inside her.

I lower my voice without thinking. "Hey... It's just me," I murmur, like that might somehow make the world less sharp for her. "No one's behind me. You're safe."

She hesitates for one long second, then another. Finally, she steps back. Just enough to clear the doorway. The invitation is so subtle that I almost miss it.

My brows lift before I can stop myself. "Are you... inviting me in?"

Her lips twitch faintly, the ghost of a smile trying to survive whatever's wrecking her from the inside.

"Well," she says softly, eyes lifting to meet mine at last, "this is your room."

Something tight in my chest loosens at that. I move slowly past her, careful not to brush too close, like one wrong step might send her bolting again.

She doesn't lock the door. Doesn't even fully close it. Like she might still run. I'm okay with that. I want her to be comfortable. This isn't about me, hasn't been for a second.

She leads the way through the room and out onto the verandah attached to the main bedroom. The French doors open, as the curtain blows in the breeze.

The sun's long gone, leaving behind a cloudless sky stretched wide and endless. The city hums in the distance, all lights and movement and life, while the ocean breeze rolls in off the water and nips at my skin.

It's calm out here. The kind of calm you don't question.

She's still wrapped in that jade-colored hoodie and matching sweats, covered head to toe like armor made of cotton and caution. Even in the warm, humid air, she's absolutely stunning.

She steps closer to the railing, and I stay a careful distance behind her, but near enough to be there, far enough not to crowd.

That little white patch in her dark hair almost glows in the moonlight, a soft silver streak against the night. The rest of her hair falls loose down her back in that messy, slept-in way—untamed, real, untouched by stylists or stage lights.

For a strange, quiet second, she doesn't look like a woman hiding from the world. She looks like someone standing right on the edge of it, trying to decide if she's ready to step back in.

"I… I'm sorry I ran, August." She finally speaks, breaking the silence that's settled thick between us. "I'm not used to being in someone else's space," she adds quietly.

I shift my weight, keeping my voice low so I don't spook her. "Elli, I want you to feel comfortable. To be comfortable."

I pause, choosing my next words carefully. "The moment Jaxon called and said he was on the way, I knew you were with him. I know we don't know each other the way you and Jaxon do, but…"

She cuts me off before I can finish. "Jaxon knows me a hell of a lot more than I know him," she says, almost to herself. "Fuck… he knows me more than I know myself these days."

Her voice drops to something barely there. "I'm scared."

That single word, "scared," lands like a punch to my chest. And suddenly I understand, this isn't about space. This isn't about couches. Or tension. It's about existing in a world that became foreign to her.

She's been hiding so long that stepping back into everyday life feels like walking across broken glass.

I turn to face her fully, really take her in this time. Her eyes are glossy, like she's been fighting the tears from the second she opened that door. Holding them back with pure will and stubborn pride.

She meets my gaze without flinching. Those big, round amber eyes look darker in the moonlight, look deeper, feral almost. Not fragile. Not broken.

Like a wolf cornered in shadow. Scared, yes. But still dangerous. Still ready to strike if the threat comes too close.

Something clicks in my head as I hold that gaze. The world sees her as fragile now. Delicate. Recovering. They're wrong.

This woman isn't weak. She's restrained. There's a difference. The fear is genuine, but so is the steel wrapped around it.

The kind of steel you only earn by surviving hell and crawling back out with your teeth bared. She isn't prey standing at the edge of a balcony. She's a predator choosing not to strike. And then, just when I think I've read her correctly, she disarms me anyway.

"I watched myself go from the happiest and most outgoing person to fighting every day to heal," she whispers. "They took from me until I had nothing left to give."

Her words land softly. But they hit harder than anything else tonight. And for the first time since I knocked on that door, I don't feel like a rugby player, or a man built to absorb impact.

The most dangerous thing in this room isn't the tension, or the fear, or even the history. It's the fact that I want to protect her, and I don't yet know whether that's a gift... or a fatal mistake.

The ocean moves behind her in slow, steady violence. The city keeps breathing like nothing in the world is wrong. And then she breaks me.

"There's something you don't know," she says quietly.

I tilt my head, already bracing. But I don't speak.

"I didn't just survive Michael," she whispers. "I became his biggest threat."

She finally looks at me then, eyes dark and unflinching.

"He didn't try to kill me because he hated me," she says quietly. "I believe he tried to kill me because I was about to expose him."

Her fingers curl into the railing so tight her knuckles bleach white.

"I found out about the money. The accounts. The laundering. Robyn wasn't just sleeping with him; she was moving everything to a shell company. I knew she would steal; I just didn't know to what length."

My blood goes cold.

"I let it happen," she whispers. And the city noise drops out of my head completely.

"I pretended I didn't see it. I pretended I didn't know where the money was going." Her voice fractures just slightly. "I guess because I was building a case. Quietly. Patiently. I was waiting for the right moment to destroy them both." The words hit me like I've been blindsided.

"And I thought." Her words fade off.

My lungs forget what they're supposed to do for a second.

I search her face in the darkness, my voice dropping to a whisper that feels like gravel in my throat. "So, what you're saying is... he didn't come after you because you were slipping away from him."

The realization crashes through me like ice water. "He came after you because his entire world was crumbling, and you were the only thing he thought he could still control."

She doesn't answer.

I rake a hand through my hair, pace once across the verandah, then stop so hard my shoes scrape against the stone.

"Fuck you were living with a target on your back," I murmur. "Buying time. And becoming a problem, he couldn't afford."

Every piece of her makes sense in a terrifying new way, the fear. The hyper-awareness. The way she watches exits. The way she doesn't trust safety unless it's earned in blood and silence.

"You were building a case," I mumble. "Against your own lover."

Her shoulders lift in the barest shrug, like it costs her nothing to say it.

"That means he's not just dangerous because of what he did to you." I meet her eyes again. "He's dangerous because of what he's afraid you still know. He made it easy."

Something cold and violent settles into my chest, but she doesn't react at all. Then her jaw tightens. Just slightly. A crack in the armor.

"Jaxon knows some of it," she admits. "Not everything. I didn't want him carrying all of it, too."

That hits me harder than I expected. "You're still protecting people," I say, disbelief edging my voice. "Even now."

Her laugh is soft and hollow. "Old habits."

The anger I've been holding back finally slips its leash.

"Ellia," I say, and for the first time, the fear breaks through my control, "if he thinks you still have proof, if he thinks you're a loose end, then this isn't over. Not even close."

Her eyes flick up to mine again, sharp despite the exhaustion. "I know."

Silence falls heavily between us. Neither of us speaks. We just stare, locked in that tense, unmoving way that feels more like a standoff than a pause. Like a predator hesitating at the edge of instinct.

A wolf deciding whether to strike... or disappear back into the dark. Then she breaks it. Too casually. Too lightly.

She looks out at the ocean, voice casual as a weather report. "I know you were on the mountain that day. I could feel you, feel him."

Something cold slides between my ribs. She turns to me, moonlight catching in her eyes.

"The nightmares come in fragments," she whispers. "Pieces that don't fit. I can't tell what's memory and what's..." Her fingers twist in the hem of her sleeve. "Was I..." The question hangs, unfinished.

Reality slides sideways, and the ocean's roar vanishes, and the coastal breeze dies against my skin. My chest freezes mid-breath.

Something murderous rises in me, the urge to craft a beautiful lie, to build walls between her and what happened on that mountain. Her unspoken question hangs between us, and I recognize its terrible shape perfectly.

My silence stretches too long, and I watch understanding dawn in her eyes before I can find the words. Her shoulders tighten, bracing for impact. The memory flashes through me, her body discarded on that mountainside, clothes askew, vulnerable in ways no one should ever be. The words lodge in my throat like broken glass.

I force them past the tightness. “Elli...”

That one word is all it takes. Her breath shudders once. But her eyes stay locked on mine. Unblinking. Waiting. And my throat locks.

Every instinct in me fractures in opposite directions: tell her the truth and destroy what little peace she still has... or lie and become the villain differently. I choose the lie.

“No,” I say.

It comes out too fast. Too clean.

“No,” I repeat, steadier now. “You weren't.” Her shoulders sag in a breath she didn't even know she was holding. Relief hits her like gravity finally loosening its grip.

“Oh,” the sound is small. Broken. I don't know if she believes me at this moment.

She fixes her gaze on the ocean. I've never hated myself more in my life.

"You were hurt," I add carefully. "Badly. But that night... that wasn't taken from you."

She nods once. Then again. Like she's anchoring the answer into her bones.

"Thank God," she whispers.

Yeah. Thank God. Because if she ever learns what really happened, what I just sentenced myself to carry alone, she will never forgive me.

CHAPTER 13

JAXON

August climbed the wide stairs to check on Ellia, the low light flickering off the white railing. I never warned him he was stepping into a trap of his own making, but soon enough, he'd learn that when Ellia's heart races past the point of bearing, she needs air like a drowning swimmer, space to draw in fresh breath.

When crowded, she doesn't burst outward; she contracts inward, a hidden implosion.

I've watched that woman splinter in silence, watched her slip behind a practiced smile, legs trembling where no one else could see.

Her stiff posture wasn't strength; it was a military maneuver, a fortress she built against panic. And if August presses too hard now, he'll shatter her, not into the brilliant, unbreakable Ellia the world knows, but into the fragile wisp she becomes when survival is all that matters.

When August visited, he kept his distance—never hovering, never pressing. But I caught his eyes following her movements, filled with a quiet determination to shoulder some of her burden. He was the only one she'd let approach on those darkest days, when even the softest footsteps from anyone else sent her retreating behind locked doors.

A shift in the humid night air warns me before I hear anything: that prickling wrongness crawling up my spine. Too much time has passed.

Ellia never stands still that long when her thoughts spin. She paces, fidgets, storms in place like thunder trapped beneath glass. Stillness means she's a bird locked in a cage with only her own heartbeat for company, and August is in that cage with her.

My jaw tightens as I replay the furtive glances they exchanged downstairs, each second stretching too long. August means well, God knows I trust him with my life, but Ellia isn't a simple rescue. She's a live wire swathed in silk.

I leave my drink on the counter with no more sound than mist settling on glass and head up the stairs. A single voice carries to me through the open doors: Ellia's, soft as a moth's wing. "Was I..."

The question doesn't echo; it detonates. I take a silent step closer, heart pounding like a war drum, and peer through the moonlit doors.

Ellia stands rigid by the railing; August faces her, shoulders slumped in the instant between truth and denial.

"No," he says, voice too swift, too immaculate. "No, you weren't."

Her exhale comes like a diver surfacing for the first time: relief carving lines in her shoulders, her bones sighing under the weight of his answer.

"Oh," she whispers.

August's gaze never wavers, but the lie cuts him open; I see the guilt, anger, and shame flicker in his eyes faster than lightning. Ellia nods faintly, sealing the answer inside her like sacred text.

I linger on the landing, watching two people I would die for fracture in opposite directions over a truth none of us can survive intact.

He lied to spare her pain, and now we all pay for that lie.

The door behind me flies open in one violent breath; August flies down the stairs so fast I feel the echo of his heat, but he doesn't look back.

Heavy footsteps pound into the garage, a single scream of tires, and then, silence again.

Ellia remains alone on the verandah, clutching a half-truth, the open French doors behind her spilling moonlight onto the marble.

I rub my forehead, bracing for what's next: a woman who believes she's safe, and a man tearing himself apart to protect her from what she can't bear to know.

I drift closer without meaning to. Through the half-open French doors, I watch Ellia retreat into the room then disappear into the master bath, trailing silver wisps of steam.

She digs through her bag until she finds her headphones, the fabric of her oversized sweatshirt whispering against itself like armor.

When she sheds first the sweatshirt, then her sweatpants, I see everything, the elegant lines of her frame, collarbones rising like wings, the gentle curve where ribs meet skin, those arms somehow both strong and defenseless. And there, etched across her body, the permanent testimony of that night's violence.

The sight stops me cold. My chest tightens as I force my eyes downward. This is the precise moment I should have left. But she pauses mid-motion, one shoulder lifting as though she can sense me there.

She wraps her arms around herself, skin flushed by the humid air and something deeper, an exposure that has nothing to do with bare flesh.

My pulse drums in my ears as hunger wraps the line I swore I'd never cross. I clench my fist, step back into the shadow, and vanish before I betray this guardian role I've upheld for a few years.

"Jaxon." Her voice is a soft plea drifting through the half-open door. My name in her mouth shatters me.

I don't respond. She calls again, and I know she is searching for a lifeline. Against every instinct, I step forward into the muted glow of the bedroom. Curtains sway in the ocean wind.

The hush of water drawing me in from the bathroom makes me pause at the threshold. There she is, seated in the tub, knees drawn tight, hair pinned in a knot, bare shoulders lifting gently with her breathing.

Headphones rest against her neck, music a distant heartbeat. She stares out the window, unseeing, lost in the horizon.

I should leave. Instead, I step onto cool tile. Our eyes meet in the window, hers measured, unstartled, as though she'd been waiting.

Moonlight finds the ridge along her back— a pale, jagged memory carved from shoulder to ribs. I've spent a year trying to forget the night that left it there.

The others have mostly vanished, but I still map their ghost-trails beneath her clothes. It's not knowledge a bodyguard should possess, the precise constellation of her healing, witnessed through bandage changes and moments when she thought no one was watching her turn away.

She breaks the quiet. "I felt you there." Her tone is steady, unguarded. "I felt you leave."

A pause, and then: "I didn't want you to leave."

My throat tightens. "I'm here," I whisper, voice softer than the ocean's sigh.

"Good."

She shifts slightly, sending ripples across the water's surface. "It's okay if you can't look at it."

I find myself staring at the condensation trails on the window.

"I know it's there," she says, voice barely audible above the water. "But sometimes I need to believe I'm more than just... what happened to me."

Her words land like stones. I rest my shoulder against the doorframe, letting the wood's cool grain anchor me.

"You are," I say, voice firm. "I remember who you were before it, and who you are now."

Silence stretches.

Then, softly: "I've never told you this..." I sense her listening. "I replay that night every time I close my eyes. Not the crash, or the blood, but the moment I almost lost you." My palm presses into the tile beside me. "I don't dream of saving you, I dream of being too late."

She turns at last, face raw, unadorned by her usual armor. Steam beads on her lashes; uncertainty trembles in her parted lips.

"I didn't know," she whispers.

"You weren't supposed to." I meet her gaze, the air between us crackling with things we dare not touch.

"I thought I was alone in this," she says.

"You were never supposed to."

My phone vibrates in my pocket, once, twice—shattering the fragile world we've built here. I glance down, then back at her wary eyes.

"You should answer that," she murmurs.

I step back into the bedroom, keeping my back to her so she won't feel abandoned. I tap the screen. "Talk."

Static, wind. Then my team's voice, sharp as a bullet: "Movement on Robyn was sighted in L.A. She bought the Bentley, matching your intel."

My blood freezes. "When?"

"A few days ago, we're tracking her now."

I close my eyes, the tub's water stilling behind me. Ellia senses the shift before I can continue. I end the call, slide back against the doorframe, and gather my resolve.

I don't break the silence, just hold her gaze, letting the weight of what I've learned assemble itself into purpose.

She watches me. At last, she asks in a careful breath, "What is it?"

"Something we've been waiting for," I say.

Her reflection in the mirror catches the flicker of moonlight.

Outside, the ocean hums on— steady, indifferent, but tonight, part of our shared vigil.

"Jaxon," she says, my name falling from her lips like a stone into still water.

I hold her gaze, every muscle in my body tensing as if preparing for a blow. The air between us thickens, charged with everything we've never said.

"Why do you call me songbird?" The question hangs between us, fragile as a held breath.

My throat tightens. "Because when you sing, I hear what freedom sounds like." I step closer, voice dropping to nearly a whisper. "Because I've watched you build fortress after fortress inside yourself, and still, something wild remains. Because the first time I saw you, I recognized that look in your eyes. The one that says you've forgotten how to trust the sky."

"I like it," she says, her fingers trembling slightly against the windowsill.

CHAPTER 14

ELLIA

My lungs stop mid- breath, replaced by a throbbing pulse between my thighs. The world contracts to the thin ribbon of space between us, to the low, inexorable timbre of his voice that vibrates through my core like a promise of what's to come.

I lock eyes with Jaxon because his gaze pins me in place—hungry, demanding—and the raw need I see there makes my skin prickle with anticipation.

The water trembles when I shift, my nipples hardening as they break the surface. My lips part involuntarily, and heat floods my skin where the water parts and air rushes in, every nerve ending begging for his touch.

Every nerve ignites: how naked and vulnerable I am, how unmoving he remains, how the air itself seems to lean closer, straining to hear.

My knees press into my chin, a shield of bone and flesh that fools neither of us. The bathwater ripples as I lean back, exhaling a breath that's been trapped beneath my sternum for too long.

Jaxon kept his promise. I can see it in the shadows beneath his eyes, the tension in his jaw. He's been digging up graves while I've been planning funerals.

He thinks I want salvation, but what I truly hunger for is the weight of the gavel in my palm. Let him believe I seek justice; what I crave is retribution.

When the moment arrives, prison bars or cemetery gates. I want to be the face they see last, the name that withers on their tongues. Not mercy. Not absolution. Just the living embodiment of every consequence they never thought would find them.

He watches me like a living weapon left too close, a mechanism bristling with potential violence yet chafing under restraint. His gaze tracks every tremor of my skin, every ripple I've forced stillness to betray, every inhale that misses its beat.

It isn't lust in his eyes. It's something wilder. I see his jaw tighten, the muscle jumping once, then clamping down like a steel trap as his eyes roam over me.

Control reasserting itself, like half a heartbeat too late. His hands curl into fists at his sides, knuckles going white beneath intricate swirls of ink that snake over tendon and bone, vanishing under the cuff of his sleeve.

Even the slightest movement twists the artwork, revealing the brute force of his containment, the friction in every locked joint. He notices me studying the tattoos, my silent mapping of every line, every hidden symbol.

The charged awareness crackles between us. He knows exactly what I'm imagining: those dark designs pressed against my skin. My pulse pounds the thought up into my throat before my courage can rein it in.

"Are you always this still?" I breathe, the words dropping like a blade between us, "or am I the exception that freezes your blood?"

The question detonates, splintering the air.

At last, something in Jaxon splinters, too. So small I almost miss it, yet seismic under the surface.

I hear his breath catch; his jaw twitches as though he'd grind his teeth down to dust. His fists clench tighter, fingers flexing with a brutal deliberation that telegraphs exactly how close he is to losing it.

When he speaks, his voice is a low rumble, a whisper laced with danger: "You shouldn't ask that."

The words aren't cold, they're the taut line of a noose, quivering just before it snaps.

I part my knees, letting them fall open in the water, a gesture both defiant and conceding. The tub ripples in response; his gaze darkens, the rip through steam.

My skin flushes despite the heat of the bath, a shiver running through me. His knuckles whiten as he grips his legs, and I wonder which of us will drown first.

The walls draw nearer, as if the room itself can't stand to witness what's coming. Inch by inch, he straightens, each movement calibrated, a predator tightening its coil. His chest swells; his scent swamps me.

He bends forward, the heat of his exhalation brushing my cheek.

"You're playing with fire," he growls, chest vibrating against the word.

I tilt my head, letting the mist curl around us like a vow.

"Yet here you are, still burning with me."

His reply is a growl, raw and controlled: "You don't know the darkness you're unleashing, Ellia."

My whisper scrapes my throat raw: "I want your darkness to devour mine whole."

Something snaps behind his eyes, the last thread of restraint severing. A sound claws up from his chest that makes my blood surge hot and terrified.

His breath scorches my neck in violent bursts; his pupils flood black like spilled ink, consuming everything until I'm drowning in that void.

"Last chance," he rasps, fingertips drifting toward me, like a magnet. "Once I start..."

I give him precisely the permission that will break him: "Stop waiting for it."

With a predator's grace, he pushes from the door and kneels beside the tub. His presence hits me like a physical pulse: the warmth of the water on my legs, the gravity of his stare, the lonesome hush between us now that the music is gone.

He reaches up, slips the headphones from around my neck, as "Say Yea" by Niykee Heaton plays, and sets them aside. Silence floods in, mercurial, intimate, unyielding. His eyes roam to my parted lips, then back to my eyes.

"Ellia," he murmurs.

My pulse stutters. "You took the music away," I manage.

"So, you can hear what you're asking for."

I swallow the words. "I'm not asking anymore."

"So, I can hear you when you try to stop me."

"I won't," I breathe.

His hand finds my throat, thumb pressing into the pulse point, drawing me closer. He turns me to face the window, where I meet his dark gaze.

The pressure steals my breath; pleasure threads through the sting. My nipples tighten against the cool air as his other hand sinks beneath the surface, seeking out bare skin with predatory precision.

His voice drops to a register that vibrates through my bones, each syllable a caress against my most private thoughts. "I have waited so long," he breathes against my neck, his lips barely grazing my skin, "for your fire to return."

The heat in his eyes burns away whatever remains of my resistance, leaving only molten need in its wake.

"I've imagined the taste of you burning against my tongue."

My back arches; a soft moan breaks free as he cups my breast with merciless rhythm, never faltering even as I writhe and buck against him. The tub's porcelain edge gouges into my spine, this barrier suddenly an agony I long to crush.

"Jaxon," I gasp, voice ragged with need.

He answers with something guttural, like a beast exulting in the chase. His hand slides between my thighs with devastating purpose, fingers circling that swollen, sensitive point where all sensation converges.

When he plunges two fingers inside me, the stretch burns exquisitely, too much and not enough. My body yields, clenching around his invasion as wetness floods between us, my arousal painting his skin with undeniable evidence of what he does to me.

My head drops back on his shoulder, and his voice drops to a harsh snarl at my ear: "Oh, songbird, I want to devour you until you have nothing left, every drop of you."

My body trembles, betraying me as his thumb lands on that electric spot inside me. I clench around him until the water quakes, splashing over the rim. My walls grip and pulse, dragging him deeper.

I try to scream, but all that comes out is a raw, animal sound as his fingers thrust deeper inside me, curling against that spot that makes my vision blur.

He leans close, teeth grazing my earlobe, voice a gravelly whisper: "You have no idea what you have done."

My back arches violently against him, my wetness coating his hand.

I acknowledge with a desperate moan, anything else dies in my throat as he squeezes, stealing my breath while his thumb circles my swollen clit with merciless precision.

He lets out a growl that transcends human terror—ancient, possessive. His teeth graze my earlobe; warm blood beads between us.

My release tears through me like wildfire, consuming everything in its path. I arch against him, my body a live wire beneath his touch, as he holds my head still with brutal tenderness.

"Look," he commands, voice rough with need, and I can't look away from our reflection—my flushed skin, parted lips, the naked hunger in his eyes as he watches me come undone against his hand.

I taste only him, his tongue claiming my mouth with savage possession, his teeth catching my lower lip until I whimper.

He withdraws just enough to whisper against my quaking skin: "Now that I have had a taste of you, there is no going back. Every scar you carry, I will erase with my touch until your flesh remembers only me."

He holds me there, tethered to the aftermath, his breathing steadying me as gravity pulls me back into my bones. He doesn't break the silence; he preserves it, makes it a sanctuary.

Slowly, the heat dulls to a molten warmth, my breath returning, my heart dragging life back into its chambers.

I register the weight of water, the cool air on my shoulders, the shock of calm flooding my chest. Tears burn at the edges of my vision. Tears for what's been undone.

Jaxon studies me with that unblinking intensity, as though he can see the war raging inside me: desire clashing with fear, hope skirmishing with regret. I know it's going to rend me apart, that I may never piece myself together again the way I was.

He doesn't let me go, not when my strength falters, limbs collapsing like spent silk. His hand slides up my arm, fingers digging in just enough to pin me to this moment, to him.

"You are mine, now," he growls, voice deceptively gentle.

The single word cleaves through my last defenses. Before I can shape resistance, he hoists me from the water.

A waterfall of droplets cascades from my skin, each a pinprick of cold.

He wraps me in a towel with clinical precision, mercy bound in threads, yet the predator's hunger still flickers in his gaze. It shatters me more than his violence.

He cradles me against his chest; my weight is nothing to his strength, my trembling body both prey and prize. He eases me onto the mattress, securing the towel around me as though I were something exquisite and fragile.

Then he leans down, breath warm against my ear: "You belong to me now."

I look away, though I feel the brand of those words sear into my soul. And I know there is no going back to 'before', and my heart hammers in my chest at that realization.

CHAPTER 15

AUGUST

I had to get out of there. The lie I told Ellia sits in my chest like a live wire. Why did I lie? Why couldn't I just tell her the truth?

I keep turning it over, every possible outcome gnawing at me.

What if the truth had pushed her deeper into the dark? Or what if it was the ammunition she needed to stay standing? I'll never know now.

But when the truth finally surfaces, and it will, she'll understand how lies calcify into their own reality, no matter how desperately we try to outrun them.

The moment I met Ellia, the world shifted. She had this presence, this quiet gravity that bent the surrounding air. An aura you don't escape once it locks onto you. I knew immediately that I needed her in my life. That kind of knowing is a curse as much as it is a gift.

Before her, it was all noise. The constant chasing. The bodies that didn't mean anything. The fan girls, the nights that blurred together into one long distraction.

I told myself it was freedom. I told myself it was control. It was just a void I didn't know how to name.

Jaxon brought me into her world like it was nothing, like he didn't realize what he was opening the door to. Maybe he still doesn't. Or maybe he does, and we're all pretending this doesn't already feel like the beginning of something that will burn whoever gets closest.

Hours slip past without names. Only the steady drain of amber from the bottle to the glass, to my throat.

The pub is loud in the way it always is, some of my teammates clustered near the back, fan girls rotating through like orbiting debris, all of it noise I usually know how to disappear into.

Tonight, it doesn't work. The lie circles in my head like a blade I can't put down. Whiskey burns a familiar path down my chest, and the edge of it feels earned. Necessary.

I should've told her. I should've let her decide what the truth would do to her instead of deciding for her like a coward wrapped in good intentions.

Laughter erupts to my left, too loud, too forced. A girl I don't recognize brushes her hand over my shoulder like she's entitled to it. I don't even look at her.

There was a time that would've been enough. There was a time I would've let the night disappear into the shape of someone else's body just to shut my head up.

I see her everywhere now, in the curve of condensation on the glass, in the way the door swings open and closed, in the spaces between words when no one knows what to say. I look for her without meaning to. I measure everything against her without permission.

The girl circles behind me and plants herself at my side, pressing her back against the bar as if she belongs there. Her elbows rest on the bar top, casually. Practiced.

"I watched you play last week," she says, smiling like she's already halfway into a story we both know the ending to. "I've been wanting to meet you."

There was a time when that line might have worked on me without any effort. I could pick and choose who I needed to fuck, but now? It's only Ellia I want. And tonight, it just makes everything worse.

"That so?" I mumble, lifting my glass instead of looking at her.

She laughs softly, undeterred. Slides a finger along the rim of her own drink. "You were incredible out there. That last play..."

"I know," I cut in. Not cruel. Just honest. I don't need the reminder.

Something flickers across her face: surprise, maybe. Then she recovers, leaning in closer, her shoulder brushing mine. The contact is deliberate, like an invitation, making me pull back.

Ellia's face flashes in my head without permission—quiet, steady, impossible. The way she looks at the world is like it's already broken and she's daring it to break her again.

The girl beside me reeks of cheap perfume and desperation, sticky sweetness that makes my stomach turn. She shifts closer, her availability hanging in the air between us like something rotting.

My skin crawls where her arm brushes mine. That hollow inside me, the one only Ellia could ever fill, contracts in revulsion.

"Buy me a drink?" She asks, lips wet with gloss.

"I'm already drinking," I say, angling away from her breath.

She studies me for a beat, something predatory shifting behind her eyes. Her fingers find my forearm, nails digging in just enough to make my skin crawl.

"I don't think you understand," she purrs, leaning close enough that I can count the pores beneath her makeup.

The sickly-sweet smell of her breath makes bile rise in my throat. "I'm not asking."

Something in me breaks clean. Not loud. Not explosive at first. Just a hard, internal click, the sound of restraint giving way.

I jerk my arm free from her grip. The movement is sharp enough to send her stumbling back a step. Glass sloshes. Someone nearby laughs nervously, thinking it's still part of the show.

“Don't,” I say.

The word lands flat and final. She doesn't hear it that way. Her hand comes back for me, greedier this time, possessive. “You don't get to tell me—”

"Touch me again, and I'll break every fucking finger you put on me."

The promise in my tone makes her pupils dilate with fear. I explode upward, stool crashing to the floor as something primal takes over.

My fist slams down, glass shattering into a constellation of razor-edged stars. Blood mingles with whiskey across my knuckles, the sting barely registering through the roar in my head.

The bar goes cemetery-silent, every eye locked on the violence coiled in my shoulders. The bouncer materializes between us, his massive frame vibrating with tension.

"That's enough," he growls, eyes never leaving mine. "Both of you. Out. Now."

When I finally make it home, I shouldn't have driven. I know that. The road is a blur I don't remember, stitched together by instinct and whiskey and regret. All of it spiraling around the one woman I can't have or even tell the truth to.

The house is dark when I pull in. No lights. No noise. No sign of Jaxon or Ellia. The quiet feels heavier than sound.

Stumbling through the garage, I clip the door on my way in, the metal groaning in protest. I freeze, listening for movement. But there is nothing. The kitchen greets me with icy stillness.

Good job, August. You really fucked up whatever chance you had with her.

The living room is wrong without them. No, Jaxon planted on the couch, watching whatever late-night news he broods over. No, Ellia curled into the corner with her quiet gravity. I check my phone with clumsy fingers.

Past midnight. I start up the stairs, trying not to make a sound and spectacularly failing. My hand clamps around the banister like it's the only thing keeping me upright. Each step creaks its disapproval.

Then I notice Ellia's door. Still open. I move closer, slow now. Careful.

The bathroom light inside is dim, soft. And there, Jaxon sits in one of the oversized chairs facing the bed. Arms crossed over his chest in that protective, dangerous way he carries like second skin. He looks up as soon as I step into the doorway.

Doesn't say a word. Just tips his head toward the bed. That's when I see her.

She sleeps beneath the covers like she's wrapped in cloud and shadow, the room holding its breath around her.

Safe, for now. Held there by the quiet vigilance of the man watching over her.

I slide into the matching chair without a word. The wood creaks softly beneath my weight, loud in the stillness, but neither of them moves. I let my eyes settle on her.

Her breathing is even, steady. The kind of peace that feels fragile and hard-won. Her hair is twisted into a messy knot, barely holding together the black and white strands that refuse to be tamed.

She's curled on her left side, facing the verandah, the door still cracked open just enough to let the night in.

The only sound is the ocean. Rolling in and out like it's governing the calm in the room, as if the tide itself is tasked with keeping her steady. She looks... calm.

I haven't seen her like this since before that night. Before the mountains. Before the violence, the terror, and the shattering of everything, leaving it permanently altered.

My chest tightens at the sight of it.

"You're drunk," Jaxon says, low and controlled.

"I fucked up, Jaxon."

He starts to shake his head, then stops. He lets out a breath like he's been holding it in for hours. "No, you didn't," he says finally. "I would've done the same thing."

His eyes flick to Ellia, still asleep. "She's strong, but knowing that..."

A pause. Heavy and deliberate. "It would've destroyed her beyond repair."

The words settle into me like wet concrete. "That doesn't make it right," I whisper.

"No," he agrees quietly. "It just makes it survivable. For now."

I glance back at her, at the steady rise and fall of her chest. "What happens when 'for now' runs out?"

Jaxon's jaw tightens. "Then we deal with what's left."

"And if she never forgives us?"

His eyes return to me, sharp in the dim. "Then we live with it," he says. "So, she doesn't have to."

"Jaxon," I start. The words jam up somewhere between guilt and longing. I don't know how to give them shape without betraying everything at once.

That what I feel for the woman who sleeps across from me isn't love, it's something far more dangerous.

He doesn't look at me right away. Just breathes out slowly through his nose, eyes still on Ellia. "I know," he says quietly. "I do too."

We sit there, the two of us, suspended in the suffocating silence of secrets too dangerous to voice.

On the bed, Ellia's body suddenly goes rigid. Her breathing turns ragged, chest heaving as if she's running from something in the dark.

The whimpers start low in her throat, animal sounds of pure terror that slice through the room.

"Nightmare," Jaxon hisses, already moving.

Her body convulses once, violently, spine arching off the mattress. A sound tears from her lips, not a cry but a scream swallowed back into flesh.

Jaxon lunges toward her, movements predatory in their precision.

"What do I..." My question dies as her fingers claw at invisible wounds.

"Don't touch her," Jaxon commands, voice razor-sharp. "Last time she woke fighting, she nearly broke my jaw. She won't know it's you, only sees them."

Jaxon hovers over her, his voice a dangerous whisper. "Ellia." His hand suspends inches from her skin, trembling with restraint. Her cries escalate to raw, guttural sounds that claw at my insides.

"Ellia," he tries again, desperation edging his voice. "They're not here. You're with me. You're safe."

Sweat gleams on his forehead as he fights his instinct to grab her.

"Michael, NO!" The name tears from her throat like something ripped from her soul. Head flailing, tendons straining against skin.

His fingers finally make contact with her shoulder. The effect is instantaneous; her eyes fly open, wild and unseeing.

For one terrible moment, I see pure animal terror in them before recognition floods back. Jaxon cradles her face between his palms, his thumbs brushing tears from her cheekbones.

"Songbird," he breathes, forehead pressed to hers. "I've got you."

I'm frozen at the foot of the bed, watching her claw her way back to consciousness. Her skin glistens with night terrors, eyes wild and unfocused like shattered glass catching moonlight.

The thing that broke her all those months ago seems to pulse beneath her skin, threatening to tear her open again.

"Jaxon, August," she gasps, my name in her mouth like a prayer or a curse.

Her fingers tremble violently against her face, fighting back tears that haven't fallen yet would drown her if they did.

Her gaze locks onto us both, a drowning woman spotting shore. Jaxon's fingers dig into her shoulders, not hard enough to bruise, but as if his grip alone keeps her tethered to this world.

"Don't," she whispers, the word raw and bleeding.

I watch it hit Jaxon like a bullet—his pupils dilate, breath catching in his throat, something primal and terrified flashing across his face as he steps back, hands raised in surrender.

"Don't leave me," she begs, each syllable ripped from somewhere vital and damaged. "Not tonight."

We move like predators answering a call, one to each side of her. Her eyes find mine first, wild and haunted. Then Jaxon's, as her breathing slows from prey-like to something human again.

Without speaking, she shifts to the center and peels back the duvet, an offering that feels both sacred and profane.

I strip my shirt off, kick away my shoes, my hands trembling with bourbon and need. Jaxon is already down to his boxers, moonlight catching on the constellation of tattoos and scars that map his torso.

A bath towel is all she has on. I slide next to her, and the fabric splits open just enough at her thigh. When I look, Jaxon notices.

His mouth twists into something that makes my throat go dry. "She was..." His voice drops low. "I got her into bed."

The king bed shrinks as our bodies claim it. My thigh presses against hers, and I feel her pulse hammering through her skin. Jaxon pulls the covers over us, his arm possessively spanning her waist. She looks between us, vulnerability and strength warring in her expression.

"Thank you," she whispers, and the words ignite something in me.

The need to protect her warring with darker impulses I've buried for months. I want to crush her against me until our heartbeats synchronize, but I know the wrong move could shatter everything she is fighting.

Her scent, lavender and something darker, more essential, floods my senses, my body hardening in response. I hate myself for it, for wanting her when she's this broken.

Her fingers dig into Jaxon's tattooed forearm; knuckles bleached with pressure. A single violent tremor passed through her, like lightning struck the ground, then vanished.

The silence that followed was so complete, so absolute, I questioned whether her scream had been real or just another phantom in my mind.

Jaxon goes silent. He leans back, his body a shield between her and whatever dangers might be hiding in the bedroom's dim corners, as if his flesh alone could stop both real threats and the ones that exist only in our minds.

His hand never leaves her; he watches her face like it might detonate or vanish, depending.

I don't know if I've ever seen vulnerability that raw, bleeding right through the mask Ellia has welded on over the months.

I don't know what to do with myself, so I fold my limbs into the space that's left and wait. Through the architecture of sheets and bodies, I can see the pearly streaks of moon drifting across Ellia's bare shoulder. Her scars are so faint, yet undeniable.

She looks like the Ellia I knew, the one who could take on the world and burn it down when she wants. The Ellia I fell in love with the first time I met her.

CHAPTER 16

ELLIA

Morning light creeps through the curtains in slow, pale ribbons, dust motes dancing in the golden beams as my eyes drift open with it, heavy-lidded and reluctant.

For a moment, I just lie there, suspended between sleep and waking, trying to name what I feel. Rested. The word tastes unfamiliar on my tongue. Almost suspicious.

Did I have a nightmare? I can't remember the usual metallic tang of fear, the cold sweat, the racing heart. Did I sleep through the night? I must have. And somehow, impossibly, I feel good. Lighter.

Like my body finally unclenched while I wasn't watching, muscles no longer coiled tight as a spring about to snap.

I'm still wrapped in the towel Jaxon covered me with. The fabric has shifted but not fallen away, soft cotton clinging to the curve of my hip, the hollow between my breasts. A quiet act of care that makes my throat tighten.

I sit up slowly, wincing only a little as the room settles into focus, the dull throb behind my eyes more habit than pain. And that's when I see them, feel them. Not just Jaxon beside me, but August too.

Both look peaceful. August's legs tangled with mine, the rough hair on his calves scratching against my skin. Jaxon's hand on my waist, his fingers splayed possessively, heat radiating from his palm like a brand.

The feeling of security and protection wraps around me like another layer, dangerous and intoxicating.

Is this why I feel like I slept through the night? Did they calm me, these two men who shouldn't be in my bed, shouldn't be in my life at all?

Slowly, I shift free from between them. They barely stir as I untangle myself. "Don't get used to this, Ellia. They're only here to protect you. Don't be ridiculous," I whisper, self-doubt churning low in my stomach.

My feet hit the floor, quiet and determined. I need to get dressed before they see my skin.

I pad over to the suitcase Jaxon brought in yesterday.

First comes my favorite black hoodie, then the matching sweatpants. I lay them neatly on the bed's edge and dig beneath for my bra and panties, a simple black cotton set to do the trick.

I glance back. They haven't moved. Good. Jaxon's hand still rests where I slept. August breathes steadily.

Seeing them like that, unguarded, exhausted, real, ignites something warm and dangerous in my chest. I creep past, each bare step deliberate. The bathroom door clicks shut with a whisper, and only then do I let myself exhale.

In the mirror, I freeze. A faint mark curves behind my ear, invisible to anyone but me, a quiet imprint of last night. Heat rushes up my neck before I can stop it, because this is a mark that I welcome, unlike the others.

I dress in a hurry: hoodie over my head, brush through my hair, teeth scrubbed as if rinsing memory and sleep. The girl in the mirror looks calmer than she feels, or maybe she's finally catching up.

Outside, I hear the bed shift. The covers lift. They're awake, and my hand hovers over the doorknob.

"Ellia." Jaxon's voice is low and tight, threaded with something that sounds dangerously like fear. My chest clenches.

I open the door. "I'm here," I murmur.

His shoulders sag just enough. "I thought you'd gone," he admits in a hush. "I thought I'd scared you off with what happened last night."

"You can't scare me away like that," I say and step closer.

We drift into each other's space without meaning to. His warmth seeps through the thin air between us, familiar and unsettling all at once. His eyes search my face, afraid I might vanish if he looks away.

Then August stirs, pushing himself upright, rubbing at his eyes, still half-lost in sleep.

"It was a nightmare, Ellia. We saw you fighting it," he says wearily, "you asked us to stay."

He fixes me with a look that is almost an accusation, but there's worry in the lines of his mouth.

Pieces of the dream started flickering in the back of my skull, fragments of voices shouting my name, someone reaching for me but not quite catching hold.

"It was just a dream," I manage, voice steadier than I feel. "Nothing new."

But the way Jaxon looks at me says he's not convinced, so I force a crooked smile, shake off the weight of his eyes, and duck around him, heading to the kitchen.

I need coffee, maybe a gallon, and distance, at least the kind measured in steps. My hands shake a little; I pretend it's from the chill of the tile, not the memory of being lost, so lost.

"Coffee?" I murmur, already moving. Slipping past them, the space between us brushes tight and electric as I go.

"Elli," August calls softly behind me. "I'm sorry I ran on you last night. I... I just needed to clear my head."

I pause at the doorway to the stairs, my back still to them. "I understand, August," I say, and mean it.

Then, softer, with a small, crooked truth I don't bother hiding. "I'm a master at running when I need to clear my own head."

I head down the stairs toward the kitchen, toward coffee and distance and the fragile promise of a normal morning, knowing full well that nothing about us is normal anymore.

Behind me, I hear August try again. "Is she talking about the nightmare, Jax?"

His voice is quieter this time. Careful. I don't hear Jaxon's answer. But by the time I step into the kitchen, I feel the shift in the air anyway.

Like the house itself has inhaled and decided not to exhale yet. Every instinct in me goes tight, coiled and alert. I won't survive this. Not them.

I drag my hands down my face, the skin pulling beneath my fingers. "Jesus, Elli," I whisper to myself. "What were you thinking?"

The memory surfaces in fragments: my voice in the darkness, asking not one but both to stay.

The kitchen is a pocket of hush and cool light. I fill the pot and set it aside, wrapping both hands around my mug. I breathe for the first time since I woke.

I don't even really drink coffee, not since everything that happened. But I miss the ritual. I miss the grounding weight of it, the grasping after a normal that no longer belongs to me anymore.

The urge to run is still thrumming through my bones, primal and unhelpful, so I let the minor tasks eat at my nerves instead.

I feel them before I see them. Counting the heartbeats between their footsteps on the stairs.

I've taken a seat at the small kitchen table, one knee drawn up like a barrier I know is useless. My pulse hasn't settled since I woke. The mug burns against my palms, but I grip it harder, needing the pain to ground me.

When they finally enter, my throat goes dry. I feel him before I see him, Jaxon, a dense gravity filling the room ahead of his actual body. I brace myself for the inevitable questions.

He's always careful not to crowd me, but sometimes it feels like the question is somehow bigger than either of us, pressing in from every direction until the only option is to answer it.

Jaxon first, black hair still damp, soft waves across his brow. His button-up clings where his skin hasn't dried properly, the fabric darkening in places I shouldn't notice. Sleeves rolled to expose forearms marked with ink that seems to move with each flex of muscle. His green eyes find mine with such piercing clarity that I have to swallow hard.

Then August. God. Shirtless. The tattoos across his chest aren't just designs but trails my fingers itch to follow. Worn jeans hanging dangerously low, that devastating V of muscle disappearing beneath denim.

I can't look away. Can't breathe right. The space between us feels charged with something that might kill me if I acknowledge it.

I press my thighs together under the table, lift the mug to hide how my lips have parted, but the steam does nothing to cool the heat crawling up my neck, pooling low in my belly.

Two storms are converging, and I'm the breaking point.

A soft "ahm" shatters the silence.

I look away, but the heat in my cheeks betrays me. Between my thighs, a desperate, pulsing ache builds as they take the seats flanking me, caged by their bodies, their proximity.

August's scent hits first: smoked cedar with undertones of sandalwood and raw leather, like expensive sin bottled into cologne. It crawls inside my lungs, settles low in my belly.

The scent of crushed mint and worn leather wafts from Jaxon, so familiar it hurts. My treacherous body recognizes it instantly, the same phantom fragrance that haunts me on those nights I wake with his name on my lips.

Their eyes pin me like twin predators. August's gaze drops to my throat, tracking the pulse that betrays me there. Jaxon watches my lips, the way they part slightly when I try to breathe. The air between us thickens, dangerous.

I panic. "When is your next game, August?" I blurt out, like I don't already know the answer. Like it hasn't been counting down in the back of my mind since the schedule was posted.

"Friday," he says, leaning forward until I can count his eyelashes. "Will you be there?"

I glance at Jaxon for escape, but find no mercy. His lips curl into that half-smile that makes my stomach hollow out, the one that sends heat spiraling down my spine like molten metal.

His eyes darken as he watches me squirm between them, pupils dilating until only a thin ring of emerald remains.

This version of me, flushed and wanting, pulse hammering visibly at my throat, is foreign to us. He's used to the girl who curls into herself on the couch, body tense and small, fingers white-knuckled around the remote as she half-watches something familiar just to drown out the screaming in her skull. Usually, it's something safe. Predictable.

I almost laugh, the sound catching painfully in my throat. My tongue darts out to wet my suddenly parched lips, and I don't miss how both men track the movement.

I keep looking at Jaxon, silently begging. His jaw tightens, the muscle there jumping beneath stubbled skin.

After a beat, he cuts through the chaos in my head, his voice a low rumble that vibrates through the air between us.

"We'll try," he says, each word deliberate.

His hand slides across the table, stopping just short of mine. "She hasn't been out in over a year. People come to her if she needs anything."

His thumb traces an invisible pattern on the wood, and I can almost feel the ghost of that touch on my skin.

August just grins, as if the rules have always been more a suggestion than a law.

"Good thing I've already got a box reserved, then," he says with that usual Aussie cockiness that always sneaks a laugh out of me when I least expect it. "Just yours, comfort for your grand re-entry."

I do laugh—softly, involuntarily. Big mistake.

Jaxon's jaw tightens immediately. The shift in him is subtle but lethal. His green eyes cut from August back to me, storm-deep and unblinking, like he can see straight through every fear I'm pretending not to feel. And the room goes quiet again.

Then, finally, he ends my spiral with soft words, but blunt enough to anchor me. "You don't have to decide right now, Elli."

I nod, sipping my coffee to hide the tremble in my lips. "Okay," I whisper, the word barely disturbing the air between us.

Jaxon's sharp glare softens at the edges when I add, "As long as you come too. Not as my shadow, but as yourself."

His jaw tightens, head tilting as he dissects every syllable I've just offered. August's grin spreads slowly and victoriously, revealing teeth that are too white, too sharp, too perfect.

"I want to, so if I'm doing this," I continue, pulse hammering in my throat, "then you're not on duty. You'll have to actually exist in the moment. With me."

The room goes silent. Jaxon's jaw tightens; August's eyes widen slightly. They stare at me like I've just torn up some invisible contract between us.

"Will there be cameras?" My voice breaks on the question.

Jaxon leans close, his breath warm against my skin. "Songbird," he murmurs, the word settling into me like a stone dropping into still water. "Don't you understand yet? Looking after you was never just a job."

His hand finds my wrist, his fingers forming a complete circle around it.

"From that first day at the awards ceremony, when you took my outstretched hand, you became a part of me. What's mine, I shield. Always."

The word detonates between my thighs, liquid heat flooding me so suddenly I have to bite back a whimper. Jaxon's attention snaps to August, something primal and territorial darkening his features.

"Answer her question. Will she be exposed?" Jaxon turns to August.

"I'll handle everything personally, love." August's voice drops an octave, his accent thickening as he drags his teeth over his bottom lip.

“Do you trust me?” August asks, raising an eyebrow.

The question hangs between us like a blade. I do trust him with parts of me I've never surrendered before. But admitting it means acknowledging other truths: how I crave them both, how I remember their bodies pressed against mine in that bed, how I've imagined their hands replacing mine in the dark.

I look to Jaxon, expecting intervention, but find only hunger. He sets his mug down with deliberate control, leans forward until I can see the flecks of silver in his irises, and waits, patient as a wolf who knows his prey is cornered.

My mouth goes dry. "I'll tell you after Friday's game."

I meet August's gaze directly, something reckless taking over. "Win, and maybe I'll show you exactly how much I trust you both."

August leans back in his chair, his hunger now unmasked and predatory. The air between us vibrates with unspoken promises.

"I need to go," Jaxon announces after breakfast, his voice clipped. "The search for Michael and Robyn continues."

His confidence about closing in on them doesn't convince me. Michael is a ghost when he wants to be, vanishing for weeks between tours, leaving no digital footprint, no trail.

Part of me understands the impulse to disappear. How many times had I fantasized about escaping to some nameless Caribbean beach, salt-rimmed glass in hand, while record executives demanded more of my blood, more of my soul?

The irony doesn't escape me now; those same executives unknowingly answer to me. My shadow identity now owns the label that once owned me.

Money talks. I threw enough at them to drown out questions and presented credentials too impressive to ignore. They sold their empire in less than a week.

Jaxon has no idea that the owner and I are the same. If he hasn't uncovered my secret, August certainly hasn't either. My shadow self remains just that, a shadow.

I never intended to become a record label owner. But after weeks of executives hounding me about album deadlines and tour dates, something in me snapped.

The third album was to be released while I was still touring America, with barely a breath before Europe. But nearly dying and having people still hunting me wasn't a reason enough to pause.

Even knowing fragments of what happened that night, they kept pushing. So, I made a call and bought the entire label.

I have drifted across the estate for hours, restless yet content. Jaxon hunches over screens in his surveillance sanctuary while August's grunts echo from the gym. The rhythm of their presence has begun to feel dangerously like home.

I finally collapse into a weathered Adirondack chair at the property's edge, where the manicured lawn surrenders to the cliffs' drop and endless ocean beyond.

"Found you at last, beautiful." August's voice materializes behind me, followed by his footsteps crossing from the French doors.

His shadow falls across my shoulders before he does. August sinks into the Adirondack chair beside me. He's still shirtless. Hair damp, gym sweat wicked away from the sharp wind off the water.

Sprawling out in typical August fashion—legs long, arms draped over the arms, eyes facing the ocean but angled sideways to watch me.

He waits just long enough for it to get awkward and then asks: "You ever get tired of staring at the water?"

I snorted, but the edge of a smile threatened. "Only when it stares back," I say.

My throat constricts as I force the words out. "August," I whisper, my voice cracking. "Friday night terrifies me. Not just scared, terrified."

His eyes darken, pupils dilating as he leans forward. "I've handled everything personally, love."

His accent thickens, voice dropping to that dangerous register that makes my skin prickle. "Every camera, every security detail. If anyone so much as points a lens in your direction, they'll regret it."

I slide my trembling hand over his. His skin burns electric against mine, and his entire body goes rigid, like a predator sensing movement. His gaze tracks my touch with such intensity that I can almost feel it branding my skin.

"I'm in recovery, to the world," I breathe, squeezing his hand until my knuckles whiten. "And I want it to stay that way until I decide otherwise. On my terms. Mine alone."

August says, "I will kill anyone who hurts you."

His hand tightens over mine, his thumb on the frenetic throb of my pulse. He studies me like a puzzle he could spend his life taking apart, one fragile, breakable piece at a time.

"I know what it's like, you know. The pressure." His eyes never leave my face. "The difference is, the world does want you back. Even if you don't want to."

The wind whips at my hair, tangling it into ropes that sting my cheeks. I want to believe him. I move my hand away, the movement sharp enough to make August flinch, and curl my legs beneath me like armor.

"It's not that simple. If Michael finds me..." My voice splinters.

The thought of Michael seeing my face, seeing me alive, before Jaxon can put him in the ground makes something feral rise in my chest.

It's different from when I was planning my comeback. But my comeback came with security, watchful appearances, and on my terms. This is nothing like a comeback. It feels like chaos waiting to happen.

August's hand shoots out, gripping my chin with fingers that could crush bone but hold me with devastating restraint.

"Look at me." His voice drops to that place where promises and threats become indistinguishable. "Michael will never touch you again. If he tries, I'll carve him apart while he's still breathing."

His eyes burn into mine, pupils blown wide with something darker than protection. "Do you understand me? You're ours now."

I don't move. His grip brands my skin like a hot iron, each fingertip a separate point of delicious pain. I raise my head with deliberate slowness, keeping my lips a whisper away from his, close enough that the mint on his breath crystallizes in my lungs with each inhale.

The heat radiating between us makes the ocean air feel arctic by comparison.

For months, I've constructed walls around myself, brick by meticulous brick, but now they're crumbling under his touch, mortar turning to sand.

My control, that precious, hard-won control, hangs by a thread so frayed I can almost hear it snapping.

CHAPTER 17

JAXON

I have been at my computer for days now. The blue light burns my retinas, leaving ghosts of images when I close my bloodshot eyes. Each monitor is on a distinct trace, casting an eerie glow across my unwashed skin.

L.A. was bust for Robyn. Once that tracker was pulled from her Bentley, leaving nothing but static on my screen, she vanished like smoke.

However, I found Michael in New York. His face appeared on grainy CCTV footage, a phantom moving through crowds, captured frame by frame on traffic cams as he crossed rain-slicked streets. No trace of Robyn, though.

Every angle suggests that he is alone, a solitary figure in a city of millions, unaware of my watching eyes.

"Any news?" I hear Ellia's voice over my shoulder. She is standing in the doorway, hands twisting in her sweatshirt, like she is trying to ground herself.

"I believe I found Michael in New York. He's using cash," I said. "No credit cards, no bank accounts, and he's hopping hotels like he's allergic to sheets."

I gestured at the side display, which showed a sprawl of surveillance stills and timestamps, the digital breadcrumbs of a man who, for all his intelligence, didn't realize how deeply the city had been wired for watching.

Ellia stepped closer, and the smell of lavender and vanilla filled the stagnant air. She leaned in, scanning the screens, her face drawn and shadowed.

I watched her eyes track Michael's movements. One frame showed him ducking into a subway station, another crossing a neon-lit intersection, his face half-obscured by a hood.

"Enhance that," Ellia said, voice low.

She pointed at a blurry shot of Michael exiting a deli, a brown paper bag clutched in his fist, his hair longer than I remembered. He was thinner too, bones more defined along his jaw.

Her fingernail tapped the screen where his gaunt face appeared. "What are you hunting in New York?" She breathed, her voice barely disturbing the air between us.

She turns to look at me, her amber eyes no longer soft but burning with something feral. "You need to eat, Jaxon." The words hang between us like a threat.

I've been locked in this digital cave since dawn, my body forgotten. The monitor reads just before midnight. I stand, joints cracking like gunshots in the silence.

Ellia doesn't step back. She's close enough that I can feel the heat radiating from her skin, smell the lavender beneath the sweat at her throat. She's only several inches shorter, but I could consume her whole if I wanted to.

"August ordered takeout. We're watching a movie," she says, her pulse visible to her neck.

"You look different, songbird." I step closer, eliminating what little space remains between us. My voice drops to a whisper. "What happened to you?"

Her breath catches. "I..." The word dies as her pupils dilate.

I can practically hear the blood rushing through her veins, see the calculations behind her eyes as she weighs her options.

Her lips part, but the words catch in her throat. "About last night..." she whispers, voice trailing into silence.

I lean down until my breath warms her ear. "Which memory haunts you, songbird? The way you trembled against the porcelain when my fingers made you come, or how you begged me not to leave your bed?"

"I never begged," she counters, but her voice wavers. "I just... I haven't slept that deeply in years."

I withdraw just enough to see her face, still close enough that the electricity between us crackles like a live wire.

"And tonight?" The question hangs between us, dangerous and weighted.

She doesn't answer with words. Instead, her lips curve into that knowing half-smile that turns my blood to fire. I recognize the silent acceptance in her eyes, even as I recognize the fear behind it.

One wrong move, one moment of pressure, and she'll vanish like smoke.

With that, she turns and slips from the room, the ghost of her warmth lingering where she stood. Something cracked inside her last night, a hairline fracture in her armor. Her silence speaks volumes; her body betrays what her lips refuse to admit.

August messaged me after their conversation by the water's edge, his text confirming what I already sensed: she's changing.

The fortress she built after what happened on the mountain, those walls she erected without warning, they're beginning to crumble beneath our persistent siege.

I joined Ellia and August in the living room after a much-needed shower, my skin still flushed and damp, hair dripping cold rivulets down my neck.

The scent of my soap, sandalwood, and something sharper, clung to me like a second skin.

"Hey mate, Ellia picked Gone Girl," August drawled, rolling his eyes as he draped himself diagonally across the cream sectional.

One arm stretched possessively along the soft back cushions, his fingertips grazing the plush fabric.

I eased into the gap beside Ellia, nudging her gently between us. Her charcoal sweatpants pressed warm against my thigh, the cotton's faint raindrop pattern soft under my palm.

She leaned toward August, but when my shoulder brushed hers, I felt her breath hitch. In the flickering glow of the television, her eyes ignited, a liquid amber spark dancing in the shadows.

"If I remember correctly, you've seen this hundreds of times over the last year," I murmured. Her lips curved into a secretive smile, the light in her eyes brightening.

Back in Idaho, she'd cocoon herself in familiar stories, Vampire Diaries rewound endlessly, every twist and line memorized.

Musicals, she would tap her fingers along with. And classics, when reality tightened around her. She'd press play and let the fictional world steady her racing thoughts. Yet of all her comfort shows and musicals. Action and suspense held her heart most fiercely.

August, surprisingly, seemed enthralled this evening. I remembered him skulking at the doorway the last time the movie played, equally entranced by her soft expressions and the unfolding drama on-screen.

He'd never understood her Vampire Diaries obsession; that always made me smile. He'd return from his clandestine watch with a lopsided grin, shaking his head.

"She's only here for Damon," he'd quip, as if the darkest vampire in a suburban supernatural series could rival the depth of her own longing.

And, in a way, he wasn't wrong; she craved mystery and intensity, qualities scarce in the polished arena of her music career.

Every muscle in me coiled with tension. Ellia's nearness was exquisite torture; each subtle shift, the gentle press of her hip at my side, sent electric sparks through my veins.

My jeans felt impossibly snug, the heat pulsing through my veins. From the corner of my eye, I met August's gaze across her slumped form: his jaw was rigid, pupils dark and wide, the unsaid hunger between us thick as smoke.

Midway through the film, Ellia finally succumbed to sleep. Her head lolled against August's shoulder, warm breath fluttering across his neck like a whisper.

The soft curve of her ass pressed into my thigh, pliant and comforting. Her feet are resting on my knees.

I froze, afraid that the slightest movement would shatter this fragile moment of vulnerability. After so long spent fleeing her nightmares, tonight she could rest, cradled by the glow of the screen and the silent promise of our shared stillness.

When credits roll, August's eyes lock with mine; possessive, desperate. A silent negotiation passes between us. I give him an almost imperceptible nod before sliding my arms beneath her.

As I lift her, she melts against my chest, lips parted in unconscious surrender, her pulse flutters beneath my fingertips like a captured bird.

August follows like a shadow, extinguishing lights as he moves through the house. His footsteps whisper across the floor, halting at the edge of the bed where darkness pools deepest.

"She wants us both tonight," I murmur, my voice barely disturbing the air.

"Did she say that?" Doubt threads through his question, his silhouette tense against the moonlit window. "I thought last night was..."

I circle the bed like a predator, lowering her body to the center of the mattress. "Not explicitly." My fingers linger against her skin. "But when I asked, her eyes told me everything her mouth wouldn't."

August hesitates only a moment before approaching the opposite side, his hands already finding the hem of his shirt. The moonlight catches the movement, illuminating the hunger in his eyes. I begin to undress as well, the sound of fabric sliding against skin filling the silence between us.

August's eyes glint in the darkness as he slides next to her.

"She's changing, Jax," he breathes, voice thick with hunger. "I can smell it on her skin."

I press myself against her other side, my chest flush against the curve of her spine. Her heat burns through the thin fabric separating us. Each slow breath she takes draws her body tighter against mine.

"She's remembering who she was," I whisper, my lips grazing her shoulder. "Before she buried herself alive."

We fall into predatory silence, our eyes tracing her curves between us, memorizing the rise and fall of her chest as the darkness wraps around us like a shroud, exhaustion finally claims its prize, dragging us under one by one into dreamless depths.

Early morning, I woke to the soft heat of her breath against my skin, her head nestled in the hollow of my chest as if it had always belonged there.

My arms had become a cage around her delicate shoulders, protective and possessive. August had gravitated toward her in sleep, his broad chest pressed against her spine, one heavy arm draped over the curve of her waist and my abdomen.

I remain perfectly still; muscles locked with restraint. When she wakes, this fragile peace might shatter. She'll find herself caught between our bodies, limbs entangled, with no easy escape.

The irony isn't lost on me, this woman who built walls around herself for years, who carved out solitude like it was salvation, now lies suspended in our shared gravity.

Even at her lowest, when grief hollowed her out and left her raw, she never truly broke. Only August and I were permitted to witness those cracks in her armor, those moments of vulnerability she hid from everyone else.

Perhaps that's the root of her tension with Faith. Now she breathes softly between us, adrift in unmapped waters.

Her body starts to tense against mine before I even open my eyes. Soft, sleep-warm moans escape her lips as she stretches between us, her spine arching like a cat's. August's fingers tighten possessively around her hip, his face buried in her hair.

I trace my fingertips along her arm, feeling her shake under my touch. "Good morning, songbird."

Her eyes snap open, disoriented, then alarmed. She registers her head on my chest, her legs tangled with August's, trapped between our bodies.

"I... I'm sorry. I didn't..." The words die in her throat.

I capture her chin, my thumb pressing against the fullness of her lower lip. "Don't ever apologize to me, Elli." My voice drops to a dangerous whisper. "Not for this."

She extracts herself from our tangle of limbs, the fabric of her hoodie damp with sweat where our skin touched. Even in sleep, her body had burned between us, radiating heat that had me kicking off covers throughout the night.

With calculated movements, she slides from the bed, casting one backward glance before disappearing into the bathroom. The shower hisses to life moments later.

August's gaze remains fixed on the closed door, his jaw clenched tight. "Mine," he growls, the single word vibrating with possession.

I let his claim hang in the air between us. There's no rulebook for this: two best friends falling for the same woman.

I remember Ellia's words from years ago, her voice soft in the darkness of my car: "The heart isn't a vessel with limited capacity," she'd said, fingers tracing invisible patterns on the window. "It expands."

Back then, I'd nodded without understanding. Now, watching August's eyes track the bathroom door, I finally do.

Ironic that she never applied this philosophy to Michael. Whatever happened there remains locked behind her eyes, a story written in a language she's not yet ready to translate for us.

I knew August would fall for her the moment they met. I saw it in his eyes, the same freefall I'd experienced. I never intended to share her, but now I can't imagine any other way.

I drag myself from the bed, muscles taut with restraint. "Need to cool off," I mutter, not meeting August's eyes as I yank my jeans over my still-hard cock.

August remains motionless on the rumpled sheets, his gaze fixed on the bathroom door like a wolf scenting blood on the wind.

The moment I'm alone, I strip bare, my clothes hitting the floor as steam fills the space she left behind.

I braced my palm against the tile, the cold bite of ceramic grounding me for all of a second before the thought of her, pressed between us, soft flesh and fire, crashed into me again.

My cock was already thick and aching in my fist, but it wasn't enough: I needed her voice, the velvet rasp of it, the way she said my name when she was right at the edge. I squeezed tighter, stroking, slow at first, then desperate, chasing the memory of her heat.

Behind the hiss of water, her phantom haunts me: another shower, another body, August's hands claiming territory I've marked as mine, or perhaps her own fingers exploring the slick heat I've dreamed of tasting.

The vision sears itself behind my eyelids with such violent clarity that I have to bite my lip bloody to keep from calling her name. My forehead presses against cold tile, a futile anchor as my breath fractures into ragged, animal sounds.

"Ellia," her name rolling off my tongue.

Steam rises from my skin like something burning alive, but the scalding water is nothing compared to the inferno raging beneath.

My restraint shatters completely. Release tears through me with brutal force, my body convulsing as pleasure borders pain, marking the wall with evidence of my obsession.

Her name becomes a prayer, a curse, a promise whispered into steam.

CHAPTER 18

ELLIA

By the time Friday rolls around, I wake crushed between two male bodies, their possessive limbs caging me like predators who've caught their prey.

Their arms and legs snake around me, muscles taut even in sleep, as if they fear I'll vanish if they loosen their grip.

Each morning, I've surfaced from unconsciousness with my skin burning where it meets theirs, my breath shallow from their weight, yet somehow more alive than I've felt in years.

There's a dangerous comfort in being claimed by these men. I crave with an intensity that terrifies me, their presence anchoring me to reality when my mind threatens to drift into darkness.

The nightmares that once clawed at my throat can't reach me when I'm pinned between their heartbeats.

The day had started with deceptive calm, their scent still clinging to my skin, my body still aching pleasantly from their attention, but with each passing hour, thoughts of tonight's game slither into my consciousness like poison.

My lungs constrict. My hands tremble. That familiar void yawns beneath me, hungry and patient, waiting for me to tumble back into its suffocating embrace despite how desperately I've clawed my way toward the light.

I slide from between their bodies, the sheets whispering against my skin. "About tonight's game," I murmur, my voice barely audible over the thundering of my pulse.

"Everything's handled, baby girl," August growls, his fingers grazing my wrist with deceptive gentleness.

"I know, but I..." The words evaporate on my tongue. I pivot toward the bathroom when his grip suddenly locks around my forearm like a vise.

My head snaps back, eyes narrowing into daggers. August releases me instantly, palms raised in mock innocence, but the predatory gleam in his eyes remains.

Jaxon's voice slices through the room. "Back off." He crosses the floor in three long strides, his shadow stretching before him like something alive.

Before I can breathe, August lunges forward. They square off, circling, muscles coiled tight as springs. Two predators, territorial and primal. I can't move, can only feel my pulse hammering against my ribs, ashamed at how their raw aggression makes something low in my belly tighten.

August is on him in a breath, snarling, shoulders squared, like two wolves determined to tear each other's throats out. I stand frozen, heart galloping, some obscene part of me thrilled by their ferocity.

"Touch her like that again, and I'll end you," Jaxon's words scrape out, stripped of civility.

August's lips curl back, his tongue darting across them as though sampling violence. "She doesn't belong to you."

"I'm the only thing keeping her from drowning," Jaxon spits. "You're just here for the ride."

A hot, electric silence. August's eyes flick to me—hungry, defiant, as if daring me to choose. My skin prickles. I want them both, want their war, want that violence to devour the gnawing fear that tonight brings.

"Stop," I say, stepping between them, my body a fragile barrier against the storm of testosterone and rage.

Their heat radiates against my skin from both sides, making it hard to breathe.

"What the fuck is wrong with you two?" The words tear from my throat, sharp and venomous, my tongue tasting the acid of my fury.

Jaxon's breath scorches my scalp as he growls, "You don't get to put your hands on her like she's property."

"It wasn't like that," August's voice drops dangerously low, his eyes never leaving mine. "You felt it too, didn't you? Like a current of electricity?"

I nod, just slightly. I press my palms against both their chests, feeling twin heartbeats hammering against my skin.

"Enough. I can't be the battlefield where the only two people I trust tear each other apart." My voice breaks on the last word, betraying more vulnerability than I intended.

I step back, creating distance between us. "I need a shower," I say, my voice steadier than my pulse. "And you two need to get your heads straight."

My gaze flicks between them, catching the heat still smoldering in their eyes. I swallow hard. "This isn't some competition where I'm the prize. I want both of you, more than I should, but not like this."

They retreat like wolves denied their kill, the air between them still crackling with hostility. My lungs finally expand. What the fuck was that, Ellia? The question echoes in my skull as I shake my head at them both.

"A shower sounds perfect," August murmurs. His boxers hit the floor with a whisper. My gaze betrays me, dropping to his already massive, hard length as he stalks toward my bathroom.

"I meant in your own shower, August," I manage, but the words feel hollow in my mouth. He turns just enough to flash that dangerous smirk that makes my thighs clench.

Steam billows from the bathroom as the shower hisses to life. I whip around to Jaxon, pulse hammering in my throat. He holds my gaze for one brutal second before his lips curl into that knowing smile that makes my stomach drop.

Without breaking eye contact, he strips, peeling away fabric to reveal the battlefield of ink and old scars carved across his flesh. My breath catches as my eyes betray me, again, dragging down the topography of his body until they lock on his hardening length.

The contrast is jarring: that untouched flesh against the storm of black ink that devours everything else, like he's saved that one part of himself from the darkness that's claimed the rest.

'Ellia, this is a mistake.' The warning dissolves on my tongue as my feet carry me forward.

Steam caresses my skin like phantom hands as I cross the threshold. Water cascades down their bodies, rivulets tracing the ridges of abdominals, disappearing into the dark thatch between powerful thighs.

August's eyes lock on mine, pupils blown wide with hunger as his hand slides down his slick torso. Jaxon turns, water sluicing off his shoulders, his cock already thickening under my gaze.

My nipples harden painfully against the thin fabric of my shirt as I peel it upward. Heat pools between my thighs, my body's betrayal more complete than my mind's. The air between us thickens with possibility, and with need.

I turn away, heat blooming across my cheeks as I slip my thumbs beneath the elastic of my waistband. I ease the fabric down inch by inch, bending forward with deliberate grace, knowing they can see everything I'm offering.

My pussy throbs with each inch revealed, already slick and swollen with need. The growl from both men over my shoulder, as I step free, completely naked now, my nipples hardening under their predatory stares.

My thighs quiver, not from cold but from the raw hunger radiating from both men.

Jaxon extends his hand, water streaming down the corded muscles of his arm. His cock stands rigid against his abdomen, a bead of precum glistening at the tip. I wet my lips, eager to taste him.

I take his hand, and he pulls me under the spray, my breasts colliding with his chest.

Behind me, August presses his hard length against the curve of my ass, his breath hot on my neck. His hands slide up my sides, thumbs grazing the undersides of my breasts as he growls against my ear, "I've been waiting to taste every inch of you."

August's mouth found the slope of my shoulder, teeth grazing flesh as he steadied me against Jaxon's chest. My body jerked with the shock of sensation; heat and the relentless press of their hands, and I caught myself gasping, almost sobbing, at the force of it.

Jaxon's lips crashed onto mine, tasting of steam and salt, his tongue parting me, owning me, while August's hands slid over my hips and around my belly.

My head fell back onto August's shoulder as Jaxon kissed me, his thick cock nudging at my thigh. August's fingers danced lower, knuckles grazing the slick crease between my legs, and I whimpered, all thought eviscerated by the two of them pinning me.

Jaxon's hands cupped my breasts, thumbs circling my nipples until they screamed for more, while August parted my thighs with practiced, brutal insistence.

His hand slid between my thighs, fingers parting my pussy lips, and I moaned into Jaxon's mouth.

The sound vibrated through his lips, and he groaned back, rolling my nipples between his calloused fingers as August's thumb circled my clit.

It was chaos, water crashing against my skin, hands and mouths devouring every exposed inch, my body torn between the pressure of August at my back and Jaxon's insistent grind at my front.

"God, you're so fucking wet," August rasped, and the tip of his cock nudged against the crease of my ass, hot and thick, as he pressed his palm more firmly onto my mound.

My knees buckled, and Jaxon caught me, pinning me tighter to his chest, his hands anchoring my hips as August's fingers thrust inside me—one, and then two, stretching me until I whimpered.

Jaxon's lips moved to my ear, his voice a dark threat against the pounding in my skull.

"Let him get you ready, Ellia. I want to hear how much you need it." His breath was a wild animal in my ear—hungry, desperate, edged with something close to violence.

August's fingers fucked me mercilessly, curling and twisting inside me as his thumb ground perfect little circles against my clit. I was sobbing now, helpless, the world reduced to the wet slapping of August's hand and the hard planes of Jaxon's body caging me.

My arms clung to Jaxon's shoulders, nails digging into the ink-drenched skin. The feeling of being utterly pinned, one man in front, one behind, should have terrified me, but all I wanted was more.

August groaned against my neck. "Fuck, Jax... she's squeezing my fingers. So, fucking tight."

His teeth closed over my shoulder, biting down just shy of pain. Jaxon's cock ground against my stomach, smearing pre-cum into my skin, and I felt the tremor run through his whole body.

"Look at me," he said, his voice a command, and I obeyed, even as August's fingers pumped in and out, "Let him hear you."

"Don't come yet," August ordered, voice guttural.

A sound between a whimper and a sob escapes me. My chin dips in a weak attempt at nodding, but my body has surrendered to sensation.

August's arm locks around my waist like an iron band, his grip the only thing keeping me upright as my legs tremble and threaten to give way beneath me.

"I'm going to taste every drop of you," Jaxon growls against the hollow of my throat, his breath scorching my already fevered skin.

August buried his face in the crook of my neck, teeth scraping a line up my jaw as his fingers twisted mercilessly inside me, the sound of my own whimpers ricocheting off the tile.

Before I could process his threat, Jaxon knelt. His hands manacled my thighs, spreading me wide as steam curled around us.

My pussy is throbbing as Jaxon studies every inch.

He looks up, eyes gone ravenous, and hooks my thigh over his broad shoulders.

The first swipe of his tongue made me scream, no preamble, just a rough, greedy lick from clit to entrance that left my whole body spasming, pulling them closer by their hair.

He growled as he sucked my clit into his mouth, the vibration so intense my vision whited out at the edges.

August's fingers never left me; he fucked me with them as Jaxon's mouth devoured my cunt, each thrust and pull orchestrated between them so that I never once stopped feeling claimed, wrung out, ruined for anyone but them.

My hips bucked helplessly into Jaxon's face, his tongue relentless, his dark hair plastered to his skull as he looked up at me, daring me to come.

"You want to come, Ellia?" August murmured in my ear.

"Mmhmm," I moaned as Jaxon licked up everything I gave him, his hands bruising my hips as he sucked my clit, refusing to let me go soft.

"You taste like fucking salvation," he growled against my flesh, pupils blown so wide his eyes looked black. "I could die here and never regret it."

August's hand clamped over my belly. My entire body jerked under the dual assault, Jaxon's mouth devouring every inch, August's finger fucking me as his cock rutted against the slick, desperate place between my thighs.

I moaned, wordless and raw, and August's breath split the air behind my ear, a guttural, animal sound. "You hear that, Jax?" August taunted, voice thick and shaking.

"Please," I whimper.

Jaxon's answering growl reverberated against my cunt, the vibration so sharp and greedy I nearly blacked out.

"You need to come, songbird?"

"Yes, fuck... Please," I begged, almost sobbing, and the sound that ripped from my throat was more animal than human.

My fingers tangled in Jaxon's hair, pulling him harder against me, all shame burned away by the relentless need clawing at my insides.

Jaxon's tongue traced savage circles around my clit, and the pleasure was so bright it bordered on pain. I could hear August behind me, panting like a beast, his cock rutting against the slickness of my ass as the muscles in his forearm flexed around my waist, holding me wide open for Jaxon's greedy mouth.

"Fucking beautiful," August moaned, as if the sight of me unraveling was enough to push him to the edge.

He nipped at the curve of my shoulder, then dragged his teeth up to my ear. "You're gonna soak his face, sweetheart. Look at you...so desperate, so fucking perfect."

Jaxon growled again, "Come now," he ordered, a dictator from between my thighs, and my body obeyed before my mind could even catch up.

I shattered against his face, the orgasm ripping through me like a live wire. My knees gave way, my arms flailing against the wet tile, and August cradled me from behind, his arm a lifeline around my waist.

I screamed, throat raw, fingers scrabbling for purchase in Jaxon's black hair as he devoured every last pulse of pleasure.

The tile threatened to crack under my scream. They didn't let up for a second, not until I was wrung out, twitching, the world reduced to white noise, and the animal sounds of our bodies.

Jaxon pushed to his feet, water streaming from his sharp jawline, his eyes wolf-bright as he loomed over us. His mouth glistened with me, but he didn't wipe it away.

August's teeth scrape against my pulse. "You're ruining us," he growls, his voice shattered.

His hands grip my shoulders, spinning me so violently that I gasp as my back hits the tile. His mouth crushes mine, stealing what little breath remains in my lungs.

"She belongs to us both now." Jaxon's shadow falls over me, his voice closer, dangerous. "Songbird."

"I want to watch you taste yourself from his mouth," August commands, his fingers digging into my hips. "Show me how much you need it, love."

I tear myself from August's bruising kiss, spinning toward Jaxon's waiting mouth like a compass finding north. He kissed me like a man starved, his tattooed hand caging my jaw, holding me steady as his tongue swept in, dominating. I moaned, helpless.

August's hand was twisted in my hair, yanking my head back and forth between their mouths, my body a rag doll in their grip, my own will dissolving into the steam and hunger and the low, animal sounds pouring from my throat.

'You love being their plaything,' my mind sneered, but the words felt as far away as a voice underwater. I wanted this. I wanted to be ruined, to be nothing but what I was in their hands.

Jaxon tears his mouth from mine, leaving me cold despite the steam. "Time for you to finish your shower," he says, voice rough as gravel. "Alone."

My body betrays me with a desperate sound, half plea, half protest, as they step away, the sudden absence of their heat against my skin like a physical wound.

CHAPTER 19

JAXON

August kept his promise to Ellia, sparing no expense on security measures. The private viewing box featured one-way glass, while men and women in civilian attire, their earpieces and vigilant postures the only betrayal of their purpose, maintained a protective perimeter around them.

Ellia sank into her seat, the leather yielding beneath her with a soft creak as I poured amber liquid into a crystal tumbler, watching as she curled her fingers around the glass with a familiarity that made something twist in my chest.

The whiskey caught the light as she raised it to her lips, her eyes meeting mine over the rim with a challenge I couldn't quite decipher. Her eyes have caught mine lingering too many times today, a silent acknowledgment passing between us each time.

After her shower, she emerged not in those threadbare sweats I've grown accustomed to seeing, but in a thin t-shirt that barely skimmed the curve where thigh meets flesh.

She paired it with loose sweatpants, a concession that still felt like victory. Progress, I think, the word tasting dangerous even in the silence of my mind.

August had to get to the stadium right after our shower this morning. He moved like a caged animal suddenly released, all restless energy and sharp movements, leaving the scent of his expensive cologne hanging in the humid air between us.

His smile was stretched so wide across his face that I could see the pink of his gums, the whiteness of his teeth, almost predatory under the hallway light.

Ellia's descent down the staircase this afternoon was a calculated assault. Each step brought the whisper of expensive fabric against skin, the black button-down molded to her body like a second skin.

The corset, over a fitted black button-up, midnight satin laced so tight her ribs might splinter, transformed her silhouette into something lethal. She paired it with black slacks and her favorite boots.

I tracked the shallow rise and fall of her chest, counting seconds between breaths. Those ribbons trailing down her spine seemed to beckon my fingers.

Her hair fell in dark waves around her face, framing features I barely recognized beneath cosmetics she hadn't worn since before everything fell apart, and that singular white streak tucked behind one ear like a secret only I was meant to find.

My lungs seized, oxygen burning away like paper thrown into flame. The room contracted to just her, just us, as my fingers flexed involuntarily at my sides, nails biting crescents into my palms. I wanted to shred that fabric from her body, to mark that skin until she couldn't remember a time before my hands had claimed her.

The control I'd maintained around Ellia—that careful, suffocating restraint—was fracturing, hairline cracks spreading through my resolve with each heartbeat that thundered against my ribs.

My instincts scream to work, to scan for threats, to calculate exit routes, but tonight I'm forcing myself to be still. The woman beside me is the single point in this universe I would reduce everything to ash for, and I watch her with the intensity of someone memorizing what they fear might disappear.

The teams burst from their tunnels, igniting the stadium with a volcanic roar of voices. I follow Ellia's gaze as it locks onto August, the man who somehow helped me chisel through her defenses. Her face transforms, illuminated by something I can't give her.

August stretches, his movements fluid and practiced, but his eyes flick toward our box too frequently. Each glance is a liability I can't afford.

Women across Australia fantasize about August, his touch, his attention, the possibility of a night with him. Yet since Ellia entered his orbit, the revolving door to his bedroom stopped.

When I first mentioned my client, he showed nothing beyond professional courtesy. Everything changed after that concert with me, as if he'd glimpsed something in my eyes that revealed what she truly meant.

She turns to me, the rigid line of her shoulders softening almost imperceptibly. "Strange," she murmurs, her gaze tracking August as he takes his position on the field, "to finally witness in flesh what I've only ever seen through screens."

The confession hangs between us, intimate despite its innocence.

The crowd surges to its feet as the referee produces the coin, a collective breath held in suspension before the metallic flash catches the stadium lights and spins upward, destiny balanced on its razor's edge.

Her fingertips trace the rim of her glass as she leans closer. "Tell me, Jaxon," she murmurs, her breath warm against my ear, "just how violent is this game?"

The question hangs between us, deceptively casual.

I know she's seen August play before, studied him through screens in the darkness of her room. This is safer territory than the nightmares that leave her screaming in the night, or any mention of the man whose throat I've promised myself will open beneath my blade.

Ellia smiles, the corner of her mouth curling knowingly. She tilts her head, eyes half-lidded, her voice dropping so only I can hear.

"I want the version where men bleed for each other's approval. The version where someone always loses more than the game."

The way she says it, like a dare, like she wants to see if I'll flinch, sends a hot pulse through my chest. I lean closer, our knees touching beneath the small table, and her clothed skin is electric where it brushes mine.

"You get off on the violence?" I whisper, low and dangerous. "Or do you just want permission to root for the bloodier one?"

"Maybe both," she says, her lips ghosting the rim of her glass, the whisky catching on the gloss. "Or maybe I'm just curious. "

The first half unfolds with savage intensity, August's team clinging to a narrow nine-point lead. Each time his body collides with the earth, limbs twisted at angles nature never intended, the impact reverberates through the stadium.

Ellia inches forward in her seat. Her knuckles bleach white against the armrest, pupils dilating with each hit.

The television broadcasts she's accustomed to sanitize this violence with well-timed cuts and commercial breaks. Here, there's nowhere to hide from the sound of sinew straining against bone, from the primal roar that follows blood on the field.

Ellia stands at the glass barrier, her breath fogging the surface with each exhale. The clock ticks down the final minutes of the first half.

I move behind her with deliberate slowness, pressing my body against hers until she's trapped between me and the one-way wall. My lips brush the shell of her ear, teeth grazing the sensitive skin.

"I've been watching those thighs of yours," I whisper, voice rough with intent. "The way they clench every time August draws blood. Does violence make you wet, songbird?"

Her body trembles against mine, a small, involuntary shudder that travels from her spine to my chest.

"Tell me," I demand, one hand sliding possessively around her waist, "should I make you fall apart right here while you watch him destroy other men?"

Her head falls back against my shoulder, throat exposed like an offering. In the glass, her reflection fractures—eyes half-lidded, mouth slack with want.

A sound escapes her, raw and primal, vibrating against my chest where her spine presses into me. When she merely nods, I tighten my grip on her jaw, forcing her to meet my reflected gaze.

"Use your words, Ellia." My voice is barely recognizable, stripped to something ancient and possessive.

"Yes," she gasps, the single syllable breaking as my hand slides lower, claiming her through thin fabric.

My other arm braces hard against the glass, veins standing stark against skin as she clutches me, nails digging half-moons into my flesh.

She stiffened in my hold, hips bucking back for friction even as her hands clawed at the glass, leaving trails of condensation in their wake.

The stadium noise fell away, replaced by her ragged breaths and the slick heat blooming beneath my palm. I pressed her tighter, fitting my thigh between hers and locking her into place, an animal caught, and loving every second.

"Jaxon," she hissed, the syllables knife-sharp and needful.

I slipped my hand beneath the waistband. Her cunt was already wet, the proof of her need soaking my fingers before I even reached her.

I worked her slowly at first, thumb circling her clit in measured torture, grinning at the way her whole body stuttered and flexed.

Her hands scrabbled for purchase, palms flattening against the glass, and I made her watch, made her see the want painted across her face, the way her lips parted, and her eyes went dark.

"I need to feel you," she breathes.

I pulled her back, forcing her flush against my chest, and put my mouth to her ear, the kind of whisper meant only for her. "You'll have to beg me for it, songbird."

My fingers moved in slick, measured circles, every slow drag calculated as a lesson in patience. She whimpered, hips rocking helplessly against my hand, and I let her ride my palm, her thighs trembling, her cunt throbbing as I denied her every time she got close.

Her head lolled back, eyes glassy and unfocused. "Jaxon, please..."

The words fell out thick and desperate, edged with the kind of need I used to think she'd never let me see.

I tightened my hold, my grip on her jaw just shy of bruising, and watched her reflection. She looked utterly ruined, smudged liner running at the corners of her eyes, mouth open in a silent sob of pleasure.

"Keep watching him," I commanded, nodding toward the field, where August's body was already steaming with aftermath, sweat shining across his arms and brow. "Keep your eyes on him while you come for me."

She tried to turn, to bury her face in my neck, but I forced her chin forward and ground my palm hard against her clit.

Through the glass, her reflection warped into something feral.

"Look at him. Picture what he'd do to you if I let him. Tell me who you want more, right fucking now."

Her breath caught, nails scratching desperate patterns on the glass. "I...can't..." She stammered, legs shaking, caught between the violence on the pitch and my hand working her from behind.

The game had devolved into chaos, the scrum a tangle of flesh and rage, her head leans back resting on my chest, and I can see her reflection in the glass, her lips parted, and a slight moan escaping her lips.

She nods.

"Use your words, Ellia."

"You," she breathes.

My hand slipping down, my other hand bracing against the glass. She uses my arm for leverage.

August's head snaps up, eyes locking with mine through the tinted glass. Blood trickles from a split in his lip, his chest heaving with exertion as his gaze burns through the barrier between us.

Something primal flashes across his face: recognition, hunger, rage, as if he can smell her arousal through the reinforced glass and hear the desperate sounds she makes as she fractures against my fingers.

My fingers press into the soft hollow beneath her jaw, angling her face toward the field where he stands. His nostrils flare, jaw muscle twitching beneath sweat-slicked skin. Something primal passes between us, two predators acknowledging territory.

The stadium's massive screen captures his face in high definition; his eyes locked on our darkened box. 70 thousand heads swivel in unison, following his stare to where we stand behind the glass.

I sink my teeth into the soft flesh beneath her ear, my voice a guttural command against her racing pulse. "Look at him while you shatter for me."

Her body went rigid, her breath stuttered, and all at once she shattered, hips grinding back, cry muffled as I bit down on the tendon at her neck, tasting salt and perfume and the sharpness of skin.

The glass trembled with the force of her collapse against it. I let her ride it out, pinning her in place until the aftershocks had wrung every tremor from her.

Only then did I release her jaw, pressing her face to the barrier, letting her see the stadium, the chaos, the man on the field staring up at us as if he could feel every pulse of her orgasm through the glass.

My hand was slick with her, a wet heat that made my self-control threadbare. I forced my own hips back, enough to keep from rutting against her like the animal she'd conjured in me. But she surprised me, twisting in my grip, hands scrabbling for my buckle with the desperation of someone half-starving.

Eyes wild and glassy with tears, and fumbled me out of my slacks. I caught her wrists, pinning them above her head.

She moaned, low and vicious, as I pressed her hands to the windowpane and kept them there with a single, bruising grip.

I glance at the scoreboard. "The clock's running down," I murmur, slowly withdrawing my fingers from her slick heat.

A sound escapes her throat, something between protest and desperation, as her body instinctively arches, seeking to reclaim my touch.

The other team had scored while I was buried in her pleasure, my attention consumed by the woman I'd kill for.

On the field below, August sprinted with the ball, his muscles coiled like a predator's, when a mountain of a man slammed into him from below.

The sound reached us even through the glass, a sickening crack as August's skull connected with the man's shoulder. Both bodies crumpled to the turf, the larger player clutching his shoulder and writhing like a wounded beast.

The stadium went quiet as August lay motionless, a crimson halo spreading from his temple, soaking into the artificial grass. His limbs splayed at unnatural angles, a broken doll discarded.

Players converged from all directions, their faces masks of horror. The medics swarmed the field with their stretcher and equipment, moving with the practiced urgency of those who've seen death before and recognize its approach.

Ellia's body goes rigid against me, her post-orgasmic bliss evaporating as she watches August's blood spread across the field. Her teeth savage her bottom lip until I see crimson bloom there, too.

"Jesus Christ, Jaxon," she chokes out, voice stripped raw. "He's not fucking moving."

Tucking myself back in, she whips around to face me, pupils blown wide with panic. My phone is already in my hand, fingers stabbing at the screen.

The line connects, and I bark into it: "Lucas, what the goddamn hell just happened down there?"

Ellia presses against me, ear to the phone, her heartbeat a frantic drum I can feel through her skin. I listen, my jaw clenching tighter with each word from Lucas, lead security from August.

The medics haul his broken body onto the cart, and August's arm slips free, dangling lifelessly over the edge. Blood drips from his fingertips, marking a trail as they rush him away.

Ellia claws at my chest, her nails breaking skin through my shirt. "Get me down there now," she hisses, voice cracking like glass under pressure.

Her entire body convulses against mine, tears carving mascara-stained ravines down her cheeks.

In all our years, through her recovery, through that bastard who left her scarred, I've never seen her shed a single tear. Yet here she stands, coming apart for a man whose name she can barely whisper without her pulse betraying her.

The truth bleeds between us, sharper than any blade: she loves him enough to shatter for him.

I gripped her by the chin, forced her to look at me. “He’s not dead. He’s not. But you have to keep it together, Ellia.”

Even as I said it, my own hands shook. It was the blood, the sudden stillness of August’s body that had rewired both of us: we were off-script, exposed, raw.

She blinked at me, wet lashes clumping together.

“I have to go down there.” She said it like someone begging for a hit, shaking with withdrawal.

I didn’t hesitate. I snatched her by the hand and dragged her through the box as security leapt to attention.

“Clear the tunnels,” I barked into my shoulder mic. “We’re coming through.”

Agents in black suits and civilian attire peeled open the path, their bodies slicing the crowd in two. I pulled Ellia to my side, shielding her the best I could, neither of us caring that her shirt clung to her body with the sweat of the moments before.

We burst into the injury room in under three minutes, the air thick with antiseptic and copper-scented blood. Security formed a human barricade outside, their shoulders touching as they blocked the vultures with their cameras and questions.

If a single lens captured her here, mascara-streaked and trembling, her blouse still damp from our encounter, the image would explode across every screen worldwide by morning. Michael would see it. Michael would know exactly where to find her after all these months of hunting.

Ellia's fingers dug crescents into my wrist as she pushed past me, her breath coming in shallow gasps that barely disturbed the clinical silence.

Her eyes fixed on August's motionless form, the pristine white sheets already blooming with crimson constellations beneath his head.

She didn't give a single fuck who saw her or what it might cost; her freedom, her safety, her life. She had one singular, devastating purpose that eclipsed everything else: the broken man on that table who hadn't yet opened his eyes.

The medic's gloved hands press a blood-soaked gauze to August's temple. "Pulse is thready, but he's breathing," he barks, not looking up as they heave the stretcher.

Ellia stalks them like a predator, close enough to smell the metallic tang of August's blood, her body vibrating with barely contained violence.

When the gurney wheels catch on a threshold, she lunges forward, gripping the medic's wrist hard enough to leave marks.

"Where," she hisses through clenched teeth, "are you taking him?"

Her presence electrifies the room, every pair of eyes suddenly locked on her disheveled state, the unmistakable flush of recent pleasure still coloring her throat, mascara tears tracking down her cheeks.

A meaty hand clamps around her forearm, fingers digging into the tender flesh where her pulse hammers wildly. "Ma'am, only medical personnel beyond this point. We're transporting to Royal Prince Alfred."

The words barely register before I'm there, my body between them, my hand crushing his wrist until his fingers spring open like a trap releasing its prey.

"Touch her again," I snarl against his ear, "and they'll need another ambulance."

“Ellia, we need to go now.”

She lunges forward, feral, her body molding to mine as I carve through the crowd like a blade. "Clear a fucking path!" I snarl at August's security team, their faces blanching at the blood in my voice. "Car. NOW."

The Audi R8 engine screams as I hammer through Sydney's streets, the speedometer needle trembling past 140.

Red lights blur into streaks as we blow through intersections. Her perfume lingers in the passenger seat.

Ellia's fingers dig into my forearm as I downshift, her nails breaking skin. Each sob that tears from her throat feels like it's being ripped from my own chest.

The taste of copper floods my mouth. I've bitten through my cheek watching her splinter apart, powerless to stop it.

The hospital looms ahead, its façade crawling with vultures.

"They'll devour you alive in there," I warn, voice raw. "Every camera, every witness, they're all loaded guns pointed at your head."

"I know," she whispers, the words like shattered glass.

Her tears carve fresh tracks through the dried ones, her mascara a black river of grief. "I don't care if I burn for it."

The security team flanked us on all sides, their black suits forming a movable wall that parted only at the automatic doors.

Ellia's raw keening filled the foyer as I dragged her into the glare of the lobby, past the nurses who recognized us, past the cluster of bystanders with phones outstretched like crucifixes.

I glanced up at the television bolted to the ceiling, August's bloodied face filled the screen, the Chyron screaming: TATE'S CAREER ENDING IN TRAGEDY? I jerked my gaze away, bile churning in my throat.

August breathes this sport like oxygen. When he's benched, his restlessness becomes a storm we all weather. The first ball he ever held was before his tiny hands could grip bicycle handlebars.

We hit the elevator, and Ellia slammed the button for ER, her hands shaking so violently I had to wrap both arms around her to keep her upright. Every surface in this place reeked of antiseptic and dread.

She was incoherent, sobbing into my chest, her words an animal whimper that looped in my head on repeat: "He can't die, he can't."

CHAPTER 20

ELLIA

Jaxon's arm locks around me like a vise as we storm into the ER. My tears have dried to salt tracks on my cheeks, but the hollow ache in my chest remains as the elevator doors slide open with a soft hiss.

The nurses behind the desk recognize me instantly, their eyes widening with what might be pity or fear. I don't give a damn which.

"August Tate," I demand, my voice scraping raw against my throat. "Where is he?"

A nurse with pinched lips rounds the station. "This way, Ms. Delvine," she says, her practiced calm only making my skin crawl.

"What happened to him?" The words tumble out as Jaxon's fingers dig into my waist, anchoring me.

"He's stable," she replies, hesitating just long enough to make my heart stutter. "For now. The concussion is severe, and the laceration near his temple required significant suturing."

She guides us toward the Family Room, her shoes squeaking against the too-clean floor.

The nurse's eyes flicker away from mine. "The doctor will explain more," she murmurs before abandoning us to the sterile purgatory of the waiting room.

I pace like a caged animal, my heartbeat thundering in my ears. The walls pulse inward with each breath. Jaxon's eyes track my movements, predatory and concerned.

"Songbird," he growls, "he will survive this."

"He fucking better," I snarl, my voice breaking as I whirl to face him. My fingers tremble violently. "I can't..." The words catch like barbed wire in my throat.

"August and you are all I have left in this godforsaken world."

My chest heaves with the confession. "This year has been gutting me alive from the inside out, and I've been drowning in silence while pretending I could breathe."

Jaxon's hands seized my shoulders, spinning me so my back hit the wall. His grip was bruising, and I wanted him to hurt me, just a little, so I could focus on anything but the sickening, frantic need knifing through my chest.

His forehead mashed against mine, our breath commingling, wild and hot.

His thumbs were cleaning the wet and dried mascara when he said, "Do you hear me?" he demanded, voice a low, electric snarl.

"You don't get to self-destruct. Not while I'm still breathing. Not when I've finally dragged you back from the edge of oblivion. Not when you've only just clawed your way into my arms."

My hands fisted in his jacket, pulling him closer, desperate for the anger and the heat, for the only reality that made sense, his.

"If you tell me to calm down, I will bite you," I spat, lips trembling. "I will take a chunk out of your jugular, Jaxon, I swear."

He kissed me like a dare, teeth clashing, his tongue forcing mine into submission. It was ugly and ravenous, the kind of kiss that I needed in this moment.

A throat cleared behind us, the sound slicing through our violent intimacy like a scalpel.

We broke apart to find a man in a white coat watching us, his expression unreadable behind wire-rimmed glasses.

"Are you here for August Tate?" He says studying both of us.

"Yes, how is he?" Jaxon asks.

"He is awake. "He's asking for Ellia, actually."

The doctor's gaze moved past Jaxon and landed on me, as if he could see the raw need, the panic flickering behind my eyes.

"He's lucid, but the head injury is significant. He's not to be upset."

The doctor's frown deepened, as if I were a recalcitrant child and not a grown woman with my insides strung out on piano wire.

"You can see him. Briefly. One at a time."

He left before we could argue, the click of his shoes vanishing down the corridor.

Jaxon started to follow, but I grabbed his sleeve. The look we shared was all knives and bruises, but I shook my head.

"I need to see him," I rasped.

I needed to see him alive with my own eyes, or I would tear the world down.

The doctor pushed the door open, and I slipped inside, oxygen fleeing my lungs at the sight before me.

August's massive body looked wrong against the sterile white sheets, diminished somehow, his head lolling with drugged heaviness.

Each step toward him felt like wading through quicksand. My fingers found his before my mind caught up to the movement, his skin cooler than it should be.

"There's my beautiful girl," he murmured, voice thick with sedatives and pain.

Something feral clawed beneath my ribcage, threatening to shred me from within. I swallowed it down, anchoring myself to the steady beep of his monitor. He's awake, and he's breathing.

"You scared me," I whisper, my voice like shattered glass. My fingers tighten around his until my knuckles blanch white. "I thought I was going to lose you."

"You shouldn't be here, love." His eyes, glazed with medication, still burn into mine with an intensity that makes my breath catch.

"Don't you dare." The words tear from my throat, raw and primal. "There was never a choice. I would have crawled through hell on broken glass to get to this room."

I lean closer, my lips almost brushing his ear. "I need to see you breathing. I need to feel your pulse under my fingers to know you're still mine."

The confession rips from me like a wound reopening.

The door crashes open behind me. A nurse materializes, her eyes tracking my every movement like I'm prey.

"He needs his rest," she hisses, each syllable slicing through the air between us.

Her fingers twitch at her sides, eager to tear me away from him. I catch how her gaze softens when it lands on August, lingering on the curve of his jaw, the width of his shoulders beneath the hospital gown, before hardening back to ice when it returns to me.

Something possessive and violent unfurls in my chest. The way she looks at what's mine makes my teeth ache to sink into flesh.

I lean in until my lips brush his ear, my voice a razor-edged whisper. "You better come home to me, or I swear to god I will follow you into death and drag you back myself."

The nurse flinches as she rounds the bed, her knuckles whitening around the blood pressure cuff.

August's eyes darken to midnight, that half-cocky smile spreading across his bruised face like a bloodstain. Heat floods between my thighs, primal and violent, even as tears threaten to drown me.

August's hand gripped mine with an unnatural strength, so hard the bones ground together, so hard I wanted to wince but wouldn't give the universe the satisfaction.

"Don't let them take you away from me," he muttered, and I realized the nurse's presence was as harshly felt in him as in me.

We watched her together, the way she fussed over the I.V. and double-checked monitors, her movements crisp and efficient, but there was a flicker in her eyes; a hunger, a wanting every time she looked at him.

The urge to claw her face was almost physical. Instead, I smiled, the smile I'd perfected on stage and in interviews, the one that said fuck around and find out.

"He needs rest," she repeated, voice syrupy now that August's attention was on her and not me.

I lean in, my lips grazing the shell of his ear. "Dawn will find me at your side," I promise, the words a vow etched in blood.

When I kiss him, I taste copper and desperation.

Each backward step feels like tearing open a fresh wound. The nurse watches with predatory satisfaction as I retreat, but her smug smile falters when our eyes lock.

Something dark and possessive flashes across my face, a silent promise that her presumption will have consequences when I return to the ward.

I slam through the door to the family room, Jaxon's name a jagged shard on my tongue. The words die in my throat as I collide with a wall of August's teammates.

Their massive frames crowd the small space, smelling of sweat and fear, eyes rimmed red and hollow. The fluorescent lights cast shadows beneath their cheekbones, turning warriors into ghosts.

"Ellia." Jaxon materializes from their midst, his hand finding the small of my back, steadying me when I hadn't realized I was swaying. "The doctor has informed them of his condition."

Their eyes bore into me like drills seeking oil, each gaze a physical violation. No hiding now, they've caught me in my raw, feral state, my mask of composure shattered at their feet.

The weight of their collective judgment presses against my chest until breathing becomes an act of defiance.

"He'll pull through," said the smallest of them, whose name I always blanked on, his gaze fixed past me at the vending machine as if daring it to vend something worth his pain.

"He's too stubborn to die."

There was a ripple of agreement, a shuffling of feet, a collective exhale as if they'd reached some unspoken consensus about August.

My throat closes around the words, the taste of his blood still on my lips.

"No one can know I was here," I finally manage, voice like gravel dragged across silk. "If this gets out..."

I leave the threat unfinished, my eyes meeting each of theirs in turn, daring them to challenge the darkness they see there.

Every pair of eyes burns into my skin as I step into the center of their circle, the air between us thick with unspoken accusations. One player—Reed, with his perpetual sneer—edges forward, sweat beading along his temple.

"We heard you..." his voice drops to a rasp, "didn't make it off that mountain alive."

My eyes lock with Jaxon's. Without a word, he slides the deadbolt into place, his back pressed against the door like a sentinel. The click echoes through the silence.

"I didn't, actually," I whisper, feeling the phantom cold of death crawl up my spine. "My heart stopped for a couple of minutes."

I press my palm against my chest, feeling the thundering proof of life beneath my fingers.

"Jaxon broke three of my ribs, forcing it to beat again. He breathed into my lips until blood frothed between his teeth, as August nearly killed us all getting down that mountain."

"After that," I say, my voice steady as stone, "there's nothing but darkness. If I'm breathing today, it's because of what they did on that mountain."

I pivot slowly, meeting each pair of eyes in the room, feeling Jaxon's presence like a shadow behind me.

"No one was supposed to know I survived. Because it wasn't an accident." The words hang in the air, dangerous and electric.

Audible gasps from everyone in the room at the confession I just made.

Jaxon steps forward, his voice dropping to a register that makes the hairs on my arms rise.

"This stays buried. You're his brothers on the field, but this secret dies in this room. Her team is already containing the situation. She resurfaces when she chooses, not by anyone else."

The coach approaches, his calloused fingers closing around mine with unexpected gentleness.

Jaxon's body heat radiates against my back, his breath a warning on my neck.

"Ellia," the coach says, his voice gravel-rough, "your secret is safe with us."

He turns, his expression hardening as he addresses his team. "And if I hear so much as a whisper of her name outside these walls, I'll end your fucking season. Permanently."

The words "thank you" scrape my throat like broken glass.

I pivot sharply, the movement precise as a dancer, and stalk toward the exit.

Their eyes burn into my back, but I refuse to grant them the satisfaction of my acknowledgment. August trusts these men with his life on the field.

Tonight, I'm trusting them with something far more precious: my resurrection.

Flashbulbs detonate against my skull like artillery fire, burning holes through my vision until I'm half-blind.

"ELLIA! ELLIA!" My name rips from their throats like they're tearing pieces of me away with each syllable.

Bodies slam against me with bruising force, microphones stabbing toward my face, hungry for flesh. Jaxon's jacket comes down over my head, still fever-hot from his body, smelling of sandalwood cologne and the acrid tang of his terror-sweat. His arm crushes across my collarbones with such force I can't breathe.

"Ellia, why did you fake your own death?"

The question cuts through me like a serrated blade. Jaxon's muscles lock against mine, vibrating with rage before he shoves me toward Jenkins.

"Are you with August Tate?"

The absence of Jaxon's heat against my skin vanishes beneath the wet crack of cartilage giving way. His knuckles disappear into the reporter's face, and blood arcs through the air like stage lighting gone wrong, hot droplets spattering across my cheek beneath the jacket's shelter.

The man crumples with a sound like a sandbag hitting marble.

Security surges forward, a black-clad tide. Jenkins' arm locks around my waist, dragging me backward as he fights the door handle with his free hand. My body slides across leather seats still cold from the night air.

Through the windshield, I watch Jaxon carve a path through the chaos, his shoulders hunched like a predator's, faces contorting in fear as he approaches.

Lucas barks commands at the remaining security team, his voice tight with something between panic and rage.

CHAPTER 21

ELLIA

Silence has infected the house like a disease these past few days, and I've found myself drowning in tears that burn unfamiliar tracks down my cheeks, more than I've allowed myself since before the mountain.

My stage face, that perfect mask of control I perfected under the lights, has finally betrayed me, cracking open to reveal the raw creature beneath.

Each morning, Jaxon drives me to August in predawn darkness. My first victory was ensuring that the nurse disappeared from the night shift.

She now delivers babies three floors away, far enough that she'll never again look at what's mine with hunger in her eyes.

Jaxon's jaw flexes once before he speaks, pulling me from my thoughts. "He comes home today." The words hang between us like a blade. "Three o'clock."

My heart slams against my ribs. "I'm coming with you."

"You're staying here." His voice drops to that register that makes my skin prickle with warning. He steps closer, the heat of his body radiating against mine. "Your face is still burning through the internet like wildfire. Every second you're visible is another second we're fucked."

"I don't care," I hiss, my fingers curling into fists so tight my nails break skin.

Blood wells in my palms.

Jaxon's hand shoots out, fingers wrapping around my throat, not squeezing, just holding, his thumb resting against my pulse point. Backing me into the cold marble kitchen counter.

"It's not a question." His breath fans hot against my face. "You will stay here. Do you understand me?"

I swallow against his palm, feeling the slight pressure increase. He's right. My team is working overtime, scrubbing every trace of me from the digital world, replacing leaked photos with carefully curated ones from last year's appearances. But it's not enough. Not yet.

I nod, my pulse hammering against his fingertips like a caged animal. His pupils dilate until his eyes are almost black, swallowing me whole.

"Good girl," he breathes, the words slipping from his tongue like a benediction and a threat.

My whole body tingled with shame and need. I hated how good it felt to obey; I hated how much I craved the gravity of his command. He saw right through me, to the feral thing I'd become, and that only made me want him more.

"You like it when I make it easy for you," he said, not a question.

"When I take the choice away."

I nod once more.

"Say it," Jaxon commanded, voice low and terrible. "Say you'll do as you're told."

I swallowed. My throat was raw, ached for violence or for mercy, maybe both.

"I'll stay," I managed, hating the way my voice trembled. "Only because you asked nicely."

The last bit was a lie. He knew it, and I knew it.

His mouth twisted with a smile that was more threat than comfort.

"That's my girl," he said, and his hand slid up, cupping the side of my face.

He leans in. His lips are a brutal line against my jaw, pressing a streak of heat down to the place where his fingers hold me captive.

"I have been trying," he growls, "to be gentle with you."

He must've seen it in my eyes, that brittle flicker of need, because his grip tightened and his other hand drove into my hair, twisting at the roots until my scalp hummed with pain.

I gasped, a fractured sound, and his lips crashed into mine like a car wreck, metal on metal, the taste of blood immediate as my teeth bit through the soft of his lip. My shame was gasoline; his anger was the match.

"But that's never what you want, is it, songbird?"

He gripped my throat just a hair tighter, until the pulse in my ears was thunder and my vision rimmed with stars.

"No," I rasped, kissing me again, slower this time, savoring my surrender.

His tongue was a brand, a demand, and I gave in, pressing every inch of my body against his as if I could crawl inside his skin and find shelter from the storm.

"You want me to hurt you?"

"I want what you give me," I managed to gasp, because he demanded truths and I couldn't bear to disappoint. "I want to forget everything except you and this..."

He wrenches his hand from my hair, leaving burning roots in his wake as his fingers drag down my throat, my collarbone, leaving a trail of fire that makes me gasp.

His tattooed knuckles, still raw from the reporter's face, scrape across my skin like he's marking territory, each black line of ink a promise of violence barely contained beneath his skin.

His gaze raked over me like claws, pupils blown wide with hunger as his finger trailed a slow, deliberate path down the curve of my breast.

When he reached my nipple, already hardened beneath his touch, he circled it once, twice, the callused pad of his thumb sending electric currents straight to my core.

"Tell me, songbird," he whispered, his voice a dangerous rasp against my ear. "Have I already made you ache for me?"

I don't have time to answer before he tears my shirt up and over my head, the fabric ripping at the seams. My bra follows, the clasp snapping under his violent fingers.

"Fucking beautiful," he growls, voice thick with something primal.

His mouth descends, teeth grazing my nipple before his tongue soothes the sting, sending lightning through my veins. His hand tightens around my throat, thumb pressing into my windpipe just enough to make each breath a struggle, and a gift.

My body arches toward him, betraying every rational thought, craving the danger of his touch like a death wish. The line between fear and desire blurs until I can't remember which is which.

My fingers claw at his belt buckle, desperate and clumsy. When he doesn't stop me, triumph surges through my veins. His thick, heavy cock springs free into my trembling hands, the velvet-smooth skin stretched taut over rigid heat.

I drop to my knees, my mouth already flooding with saliva as I stare up at him, silently begging for permission to worship him with my tongue, to choke myself on his length until I can't breathe.

His hands fisted in my hair, wrenching my head back so I had no choice but to stare up at him. His eyes were wild, pupils swallowed by black, a smirk carved devilish into his mouth, blood still trickling from the split in his lip.

"Open," he ordered, his cock already pressed thick and hot against my lips.

I obeyed, my tongue darting out to taste salt and musk as he forced himself between my lips with brutal efficiency. The blunt head slammed against the back of my throat, stealing my breath and sending stars exploding behind my eyelids.

I gagged violently, tears streaming down my cheeks, but he only growled and drove deeper, his fingers digging into my scalp.

My jaw stretched to breaking point as he buried himself to the hilt, my nose almost crushed against the hard plane of his abdomen, inhaling the heady scent of his sweat and arousal.

"Look at me," he demanded, voice savage.

My lashes fluttered upward, locking onto his.

He held me there, suspended between consciousness and oblivion, my lungs burning for air I couldn't take.

His thumbs stroked my temples with a gentleness that felt like mockery as my throat convulsed around him.

I couldn't breathe, couldn't think, could only surrender to the exquisite agony of being consumed.

"You love this, don't you? You want to choke on me until you pass out. That's what you want?"

I moaned, the sound raw and wanton, needing more than I dared say, and he heard it in the shudder of my breath.

"What is it, songbird?" he taunted. "Can't sing with your throat full of cock?"

He didn't wait for an answer. "Christ, look at you," Jaxon hissed, head thrown back for a moment before his attention snapped down, pinning me in place.

"Fuck," Jaxon groaned, his voice raw. "No one will ever ruin you the way I do. No one will ever know how you beg for this, how you need it."

He fucked my mouth like he wanted to erase my mind, his grip in my hair a chain to hold me upright as he pounded in and out, cock tearing my throat raw.

Saliva and tears streamed down my chin, streaking my neck and chest in messy, humiliating rivulets.

My arms wrapped around his hips, nails biting through his shirt, anchoring myself to the violence of him. I craved the pain, the helplessness, the singularity of focus that forced the rest of the world into silence.

I felt his muscles seize beneath my clawing fingers, his body going rigid as steel. His growls transformed into something feral and unrecognizable, the sound of a man coming undone.

The tendons in his neck strained against his skin as his words dissolved into guttural, animal sounds that vibrated through my skull and down my spine like electric currents.

He wrenched my head back, holding me by the roots of my hair, and I felt the thick tremor of his cock flex on my tongue.

"You're going to swallow every drop," he snarled, baring his teeth. "Not a fucking drop wasted, or you won't get to touch me again, understand?"

The threat set my nerves on fire. I braced myself, flattening my tongue and relaxing my jaw, letting him fuck my face until I couldn't even whimper.

My eyes streamed, my vision blurring with tears and smeared mascara, and I wanted him to see every second of it: how completely I was his, how desperate I was to be ruined by him.

His thrusts grew ragged, hips jerking as his breath fractured into harsh, animalistic grunts. The hand in my hair trembled, but his hold never loosened.

"Fuck, Ellia. Fuck, fuck, fuck..." The words dissolved as hot stream coats the back of my throat.

His head fell back, exposing the column of his throat, and a shudder ran through him as he let out a moan so raw it sounded like a sob.

His fingers loosened their grip on my hair as he withdrew, his cock leaving a trail of heat across my swollen lips.

"Open," he commanded, voice hoarse.

I parted my lips, tilting my head back to show him my empty mouth, the evidence of his pleasure already sliding down my throat. His eyes darkened at the sight, a muscle twitching in his jaw as he traced my tear-streaked cheek with his thumb.

He pulled me up, hand still locked in my hair, until I was standing again, our faces inches apart.

I was panting through my nose, throat on fire, makeup and saliva streaming down my chin and neck.

He kissed me, slow and filthy, lapping up his own taste from my tongue and lips, and it made my knees buckle.

There was nothing gentle with him anymore, only the bright, clean violence of his want and the invisible shrapnel of my own humiliation.

"You're perfect when you're ruined," Jaxon whispered, settling his hands on my hips. "That's all I ever wanted. For you to give in."

I hated him, and I loved him, and I wanted to tear his face open with my teeth. Instead, I twisted my arms around his neck and crushed my mouth to his, letting him taste every part of himself that lingered on my tongue.

I wanted to be his weapon, his sin, the thing he couldn't let go of.

"I'd slaughter anyone who touched you," he whispered, his voice a blade wrapped in velvet. "Now go wash yourself for August."

A small slap on the ass to get me moving. The tenderness vanished as quickly as it had appeared.

His lips brushed my forehead, the gesture almost cruel in its gentleness. I left my clothes scattered across the kitchen marble like abandoned skin.

My legs trembled beneath me as I climbed the stairs, the weight of his stare burning into my naked flesh with each step I took, marking me as thoroughly as his hands had moments before.

CHAPTER 22

AUGUST

I had been fighting with the medical staff for days, demanding they discharge me from this sterile prison.

They insisted on keeping me captive while they watched for cerebral edema, as if the threat of my brain swelling against my skull outweighed my need for freedom. But each morning, in those quiet hours before sunrise when the hospital corridors fell silent, Ellia would slip into my room like a shadow.

"If you die," she'd whisper against my ear, her breath warm on my skin, "I'll never forgive you."

I'd lie there, knowing she meant it. What she couldn't say, what I wouldn't make her say, hung between us like smoke.

After everything she'd survived, I refused to be the reason she slipped back into that darkness. Besides, knowing Ellia, she'd find a way to torment me even in the afterlife if I dared to leave her behind.

By the time Jaxon arrived, I was already clawing at the hospital doors like a feral animal. My I.V. port still leaked crimson down my forearm.

"Jesus Christ, slow down," he hissed, gripping my shoulder with enough force to bruise. "You'll tear your stitches."

"Tell me about her," I demanded, collapsing into his car.

My breath fogged the window glass. "The truth."

Jaxon's knuckles loosen around the steering wheel. "She doesn't sleep much, always asking about you," he finally said. "Thinks every shadow is the one that's coming to finish what they started. The only thing keeping her from completely shattering is knowing you're coming back to her."

The night after the tackle, when she slipped into my room, her face was raw, cheeks hollowed by grief, eyes swollen and bloodshot.

Something inside me cracked. I'd sworn a silent oath to shield her from pain, yet here I was, the source of it. Not from my fists or cruel words, but from my body broken on that field. I'd forgotten that in this brutal game, my opponent's violence could wound her just as deeply as it did me.

Pulling up to the house, I feel the atmosphere change, not lighter than I'd expected, but charged with a different kind of tension. The air feels too still, like the pause before lightning strikes.

Ellia waits on the front steps, her thin white t-shirt clinging to her frame, revealing the sharp angles her body has become. I glance at Jaxon, who catches my eye.

"She's fighting," he says, voice low. "But she flinches when anyone looks at her too long. Covers herself. She needs to hear she's still beautiful, and not just from me."

Ellia exists beyond language. I've tried for years to find the right words, in poetry, in songs, in the breathless space between kisses, but nothing captures the precise geometry of her smile or how her generosity makes gravity feel optional.

Every time I think I've found the perfect description, she shifts like light through water, becoming something even more impossible to name.

I slide out of the Audi without a backward glance at Jaxon. My body aches with each movement, but I don't hesitate. When I reach her, I lift Ellia into my arms despite the pain shooting through my head. She weighs nothing now, a ghost of herself.

Her breath catches in her throat as my arms lock around her, and her legs instinctively circle my waist, clinging to me like I'm the only solid thing in her world.

"The doctor said no heavy lifting," Jaxon calls from behind me, his voice sharp with concern.

Her body goes rigid against mine. "Heavy?" The word escapes her lips like venom, each syllable dripping with rage and something far worse: shame.

I lower her to the ground, feeling her slip from my grasp like water.

She doesn't look at me as she retreats, her spine a perfect line of fury.

The door doesn't just close, it slams with such force I feel it reverberate in my still-healing skull.

In the sudden silence, I turn to Jaxon, watching as his fingers claw anxiously through his raven hair, his eyes fixed on the door as if he's just sealed something terrible behind it.

I stare at Jaxon. "You really fucked that up."

"Back off, August," he growls, eyes darkening. "Not now."

I push open the door, my skull throbbing with each step. So much for my homecoming.

Inside, I find Ellia stalking the living room like a caged animal, her knuckles white where her nails dig into her palms. She won't look at me.

Behind me, Jaxon closes the door with deliberate softness, as if the smallest sound might detonate her. When she finally speaks, her voice crawls up my spine—raw and dangerous, barely human.

"Who the FUCK gives you the right to talk about my body?"

The veins in her neck stand out, pulsing with rage. Her eyes lock onto Jaxon with such feral intensity that I instinctively step between them.

"It's comments like that," she chokes on the words, her entire body trembling, pupils blown wide with fury, "that makes me wish I could tear off my own fucking skin."

I step between them; palm raised toward her like I'm taming a wild animal.

"Ellia," my voice drops, rough with warning, "he fucked up his words, not his meaning." My skull throbs with each syllable, but I don't back down. Behind me, Jaxon's breath comes shallow and quick.

"What I meant," Jaxon says, each word measured and careful, "is that the doctors said August can't lift anything heavier than a gallon of milk without risking a brain bleed."

Her breathing slows, but the rage still radiates from her skin like heat. Her eyes remain wild, pupils dilated against the amber. When she steps back, I seize the momentary truce and turn to Jaxon, my gaze conveying everything words can't.

"I need to wash this hospital stench off me and lie down before my skull splits open," I say, each word deliberate and heavy.

Steam billows as the shower door slides open with careful precision. I turn, water streaming down my bruised torso, to find Ellia standing there.

Her eyes, still burning like fire, search mine with a vulnerability that makes my chest ache.

"I didn't mean to..." The words catch in her throat.

"I know." My voice drops to a whisper that barely carries over the rushing water. "Come here."

She hesitates only for a heartbeat before peeling off her clothes, each movement deliberate and raw.

When she steps into the shower, I move back, giving her space while the water creates a veil between us that somehow feels safer than air.

She walks into the rain shower head, her black hair slicking to her wet skin. Her scar, still raised and pink from where that asshole sliced her open.

I reach for her, and she walks into my embrace, her head on my chest.

She stays pressed to my chest, letting the water batter us both, the heat ramping until our skin prickles. Muscle memory kicks in; I cradle her head and let my other hand find the hollow at the small of her back.

I want to say something comforting, or clever, something to cut the tension and rinse the pain out of the air the way scalding water rinses hospital tape from my skin. But the words stick. Her ribcage expands against mine, a staccato rhythm, and she trembles even as she stands her ground.

"I hate seeing you like this," she murmurs into my sternum.

I feel her lip's part against the wetness. "Like something they scraped off the field and forgot to put back together."

I laugh softly. "Not even death can separate me from you." My head is spinning, vision warping in the cloud of steam and the scent of her.

I pressed my forehead to hers. "You think I see you as broken?" My voice was nothing but a rasp. "You think I want anyone but you?"

She slid a hand between us, splaying her palm over my chest.

"The thing is, August," she whispers, her voice like a blade against my throat, "I am shattered. Irreparably."

She retreats under the adjoining shower head, steam curling around her body like ghosts. Water streams down her face, and I can't tell if it's mixed with tears.

"Every mirror shows me the pieces that don't fit anymore."

I close the distance between us in one step, pinning her against the slick tile.

"Broken things stay broken," I growl, my fingers digging into her hips. "But you? You're fucking forged in fire. I see you burning even when you think you're nothing but ash."

She remains silent, her fingertips tracing the contours of my chest, sliding downward with deliberate slowness.

"Turn around," she whispers, the words barely audible above the rushing water. "Let me take care of you."

I pivot under her command, feeling the heat of her body behind me as she lathers the soap between her palms. In the foggy mirror across the bathroom, I glimpse her reflection, the way her eyes darken when they linger on each bruise marking my skin, the same haunted look she wears when examining her own scars in private moments she thinks I don't witness.

Her fingers dig into my bruised flesh, her voice a raw whisper against my back. "The world will never see my skin again, August. The media, they're circling like fucking vultures, waiting to carve me up for clicks."

Her hands tremble as they slide around my ribs, soap slick between us. She presses her forehead between my shoulder blades, her breath hot and uneven.

"Some days I can barely look at myself in the mirror, let alone let you see me. This body...it's a battlefield I lost." Her voice breaks. "I'll never be whole again."

"Ell..." I start, throat tight.

"Don't." The word slices through steam.

Her nails bite into my hips, anchoring me in place.

"Just listen." And I do, because the tremor in her voice holds me captive more effectively than any restraint.

Her lips brush the shell of my ear, voice fracturing. "I'm terrified of what happens when I let myself love you. Both of you. It consumes me until I can't breathe."

Her fingers dig deeper, marking me. "You and Jaxon..." she chokes on his name, body trembling against mine. "I never meant to drag anyone else into my darkness. Not you. Not him."

Her voice splinters. "And I can't." The words tear from her throat like barbed wire. "I can't fucking love."

Her fingernails scrape down my back, leaving trails of fire. "I can't love you. I can't..."

Her knees give out, and she collapses, naked and trembling, to the shower floor. The loofah crushed against her sternum like a shield. Her lungs heave but barely take in air, each sob ripping through her body with such violence I fear she might shatter completely.

I've never seen such raw devastation on a human face; it's like watching someone die from the inside out.

The bathroom door creaks open. Jaxon stands frozen in the doorway, steam billowing around him.

One look passes between us, and I know.

Jaxon crashes to his knees beside her, fully clothed, water instantly soaking through denim and cotton.

His eyes meet mine over her shuddering form, raw terror reflected at me. We're balanced on the blade's edge; one wrong move and she'll slice herself open.

He doesn't hesitate. He pulls her against his chest until she gasps, while her hands hover at his sides, trembling, afraid to touch what might shatter completely.

"I can never be loved," she howls, the sound tearing from somewhere primal and wounded.

Her sobs ricochet off the tile like bullets, each one puncturing the steam-thick air between us.

She collapses into Jaxon's arms, her fingers digging into his neck hard enough to draw blood, anchoring herself to him like a drowning woman.

The sound ripping from her throat isn't human—it's primordial, the kind of scream that reshapes your nightmares.

My knees buckle as I watch them, my chest splintering open. Water streams down my face, hot as acid.

"I just can't." The words explode from her like shrapnel, each syllable tearing flesh. Her body convulses against him. "He told me I would always be damaged."

Her voice fractures, dissolves into something worse than screaming, a hollow, guttural keening that scrapes against the tile walls.

"And I can't... He broke me so I could never love again." The words die as she chokes on them, her body seizing with such violence that Jaxon's arms strain to contain her.

Jaxon crushes her against him, his soaked shirt tearing under her clawing fingers.

"I know, baby, I fucking know," he chants, voice cracking like glass underfoot.

His jaw clenches so hard I hear teeth grind.

"Please don't..." The words strangle in his throat as his eyes meet mine over her convulsing body, wild with terror, pupils blown black.

His lips tremble violently against her temple, tears cutting clean tracks down his face, mingling with the water.

I lunge for the towels, my hands shaking so violently I nearly tear the fabric. I wrap one around my hips, suddenly aware of my nakedness looming over her broken form, a primal threat I never meant to be.

The second towel I drape over them both like a shroud, watching as Jaxon rises with her trembling body clutched against his chest.

Her sobs carve through the steam-thick air, each one a serrated blade between my ribs.

Jaxon's eyes lock with mine over her head, something feral and protective darkening his gaze as he carries her toward my bed, leaving wet footprints like blood trails across the floor.

Jaxon set her down on the bed and knelt beside her, his hands trembling uselessly in the sheets. I lingered at the threshold, towel clenched at my hips, feeling like a trespasser in my room.

Ellia curled on her side, knees drawn to her chest, still heaving but silent now. I watched her back flex with every ragged breath, the ridges of her spine as sharp as the edges of her voice.

I wanted to touch her, comfort her, fold her up and tuck her into the safety of my chest the way I did, but I was afraid to set her off again. I was afraid to make her hurt more.

Jaxon's head hung low, his brow pressed to the mattress as he tried to catch his own breath. I could see the muscles corded in his neck, jaw working as if he could chew through the pain for both of them if he just clenched hard enough.

Without a word, I rummaged through the dresser, fingers numb as I pulled out whatever dry clothes I could find.

I fumbled with the sweatpants, my fingers refusing to cooperate as I pulled them over damp skin, then tossed a pair toward Jaxon.

The gentle thud of fabric hitting the floor between us felt obscene against the suffocating silence that had replaced her screams.

Ellia's body begins to surrender to exhaustion, her chest still hitching with aftershocks of grief as she slips into unconsciousness.

The duvet engulfs her tall frame like a shroud, hiding everything but the damp tangle of her hair against my pillow.

I catch Jaxon's eye and tilt my head toward the door. He rises halfway, then freezes, gaze anchored to her tear-ravaged face, the wreckage of something once whole now collapsed in the center of my sheets.

I rake my nails down my face hard enough to leave welts. "What the fuck just happened in there?" My voice scrapes out, barely above a whisper but vibrating with rage.

Jaxon's face contorts, a battlefield of terror and fury. His pupils are blown wide, nostrils flared.

"She finally shattered, August." His voice was low and controlled.

"Remember what I told you? Not one goddamn tear in that hospital bed while they catalogued every violation on her body. Nothing during recovery when the nightmares had her clawing her own skin open. Nothing. Ever." His voice drops to something primal, each word a blade between us.

Pacing like a caged animal, I place my palm on the wall, anchoring myself. My injuries are insignificant to hers.

"Thank fucking god she was in that medically induced coma." My voice drops to a guttural whisper. "If she had been conscious when they..." The words strangle me, acid burning up my throat.

Jaxon's eyes flash black in the half-light.

"I know, August," he hisses through clenched teeth. "Every night I wake up drenched, terrified she'll discover what they did to her while she was lifeless on that hill."

He takes a deep breath.

"They warned me," he goes on. "The psych team. Said this could happen. Delayed response. The mind catches up once the body's no longer in survival mode."

His eyes lift to mine, red-rimmed, mercilessly honest. "I still wasn't ready."

"We don't leave her alone," I say. It isn't a suggestion. "Not tonight. Not for a while."

Jaxon nods once. Sharp. Final.

"Good." I push off the wall, forcing breath back into my lungs. "Then we hold the line. We let her rage. We let her grieve. We don't rush her back into being palatable."

A muscle in my cheek twitches. "And if she remembers more?"

"Then we're here for that too," he says. "Every ugly inch of it."

CHAPTER 23

AUGUST

I lay stretched out on the couch, one arm slung over my eyes, trying to breathe through the hammering behind my temples. The headache pulses in time with my heartbeat—sharp, relentless, punishing. Every throb feels like a reminder of how useless I am here, separated by walls and rules and Jaxon's quiet authority.

I'd argued. Of course, I had. Fought him on it with teeth bared and voice raw. But he'd stood his ground, steady and immovable, the way he gets when chaos needs containment.

"I've got her," he'd said. Not dismissive, but protective. Final. And he does. I know that.

Still, it doesn't stop the ache in my chest. I wanted to be near her. Not to speak. Not to fix anything. Just to exist in the same space. To feel the rise and fall of her breathing, to anchor myself to the simple fact that she's here—alive, warm, real. To let my body remember what safety sounds like.

Jaxon prowls down every hour like a sentinel, his eyes scanning me for cracks. Each time he appears in the doorway, shoulders filling the frame, I catch glimpses of what war looks like when it wears human skin. He bleeds control from every pore while the rest of us hemorrhage.

Jaxon came down one last time to inform me she is awake. A quiet nod as I stare up at the ceiling. How did everything go so wrong so fast?

She is going to need her space, but that promise Jaxon and I declared will not be broken. Her grief is our grief. Her rage also belongs to us.

The bedroom is a tomb of silence when I enter. She lies with her back to me, shoulder blades jutting like broken wings beneath her skin, each breath making her ribs expand and collapse in violent rhythm. Her hair spills across the pillow in a dark tangle, still damp at the roots.

Jaxon's abandoned chair stands sentinel beside the bed, while the sheets, now dry but bearing the memory of her earlier storm, coil around her legs like pale serpents waiting to strike.

I hover at the edge of the bed, unwilling to breach her perimeter, but she senses me there. She doesn't roll over. Doesn't flinch. Just says, so quiet I almost miss it, "You wouldn't have let it happen, would you?"

I moved closer, the mattress giving under my weight. "No," I answered. "But I couldn't stop it either."

She turns. All the fury is gone now; it's something way worse. She's not looking for comfort, or even absolution; she's looking for the truth, no matter how much it hurts.

"Will you lay with me?" The words scrape from her throat like broken glass, barely audible but carrying the weight of a scream.

Her fingers clutch the edge of the sheet, knuckles bleached white, trembling with the effort of asking for what she needs.

My body responds before my mind can catch up. I lift the covers just enough to slide beneath them, careful to disturb nothing on her side. I settle onto my back, one arm crooked behind my head, barely breathing.

She inches backward, eliminating the space between us millimeter by millimeter. The silent request in her movement is unmistakable.

When I finally press my chest against her spine, her skin is winter-cold from exposure, pulling her in close enough for my heartbeat to synchronize with hers.

I move with the caution of someone approaching a wounded animal, each shift of muscle telegraphed to avoid startling her.

"I'm sorry," she whispers, the words barely a ghost against the darkness.

"Don't," I murmur against her hair, feeling each strand catch against my lips. "Whatever breaks you apart tears through me too."

Against my chest, her ribcage expands with a ragged inhale that seems to pull all the oxygen from the room.

Her breath catches, a sound like prey in a snare.

"In that hospital, when I finally opened my eyes..." Her throat convulses against my forearm, muscles working desperately. "I searched for you. For Jaxon. No one else."

My arm locks around her waist with savage possession, fingers digging into the hollow beneath her ribs until I feel the flutter of her pulse against my fingertips.

I want to crack her open and pull her inside me, beneath my sternum, where nothing could ever touch her again. Her heartbeat hammers against mine, our bodies vibrating at the same desperate frequency.

"Will you tell me about that night?" The question tears through the dark like a bullet.

I sense Jaxon before I see him, a shift in the air pressure, the presence of something lethal. As he materializes on the other side of the bed, looming over the chair, his shadow stretches across her like a claim.

My eyes lock with Jaxon's across her body. His jaw clenches, nostrils flaring with each measured breath. The unspoken warning in his gaze is unmistakable.

"Are you certain you want this?" I whisper against her ear, my lips barely grazing her skin.

"I need to know," she breathes, the words vibrating through her back into my chest. Some truths will shatter her. Some horrors neither of us can bear to voice.

Jaxon settles into the chair beside the bed, leaning forward until his massive shoulders block the moonlight streaming through the window. His shadow falls across her like a shroud, his presence both guardian and executioner.

I inhale slowly, tasting copper on the back of my tongue. The confession burns like acid waiting to be spilled.

"Jaxon put a tracker on your bike."

The words hang between us, heavy and irrevocable. Against my chest, her body goes rigid, a prey animal sensing danger. Her fingers find mine in the darkness, trembling as she draws them to her mouth, pressing my knuckles against lips gone cold.

Her voice, when it finally comes, is barely a whisper against my skin. "I had suspected."

The truth scrapes my throat raw as it emerges. "He knew he couldn't trust Michael. The tracker wasn't about control— it was insurance." My voice drops to a whisper. "Protection."

Jaxon's eyes catch the moonlight like a predator's in the darkness, pupils dilated to swallow every shadow.

"When midnight passed, and you hadn't returned," he says, voice dropping to a frequency that vibrates through bone, "my blood turned to ice. You've never missed your time of arrival, not once in the three years I worked for you."

"August was already moving," he continues, jaw clenched so tight I can hear his teeth grinding. "Your tracker's signal died halfway down the Summit."

Her fingers dig into my hand with such force that I feel the arcs of her nails breaking skin. Her entire body trembles against mine, a violent shiver that won't subside.

"We drove like demons were chasing us. When we reached the last ping location." His voice fractures, a hairline crack in steel.

"There was blood on the guardrail," I finish, the words tasting like copper in my mouth. "Tire marks carved into asphalt like someone tried to run you off the road. We followed the broken pieces of your bike down the side of the slope."

“Where was Michael?” Her voice cracks like thin ice, and every syllable seems to warn of a descent into darker depths.

Jaxon's eyes meet mine across her trembling body, obsidian meeting steel, a silent agreement passing between us about how much horror she can bear to hear.

"There was no sign of him," I finally say, feeling her exhale against my chest, her breath warm but shallow. "When we found you at the bottom of that ravine, you were splayed across jagged rock like something discarded. Your legs bent at unnatural angles. The moonlight caught the white of bone piercing through your riding jeans."

"We found your helmet before we found your body," Jaxon's voice drops to a guttural whisper. "The visor had cracks, blood matting your hair to your scalp, your lips already turning blue in the flashlight beam."

"Jaxon straddled you on that blood-slick stone," I continue, feeling her pulse hammer against my palm. "When he compressed your chest, your ribs gave way like brittle branches. Three broken ribs are what the doctor confirmed. For three minutes, nothing. Just Jaxon's labored breathing and my own prayers turning to curses in the dark."

Her body coils against mine, spine arching as if reliving the trauma.

"When you finally gasped," Jaxon says, "it was like watching someone claw their way back from the dead. We carried you up that slope, unconscious. In my arms, you went limp again. No breath. Nothing."

"I drove blind with panic," I whisper into her hair. "One hand on the wheel, the other reaching back to feel for any sign of life while Jaxon breathed for you in the backseat."

"I examined the wreckage," he says, his voice scraping low. Our eyes lock across her body—a wordless exchange. "Your brake lines were severed. Deliberately." The revelation lands like a blade.

Against me, her body seizes, a current running through her frame. Her spine snaps straight with an audible crack as she tears herself from my chest.

CHAPTER 24

ELLIA

The memory hits me like a truck, Michael slashing my brake lines while pretending to take a piss in the bushes. I bolt upright, sheets falling to my ankles as my feet slam against the floor.

Pulling on August's discarded shirt that lay at the foot of the bed.

"He cut them on the ridge," I gasp, heat radiating from my skin.

"When he went back to the bikes. I thought he was just taking a leak."

Jaxon and August are instantly beside me, their bodies tense.

"You remember?" Jaxon's voice cuts like shattered glass.

My mind races. Yes, I fucking remember. The pieces click into a horrible place, why he insisted we didn't need gear that day.

My palm presses against my forehead as fragments of memory crystallize.

"I do," I say, shaking my head. "From before the crash."

I take a much-needed breath before I continue, "My phone...the photos from that night. There has to be evidence."

I'd avoided those pictures after the accident, couldn't stand seeing glimpses of who I used to be.

"Where are you going?" Their voices echo behind me, tense and urgent.

I didn't answer. I'd hidden my phone in my suitcase, tired of labels and whispers. I hate being tied to a tiny mobile device, thank fuck for some people in my life who understand I am not the one glued to any kind of device.

"Aha." I yank the device from my suitcase pocket, a spark of triumph cutting through the chaos. "Found it. I took pictures that night."

My thumb swipes frantically through the gallery, searching for that final evening, the last photos before my camera roll goes dead.

After the accident, I couldn't bear to document anything. Every potential memory felt like another thing I might lose.

"Ellia, that phone was pulverized in the crash," August says, worry creasing his forehead.

"True," I snapped. "But my cloud didn't."

I scrolled through photos—sunlit adventures, laughter, freedom.

"Here. Look." I shoved the screen into Jaxon's chest.

They flip through the shots. August's expression darkens into something feral, unfamiliar. "Ellia... have you seen these?"

His oversized shirt slides off my shoulder as I shiver. I fumble for my sweatpants, my trembling fingers betraying me as I struggle to guide each foot through the fabric, the cotton twisting against my skin like it's fighting back.

"See Michael talking to Robyn in this selfie?" Jaxon hands me the phone. "She was up there with you."

"No," I breathe. "We spent hours together, and I never saw her."

"Look again."

Jaxon opens another photo. My bike's silhouette in the foreground, Robyn crouched behind a pine, eyes locked on me.

Rage and dread crash together in my chest. Of course, she was spying; of course, both of them were in on it.

"Let's enhance these," Jaxon grits out. "I want every detail."

August and I follow Jaxon to his computer cave.

He hooks the phone up and starts downloading. "Wait... don't grab them all. Some are private." I fold my arms and scowl.

He smirks, leaning in so close I feel his breath. "I love it when you get huffy. It suits you. But you're always..." He falters, eyes darkening.

"But what, Jaxon? Depressed? Numb? Crazy? Say it." I step into him, my pulse pounding.

The glow of the screen illuminates his face, and the storm brewing between us. We both move forward, closing the already small space between us.

Chest to chest, his hands carved the small of my back and yanked me so hard I nearly toppled. My knees bumped the battered rolling chair, and he pressed me against the edge of the desk, sending a static shudder up my spine.

The computer screen's cold light flickered, parsing the evidence we'd just found: Robyn's feral little face, blown up and pixelated, watching from the dark.

But it was Jaxon's face I was watching now, and it was a storm front—thunderous, hungry, all the patience burnt away.

"You're not crazy," he said, voice hoarse. "You're dangerous, and you are ours."

His mouth crashed into mine. Not a gentle apology, not a lover's slow burn, but an unmaking.

He tasted like coffee and mint, and all the years I'd spent pretending I didn't want this.

August's eyes burn into my back like twin brands. Jaxon tears his mouth from mine, our chests heaving. He growls, vibrating against my collarbone.

He pivots to the screens, jaw clenched. We crowd forward, the air between us electric and suffocating. August's finger jabs at the monitor.

"Look."

My stomach drops. There I am—naked, writhing with Michael in my Nashville loft, his hands everywhere I now wish they'd never been. The intimate betrayal hits like a physical blow.

Their eyes drill into me, predatory and possessive. The walls begin to contract. My lungs seize.

"What?" I retreat, shoulder blades hitting the wall. "It was just something he liked."

"We'll revisit that," August says, voice dangerously soft. "But focus. Do you see it?"

I force myself forward, pulse hammering in my throat. There, in the corner of the frame, is Michael's banking app. Colorado Twin National Bank. The balance makes my blood freeze.

"40 million dollars," Jaxon whispers, the words slicing through the room. "Was that typical for your band?"

"No." My voice sounds hollow, distant.

August moves closer, his heat at my back. "Did you share accounts with him?"

The question dangles between us, heavy with accusation.

Six months into our relationship, Michael had pushed me to merge our bank accounts. Something in my gut had revolted against the idea, a primal warning I couldn't name. The timestamp on this photo tells me everything: three days before he tried to kill me on that mountain.

A terrible thought washes over me. He'd gone back to Colorado. His sanctuary. His hometown. The place he always swore he'd retire to when he had enough money.

Enough of my money.

Rage pulses through me like electricity, turning my blood to acid.

My feet wear paths in the tile as I pace, each step harder than the last.

"WHAT THE ABSOLUTE FUCK!"

The scream tears from my throat, raw and feral. My nails bite crescents into my palms as I yank at my hoodie, choking on fury.

I bolt for the back door, their voices calling my name like a funeral dirge I can't stand to hear anymore.

Outside, the night air does nothing to cool the inferno inside me.

Michael. His name tastes like poison. He didn't just take; he hollowed me out. My body. My money. My fucking soul. The thought of his hands on me, in my accounts, makes bile rise in my throat.

Jaxon materializes behind me, his presence a dark current against my skin before I hear him. "Elli." His voice is gravel and smoke. "Look at me."

I can't. If I look at him, I might shatter.

He grips my jaw, forcing my face to his.

"While I still draw breath," he whispers, each word a knife edge, "they will bleed for what they've done."

His vow hangs in the air between us, heavy as a storm cloud.

$40 million. Gone. Not just skimmed from, but completely emptied. I'd suspected Michael was dipping into my accounts, but never imagined he'd drain everything to the last cent.

Just like the first time his fingers closed too tightly around my wrist, I'd known then what would follow, known I should run, but stayed anyway.

"What now?" I manage to choke out. "That offshore account was one of my smallest, but he still wiped it. He was funneling money to Robyn all along. And I let him."

His fingers find my throat, his thumb settling over my racing pulse as he draws me in until I can feel his exhale on my lips.

"We know where he banks. They'll slip up."

Each word grazes my mouth like a promise. "And when he does, I'll tear him apart so thoroughly his own mother won't recognize what's left."

His touch traces the delicate hollow of my neck, awakening something ancient and wild that makes me freeze beneath his hand.

I try to look past him. "Where's August?"

Jaxon's eyes pin me, dissecting every micro-expression on my face. "He needed to rest."

His eyes gleam with recognition.

"There it is, that wildfire I thought was extinguished." His thumb presses harder against my pulse.

"You're clawing your way back to me." Not a question, more like a verdict.

He searches my face like he's excavating for something precious beneath the rage. I am hollow except for the inferno.

"Let me hear you."

"I don't want words," I hiss, teeth bared. "I want you to burn everything else out of me until there's nothing left but ash."

His pupils dilate until his eyes are almost black. He's hunting for me in there, behind the fury, behind the emptiness. I don't know if I exist anymore, but whatever remains is nothing like the ghost I've been since that blood-soaked summit.

His grip slides from my throat in one fluid motion, fingertips scorching a path down my body. In a single violent movement, he hoists me up by the backs of my thighs, my weight meaningless against his strength.

"I worship you," he growls against my mouth, "but what I'm about to do to you will be absolutely fucking sacrilegious."

I crash my mouth to his, teeth clashing, tasting copper. I need to feel him obliterate everything else; every betrayal, every violation.

He drops to his knees at the cliff's edge, the ocean roaring sixty feet below us like a hungry beast. The salt air whips my hair as his fingers dig bruises into my hips.

He tears my shirt over my head, exposing my skin to the night. His mouth finds my throat, teeth scraping the tender flesh beneath my ear as his hand wraps around my neck. My pulse hammers against his palm.

"Now that I've tasted you," he growls, breath hot against my ear, "I'll devour you until there's nothing left."

I arch into him as he tightens his grip, cutting off just enough air to make stars bloom behind my eyes, and my body liquefies, primal and desperate.

"Scream for me," he commands, voice raw. "Let me hear what I'm doing to you. Let everyone know who you belong to."

I try to nod, clawing at his shoulders.

"Words," he demands, squeezing harder. "Give me your voice."

"Yes...Jaxon...please," each syllable tears from my throat like a confession.

His eyes flash with savage approval. "Good girl."

He tears my sweatpants with a single savage motion, the sound of ripping fabric like thunder in my ears. My spine bows violently, a live wire arching toward its ground.

"Open. Your. legs." Each word falls like a command to the universe itself. His fingers dig into my flesh, branding me, claiming territory.

"Christ, songbird," he growls, his voice dropping to something ancient and feral, "you're fucking drowning for me."

His mouth descends, teeth grazing my nipple before he takes it between his lips, and the sensation detonates through me like white phosphorus, burning everything in its path.

Each kiss leaves fire in its wake. His fingers twist my nipple with cruel precision while his other hand claims me below, the sudden invasion making me cry out so loudly he growls against my fevered skin. Teeth grazing my hip bone as he inhales deeply.

"You smell delicious," he murmurs, voice thick with savage hunger.

I couldn't help the wild sound that tore from between my teeth. Jaxon's tongue was hot and brutal, lapping at me with unyielding intent, almost as if he could drag the poison out through my skin.

His grip kept me caged to the earth. The cliff's wind clawed goosebumps across my naked body. It was all raw nerves and open air.

My hands clutched fistfuls of his hair, desperate to anchor myself to something that wasn't slipping away. He pulled back for a breath, face slick with my arousal, eyes black as tar pits.

Jaxon guides me even closer to the cliff's edge, his fingers working their magic inside me. I dangle precariously, the ocean's roar rising from below as I clutch his hair, my pulse racing with both fear and desire.

He raises his gaze, his mouth glistening. "Let your head fall back," he commands, his voice vibrating against my most sensitive flesh.

Wide-eyed with anticipation, I meet his impatient smirk before surrendering to his demand, allowing my head to tilt over nothingness.

Each skilled movement brings me closer to the edge in every sense, as the coastal winds whip through my hair, he devours me with relentless hunger.

He got off on the way I shook, the way my body bucked with every relentless pass of his tongue, every calculated bite. With each breath, I was further from Ellia the victim, closer to the animal inside.

"I want you to come so hard they'll think someone's being murdered," he growled, then devoured me again with savage hunger.

When he thrust his finger harder inside me, the invasion tore a scream from my throat that echoed across the cliffside.

He groaned against my flesh, the vibration shooting lightning through my core as he worked deeper, curling his finger to scrape against that exquisite spot that made my vision fragment.

The second finger stretched me, his mouth never relenting as he sucked my clit between his teeth, applying just enough pressure to dance on the knife's edge between pleasure and pain.

His feral sounds against my flesh told me he was consuming me, not just pleasuring me. My inner walls clamped down on his fingers with brutal force as the orgasm built like a tsunami.

When it crashed through me, my entire body convulsed violently over the edge, my voice shattering into primal, broken sounds.

“Jax..." My voice shattered, replaced by primal sounds I'd never made before. "Don't stop.”

He only growled deeper and worked me harder through each devastating aftershock, refusing to let me come down from the height.

Something in me snapped as his tongue worked me, as if my body had its own agenda and every cell was in mutiny.

I didn't care that we were on the cliff, exposed to ocean wind and the black sweep of night, maybe even visible from the road below if headlights crested the rise.

I wanted this humiliation, this devouring. I wanted to be witnessed.

I ground my hips into his face until his jaw creaked and my thighs ached from the effort, and even then, Jaxon only groaned, greedier.

He spat into me, rough and obscene, and lapped it back with the flat of his tongue.

The noises he made were animalistic, guttural, and they unlocked something feral inside me.

I met him sound for sound, my voice shredding itself and reforming into something that belonged to the wind and the void.

He curved his two fingers deeper, and the pleasure-pain was so dense it became indistinguishable from panic.

I collapsed, boneless, legs still splayed open, my lungs shivering in the cool night air.

Jaxon hovered over me, his mouth slick, his jawline shining with my wet. His voice rasps like a blade against stone. "Taste yourself."

I seize his hair and slam our mouths together, invading him with my tongue, reclaiming my essence from his lips, his teeth, the hollow of his cheeks. The taste of my arousal mixed with his saliva ignites something primal in me.

My fingers find his shirt, and I tear at the buttons, fabric shredding beneath my nails until his chest is exposed, my palms burning against his skin.

My hands tear at his belt, fumbling with the buckle, a feral hunger making my movements desperate and uncoordinated. My breath catches as he snarls, the sound reverberating through me like thunder, and with one savage motion, he's exposed.

Heat floods my core at the sight of him, my muscles contracting involuntarily. My body recognizes what's coming, the exquisite stretch, the delicious intrusion, and responds with a flood of slick anticipation.

He leaned over me, bracing his hands hard on either side of my head, so the only thing I could see was the black canopy of his body and the endless ocean behind.

“I want you to beg,” he whispered, his lips dragging across my jaw, “until my name is the only one on those pretty little lips of yours.”

The word "yes" escaped me like something ripped from my chest. "Jaxon," I gasped, my voice breaking on his name.

"Please." My breath came in shallow bursts as I felt him against me, impossibly hard, poised at the threshold of my body.

He gripped my jaw in one hand and fit the head of his cock to me, thick and hot, rubbing a slow, obscene figure-eight between my folds.

He didn’t ask permission. He didn’t check if I was ready. He pressed forward, and the first inch was always a war. I gasped, clawing at his biceps, nails raking angry red trails through his tattoos, but he didn't stop.

I shuddered as he forced more of himself inside, the stretch so sharp it bordered on cruelty.

"Is this what you want?" His voice was barely more than a snarl. "You want me to fuck you empty right here on this cliff?"

I barely nodded as I was biting his arm.

“Yes, Jaxon,” words caught in the moans, “Please, Jaxon.”

"Then tell me," He demanded, dark and wild. "Tell me who you belong to."

"You," I hissed, voice breaking on the word. "You, Jaxon. Only you."

He leaned in, forehead pressed to mine, eyes black and bottomless. “Look at me,” he demanded, voice a sandpaper scrape. “Don’t ever fucking look away.”

I obeyed. I had no choice. The world shrank to this: his sweat mixing with mine, our breath tangling in the night, the pulse of blood roaring in my ears.

He fucked me slow and deep at first, each thrust a deliberate act of possession, then harder, rougher, until I was nothing but wreckage beneath him. My body threatening to fall over the cliff.

“Say it, Ellia. Louder.”

“Please, Jaxon. Fuck me, make it hurt.” The last word fell out of me, ragged as a torn banner.

He grinned like a wolf and drove forward, burying himself to the hilt. My scream shattered the night. He stilled, forcing me to take every impossible inch, and waited until the tremors in my thighs became convulsions.

"I could wreck you," he whispered, voice gone velvet and murder. "I could leave you out here limp and leaking for the world to see."

"Do it," I snarled, digging my heels into the small of his back, forcing him deeper as my orgasm tore through me like wildfire.

My inner walls seized around his thickness, milking him mercilessly. Jaxon threw his head back, throat exposed, a primal sound ripping from his chest.

"That's it, songbird. Let me hear you break," he growled, sweat glistening on his collarbone.

In one fluid motion, he hoisted me up, my legs vice-tight around his waist, his cock still buried to the hilt as he carried me to the retaining wall overlooking the deadly drop. The cold stone bit into my flesh as he perched me on the edge.

"Every scar on this body belongs to me now," he whispered against my shoulder, teeth grazing my collarbone. "I'll fuck the memory of who marked you right out of your skin."

When he withdrew suddenly, I felt hollowed out, desperate. The whimper that escaped me was pathetic and needy. His hand found my throat, thumb pressing just beneath my jaw.

"You're going to sing so loud the whole fucking world will hear who owns you," he commanded, spinning me around and bending me forward until my torso hung over the abyss.

The sixty-foot drop yawned beneath me, my hair whipping in the updraft. "Christ, you're magnificent like this, spread open and dangerous."

His fingers traced each raised line on my back with reverent cruelty before he slammed into me from behind with such force that my vision blurred. His hand tightened around my throat as he pulled me back against him, my thighs barely maintaining contact with the wall's edge.

"Mine," he growled. Thunderous, almost drowning out my own noises. His lips brush my ear, teeth grazing the shell. "I'm going to flood this tight cunt until you're dripping with me for days."

The promise vibrates through my bones, dark and possessive.

I can only manage a desperate nod as his grip constricts around my throat, blood pounding in my ears as oxygen becomes precious.

My vision narrows to pinpricks of light against the vast darkness below. My orgasm builds like a gathering storm, electric and unstoppable.

"Every. Last. drop." Each word is punctuated by a brutal thrust that pushes me closer to the precipice, both literal and figurative.

My body betrayed me gloriously, inner walls seizing around his thickness as oxygen deprivation heightened every sensation to unbearable intensity.

His rhythm faltered, becoming savage and primal as he came with me. I clawed at his restraining hand, not to escape but to feel the exquisite danger of his control as my consciousness began to float away from my body.

His grip relents just as black spots bloom across my vision.

"Breathe for me, Elli," he commands, the words swimming through my oxygen-starved brain.

My lungs burn as they fill, each gasping inhale scraping my raw throat. He yanks me back against his sweat-slick chest, spinning me to face him, my legs trembling and useless.

"You take my darkness like you were made for it," he growls, eyes gleaming with savage pride. "Every. Brutal. Inch."

I can only manage a drugged, delirious smile, my body still pulsing with aftershocks. His teeth graze my jugular, not quite gentle.

"Such a good girl," he whispers against my thundering pulse before lifting me, my limbs hanging like a broken doll's as he carries his conquest back to the house.

CHAPTER 25

JAXON

I carried Ellia into the house, her body draped across my arms like a discarded marionette, head lolling against my chest. The only sign she hadn't completely surrendered to unconsciousness was the occasional flutter of her eyelashes against tear-swollen lids.

The day had hollowed her out. I could feel it in the shallow rise and fall of her breath against my neck, in the way her fingers curled weakly into my shirt as if she might dissolve completely without that anchor.

The memory of her collapse in the shower, knees giving way, shoulders heaving with sobs that seemed torn from somewhere primal inside her, made my jaw clench.

August's silhouette appeared at the top of the landing, his face half hidden in shadow. He winced, pressing fingers to his temple as he watched us ascend, but his eyes never left her face. August's lips curled into that familiar predatory smirk.

"You broke her pretty damn good." His words hung in the air, not a question but an approval.

"I hope the whole fucking world heard her." I shouldered past him toward his bed. "How's your head?"

He dragged his palm down his face, but the gesture couldn't quite erase the darkness in his eyes.

"Better now that she's here."

August pulled back the covers, and we lay her down together, a ritual that felt both tender and obscene. As we drew the blankets to her shoulders, she shuddered with a soft moan that vibrated through my fingertips.

The sound confirmed she'd finally surrendered to unconsciousness. I stepped back, adjusting my loosened pants riding low on my hips.

"Keep her warm," I murmured, already turning away. "I have some work to do."

I stalk to my computer, my jaw locked so tight I taste blood where I've bitten the inside of my cheek.

The screens flicker to life under my trembling fingers, and there she is, Ellia sprawled beneath Michael, her lips parted, his hands on her body. The image burns into my retinas like acid, and my vision narrows to pinpricks of red.

I slam my fist into the desk, sending coffee splashing across papers. The pain barely registers. "I'll flay him alive," I whisper, the words scraping my throat raw. "I'll make him beg for death before I'm done for touching what's mine."

The photo remains on the left monitor while I pull up her life on the others, a digital shrine to everything she was before him.

Each file I open carves another wound. Photos of Ellia on stage, radiant under spotlights. Award ceremonies where she outshone everyone. Magazine covers capturing a confidence that's been systematically extinguished. The contrast between then and now slices through me like a serrated blade.

The evidence of Michael's sabotage glows from my screens, emails redirecting her opportunities to his other accounts, contracts with poison clauses highlighted by my software, and bank statements showing systematic withdrawals to offshore accounts in his name.

The bastard constructed walls around her, brick by digital brick, until she could see nothing but him.

There are even photos taken of her bruised and beaten body in various stages of healing. That fucker laid his hands on her, and not in a pleasurable way. I'm going to fucking kill him, bring him back from the dead, and tear his skin off him while he screams for mercy.

My molars grind against each other as acid burns up my esophagus. I had sensed the wrongness in him from the beginning, that predatory stillness behind his smile.

I'd walked away from violence once, thinking I could build something better than my blood-soaked past. That hesitation cost her everything. It won't happen again. When I find him, his suffering will be an echo of hers, but his will end.

I comb through her digital footprint with surgical precision, each click bringing me closer to the truth. Her messages reveal nothing but industry talk until a hidden account tucked behind layers of encryption appears. The name "Kingston Sage" glows on my screen like a confession. My breath catches.

The folder unfolds before me: correspondence, financial transactions, contractual agreements, a shadow life completely divorced from the music world I thought defined her.

My fingers hover over the keyboard, suddenly cold. The woman I've been protecting is a stranger wearing Ellia's face.

"Who the hell are you, really?" I whisper to her ghost in the machine.

The digital trail went cold exactly one year ago. Urgent messages pile up like bodies: "Kingston, we need to discuss the potential businesses," and "Ms. Sage, please confirm receipt of payment," all met with deafening silence.

Whatever secret empire she had built alongside her music career collapsed simultaneously, as if someone had cut both puppet strings at once.

Michael must have discovered what she was hiding. The offshore accounts I've uncovered hold sums that make her platinum records look like pocket change.

One more click reveals a document that freezes the blood in my veins: a purchase agreement for Midnight Sound Records, the very label that launched her career.

The timestamp shows she acquired it six months ago, after her disappearance at the mountain retreat. This single transaction breaks her digital silence, a lone ripple in a dead sea.

The digital breadcrumbs paint a portrait I never imagined—quarterly reports showing Ellia's shell company acquiring controlling interest in failing tech startups moments before patent approvals, leveraged buyouts of family businesses executed with the cold efficiency of a corporate assassin, offshore accounts funneling millions through tax havens in the Caymans and Bermuda.

Each transaction lines up with those mysterious account numbers, creating a web of financial power that stretches across continents. Two hundred separate businesses under her control, and I'm still uncovering more with every click.

My chair creaks as I lean back, fingers laced behind my neck, staring at the empire she built in shadow. The woman I thought I knew had been playing a game of corporate chess while the world watched her sing.

The screen before me pulses with the ghost of her ambition, a fortune built in shadows.

Exhaustion claws at my consciousness after hours hunched over the screen. I drag myself from the desk, my body leaden with fatigue, and find myself frozen in August's doorway.

Ellia lies exactly where I placed her, but now August's body curves around hers like a shield, his arm draped possessively across her waist. The sight ignites something primal in my chest, jealousy and desire tangled into something dangerous.

I linger in the threshold, watching their synchronized breathing. August and I, we're both tethered to her now, caught in her gravity.

My gaze lingers on the tableau they make: my best friend and the woman who has carved herself into both our souls.

This woman who built empires in secret, who survived Michael's systematic destruction, who lies broken but undefeated between us.

I clutch the doorframe, blood draining from my knuckles, frozen between two worlds, the Ellia I thought I knew and this shadow empress whose secrets August and I would still take bullets for without hesitation.

I move to the empty side of the bed and strip off what remains of my clothes, the buttons Ellia had torn off earlier now completely missing.

My movements are measured, careful not to disturb her, finally peaceful form or August, whose concussion demands uninterrupted rest. The silence between us feels both necessary and unbearable.

The mattress dips beneath my weight as I settle beside her, leaving calculated inches between us as I fix my gaze on the shadows playing across the ceiling.

Sleep evades me. Then, her fingers emerge from beneath the blanket August has tucked around her, blindly seeking in the darkness.

When I turn toward her, her hand finds mine with unexpected certainty. I draw it to rest against my chest, where my heart betrays me with its quickened pace. A soft sound escapes her parted lips, not quite a word, but a surrender that cuts deeper than any confession could.

CHAPTER 26

JAXON

Midday light sliced through the blinds when I finally opened my eyes. Sometime during the night, Ellia had migrated across the sheets to nestle against my chest, her breath warm against my skin.

August lay sprawled on his back beside us, one arm flung overhead, his face slack with deep sleep. The three of us, tangled in this strange new constellation.

Ellia stirred against me, her eyelashes fluttering against her cheeks. I pressed my lips to her temple, breathing in the scent of her.

"I actually slept," she whispered, voice rough as she propped herself up on one elbow, eyes wide with the realization.

"You did." The corner of my mouth lifted as hers did the same, a mirror reflection.

The smile transformed her, not the practiced stage smiles I'd seen in a thousand photographs, but something genuine that made my breath catch.

And I would burn cities to the ground to protect that smile. To keep it from disappearing again.

She rises from the bed, her body bare and unapologetic in the harsh midday light. The map of scars she despises so much catches the sun, silver tributaries across her skin that tell stories she's tried to erase. Her hair falls in wild cascades down her spine, a dark curtain against pale flesh.

"Beautiful," the word escapes me before I can trap it behind my teeth.

She glances back, one shoulder angled toward me, vulnerability and defiance warring in her eyes.

"I heard that," she murmurs, voice still sleep-rough. "I need a shower."

The word hangs between us. Beautiful. I'll repeat it like a fucking prayer until it sinks beneath her skin and takes root where self-hatred has grown for too long.

August stirs beside me, his eyes still heavy with sleep. "Whatever magic you worked on her last night, Jax..." His voice trails off, thick with meaning. "She needs more of that."

I drag my fingers through my tangled hair, something dark and possessive unfurling in my chest at his words.

"We need to define what this is between the three of us," I say, the words scraping my throat raw.

His exhale fills the room as he pushes himself upright, muscles tensing beneath sleep-warmed skin. His eyes meet mine, unflinching.

"She's not naïve, Jax. She knows exactly what's happening here between the three of us."

Rising from the bed, throat dry. "I need a shower."

My body aches to follow her, but something fragile has just awakened in Ellia. Crowding her now might shatter whatever strength she's gathering, and now that I have had a taste of her, I want more. I need more.

Later, I'm alone in the kitchen when I hear the coffee machine's mechanical heartbeat. The scent seems wrong for the late afternoon shadows stretching across the floor, but I know we both need the artificial alertness after last night's revelations.

"Hey." The single word slides across my skin.

I turn to find Ellia lingering by the island, her wet hair darkening the shoulders of a thin t-shirt that barely reaches mid-thigh. The white streak in her hair catches light like polished silver.

My gaze follows her bare legs that extend endlessly beneath the hem, no fabric to hide the curves I memorized in the darkness. Something untamed stirs in me, a desire to claim every inch of her skin, to banish clothes entirely from our shared space.

I extend the coffee toward her. Our fingers brush, a jolt of electricity races up my arm and settles low in my stomach. Her eyes flicker to mine for just a heartbeat before she murmurs, "Thank you," as she retreats to the table.

I follow, settling beside her as she draws one knee to her chest like armor. The steam from her cup rises between us, a fragile barrier.

My voice drops to something dangerous and intimate.

"Ellia."

Her name feels heavy on my tongue. "I went through your phone last night."

The cup freezes against her parted lips. I can see her pulse quicken at her throat as I lean closer, close enough to taste the air she exhales.

"There's my girl," August's voice cuts through the tension.

He prowls into the kitchen, jeans riding low on his hips, torso bare and marked with last week's shadows.

Ellia's eyes flick to August, wide and unguarded. A flash of vulnerability trembles across her face.

"Hey, August," she whispers, voice fracturing.

August, massive as a linebacker, storms to the fridge. "I haven't eaten anything real in over a week," he growls, yanking it open.

Ellia smirks, an electric bond of shared history passing between them. She turns back to me.

"About your phone," I enquire as if I am running headfirst into uncharted territory.

August plops into the chair opposite her. "What about her phone?" he demands, voice low and dangerous.

Ellia's gaze darts between us, panic skittering under her skin.

I keep my eyes level, my tone clipped. "Something popped up last night," I say. "On your phone."

Time fractures as her mug pauses midair. Her shoulders coil like an animal sensing a storm. And I can see it in her face, she knows what I am asking about. But I press on.

I lean forward, voice a razor's edge. "It wasn't the photos. Or the messages."

Her head snaps up, eyes blazing. August's jaw clenches. "Then what the hell was it?"

She swallows. "You went through everything?" Setting her coffee on the table.

"I went far enough."

Ellia exhales slowly, forced control. "You don't know everything."

"No," I admit. "But I know enough to stay careful."

Silence crackles between us—thick, electric. I drop my voice lower.

"What you built," I say, "wasn't small."

My words land like blows.

"And for six months," I continue, as if marking dates on a calendar, "you were supposed to be recovering."

Ellia doesn't flinch. Her gaze drifts to a crack in the table, her escape.

"Okay, listen," she suddenly leaps up, one hand pressed to her forehead, the other to her hip, T-shirt riding up as if she forgot what she wore. "Music..."

August's confusion cuts through her panic. "What is happening right now?"

"How can I explain this correctly?" She murmurs.

She whirls to face us; one finger raised in a silent plea for patience. Before either of us can respond, she's gone, bare feet slapping against the floor as she races from the kitchen.

August and I stare at the doorway where her silhouette had been, as if her ghost might still linger there.

August exhales, tense. "This is going to be bad. I can feel it."

I rub my temples. "Give her a minute. This is the furthest she's come in a long time. I'm not trying to ruin it. But I also need to know what she has hidden."

When she returns, her phone quivers against her palm as she slides back into her seat. Her thumb swipes across the screen, her mouth a taut seam of tension.

"Everyone thinks music was all I ever wanted. It was, but I wasn't stupid about it. Before I could even get a driver's license, I created a safety net—something to catch me if the spotlight ever went dark."

She pauses on a document, then places her phone between us, screen up. "Legally, I'm Kingston Sage."

Her hands rise, palms outward, as if pushing back the air. Leaning back in her chair, "I had this business before anyone discovered me as a musician. I never expected to make it big."

She stands again, hunting for the right words. I don't interrupt, though I've already seen the documents, the contracts, the dozens of shadowy names.

August's voice slices through the tension. "Baby, if you don't want to tell us..."

He glares at me. I do not answer. My eyes lock on Ellia, wondering if she can survive the truth she's about to unleash. The white streak in her hair catches the light as she moves, a silver flash against the darkness.

She takes a deep breath, "You know how most musicians branch out into makeup, beauty lines, or perfumes."

Her voice is tight, controlled, but her fingers twist the hem of her t-shirt until I hear a thread snap.

"That was never me." Her laugh is brittle glass. "I became a private investor well before seventeen. They called me a shadow investor because I hunted in smaller businesses."

Ellia's bare feet wear a path in the marble as she paces, her gaze fixed on the shadows in the corner. Her voice has taken on an edge I've never heard before, something cold and precise. I lean back, one arm braced across my stomach, the other propping up my jaw as if holding my head in place.

"I went in the opposite direction." Her gaze drifts to the window, then pulls away. "When I was a child, my father taught me everything I know about that world." She pauses, then looks between us.

"Have you ever heard of Ryan Brooks?"

"No," August answers immediately, brow creasing. Direct. Certain.

"Yes," I say, already seeing the shape of it. "He's known for buying into struggling companies, restructuring them, rebranding, and turning them profitable without a full takeover."

She nods once. Her father's real name was Oliver Delvine. Retired now, but once a formidable attorney in Georgia, owner of a civil practice in Savannah. A man who understood leverage.

She resumes pacing. August looks lost, but not for long. He grew up in Australia; this name means nothing to him. Yet.

"By nineteen, I made my first million," she continues. "Not visibly. I guided investments through layered channels or, umm, rebrands, quiet acquisitions, companies already fractured by broken contracts."

Her breath leaves her slowly, like she's finally setting something down. "I kept my real name out of it. Well, because women aren't taken seriously in that world. Not at that level."

“I may be worth billions.” She can’t look at us as she says it, fingers knotting together, twisting until her knuckles pale. Her expression tightens as the admission itself hurts. “And I own hundreds of companies.”

August bolts upright so fast his chair crashes to the floor behind him. “You what?” The word comes out raw, disbelieving.

I don’t move. Don’t speak. I’m still processing the scale of it. I knew about the volume, the hundreds of deals, the constant motion. I just never imagined the reach. Not like this.

I lean forward, my voice dropping to a dangerous whisper. "Define 'companies,' Elli." My fingers drum once against the table, the sound sharp as a gunshot in the silence.

She watches August prowl the kitchen like a caged predator before answering.

"The usual suspects, like nightclubs, underground bars, tattoo parlors, maybe more." Her eyes flick to August, seeking alliance. “On every continent.”

“Jaxon, did you know?” August laughs a little while trying not to panic.

I shake my head, rising from my chair. “How come I did not know about this? I have worked for you for years. I went everywhere with you.”

She steps into my space, her hand finding my waist in a gesture that feels more steadying than intimate.

"I conducted those transactions in shadows," she says, voice barely above a whisper. "No one has ever seen Kingston Sage's face. And I want to keep it that way.”

She taps her sternum once with her finger. "No one could connect that name to me."

Her attention shifts to August, who's pacing like a caged animal. "You should sit down," she tells him, moving toward him with careful steps.

"Your injury..." But we both know his mind is racing too fast for caution now, processing revelations that change everything.

“Maybe,” I say softly, twisting a strand of hair around my fingers. “But I could have kept that part hidden.”

She lets go of my waist and turns toward August, who’s still visibly trying to catch up. “And I would never know what genuine love looked like.”

"So, you think we'd only want you for the money?" August snaps, raking a hand through his hair. "For the name? Is that what you're saying?"

Her face tightens, pain and regret crossing her features before she can hide them.

"No," she says flatly. "I think you'd never know which part of me you were choosing."

August opens his mouth, but closes it.

Her eyes dart between us, sharp as thrown daggers. "There's a difference between being careful and being dishonest," she says, voice steady despite everything. "Michael only discovered what I allowed him to see. Even then, I doubt he comprehends the true scale of what I control."

August paces, hand raking through his hair. "I'm just trying to understand how this was happening right in front of us."

Ellia doesn't move. Her voice comes out sharp. "Because you weren't looking for it."

"That's not fair."

She meets his eyes. " It's the truth. You thrive in the spotlight. I built my empire in shadows."

The words hang between them—not an accusation, just reality carved from years of practice.

"So, I couldn't possibly get it?" August's jaw tightens.

"No," she says with quiet finality. "Your face is on billboards across Sydney and beyond. People recognize you in airports. I created Kingston Sage precisely so no one would ever look at Ellia Delvine."

He lets out a harsh breath." I understand scrutiny better than most."

"Understanding scrutiny," she says, her voice finally cracking, "is not the same as knowing how to vanish because your survival depends on it."

I shift my weight, and suddenly her fury pivots.

"And you," she hisses, finger jabbing toward me. "Treating my life like some corporate problem to solve?"

"I needed clarity," I say.

"You needed control," she shoots back. "And you crossed a line."

August's hands fly upward. "Just tell me what's happening. I feel like I'm standing outside a locked room."

Ellia exhales, the sound like a blade unsheathing.

"Michael discovered my financial trail."

My body freezes. August's too, his shoulders suddenly rigid.

"The forty million, you know," she continues, each word precise as a surgeon's cut. "He didn't stumble onto it. He hunted it down and drained it. But really, I didn't know he'd drain the whole damn thing to be obvious, but that wasn't enough."

Her eyes slice toward me. "He became obsessed. More zeros. More accounts. He attacked my systems night after night, but my encryption held against whatever he thought he'd find."

The room fills with a silence so complete I can hear the hum of electricity in the walls.

"The affairs, the theft...I saw it all," she says, gaze locked on August, whose expression transforms into horrified comprehension. "That account? A trap. My smallest holdings. When I realized his appetite was bottomless, I left the door unlocked."

August's voice cracks. "Ellia, why did you stay with him?" His eyes search her, desperate for an answer I'm not sure she will give.

She traces the scar at the corner of her mouth, feeling the ridge of healed tissue. "I thought the bruises were love," she whispers, voice barely audible. "That the blood was devotion. But that morning I woke up in the hospital, when you were there instead of him, I finally understood what I'd been surviving wasn't love at all."

August steps closer, his shadow falling across her. "Did he..." He can't finish the question.

She turns away, tears burning. "Please don't make me say it out loud."

"So why did you buy the label?" I ask, changing this topic, she clearly isn't ready for.

Her eyes dart between us both, fingernails digging into her palm. "I was tired of being controlled. Every album, every appearance, every breath was dictated by suits who'd never written a single lyric."

Her voice drops. "So, I liquidated investments no one knew about and became the suit. Now Kingston Sage signs their paychecks, and they don't even know it's me."

CHAPTER 27

ELLIA

By the time my manager, publicist, and agent land in Australia, August is officially out for the season, and my anonymity is, too. Headlines plastered across the country.

Australia has decided there's a story to tell, and it has my face in it now. Headlines speculate. Screenshots circulate. Mystery woman in the private box. Hospital sighting confirms romance: Ellia Delvine linked to August Tate.

The cameras caught me mid-instinct—leaving the box, crossing the concourse, breaking cover without thinking, or maybe I was, but either way, once the image exists, it doesn't matter how carefully you lived before it; it's out there now.

I sit, quiet, overlooking the water, while my team works the angles, statements softened, timelines blurred, access restricted. They talk about containment. About optics. About whether we lean in or disappear.

Jaxon doesn't talk much at all these days. He watches. Tracks more exits. Adjusts his position without realizing he's doing it. His attention has narrowed—on my body in space, on proximity, on risk. The way I breathe. The way I move through a room. As if vigilance alone could fold me back into something untouchable. But I refuse to go back to that nothingness.

It doesn't. I feel the weight of more eyes now, even when no one's there. Feel the shift in the air when a secret stops being quiet.

And somewhere between the press outside and the men inside the room watching me like a perimeter, I understand this isn't about a rumor.

It's about exposure.

"We're not debating this." Jo's voice cuts clean through the air behind me.

She crosses the patio fast, heels striking concrete like punctuation. I don't turn, but I don't need to. I already know what's coming.

"You have two options," she continues, stopping so close I feel the air shift between us. "Either re-enter public life now, controlled, on our terms, with the unreleased album we've been sitting on."

I look up to find Jo's manicured nails drumming against her tablet, her blonde pixie cut catching the light.

On anyone else, that severe style might look harsh, but Jo wears it like armor, perfectly matched to her compact frame and the take-no-prisoners confidence that makes men twice her size step back when she enters a room.

There's something almost predatory in how she commands space despite being nearly a head shorter than me.

"Or you announce your retirement, break clean, definitive, then vanish again. No ambiguity. No half-measures."

Silence stretches. The ocean keeps moving. Indifferent.

"Because right now," Jo adds, voice flat, efficient, "you're exposed without a narrative. And that's the most dangerous position you can be in."

"I wouldn't recommend either option." Jaxon's voice cuts in from behind us, too calm, too certain.

Jo turns, irritation flashing. "Excuse me?"

"He's in Australia," Jaxon says, eyes never leaving mine. "Michael." The word hits harder than the ocean wind.

"He crossed into Sydney forty-eight hours ago," Jaxon continues.

Jo's posture shifts, professional mask cracking just enough.

"You're sure?"

"I'm tracking him," Jaxon replies. "And he's not here for the media."

"Then why is he here?" I ask.

Jaxon finally looks at me. There's something dangerous in his focus now; protective, intent, absolute.

"Because," he says quietly, "you stopped hiding."

"Ellia, if he finds you," Jo starts, then stops.

"I know," I cut in, the words breaking free before I can stop them. "I fucking know, Jo."

"The record label isn't going to like this, Ellia." Jo offers a sincere look.

I don't hesitate. "I own the label, Jo. So, fuck off with that label bullshit."

The silence that follows is sharp.

Jaxon steps closer, measured. “She’s right,” he says carefully. “There’s no board to appease anymore. No outside pressure.”

Jo blinks, once. Surprise flickers, then calculation snaps into place.

“Okay,” she says, recovering quickly. “Then that changes the approach.”

She straightens, already pivoting. “If you control the asset, we control the narrative. No denials. No speculation.” Her eyes lock on mine. “We move you forward, not back.”

“We announce a limited re-entry,” Jo continues. “One appearance. One statement. Enough to anchor the story before someone else does.” Jaxon’s gaze flicks to me, questioning but restrained.

“And if I say no?” I ask.

Jo doesn't flinch. "Then we fortify rather than spotlight," she says, her voice cooling to executive precision. "But either way, the clock's running."

She glances at her wrist, where platinum glints against tanned skin. "Your decision needs to be made yesterday."

“Jo, I need to discuss something private with Jaxon.”

After a minute of her waiting for an answer, she realizes she won’t be getting it anytime soon. Throws her hands in the air, turning on her heel.

“Jaxon, I need to ask you something.” I pull him into the Adirondack chair beside me. “I know it has been chaotic, and I have been wondering. You and August?”

The question hangs in the air until he understands what I am asking.

His shoulders tighten as he runs a hand down his face. Leans forward and lets out a laugh, as if it is a relief.

“Elli, we are two best friends who fell in love with the same woman,” he says as he twirls a strand of my hair.

He exhales, slow, measured. “This wasn’t something we planned. It was watching you, separately at first. Noticing the same things. The way you moved, the sparkle in your eyes when you lit up a room without trying, the way our bodies reacted when close to you.”

His thumb brushes my knuckle, absentminded, reverent. “We both realized we were orienting our lives around you. At some point, pretending it wasn’t happening felt dishonest. So, we stopped pretending.”

A faint smile ghosts across his mouth. “We talked it through. Carefully. Brutally honest.”

His eyes lift to mine. Steady. Certain.

"We didn't make rules about you," he says. "We made them about ourselves. About not competing. Not taking from each other. About protecting what mattered."

"What mattered?" I ask quietly.

"You," he answers without hesitation. "Not as something to claim, but as someone worth choosing every day."

His fingers are unmoving in my hair, as if holding the moment in place.

"We came to an understanding because loving you didn't divide us," he adds. "It clarified us."

The words settle warm and heavy in my chest, the kind that don't demand anything, only stay. And somehow, that makes them impossible to resist.

I gesture between us and toward the house where August rests. "So the arrangement is just... with me? You two aren't..." The question hangs incomplete in the air between us.

My fingers twist together in my lap. There's no guidebook for this conversation, no script for navigating whatever this is becoming.

Jaxon watches me struggle, his expression softening.

"August and I share many things," he says finally, voice low and deliberate. "But not each other. We're devoted to you—separately, differently, completely. What exists between us is friendship and respect, nothing more.

"His eyes hold mine, unflinching. "What exists between you and me belongs only to us."

I nod slowly, understanding clicking into place. These two men orbit around me without ever crossing paths themselves.

"I need to ask you something else," I say, drawing a deep breath to center myself. "But it depends on what August thinks, too." My gaze locks with his, unwavering.

"What if I return to public life after all? Before, I would have faced the cameras alone."

A small, nervous laugh escapes me. "But now..."

My attention drifts toward the ocean, words failing as the real question hangs unspoken between us.

His palm finds my knee, heavy with intent but careful not to possess. "Let them see August standing guard in the light," he says, voice like gravel. "I prefer to move unseen."

The silence between us thickens.

"Just remember," he continues, leaning close enough that his breath warms my skin, "shadows don't mean I'm far away. They mean I'm exactly where I need to be."

His thumb draws invisible spirals against my thigh, each rotation a wordless vow.

I smile, relief easing through me, not because he agreed, but because, of course, he did. He's always been strongest at my back, watching angles I don't have the space to see.

"How do you think August will take it?" I ask quietly. "Because if what you said is true, and Michael is already here, then this can't wait."

He doesn't answer, just a soft chuckle and a kiss on my forehead as he rises. Jaxon keeps his arm around my shoulders as we head back inside, steady, like he's bracing me against something unseen. No ownership. Coverage. The kind that anticipates impact before it happens.

The moment we step through the door, the noise hits. August's voice carries from the living room, half-amused, half sharp.

August leans against the doorframe, arms crossed, a smirk playing at his lips. "I love you all, truly," he says, "but this is my house. Not a command center."

Jo doesn't miss a beat. "Your house is currently a liability."

"A $2million dollar liability with an infinity pool," August fires back with a wink.

Faith and Abby flank Jo like sentries, but August saunters between them, untouchable. When he catches me watching, he throws me a look that says he's enjoying this little power play.

I catch Jaxon's eye; his face remains impassive, but I recognize the calculation behind his stillness.

The security sweep came back clean. No surveillance equipment detected. No suspicious vehicles idling at the curb. No strangers loitering beyond the perimeter. Jaxon wouldn't have risked bringing me here otherwise. His protective instincts run too deep for careless moves.

August's attention shifts to us, his expression softening at the edges. "There," he says, gesturing my way with an open palm. "Living proof everything's under control."

"Temporary," Jo counters, voice like ice. "Keep dismissing the threat and see how quickly that changes."

I move into the center of their battlefield. "Jo's assessment is correct," I say, keeping my voice steady despite my racing pulse. "Once this location becomes a target, they won't simply observe; they'll dismantle my life piece by piece until they finish what they started."

The room stills completely, tension crystallizing around us. "Jaxon and I have formulated a strategy."

Every eye burns into me, pupils dilated with something between fear and anticipation. I lock eyes with August, his jaw clenched tight enough to crack.

"August..." My throat constricts around his name.

Jaxon's hand finds the small of my back, steadying me as I step forward. My heartbeat pounds like a trapped thing beneath my ribs.

The words catch in my throat. How can I explain to the world that I stand beside August in the spotlight while carrying Jaxon's invisible marks beneath my clothes, too?

This secret feels dangerous, metallic on my tongue, uncharted territory with two men.

“August, Ellia has decided to step back into the public.”

Mouths wide open, staring directly at me. Time for them to start earning that paycheck again.

The room goes still. Every head turns. Every conversation dies mid-breath. August’s mouth falls open as he looks straight at me, disbelief flashing across his face.

“They’ve already seen you,” Jaxon continues. “At the game. At the hospital.” A beat. “So, the question is, do you want to go public too?”

Silence presses in.

August doesn’t answer right away. He just stares at me, unreadable, the seconds stretching long enough to make my chest tighten. Long enough for doubt to creep in. Long enough for me to wonder if I’ve miscalculated everything.

Then he exhales sharply and breaks into a crooked grin. "Well," he says, voice light but eyes locked on mine, "would've been rude to pretend I didn't notice you standing next to me on national television."

A few stunned laughs ripple through the room, more release than humor.

He steps closer, confidence settling back into place. "If you're stepping out," he adds, cocky as ever, "I'm not leaving you standing there alone."

He crosses the room in two strides and scoops me up without hesitation, arms locking around me like it's the most natural thing in the world.

The urgency in it steals my breath—protective, certain, unafraid of witnesses. Before I can speak, before anyone can, he kisses me.

Every set of eyes locks on us, stunned into silence by the clarity of it.

August rests his forehead against mine, voice low but steady. "Guess that answers that," I whisper.

That's when Abby claps her hands—sharp, loud, cutting through the moment like a starter pistol.

"Alright," she snaps, already moving. "That's the headline."

Phones come up. Laptops open. Strategy ignites.

"First story goes to The Sydney Morning Herald," she barks. "Clean, controlled. 'Season Ends, Relationship Begins.' No speculation. No commentary."

She turns to the room. "No one leaks photos. No one speaks off the record. We give them one image, one quote, and we starve the rest."

I'm still locked in August's embrace when Faith's eyes find mine, clinical, triumphant. "Congratulations," she says, voice crisp as autumn frost. "The narrative belongs to you now."

August's smile turns wolfish against my temple.

But beneath the tactical chatter, beneath the sudden flurry of movement, something fundamental shifts, like a key turning in a lock that can never be closed again.

The room blurs into peripheral motion while August and Jaxon become my entire world. They orbit me like twin gravitational forces.

"Time to fly, songbird," Jaxon murmurs, his mouth barely brushing mine, the ghost of a kiss that burns hotter than contact.

August's chest presses against my back, his breath on my neck radiating possession without a single touch.

Faith's throat-clearing cuts through the moment like glass. Her eyes narrow to blades as she extends her pen toward Jaxon with surgical precision.

"Are we including him in this equation?"

The word "NO" erupts from all three of our mouths at once, a perfect chord of denial.

Our eyes lock in that moment of shared refusal, and something electric passes between us, the silent understanding that whatever else happens, this triangle remains ours alone, invisible to everyone beyond its borders.

CHAPTER 28

ELLIA

By late afternoon, the living room barely resembles the place August calls home. It's been overtaken with papers, phones, and voices colliding over headlines and optics. Jo, Faith, and Abby move through the space, talking over one another, circling the same arguments from different angles.

"STOP!" I shout. The word cuts through everything.

The noise. I don't miss the fucking noise. It's not why I stayed hidden, but right now, it's reminding me why I did. I need quiet. I miss it.

"This is the headline," I say, voice tight, anger buzzing under my skin. "August Tate Confirms Relationship with Ellia Delvine. Following Season-Ending Injury."

I don't raise my voice. I don't have to. "That's it. Stop overthinking it."

I can feel myself vibrating with restrained fury. They're worried about phrasing. About tone. I'm worried about survival.

Michael is already in Australia. Jaxon has pulled his people in from everywhere. And August is at my six o'clock wherever I move, never leaving my blind spot uncovered. The headline is the least of our problems.

"Hey." August steps into my line of sight. "Eyes on me, love."

He closes the distance between us, cutting off everyone in the room.

Leaning down, his breath hot against the pulse hammering beneath my skin. His lips graze my ear, teeth catching the sensitive lobe.

"Come with me," he commands, voice like gravel.

His fingers lock around my wrist as he pulls me from the cacophony below.

August kicks the bedroom door shut behind us, before I can draw breath, he's pinned me against it, one hand tangled in my hair, yanking my head back to expose my throat. His mouth crashes against mine, devouring, punishing.

There's nothing gentle in the way he consumes me. When he finally releases me, my lungs burn, vision blurring at the edges as I gasp for air.

"I need to taste you," he growls, the words vibrating against my throat.

His other hand slams against the door beside my head, the impact reverberating through the wood. His body cages mine completely, the heat of him scorching through my clothes as his thigh forces my legs apart.

The door at my back is the only thing keeping me upright as my knees threaten to buckle.

His mouth is on my neck, open and determined. I feel each scrape of teeth as I arch, helpless to the pressure, my nerves sparking like live wires.

He bites me, hard enough to bruise, and the shock travels straight to my core.

"You're so fucking beautiful when you are angry," August rasps, voice shredding the composure I have left.

His hand leaves the door, trailing down until he's dragging my pants past my hips. His palm is rough, unyielding. Fingers grip the edge of my panties and tear.

"Look how wet you are."

A violent sound that makes me gasp, and he laughs a dark, triumphant noise. The cool air hits me, and I realize I'm already dripping. I'm embarrassed and proud at once. I want him to see.

"Look at you," he murmurs, mouth on my ear, his fingers sliding straight to where I'm soaked.

He plunges two fingers inside me without warning, curling them until I'm writhing against the hard line of his body. He holds my gaze, refuses to let me look away.

"You need it rough," he says, not for confirmation but as a statement of fact. "You need me to take."

His thumb circles relentlessly, never easing up, and my head knocks back against the door as pleasure claws through my stomach.

"Say it, Ellia," August demands. "Say you want me."

I hate that I can barely get the words out, my voice a strangled whimper. "I want you."

"Not enough." His fingers piston faster, the heel of his palm grinding until my vision shorts out. "Tell me, Ellia. Tell me who you belong to."

My ego is a crumbling wall, all the bricks knocked loose by the rhythm of his hand.

"You," I choke, "it's you, August. I belong to you."

"Good girl," he growls against my mouth, the words vibrating through my bones like a threat. Two words, and I am melting in his arms.

My fingers dig into his forearm as he drives deeper, harder, my other hand clawing at his shoulder for any anchor in this storm.

I'm hanging on the precipice, suspended between agony and ecstasy.

"There you are," he demands, his voice dropping to something primal. "Let me see you shatter."

His command slices through my last thread of control. His praise burns through me like wildfire, consuming everything in its path. My body convulses around his fingers as pleasure tears me apart from the inside out.

He doesn't give me space to fall apart. His hands are under me, lifting, and suddenly I'm weightless, spun toward the bed. My sweats tangle around my knees before they hit the carpet.

The thin shirt is yanked over my head, my arms caught and then freed as he tosses it aside. He strips away his own clothes with the urgency of a man starved for years instead of hours. Muscle and heat and sweat, so close I can't see straight.

He lays me on the edge of the bed, his hands spreading my thighs until I'm completely exposed. His eyes devour me, pupils blown wide with a hunger that makes my pulse spike.

"You have no idea what you do to me," he growls, voice thick with need. "That's it, love. Don't you dare hold back. I want to hear every sound I wring from that pretty throat."

The revelation staggers me, that praise alone could demolish my defenses so completely. I'm helpless in his grip as his mouth claims me without mercy, his tongue pressing flat against my swollen clit before he draws it between his lips.

The suction sends lightning through my veins. When his teeth graze that tender bundle of nerves, my spine bows off the mattress in a violent arch that feels like surrender.

"Fuck...August!" I scream, fingers tangling in his hair, not knowing if I'm trying to pull him closer or push him away from the overwhelming sensation.

He moans against my flesh, the vibration shooting straight through me as he slides two fingers inside, curling them against that spot that makes my vision blur. My inner walls clench around him immediately, orgasm building with brutal speed.

"Do not come until I tell you," He commands, lifting his face just enough that I can see my arousal glistening on his lips, his chin. "I own this pleasure. You come when I say."

A broken sound tears from my throat, somewhere between a prayer and a curse.

His eyes darken as he rises to his full height before me, muscles tensing beneath his shirt. "I'm no deity, love," he growls, voice dropping to that register that makes heat pool low in my belly, "but by the time I'm done with you tonight, you'll be calling my name like a prayer."

His fingers withdraw with excruciating deliberation, my slick arousal glistening on his skin as my inner walls clench desperately around nothing. The sudden emptiness leaves me hollow, aching, my body betraying me with a whimper that sounds like begging.

"Please," I beg, voice raw and desperate, "don't stop."

"I'm just getting started, baby girl," he promises, voice dropping to a dangerous growl that vibrates through my bones.

August's eyes flick over my shoulder, his lips curling into a predatory smirk. I whip my head around, heart seizing in my chest, but his hand clamps my jaw, forcing my gaze back to him.

"Eyes. On. Me. Love." Each word punctuated like a blade against my skin. The soft click of the door shutting behind us turns my blood to ice.

"August," I whisper, terror strangling my voice as I scramble backward on the bed, arms crossing desperately over my naked body, knees drawing up to shield myself. "Who the fuck is that?"

August's gaze turns midnight-dark as he reaches for my shirt. "Do you trust me?"

I nod, and the cotton surrenders with a violent tear.

Between his deft fingers, my shirt becomes nothing but ribbons, methodically shredded as his knuckles flex with each precise twist.

"That's my only decent..." The words die in my throat as he grabs my wrists, binding them together with practiced efficiency.

The fabric bites into my skin, not painfully but unmistakably secure.

"What the fuck, August?" My voice trembles between anger and arousal.

He rises in one predatory movement, his cock inches from my face, thick and rigid. A bead of pre-cum glistens at the tip, and my mouth waters involuntarily. The musky scent of his arousal fills my nostrils, making my head swim.

The silence stretches between us as my focus splits between the makeshift restraints binding my wrists and the heat radiating from his skin.

His hand finds my jaw, tilting my face upward until our eyes lock. The pad of his thumb traces my bottom lip, applying just enough pressure to part it further.

Once my wrists are bound together, he slides his hands up the back of my neck, grips my hair with bruising force until my scalp burns, and my throat is exposed. His teeth graze my bottom lip, not quite biting, a predator toying with prey.

The smile I feel against my skin isn't gentle; it's possession. My thighs clench involuntarily, the slick heat between them betraying how desperately I crave what's coming. My pulse hammers against the makeshift restraints, each heartbeat a surrender.

"Close your eyes," he commands, voice like gravel over steel.

The last strip of fabric dangles from his fingers, a promise, and a threat.

I obey without hesitation, falling into darkness as if into his arms. The blindfold slides across my face, cool cotton against feverish skin. He secures it with a sharp tug that makes me gasp, tight enough that shadows become my entire world. Blind, bound, and his.

His fingers dig into my hips, branding heat through thin fabric as he pulls me against him. "I saw how you looked at me," he whispers, his breath scorching my neck. "By morning, every inch of you will know exactly who you belong to."

My protest dissolves into a gasp as August lifts me with one powerful arm, my weight nothing against the coiled strength of his muscles. The room spins in a blur of shadows and light before my back meets cool sheets.

He spreads my legs with deliberate slowness, stretching me until the tendons in my inner thighs burn with sweet agony.

I feel the rough scratch of what must be my torn shirt as he binds each ankle to the opposite posts of the bed. The fabric bites into my skin as I test my bonds, finding myself utterly immobilized, splayed open like an offering.

His calloused fingertips trace scorching paths up the sensitive skin of my inner thighs, leaving goosebumps in their wake before he seizes the flesh with bruising force.

The pain blooms like dark flowers beneath my skin as he drags me toward the edge of the bed, positioning me precisely where he wants me.

"You should see how pretty you are," he growls, his voice a dangerous rumble that reverberates through the hollow of my pelvis.

His hot breath ghosts over my exposed sex, each exhalation sending electric currents straight to my core.

"Your pussy glistening pink and swollen, begging for my mouth. Tell me who you belong to."

"August, I..." My voice fractures as his tongue delivers a single devastating stroke against my throbbing clit.

"Oh god," I pant, each syllable torn from my lungs as pleasure crashes through me in merciless waves.

"I said," he murmurs against my flesh, the vibration of his words sending shudders through my bound body, "who do you belong to now?"

"You, only you," I surrender, the confession ripped from somewhere unnatural within me.

His forearms lock around my thighs like iron bands, thumbs spreading me wider, exposing every secret part of me to his hungry gaze. In the darkness behind the blindfold, I've never felt more seen.

My bound wrists are wrenched above my head, the fabric cutting into my flesh as August's tongue continues its relentless assault between my thighs.

Someone else is here. I can sense him before I could feel him. My pulse thunders in my ears as unseen hands secure my arms to what must be the headboard, stretching me taut as a bowstring.

"August..." My question dissolves into a gasp as familiar lips crash against mine, tasting of whiskey and danger.

The kiss is brutal, teeth scraping my bottom lip until I taste copper. When we break apart, hot breath scorches my ear, a low growl vibrating through my skull like a predator's warning.

My nipples harden painfully as another strip of fabric is forced between my teeth, the cotton soaking with my saliva as it's knotted tight behind my head.

I try to form Jaxon's name, but it emerges as a pathetic, muffled whimper. A gentle kiss, incongruously tender, presses against my forehead before the heat of this second body withdraws.

The mattress shifts, and I strain against my bonds, suddenly terrified of the pain and pleasure I am about to receive.

My pussy clenches violently around nothing as August's mouth abandons me.

"I said you are not to come until I tell you to," he snarls, his voice darker than I've ever heard it.

His fingers trace my entrance, collecting the evidence of my shameful arousal.

"I need to feel you," he growls, and then something blunt and impossibly thick presses against my swollen flesh, parting me with deliberate cruelty.

The head of his cock breaches me, stretching me beyond what I thought possible. He feeds himself into me with excruciating slowness, each inch a sweet violation that has me arching off the bed, desperate to take more.

A dark chuckle rumbles from his chest as his hands lock onto my bent legs with bruising force, holding me in place.

"You're so fucking greedy," he moans, driving the last inches home in one savage thrust that tears a scream from behind my gag.

"Oh my god," I sob as he fills me completely, my body trembling around the intrusion, cunt pulsing with a need so primal it terrifies me.

The world becomes sensation, a storm of pain and pleasure, and the obscene sounds of my body taking him. August fucks me hard, his rhythm relentless, each thrust slamming against the deepest part of me.

I'm drowning, gagged and blind and utterly at his mercy, nerves so raw it feels like every cell is an exposed wire. Every time he fills me, my hips jerk involuntarily, and when he pulls out, I whine and try to chase after him, desperate for the next assault.

Somewhere beyond my skin, I hear the scrape of a chair, the rustle of clothing. My heart rate doubles, a new level of panic flooding my bloodstream.

I can picture Jaxon on the other side of the blindfold, perched at the edge of the bed, watching as August ruins me, cataloguing every tremor and whimper, his lips pressed into a hard line as he tells himself this is all for my protection.

August's hand wraps around my throat, using it as leverage, his other hand squeezing my thigh so hard I knew I'd bear the marks.

His pace quickened, slamming into me over and over until the world shrank to a pinpoint of sensation—pain, pleasure, and the raw ache of being used like a fucktoy while Jaxon watched.

"That's it, Ellia," August growled, voice vibrating through my bones. "Take every inch. Let him see how perfect you are when you come undone for me."

The words hit me like a body blow. I writhed, the humiliation and heat and knowing I was on display twisting into something white-hot and desperate.

The mattress dipped at my side. A familiar hand caressed my hip, slow and appraising, thumb circling the bruising fingermarks August left behind.

The touch was clinical, then exploratory, and I moaned into the gag, hips jerking, more from the shame than the shock.

“Goddamn, Ellia,” Jaxon murmurs. “Perfect.”

His voice, the words, the way he said my name—it hit like a live wire, sparking something wicked in my gut.

Shame and want collided, knocking the wind from my lungs while August fucked me like the world was burning, and I was the only thing that could keep him alive. Each thrust was brutal, purposeful; he wanted to break me, rebuild me, make me his.

Jaxon's hands, God, I knew they were his; I could feel the difference, rested heavily on my thighs, pinning me wide so August could drive in even deeper.

I could hear Jaxon's breath, slow and controlled, but his fingers shook as he gripped my skin. He was watching every obscene detail, forced to bear witness to my destruction, and the knowledge of it made my cunt clamp down so hard I nearly blacked out.

"She loves an audience," August rasped, voice shredded with lust. "Don't you, Ellia?" He says with each thrust.

I'm fighting against the inevitable, my cunt spasming and gripping his thick shaft so hard I can feel every vein and ridge as my orgasm builds to unbearable pressure.

"Need to cum," I beg incoherently through the soaked fabric between my teeth, saliva streaming down my chin and neck.

His hand constricts around my throat, thumb digging into my carotid until my pulse throbs violently against his fingerprints. My vision swims as oxygen deprivation sends lightning through my brain, my pussy gushing around his cock, inner walls fluttering wildly.

His voice drops to a dangerous rasp against my ear. "Let go for me."

The command slices through my resistance like a blade. My consciousness fractures as pleasure detonates through my oxygen-starved body, each pulse more violent than the last.

The room disappears, and my existence narrows to the pressure of his hand on my throat and the relentless invasion between my thighs.

August's control finally shatters, his rhythm faltering as he drives himself to the hilt one last time, his entire body shuddering against mine.

We lay there for a moment, our bodies slick with sweat and release, lungs fighting for air. The absence of Jaxon's heat registers like a phantom limb. I hadn't felt the mattress shift, but the cool air rushing against my side tells me he's withdrawn.

August rises slightly, his abdomen flexing against mine as he reaches for my restraints. The shirt burns, tingles as blood rushes back into my wrists, his calloused fingertips trailing down my forearms, leaving goosebumps in their wake.

I shiver violently when he frees my ankles, the sensation almost unbearable against my hypersensitive skin.

Our breathing has synchronized into a shared rhythm, but beneath it, I catch the sound of water cascading into the tub, steam already seeping into the bedroom.

August works the sodden gag from between my teeth, my jaw aching as it's finally released. His mouth claims mine in a kiss that tastes of salt and me, his tongue exploring the tender places where my teeth had cut into my inner lip.

I wind my arms around his neck, anchoring myself to his solidity as reality slowly reassembles itself. Without breaking the kiss, he lifts me with frightening ease, one arm locked around my waist, the other cupping the curve of my ass, his fingers digging into the tender flesh.

The blindfold remains, plunging me into artificial night as he carries me across the threshold.

"Tell me if it's too hot," he murmurs, his voice a low rumble against my collarbone as he steps into the tub.

The blindfold comes off at last, discarded carelessly onto the tile floor. My eyes struggle to adjust to the soft bathroom light as we sit there for a moment, our bodies slick with sweat and release, lungs fighting for air.

That's when I see Jaxon kneeling beside the tub, sleeves rolled to his elbows, eyes dark and hungry as they roam over every mark August has left on my body. August lies with me, still pressed to his chest.

"You took him so well, songbird," Jaxon whispers, his voice rough with something between reverence and possession.

His hand cups my face, thumb brushing over my swollen bottom lip before he leans in. His kiss is different, deliberate, where August's was savage, exploring rather than conquering.

Behind me, August works a loofah over my shoulders, the soap's lavender scent cutting through the heavier musk of sex that clings to us. The gentle circles he traces down my spine make my muscles go liquid, and I collapse completely onto his chest.

For the first time in what feels like forever, I let go, let them tend to me, four hands moving in concert, washing away evidence of our sin.

When the water begins to cool, Jaxon lifts me from the tub, wrapping me in a towel that feels impossibly soft against my abused skin.

My head lolls against his chest, his heartbeat steady beneath my ear as exhaustion claims me. He lays me on the bed with surprising tenderness, tucking the surrounding sheets.

His face hovers above mine, unreadable yet somehow saying everything—desire, concern, and something darker I can't name. His lips brush my temple as he pulls the covers higher.

As consciousness slips away, I catch Jaxons's voice from the doorway, low and urgent: "Come with me. My guys are here, and they need to be briefed. She doesn't need to know right this minute."

The words float around me like smoke, but sleep pulls me under before I can grasp their meaning.

CHAPTER 29

JAXON

The command center erupts into chaos as August and I shoulder through the door. My handpicked team, the only men I trust after Michael and Robyn's betrayal, hover over monitors like hawks tracking prey. Their faces glow blue-white in the electronic light, eyes darting between camera feeds and scrolling data.

These are the men who would take a bullet for her without hesitation. They dissect every possible trail: flight manifests, charter records, credit card transactions.

But there is nothing. The bastard's a ghost, likely flying private or exploiting some security blind spot I haven't yet considered.

I clench my jaw, grudgingly impressed. His disappearing act shows meticulous planning; he knew exactly how to vanish.

"Jax, I've got something." Jenkins springs from his station, eyes wild with discovery. "Private charter. Surveillance caught him at Savannah/Hilton Head four days ago."

I snatch the printout, scanning it hungrily. "Where did he land?"

"Sydney," Jenkins says, then hesitates, throat working nervously.

"The name," I snarl, each word carved from ice. "What name did he use?"

Jenkins swallows hard. "Elliott Delane."

The paper warps between my fingers. Three syllables that mock her own—Ellia, Elliott, a perverse echo designed to taunt us. This sick homage explains our empty searches.

We'd been tracking variations of Michael Holt while he wrapped himself in a twisted tribute to the very woman he hunts.

"Find everything," I command, my voice razor-sharp. "Every footprint, every breath he's taken since landing."

"Yes, sir," they chorus, fingers already flying across keyboards.

We're running out of time. That plane needs to be airborne and halfway across the Pacific by now.

This property, the one I bought when August needed sanctuary from the sports media circus, has become our last line of defense.

I almost laugh at the thought: Australia's rugby God, the man whose face is plastered across billboards nationwide, now orbits silently around Ellia like she's his sun.

August's voice drops to a guttural whisper. "Was he alone?"

His jaw clenches so hard I can hear the grind of his teeth, his features twisting into something feral and unfamiliar. The same murderous rage burning through my veins is etched into every line of his face.

Jenkins doesn't meet my gaze. "Appears he traveled alone."

"Clear out her entire team. Now." My voice drops to a lethal whisper. "I don't care if they're here for media control. They can handle that from the fucking plane."

Michael is a predator stalking his prey, and I need her gone before he catches her scent.

I'm halfway to Ellia's room when August's hand clamps around my biceps, yanking me back.

"Think before you storm in there like a madman." His eyes darken. "We need a strategy that doesn't just buy us days, we need weeks, months."

He pauses, his eyes locking with mine in silent communication. "Jenkins mentioned Savannah, didn't he?"

It crashes over me in an instant. The coastal property where Ellia's father lives. Michael must have gone there before coming here.

"Goddammit." My palm rasps against my stubbled jaw as I drag my hand down my face.

We'd tracked him to Australia, but never imagined he'd ventured this near, like a predator circling, testing the perimeter.

While August couldn't escape the public eye, Ellia had vanished for more than a year, retreating whenever cameras appeared.

August's injury during the game, Ellia hovering by his hospital bed, and those damning headlines plastered everywhere.

She'd finally stepped back into the world because her isolation had become unbearable. I understood, even as I treasured those private months we shared. But watching her light dim day by day in that seclusion, it was destroying the very essence of her that I cherished.

I ease the door open with calculated precision, my heart hammering against my ribs. The empty bed's white sheets glow in the half-light, rumpled but abandoned.

The hinges protest with a betraying creak. August's breath warms the back of my neck as he presses close, scanning the shadows.

The verandah door stands slightly ajar, gauzy curtains dancing in the salt-tinged breeze. Through the gap, Ellia reclines in a weathered chair, her songbook balanced on one bare thigh, pen hovering above the page.

Moonlight catches in her hair, turning each strand to silky black ink, which has turned white into silver wire. Her face holds a tranquility I haven't witnessed in months; the tightness around her eyes has finally softened, her shoulders no longer braced for impact.

I retreat silently, turning to August. "You tell her," I mouth, the words barely disturbing the air between us. His eyebrow arches, but understanding darkens his eyes.

August has always approached her with a gentleness I can never seem to master. My bluntness has left too many invisible bruises between us, collision after collision of my unyielding force against her quiet strength. Still, between his gentle touch and my sharp edges, we've somehow carved out a space where she feels safe.

I stalk back to the command center, where the air crackles with tension. Jenkins hunches over three screens, his face bathed in their blue glow as his fingers fly across keyboards.

The rest of my team crowds around him like vultures, scheduling flights, barking orders into phones, and attempting to pacify Faith, a woman whose loyalty to Ellia manifests as pure, unfiltered rage.

"I am not fucking leaving when we just got the headline out," Faith hisses, her voice cutting through the chaos.

She whirls toward me, stilettos stabbing the floor as she closes the distance between us. Her manicured finger jabs into my chest, sharp as a blade.

"What the hell is happening, Jaxon?" Her breath, hot with anger, hits my face. "You knew he was here days ago."

"He's in Sydney." The words taste like ash in my mouth. "Using the alias Elliot Delane."

I watch the transformation in her eyes, fury melting into horrified understanding. Blood drains from her face, leaving her complexion ashen under the harsh fluorescent lights.

"Faith," I say, my voice dropping to a dangerous whisper, "get on the jet Jenkins is arranging. You can't protect her if he finds you both. You know what he's capable of."

She turns without a word, her shoulders curving inward like broken wings. The defeat in her posture is a lie. Her voice echoes off the walls as she barks orders to her team scattered throughout the house. If she only knew how Ellia has hardened in these past weeks, steel forging beneath that delicate skin.

August and Ellia materialize in the doorway like ghosts. His mouth hovers at her ear, lips barely moving as he whispers secrets meant only for her.

She grips his forearms, fingers pressing white half-moons into his skin as if he's the only thing tethering her to earth. When her eyes find mine, that small, dangerous smile she manages cuts across her face, the kind that makes my blood run cold and hot simultaneously.

"She's packing," August says, voice rough as gravel. A muscle in his jaw twitches. "She'll say goodbye to the team."

His eyes betray his uncertainty, pupils blown wide with fear he won't acknowledge.

"I have to stay behind." Guilt carves deep lines around his mouth. "Season's shot to hell, but obligations remain. When it's safe, when I can make the appearances without raising suspicion, I'll come for her."

The air between us crackles with the same electric tension that's always existed, this unspoken competition neither of us acknowledges. His golden-boy charm and reckless luck balanced against my calculated precision.

I've pulled him from the wreckage of his decisions more times than I can count. He is the brother fate denied me, and I am the shadow that ensures his survival.

When Ellia became my singular focus, something shifted in our brotherhood, a tectonic plate moving beneath the foundation. He recognized it before I did.

I've protected billionaires, politicians, royalty, but none of them matter like she does. For her, I would paint these walls crimson without hesitation or regret.

"August," I say, gripping his shoulders, feeling the coiled tension beneath my palms. "I got her. She will be safe."

The promise tastes like iron on my tongue. His eyes, haunted, desperate, tell me he finally understands the exquisite torture I've endured since the moment she walked into my life.

The ride to the private terminal stretched like a garrote wire between us. Ellia stared through the rain-slicked window, her reflection a phantom against the night. I gripped the wheel until my knuckles ached, stealing glances at her between scanning the road.

Her mind had become territory I couldn't navigate, a minefield where my words would only trigger explosions. I'd learned to respect these silences, these moments when she retreated to calculate her next move. But I still tensed, preparing for whatever conclusion would eventually emerge from her deliberations.

She could read anyone like an open book, except him. She'd always been blind where he was concerned. I understood the cruel joke of it all too well.

I'd seen that same blindness destroy others while remaining immune myself, until Ellia crashed into my life.

Now my heartbeat synchronized with hers, a shadow willing to wait eternally at the edges of her world. In the private cathedral of my thoughts, I'd claimed her long ago. I'd suffered through their relationship in professional silence when she first hired me, before I recognized this ache that defied all reason.

I climb the jet stairs behind her, the damp night air heavy against our skin.

"Idaho in eighteen hours, according to the flight plan," I say, noting how her shoulders immediately tense beneath the thin fabric of her sweater.

"Heathrow," she commands without turning, her voice cutting through the cabin's hushed atmosphere.

After hours of suffocating silence, the word falls like a blade. I close the distance between us, my shadow swallowing hers as I study the dangerous glint in her eyes.

"What's in London?" I ask, measuring each syllable.

I recognize this version of her, the one who's retreating into herself, building walls I'll have to tear down brick by brick.

"Something I need." Her jaw tightens, daring me to challenge her.

The pilots exchange glances before nodding in unison. "Yes, ma'am."

They disappear into the cockpit, leaving us alone in the tension-thick air.

Moments later, the flight attendant approaches with practiced caution, offering Ellia water as she curls into the leather seat she's claimed as her territory, positioned with perfect sightlines to every entrance and exit.

Hours stretch between us like a chasm. Ellia's thumb slides over her phone screen in that familiar, agitated rhythm, a tell she doesn't realize she has.

Something dark churns behind her eyes, but questioning her now would be like placing my throat against a blade.

I track her movements peripherally while surveillance footage plays on my laptop.

Jenkins has sent a video of Michael prowling the stadium perimeter like a predator testing. The complex stands empty and secured, but his presence there sends ice through my veins.

Thank fuck August's team practices miles away.

August's messages flood my phone, desperate for intelligence I don't have. Each vibration against my thigh is another promise I can't keep, another reassurance I can't offer.

Media coverage remains contained, the team's PR machine working overtime, but fan videos have surfaced: Ellia fleeing the box, panic visible even in grainy footage.

Worse, the nurse she had transferred sold her story. When Faith and Jo discovered it, they ensured her medical career ended as abruptly as her exile.

I watch as exhaustion shadows Ellia's eyes like bruises, but the feral vigilance behind them tells me sleep won't claim her tonight.

Her phone lies abandoned as she stares into the absolute void beyond the window, 30 thousand feet of nothing between us and oblivion. Her reflection floats there like a ghost trapped between worlds.

The team's hunt for Michael has yielded nothing but dead ends and phantom traces. No, Elliot Delane registered anywhere. No sign of Robyn slithering alongside him.

Jenkins has run every permutation of their names through the system until the database bled information.

"I am going to try and sleep," Ellia announces, her voice raw as she unfolds herself from the seat.

When she stretches, her hoodie rides up, revealing the constellation of scars mapping her stomach. My throat tightens at the sight of that sacred battlefield. Those marks I've claimed with my mouth, tasted the raised edges where her skin fought to knit itself back together.

The scars August and I have both worshipped like pilgrims at an altar, each of us silently vowing to shoulder the pain that created them.

I track her movements as she drifts toward the bedroom at the rear of the plane.

"Are you coming?"

The question hangs between us, her voice barely audible over the engine's hum. My laptop slides forgotten onto the seat as I rise.

Some primal part of me refuses to let her face the darkness alone, not when her body craves the weight of mine to anchor her to reality.

I follow so closely that my breath stirs the fine hairs at her nape as the bedroom door clicks shut behind us, sealing us in shared isolation.

Exhaustion clouds her eyes, but beneath it churns a restless current of thoughts I can almost taste.

She strips methodically—hoodie first, careful to keep her scars covered beneath cotton.

When her jeans slide down to reveal black lace clinging to her hips, my body responds with painful immediacy.

I roll my neck, muscles coiling with barely contained restraint.

As I pull my shirt over my head, her gaze locks onto me with predatory focus. Her eyes trace a deliberate path from the ink sprawling across my throat, down my chest, finally settling on my scarred knuckles, hands that have both protected and destroyed.

She slides between the sheets, her hair spilling across the pillow like fresh ink on alabaster. My chest constricts at the sight; this woman who carries her scars like armor, unaware of how they've carved her into something sublime.

I would tear open my flesh, break every bone in my body, just to absorb a fraction of her pain. I would become a vessel for her suffering and call it salvation.

She lies on her side, facing me, a wounded animal calculating risk. Her hands form a barrier against her sternum, protecting what's left of her heart.

"Come here," I command, voice rough with need, arms open like a confession.

She fits against me with violent precision. My lips brush her temple where her pulse hammers beneath paper-thin skin. Her scent, lavender and vanilla with an undercurrent of fear, floods my system like a drug.

When her thigh slides over my hip, the heat of her core brands my skin through the thin cotton separating us, my cock strains painfully against my boxers as primal instinct wars with restraint.

"You're safe," I whisper against her hair, tasting the lie on my tongue.

Nothing about what I feel for her, this consuming, destructive hunger, could ever be called safe.

CHAPTER 30

ELLIA

Blood-red sunlight bleeds through the sheer curtains. I can't remember when I blacked out, my wrists still raw from yesterday's restraints, my throat still aching from the gag. Yet, I feel rested.

Jaxon's arm is a vise across my chest, possessive even in sleep.

I sought his scorching presence last night like an addict seeking relief, partly from the hunters closing in, but mostly because only his skin against mine silences the screaming in my head.

I've wasted too many nights staring at ceilings before accepting this truth. Now, I surrender to it willingly.

His heartbeat thunders against my chest, his breath hot on my neck. Normally, he's awake before dawn, vigilant, but when our bodies are locked together like this, he stays until both August, and I stir. I never imagined surrendering to two men, becoming theirs completely, but now I'd kill anyone who tried to take them from me.

I drag my nails down his arm, feeling his skin prickle beneath my touch.

"Mmm, morning, songbird," he growls, teeth grazing my scalp as he inhales me like prey.

"Didn't mean to wake you," I whisper, my lips brushing the scar tissue mapping his chest.

His body is a weapon, honed not in gyms like August's, but in darker, bloodier arenas I dare not name.

His hands roam my body with desperate possession, memorizing every curve as if he fears this might be our last touch.

Sydney had been a sanctuary, but I left that haven behind for survival.

The monster who stripped me of everything lurks closer than we'd feared. Without August beside me, I'm fractured, the man who witnessed my naked soul now absent, leaving half my heart in ruins.

Those first Australian nights were brutal for both men. They watched me constantly, terrified I'd vanish into darkness, haunted by how I thrashed and screamed whenever I woke alone.

My writing had returned like a fragile bird, only to be crushed when Jaxon's men brought their discovery. I'd begged to stay, insisted I was protected there, swore I couldn't bear to flee again.

They'd pulled me back from that precipice of despair, from that yawning abyss that had nearly consumed me.

"About yesterday," I whisper, voice tightening.

His jaw clenches; he despises it when I retreat into myself, but self-preservation is etched into my bones. "I didn't mean to shut you out, I..."

The confession strangles in my throat.

"Songbird, " he begins, but I press my finger against his lips.

"I didn't want to leave," I breathe. "It actually felt like home."

The admission burns, a cruel reminder that once again, something I dared call mine was violently torn away. And now it's gone, again. They always take what's mine.

His breath hitches, a predator scenting danger. The space between us crackles with tension.

"I'm done running," I whisper, my voice raw with defiance. "Michael will find me, eventually. We both know it."

Jaxon's eyes darken, pupils dilating until only a thin ring of silver remains. "You think I can't protect what's mine?"

His fingers trace my collarbone, deceptively gentle.

"I'd rather keep you chained to my bed than lose you. At least then I'd know exactly where you are."

His lips curve into a smile that doesn't reach his eyes, the promise in his words sending a forbidden thrill down my spine.

I shove against his chest, needing to see his face fully. His grip tightens instantly, fingers digging into my flesh hard enough to bruise.

"I came back to stop running," I hiss, each word dripping venom. "Yet here we are."

In one fluid motion, he flips me beneath him, pinning my wrists above my head. His weight presses me into the mattress, a reminder of his dominance.

"Listen carefully, songbird," he murmurs, his free hand cupping my jaw with dangerous tenderness. "I won't let your stubbornness get you killed. I've hired ex-military, ex-SWAT—men who kill without blinking, to keep you breathing on whatever fucking continent we end up on."

I arch my back violently, muscles straining as I try to throw him off, in a pathetic attempt.

"It's not your fucking decision," I snarl, the taste of rage building on my tongue. "I built an empire from nothing but blood and tears while everyone else watched. Me. Not your men, not your precious security team, and sure as hell not Michael."

His weight crushes me deeper into the mattress, unmovable as stone.

The grip on my wrists tightens until I feel bones grinding together, but I refuse to whimper. His teeth scrape my jaw, breaking skin, the sting making my pulse hammer. His eyes gleam with dark satisfaction.

"Do I need to show you again who you obey?" he growls, one hand abandoning my wrist to tear at my collar, exposing my throat to the cold air.

"I know exactly who," I whisper, my lips a breath away from his, close enough to taste his hunger.

"But please..." I bite his bottom lip hard enough to draw blood, "remind me."

He slammed my arms above my head harder, bracing them with one hand while the other fisted in my hair, wrenching my face upward.

Our breaths collided, tangled, desperate, and rabid. His mouth crashed into mine, blood-salt and need, and I clawed at him, legs wrapping his hips, dragging him into the cage of my body.

The mattress groaned with our violence. The bruises from yesterday weren't even purple yet, but my body throbbed for more, for the threat and the safety wound together so tightly I couldn't tell which was which anymore.

He kissed me until my jaw ached, until the room spun with oxygen starvation and his taste. Then he broke away, panting, and I saw the wolf in him, pupils blown, lips red, a vein pulsing in his neck. He spat a smear of my blood onto the pillow and grinned, cruel and proud.

"You want a reminder?" he said, his cock pressing against my pussy, only stopping the feel of him is this thin piece of fabric.

He bit down hard on my throat, the sharp pain igniting me. I fought against his grip, but Jaxon wouldn't budge.

With one violent motion, he tore my shirt open, exposing my skin to the cold. This wasn't seduction, it was possession, pure and absolute.

His hand pressed against my chest, the weight of it holding me in place as my protests died in my throat. "I won't stand by while you put yourself at risk. Not again."

He knifed my legs apart with his knee and pressed himself against my rawest places, the cotton of his boxers a torment. I tried to buck him off with fury, but he just laughed, low and mean, and shook his head, strands of his hair falling across his brow.

"Try again, Ellia. Scream. No one will come for you, not now." With one hand, he forced my jaw open, thumb bruising the hinge, "Open your mouth, Ellia."

I obeyed. He spat in my mouth—hot, metallic with our mingled blood. I swallowed, eyes locked to his in challenge.

He tore his boxers away and drove into me with such force that stars exploded behind my eyes. His palm covered my mouth; I bit down hard, tasting salt and iron.

Each thrust slammed my spine against the mattress, the headboard crashing against the wall in rhythm with our violence. I clawed welts down his back while tears leaked from my eyes, but he never slowed.

My old knife scars ground into the damp sheets. I arched up, craving his marks over the old ones, someone claiming this body not with hatred but with a possession that bordered on worship.

"You are mine," he growled against my throat, teeth grazing my thundering pulse. "This body is mine." His voice dropped lower, vibrating through my sternum.

"How many times must I carve my name into your soul before you understand?"

His hips snapped forward with punishing precision, hitting that spot deep inside that made my vision blur. I felt myself growing slicker, arousal pooling beneath me, marking the sheets as thoroughly as he was marking me.

His hands map my body with savage possession, fingertips digging into flesh until capillaries burst beneath the surface. The pain blooms like black roses under my skin, pain I crave with an animal hunger. My nerve endings have been dying of thirst for him, parched and desperate.

"Please, Jaxon," I gasp, voice fracturing into something barely human.

His eyes lock onto mine, pupils blown so wide they've devoured the emerald, feral and unblinking. A predator's stare.

"I need to taste you," I whimper.

He wrenches my head back by my hair, teeth scraping the shell of my ear as he growls, "You want to taste me?"

His cock drives deeper, the thick ridge of his head battering that swollen spot inside me until tears leak from the corners of my eyes like a discarded marionette.

My inner walls convulse around him, gripping, pulling, begging.

"That's it, songbird. Flood my cock with that sweet cunt. Don't you dare hold back," he commands, each word punctuated with a brutal thrust.

Like a lit fuse reaching dynamite, my orgasm detonates without warning, white hot and violent. My consciousness fragments, vision tunneling as pleasure tears through me with claws and teeth.

Words fracture and die in my throat, my tongue a useless slab of meat. The world narrows to nerve endings and heartbeats.

His mouth burns against my ear, his voice cutting through my surrender like a blade heated white-hot. "Look at what you do to me, songbird. The way you take me, like you were made for this, for me. Like your body remembers mine from some other life."

Jaxon slows his pace as aftershocks ripple through my core, but his grip remains merciless.

"You'll taste me when I decide you've earned it."

A sound escapes me—half sob, half plea. Every hollow space in my body aches to be filled by him. My mouth, my cunt, even the forbidden tightness of my ass. He is heroin in my veins, cocaine on my tongue, a chemical reaction I can neither control nor survive without.

Jaxon pulls out abruptly, leaving my cunt gaping and desperate, clenching around nothing but the cold air between us.

A broken sound tears from my throat; half sob, half plea. His lips curve into a cruel smile as he watches my emptiness, my need.

In one savage motion, he yanks me up by my hair, my legs instinctively wrapping around his sweat-slicked waist, his cock sliding against my dripping pussy.

"You're going to ride me now," he growls against my mouth, teeth scraping my bottom lip. "I want to watch those pretty little hips bounce while you fuck yourself on my cock until you're screaming, until you're coming so hard the pilot thinks I'm torturing you."

I clawed my way upright, the muscles of my thighs trembling with the aftershocks of orgasm and the anticipation of the next.

Jaxon barely gave me a heartbeat to catch my breath before his hand fisted in my hair, the other bruising my hip, anchoring me atop him. His cock was slick with my arousal, leaking at the tip, and he pressed it against me with a mocking little slap before guiding it to my ruined center.

"You want to be in control, Ellia? Go on," he said, voice torn between command and challenge. "Let's see you take it. Show me you can."

The threat of it was almost enough to make me collapse. My arms shook as I braced myself on his tattooed chest and eased down, the stretch and burn of his size in this position, a sweet agony.

He was so big it felt like I'd never get all of him inside me, but I craved the pain. He grabs my face, forcing my gaze to his.

His words are a chain around my throat; I can't look away. "Let me see you come. Look at me while I fill this cunt."

I fucked myself down on his thick cock, feeling him stretch me open, every vein and ridge dragging against my walls. My clit throbbed against his pelvis as I ground down harder, desperate for that friction.

"You're so fucking wet," he growled, fingers digging into my ass, spreading me wider. " I can feel you dripping down my balls."

His thumb found my clit, rubbing merciless circles as I bounced on his shaft. My pussy clenched around him, walls fluttering as I edged closer.

"That's it. Take every inch, Ellia. I want to feel this tight pussy milk my cock," he rasped, voice raw with need.

His hands mapped my ribs, my waist, then slipped between my legs to rub raw circles over my clit, a cruel counterpoint to the deep grind of his cock.

Sparks lit my vision as my nerves melted into liquid. I didn't hold back the noise, I screamed, cracked and guttural, throat burning from the force of it.

"Now tell me why we are headed to London, Ellia." He grunts with his hands on my hips, keeping pace, my head thrown back, eyes shut, my orgasm on the brink of explosion.

I can't think, I can't tell him why. I continue to fuck myself on his cock.

His hands biting into my skin, he stills me with such force that my orgasm threatens to disappear.

"Tell me, or I won't let you cum." Those words hit, my moans turn to whimpers.

Jaxon's voice cuts through my haze of pleasure like a serrated blade. "Now tell me why we're headed to London, Ellia."

His fingers dig into my hip bones, leaving crescent-moon indentations that will purple by morning. My clit throbs against the base of his cock, my inner walls fluttering around his thickness as my orgasm builds, threatening to shatter me.

"I...I can't..." My words dissolve into a broken moan as he hits that spot deep inside that makes my vision blur.

His hand strikes upward, wrapping around my throat. With brutal precision, he stills my movements completely, his cock pulsing inside me.

"Tell me, or I won't let you cum."

His thumb presses against my carotid, just enough to make stars dance at the edges of my vision.

"Your pretty cunt is dripping down my balls, songbird. Don't make me leave you empty."

"I have a place there," I gasp, meeting his predatory stare.

A single nod, and his grip on my throat loosens just enough for me to breathe properly.

"I want to hear everything while you fuck yourself on my cock." His voice is gravel and smoke, each word a command that liquefies my spine, as he lies back watching me ride his cock.

His words ignite something primal in me. My cunt clenches, fresh arousal coating his length as I begin to move.

"No one knows about it," I gasp, circling my hips with increasing desperation.

The pressure builds low in my belly, coiling tighter with each descent.

"It's where I keep," My voice fractures as he hits that spot deep inside that turns my thoughts to static.

"What is it, songbird?" His eyes are midnight pools, reflecting nothing but hunger.

I slam down harder, impaling myself on his thickness, chasing the oblivion only he can give me.

"My digital files," I manage between ragged breaths, my clit throbbing against him with each roll of my hips. The taste of release floods my mouth—metallic, sweet. "Information you might want."

Something dangerous flashes in his eyes. In one fluid motion, he surges upward, one arm snaking around my waist while the other hand tangles in my hair.

My clit grinds against the hard plane of his abdomen as he captures my nipple between his teeth, biting down with exquisite cruelty. My head snaps back, spine arching to breaking point, his grip on me the only anchor to consciousness.

My inner walls convulse violently around him as his cock swells impossibly larger. His groans vibrate against my breast, the sound of a predator claiming its prey.

"I need you," I whisper against the shell of his ear, my confession raw and unguarded. "I've always needed you."

He stills for a heartbeat, eyes locking with mine, something unspoken passing between us, before we shatter together. My release tears through me like wildfire as his hot seed floods my depths.

I ride him through the aftershocks until I collapse against his chest, our mingled sweat and fluids binding us like a blood oath.

We remain fused, his cock still pulsing inside me as our heartbeats gradually slow. His arms form an iron cage around my body, possessive even in the aftermath. His breath scorches my neck in ragged bursts.

When I finally pull back to meet his gaze, something unfamiliar has replaced the earlier fury, a dangerous softness I've never witnessed before.

I've seen hunger in those eyes, obsession, the cold calculation of ownership, but this unguarded vulnerability terrifies me more than his rage ever could.

For one unnerving moment, he looks at me the way August does, like I'm something precious rather than something to be consumed.

"Come on, songbird," he murmurs, voice still rough from exertion. "Let's get you cleaned up before we land."

CHAPTER 31

ELLIA

When we arrived in London, I leaned forward until my lips nearly grazed the back of his neck, close enough to inhale the spiced amber of his cologne mingling with the natural salt of his skin.

I whisper an address that makes his broad shoulders stiffen beneath the midnight fabric of his tailored suit, the muscles coiling like a predator sensing danger.

"This isn't in London, Ellia," he says, voice rough with suspicion, each syllable scraping against his throat like gravel.

I smile against the electric tension crackling between us, tasting its metallic edge on my tongue. Some things can't be explained with words. They must be felt, tasted, experienced in the marrow of your bones.

I lean closer, my lips barely grazing his ear: "Manchester holds answers I can't simply tell you," I murmur. "And it's Elli to you, remember? Ellia only comes out when I've gotten under your skin."

His eyes, dark as the deep forest, lock onto mine, pupils dilating until only a thin ring of color remains. The air between us thickens as he leads me to the waiting SUV, his hand hovering at the small of my back, not quite touching but close enough that I can feel the heat radiating through my thick hoodie.

Jaxon extends his hands, palms up; scarred, calloused hands that have both protected and punished. When I place mine in his, he presses his lips to my knuckles, the warmth of his mouth lingering on my skin like a brand.

His gaze never wavers, dissecting every micro-expression that crosses my face, searching for the truth I've buried beneath layers of careful deception.

The SUV glides from London's congestion into the open motorway as I pull out my phone, my thumb hovering over the screen. Headlines flash across my notifications with my name, my face, speculation about my whereabouts. I'd foolishly believed my extended absence would dampen media interest. Clearly not.

Faith and Jo's leak has been circulating for days now. According to various "reliable sources," I've been spotted in Tokyo, New York, even Sydney, anywhere but where I actually am. Perhaps this wild goose chase works in my favor; no one's looking toward Manchester.

I composed a brief text to August: "Landed safely. Call when you can."

My thumb lingers over the send button before pressing it. His absence leaves an uncomfortable void. I've grown accustomed to navigating the world with both men flanking me.

Exhaling deeply, I release the breath I've been holding since our plane touched down.

In the rearview mirror, Jaxon's dark eyes catch mine, his attention dividing between the road ahead and the woman behind him who carries too many secrets.

The universe has a peculiar sense of humor, entangling my heart between two men while I navigate this labyrinth of secrets.

I've revealed fragments about my shadow investor to both August and Jaxon, each receiving the information like opposite sides of the same coin.

When I speak, Jaxon's obsidian gaze dissects every syllable, his fingers drumming against whatever surface is nearest, a telltale rhythm that betrays the machinery of his mind working overtime.

August, however, receives my revelations with those chestnut eyes alight, lips curved into an encouraging smile whenever Kingston's name enters the conversation.

His fascination with my clandestine empire both flatters and unnerves me. His questions probe deeper than I'm willing to allow, not because my secret has surfaced, but because trust remains a luxury I've forgotten how to afford.

Yet somehow, they've both accepted my reluctance to unveil the complete tapestry of my deceptions.

As we are nearing the address I had given Jaxon, his eyes are barely on the road at this point. I can feel his gaze burning holes into my brain. I have been biting my nails since Manchester came into view.

This is another thing on my list of secrets. And I can only hope he will be more understanding when he sees it for himself.

My apartment sprawls above Obsidian, the exclusive bar I own in downtown Manchester's most coveted district.

The kind where black-suited bouncers recognize members by face from their exclusive bracelets, where crystal chandeliers cast blood-red shadows across black marble floors, and where those lucky enough to enter during public nights must adhere to a dress code that separates the worthy from the wanting.

As Jaxon follows the GPS to Obsidian, I pull out my phone, the blue light illuminating my face in the darkened car. My finger taps through security feeds, the velvet rope line outside, the smoke-filled VIP section, the private rooms where secrets dissolve on tongues like expensive pills.

No one knows Ellia Delvine owns the bar; they whisper the name Kingston Sage with reverence, as if summoning a ghost. I've crafted this lie so meticulously that sometimes I forget which version of myself is real.

My phone illuminates with Obsidian's website. It's public night. The thought sends electricity through my veins. Outside, they'll gather like supplicants before a temple, cologne and perfume hanging thick in the night air.

I've crafted our requirements with surgical precision: women draped in tailored suits that conceal and suggest in equal measure, dark fabrics that absorb light rather than reflect it. Or evening gowns that whisper rather than shout.

The men understand their roles instinctively, as background elements in a carefully composed scene. Those who mistake the club for a display of flesh find themselves dissolving back into Manchester's mist, while inside, some A-lister caresses ivory keys, oblivious that I orchestrate every moment from the shadows, pulling strings they'll never see.

I lean forward, my lips brushing the shell of his ear. "There's a garage entrance around back," I whisper, letting my hand slide from his shoulder to rest against the taut muscle of his biceps.

His body goes rigid beneath my touch, jaw clenching so hard I can almost hear his teeth grinding. The air between us thickens with his disapproval. He despises secrets, yet my entire empire is built on them, each hidden truth another brick in the fortress that keeps me wealthy, powerful, and most importantly, alive.

When the SUV finally comes to rest in the shadowed garage, he kills the engine with a violent push of the button. The sudden silence crushes against my eardrums.

He turns to face me, the leather seat creaking beneath his weight, his eyes burning into mine with such ferocity I can almost feel my skin blister.

His jaw pulses, veins threading his neck as he swallows questions that would shatter lesser men. I lean across the console until our breaths mingle, hot and dangerous.

"When the time is right, you'll know everything," I whisper, my lips nearly grazing his. "Until then..."

I slide my hand up his thigh, feeling the muscle tense like steel beneath my touch. "Will you follow me into the dark, Jaxon? Just this once?"

His lips crashed against mine with enough force to answer any question. When he finally pulled away, I found myself leaning forward, chasing the heat of his mouth, reluctant to break the connection between us.

As Jaxon unloads our luggage, the fluorescent lights flicker across the polished concrete of my hidden garage. My blacked-out Mercedes AMG GT gleams like a predator waiting in the shadows, its matte obsidian exterior absorbing light, red caliper brakes peeking through like fresh wounds.

The custom dashboard still smells of hand-stitched leather and money. It took twelve months of impatient waiting before I could claim it as mine, the first trophy I awarded myself when Kingston Sage's empire began drawing blood.

My father's eyes widened when he first saw it, his fingers trailing possessively over the hood. I'd had one built for him, too.

The Ninja 650 crouches on the other side of the Mercedes, its aggressive lines cutting through space like a threat.

Michael's hands had once covered mine on those handlebars, his chest pressed against my back as he taught me to lean into curves until my knee nearly scraped asphalt.

Now every property I own houses some mechanical beast— Ninja or Ducati—waiting for the thunderous release of my adrenaline on empty highways.

I haven't touched a bike since that night on the mountain when my tires lost purchase, and the world spun into blackness. "Accident" isn't the right word when someone has deliberately severed your brake lines. The memory of metal grinding against the guardrail still vibrates in my bones.

Jaxon's throat clears, the sound echoing against concrete walls.

"The elevator is over here," I say, pointing past his broad shoulders to what appears to be a solid wall.

He turns, brow furrowed. "Ellia, that doesn't look..."

His words die as I wave my palm over an invisible sensor. The cinderblock facade shudders, then parts silently to reveal a brushed steel elevator chamber, its interior illuminated by crimson light that paints our faces in blood.

"Jaxon," I breathe, watching his pupils dilate with surprise.

He shakes his head slowly, a man watching his reality crumble.

I hold the elevator door, feeling my pulse hammer against my ribs as he hesitates on the threshold.

"Freight access only," I explain, voice barely above a whisper. "Direct lines to the garage, the club's private entrance, and..." my fingertips hover over unmarked buttons gleaming like black teeth in the crimson light, "...to where Kingston Sage becomes flesh."

The elevator ascends silently. His eyes never leave mine, dark with suspicion and something hungrier. The space between us crackles with tension; he's cataloguing every lie I've told by omission.

When the doors part, revealing my sanctuary, Jaxon sets the luggage down with calculated precision.

"Shoes off," I command with a curl of my lips. His jaw tightens—another minor rebellion against his need for control.

He tilts his head, a predator reassessing prey. "Since when do you care about floor scuffs?"

I don't answer. Instead, I turn towards the heart of the loft.

"When does the actual story begin, Ellia?" His voice cuts through the space between us.

CHAPTER 32

ELLIA

I press my palm against a hidden panel. Lights cascade across the loft in waves, illuminating my private kingdom. A smile spreads across my face—genuine, unguarded.

"Why the hell are you grinning like that?" he demands.

"Because I'm a ghost here," I breathe, exhilaration flooding my veins. "No surveillance. No trace. No one is hunting me. This was the first thing I built that was truly mine, not purchased, not inherited. Created."

Above the pulsing heart of Obsidian, I carved this space from nothing but ambition and ruthlessness, transforming concrete bones into my perfect fortress.

Exposed brick dominates the loft, its rough texture interrupted by bold industrial steel beams that slice through the space like surgical instruments.

Black curtains hang from floor to ceiling, absorbing light rather than merely blocking it. The reality matches the blueprint that once existed only in my mind.

The far wall showcases floor-to-ceiling stained glass windows that rotate with the press of a button, beauty weaponized by technology.

To my right, beyond the foyer, an open living room sprawls with white couches so deep they consume me when exhaustion wins. The sectional dwarfs any I've encountered elsewhere, designed for luxury that borders on excess.

My left reveals an industrial kitchen stretching nearly the full length of the loft, all stainless steel and sharp edges, with a bar that promises both elegance and danger.

Beyond the kitchen lies my bed, a fortress within a fortress, veiled only by translucent curtains cascading from ceilings that soar twenty feet overhead.

Jaxon's gaze fixes on a door left slightly ajar. I capture his hand, feeling his pulse quicken beneath my fingers.

"My closet," I murmur, "bathroom."

I press against his biceps, my fingers measuring the circumference of hard muscle.

As I push the door wider, I trigger its twin with a button press. Amber lights flicker to life, illuminating my wardrobe: comfort clothes for private moments, sweats in calculated colors, and Obsidian attire of precision-tailored suits, substantial loafers, and boots that could crush or climb.

The closet consumes the wall's hidden space, leading to a bathroom built to my exacting standards: a freestanding tub commanding the far wall, a two-person vanity centerpiece, and a shower spanning the left wall like a horizontal waterfall.

Watching Jaxon explore the bathroom, I circle the closet's perimeter.

"My first solo creation," I tell him. "Every element, from layout to design to decoration, both here and in Obsidian below."

His voice cuts through the air like a blade. "How have you never told me about this?"

Each syllable drips with accusation. "When exactly have you been sneaking away here? How long have you been keeping this from me?"

I slip past him without answering, my fingertips trailing across the wall as I move deeper into my sanctuary, sensing the weight of his stare burns between my shoulder blades.

"Ellia." My name becomes a threat in his mouth.

I brush past my music alcove, the place where melodies bleed from my veins onto paper when they threaten to drown me from within. The piano keys gleam like teeth in the half-light.

God, I've ached for this space. Thirteen months of exile while recovering.

I wrench open the stained glass windows. Night air rushes in, carrying the pulse of the city below.

"No one can see us," I say, voice low. "I own everything your eyes can touch from here."

I extend my arm to the left, sweeping over the glittering storefronts and the anonymous masses crawling between them.

"And there." My hand slices right. "This entire building stretches to the next intersection, a hollow shell when I found it."

Jaxon stalks toward me, tracking my movements with predatory focus. His breath warms my neck as he joins me at the railing.

"Five years to build this fortress," I whisper. "While my first singles climbed charts, I was already constructing my escape. A place to vanish when the spotlight became too much."

The confession leaves me lighter, almost dizzy.

He stands so close that our shoulders nearly touch. His green eyes absorb the light spilling from inside, transforming them into something feral.

He's cataloging everything—exits, sightlines, vulnerabilities— with the clinical precision that makes me certain he's killed before.

The way he studies security rotations, memorizes faces, and anticipates threats. These aren't the instincts of an ordinary bodyguard. I've never dared ask what blood stains his past. Perhaps because I already know the answer would terrify me.

The night air carries the scent of rain and distant cigarette smoke as I turn to face him.

"And down there," I say, my body leaning dangerously far over the concrete barrier, the city air rushing up to meet me.

"That tattoo shop belongs partly to me. The artists live in those windows above."

I point to the warm-lit apartments where I've watched them laugh and drink under string lights, oblivious to my existence.

"From their balcony, they might glimpse me if I stand exactly here, but otherwise, I'm invisible."

A beat.

"Whenever I disappeared to 'London,'" I continue, making air quotes, "I was really here. A ghost in my own building. No one knew except my father, my alibi for vanishing."

"Then why reveal it now?" Jaxon's voice vibrates through the space between us. "Why share your sanctuary?"

I turn to face him, lips curving upward. "Would you have allowed me to slip away alone?"

He straightens, his thumb pressing beneath my jawline, finding that tender hollow where pulse meets bone. The pressure walks a razor's edge between warning and promise.

"You still don't understand," he murmurs, each syllable a hot whisper against my temple. "I won't leave. Anyone who threatens you forfeits their life. Anyone who even glances at you wrong has already chosen their ultimate resting place. I go where you go."

His lips press against my temple, teeth grazing the delicate skin there, the vibration of his words penetrating straight to my skull.

"You're mine to protect. Mine to avenge. Nothing touches what's mine, not while blood still pumps through my veins."

His eyes darken to black pools. "I should have gutted Michael when my instincts first screamed traitor. I should have made him suffer for even thinking of betraying you."

"Promise me," I demand, the words clawing their way out of my throat.

"If I ever fail you," he whispers, seizing my hand and pressing it against his throat where I feel his pulse hammering beneath my fingertips, "I'll load the gun myself. I'll kneel before you. My life is forfeit the moment yours is endangered."

His voice drops to something primal, something that bypasses my ears and hooks directly into the most primitive part of my brain. "Test me."

I nod once, the gesture sharp as a blade.

His grip releases my chin, leaving phantom pressure behind as he leans against the railing and draws me to his side. My laugh comes out hollow, bitter.

"Trust was never the issue with Michael or my staff," I say, the memory of Robyn and Michael's betrayal turning my voice to ice. "This place is mine. Untainted. Ellia Delvine might be a fabrication for public consumption, but this..."

I sweep my hand across the expanse of my sanctuary, "...this is eternal. Obsidian wasn't just a club to me. It was my first taste of true power."

"No phones allowed in Obsidian means no digital footprint. No evidence I was ever there," I murmur, twisting out of his embrace to move inside, the night air suddenly too cold on my skin.

Jaxon stalks behind me, his presence a shadow I can feel without seeing.

"Every person who sets foot in Obsidian signs their silence away," I continue, peeling off my hoodie and tossing it over a dining chair.

The walnut-and-epoxy table gleams beneath the lights, its pale blue center like a slice of the Caribbean Sea trapped in amber.

"Your obsession with NDAs," he observes, voice dangerously soft.

I turn, meeting his gaze. "NDAs build walls between my worlds. I appear only on my terms, never on public nights unless I'm performing. Even then, no phone captures what happens in the dark."

I sink into the plush sofa facing the gas fireplace, fingers dancing across the remote. Above us, the massive screen descends from the ceiling on mechanical arms.

With a few taps, I summon the club's surveillance feeds, dozens of angles capturing every corner of my empire except the most private spaces.

Jaxon positions himself across the sectional, his eyes flicking between my face and the screens above. As the feeds cycle, some rotating automatically, others locked in place by my command, I watch understanding dawn across his features, mingled with something darker.

Jaxon's eyes narrow as he nods toward the surveillance feeds. "Obsidian. Tell me everything."

The predator I recognize emerges, calculating, assessing, hungry for vulnerabilities to exploit or defend.

"I built the loft first," I say, curling into the corner of the sofa, putting deliberate space between us. "Supervised every detail myself. The security team thought I was paranoid until I doubled their fee."

My fingers dance across the tablet, cycling through blind spots only I know exist.

"They constructed the elevator that doesn't appear on any building plans. I spent nights learning their systems, coding, encryption, backdoor protocols, until I could break into my fortress."

The corner of my mouth lifts. "Nothing exists here that I can't control or destroy with three keystrokes."

I feel his stare like a physical touch as I pull up thermal imaging of the surrounding blocks.

His eyes glitter with something dangerous as he watches me manipulate the surveillance system, rage or fascination, I can't tell which.

The mask of the helpless pop star I've worn for him this past year lies shattered between us.

"So, let me get this straight," he says, his body shifting like a predator repositioning for the kill.

He stretches his arm across the back of the sofa, angling to face me while keeping the screens in his peripheral vision.

"You're a fucking tech savant, and you kept that from me?"

I meet his gaze without flinching.

"You never asked what hides beneath the glitter, Jaxon." My voice drops to something colder, sharper. "When I was with Michael, you were a shadow at the door, nothing more. Our relationship was transactional."

I lift my chin slightly. "Michael never bothered looking deeper, either. I don't volunteer my secrets."

My mouth twists into something resembling pleasure, though my eyes remain cold. "While the world fixated on the spotlight, I constructed this sanctuary in the shadows. No one saw the blueprints or the builder. Every brick laid while you were looking elsewhere." I trace my finger along the wall. "Breathing required hiding. Michael never knew. This became my refuge from him. At first, occasionally, then almost constantly before it ended."

CHAPTER 33

JAXON

As I stare at this woman who didn't just steal my heart but carved it out of my chest years ago, I feel the obsession burrowing deeper into my bones. Every layer of her I peel back consumes me more completely.

Before tonight, I worshipped her raw power. The way she'd bleed herself dry writing songs until dawn broke, her body trembling with exhaustion.

I'd press against her back in those paparazzi swarms, feeling her pulse hammer through my palms. I'd watch her in the recording booth, gripping the doorframe until my knuckles went white as she tore herself open and poured that voice out like a confession.

I've stood in her shadow while millions flowed from her fingers to charities. To veterans. To her music family. All that generosity is making me burn with possessive pride.

She's devastated me since day one. I know with absolute certainty that she belongs to me alone. Well, August too, but we're consuming her together.

Her brilliance burns like a living flame, and I've made an altar of my life to guard it. Every additional layer she peels back drags me deeper into her gravity.

This secret she's sharing, known only to her father before this moment, is a gift I'll protect with my life.

Her voice drops to a whisper. "I can tell you anything, Jaxon. But showing you this," she trembles, her pulse visible at her throat. "This is me ripping myself open for you. I could have fled anywhere to escape Michael, but I chose here. With you."

Her hand slices through the air, then freezes mid-gesture.

"I knew... " The words die in her throat.

I cross the space between us in two strides and sink beside her on the couch. Her skin burns against mine as I seize her hand, pressing it hard against my mouth, tasting salt.

Ellia's feelings stay locked inside her until they erupt like magma. Back in Australia, when she finally broke and screamed until her voice went raw, I glimpsed what lived behind her walls.

And I'll stand vigil in the wreckage, waiting with a predator's patience, until there's nothing left between us. She can keep her barriers between her music and her empire of shadows. I'll become the sentinel at that threshold, keeping everything else at bay.

I say nothing, just devour her with my eyes.

She drags in a ragged breath. "I knew one day this wouldn't be just mine anymore. That day is now. But..."

"But what, Ellia?" My voice scrapes raw. "You still don't want me here?"

"Stop!" She grabs my wrist with bruising force. "No, Jaxon. I mean, the day I showed someone this, it would become ours."

The word 'ours' hangs between us like a promise or a threat. Her amber eyes lock onto mine, pupils expanding until only thin rings of color remain, consuming all light between us.

I grip her chin, my voice dropping to a dangerous whisper. "Everything you've built belongs to you alone. Do you understand that?"

She nods, a barely perceptible movement.

"The club, the empire, it's all yours. I only want what money can't buy: your heart in my hands and your absolute trust."

The air between us grows heavy, charged with something electric. Her eyes glisten in the low light, tears threatening to spill over those dark lashes.

In all our years, I've only witnessed her shatter completely a handful of times before. Once, when she collapsed naked in the shower with August, her screams echoing off tile as years of terror finally broke through the dam she'd built inside herself, and those black nights when Michael had methodically dismantled her, piece by precious piece, until nothing remained but a hollow-eyed shell I barely recognized, trembling under my hands like a wounded animal ready to bolt or die.

That rainy night in Manhattan floods back to me. She'd called, voice tight with controlled rage, saying she needed "breathing room from Michael's bullshit."

I was standing sentry at her penthouse door when it nearly flew off its hinges. She stormed through, mascara smudged beneath wild eyes, barely glancing my way before making for the elevator.

I followed silently, descending to the underground garage where vultures with cameras lurked outside the Four Seasons.

As the elevator doors parted, I pulled her roughly against me, tucking her beneath my jacket. Her body molded against mine, arms wrapping around my waist.

The contact sent electricity crackling through my veins, a hunger I'd suppressed since becoming her shadow suddenly roaring to life.

Her heartbeat hammered against my chest as I carved us a path through the crowd, shoving one particularly persistent photographer hard enough to send him sprawling.

I yanked open her SUV door, then did something unforgivable, dismissed her driver with a look that left no room for argument. I slid behind the wheel, blackout windows sealing us into our own dark universe while she trembled behind me.

"Anywhere but here," she whispered, and I obeyed.

I drove her through Manhattan's veins for hours, my knuckles white against the wheel. Each street I chose deliberately: the shadowed corners where I'd watched her from afar, the alleyways where I'd once neutralized threats to her safety, routes only I knew existed.

She probably thought we were lost. We weren't. I was prolonging these precious moments where she had nowhere to run from me.

Her first tears broke something primal inside me. The streetlights caught each one as it slid down her cheek, her profile carved in amber and shadow against the window.

I memorized every detail, her trembling lower lip, the hollow of her throat as she swallowed back sobs, the way her fingertips pressed against the glass like she was reaching for escape.

Neither of us spoke. The silence between us throbbed like an open wound. I tasted blood from biting the inside of my cheek, fighting the urge to pull over and consume her pain with my mouth.

I swore then, watching her reflection shatter and reform with each passing light, that when she finally belonged to me, truly belonged, I would destroy anyone who made her cry like this. The only tears she would ever shed in my arms would be from pleasure so intense it bordered on violence.

Dawn bled across the Manhattan skyline when I circled back to the Four Seasons. The vultures still lurked by the main entrance, cameras ready, hungry for her pain.

I navigated around the perimeter until I found the service entrance, a concrete maw where deliveries disappeared into the building's gut, safely beyond the reach of those parasites and their flashing teeth.

I killed the engine at the loading dock. When I pulled her door open, she reached for me with trembling fingers, her grip fierce and desperate against my palm. No words passed between us except her whispered command that security remove Michael from her suite immediately.

Jenkins drew that particular short straw. He called me later, voice tight with controlled rage, describing how Michael had torn through her penthouse like a hurricane of entitlement, his howls of betrayal echoing down two floors of hallways she'd rented for our teams, a man unraveling violently when his possession slipped from his grasp.

Ellia's voice cuts through my memories of that night.

“I want it to be yours, Jaxon." Her voice breaks on my name. "When I opened my eyes in that hospital room and saw only you and August, I knew. I just couldn't say it then."

She traces my jawline with trembling fingers.

"The world was collapsing around me, but you never moved. August came whenever he could escape the season, but you..." She swallows hard. "You witnessed every silent scream, every moment I shattered without making a sound."

I guide her onto my lap, her thighs bracketing mine, the heat of her seeping through our clothes. My hands find the hollow at the base of her spine, steadying her as she sways toward me.

Even now, raw, stripped of artifice, her eyes haunted by that year of darkness, she steals the oxygen from my lungs with her proximity.

"You have my heart, songbird," I growl against her throat, teeth grazing the pulse hammering beneath her skin.

"Words are worthless. I'll carve my loyalty into your life until you feel it in your bones. Every breath I take belongs to you. Every drop of blood in my veins exists to protect what's mine. And you, Ellia..." I tighten my grip until she gasps, "...you are mine now."

I pull her close by the nape of her neck. My lips brush over hers until I hear a small whimper.

"When I'm done, the story of us will be carved into your memory with such exquisite precision that my name will be the only prayer your lips remember how to form."

I devour her mouth with a violence that surprises us both. Her tongue slides against mine, tasting of mint and something uniquely hers that makes my blood roar in my veins.

When I finally break away, we're both panting, her pupils blown wide with desire.

"I want a tattoo," she whispers, her gaze burning into mine with an intensity that makes my skin prickle.

I pull back slightly, needing distance to process this revelation. "Of what?"

The question hangs between us, insufficient against the weight of her declaration.

The irony doesn't escape me. After everything, her complicated relationship with her own body, the scars she hides, this particular form of transformation had never occurred to me.

Her lips curve into that dangerous half-smile. "Angel wings."

She hooks one finger into her collar, pulling the fabric aside to expose the delicate hollow between her shoulder blades.

She traces invisible lines across her skin, describing the placement with such precision that I know she's been carrying this vision for months.

“I saw an angel the night I died," she murmurs. "I can't shake the..."

I press my finger against her lips, silencing her. My mind reels with the implications.

All this time, I thought I knew every moment of that night, her body lifeless beneath my hands as I fought to restart her heart. But she had traveled somewhere I couldn't follow, witnessed something I couldn't see.

I tilt my head, tracing the delicate curves of her cheekbones in the soft lamplight. Even now, her calm eyes still astonished me, given the unimaginable horrors she'd endured.

We'd never dissected that dark chapter, except only once, briefly, when she nervously asked what had transpired in Australia.

I'd understood then that she wasn't ready to delve deeper. There was so much she still didn't remember, so many fragments she hadn't reclaimed, and here I was, piecing together her own recollections of that night.

"Jaxon, just listen," she murmured, slipping from my lap to perch on the edge of the cushions. Her voice was low, urgent. "You told me I stopped breathing, three whole minutes."

I nodded, waiting for her to continue.

"So," she said, her eyes flashing like summer leaves in sunlight, " I've drafted the concept already. The studio artists across the street, I want them involved. A sequence: three minutes without oxygen. Three weeks with no sound. And then three months..." Her voice faded to nothing, leaving the thought suspended between us.

Her chest rises with a slow inhale as she stares at some invisible point beyond my shoulder.

"Three bones, shattered," she whispers, the words hanging between us like glass about to break. "Three ribs."

"You've already designed it?" I asked, eyebrows rising as her grin stretched to her ears. Without warning, she vaulted over the back of the couch, dashing to the suitcase by the door.

"I need three of them," she called over her shoulder, rifling through papers.

When she returned, she sank onto the plush white shag rug that swallowed her legs in its silky fibers. With deliberate care, she opened her battered songbook on the oversized ottoman, the one upholstered in matching white fabric.

She flipped past the dog-eared lyric pages with a guarded glance, her eyes flicking to mine. She hated anyone peeking at her unfinished songs; I'd seen her chase Michael from her notebooks more than once.

Finally, she paused, turned a page, and revealed a single sheet of heavy parchment.

"Okay," she whispered, her voice a fragile tremor as she slid the drawing toward me. "Don't laugh."

I would never laugh at her. But when the image lay before me, my breath caught.

Against the velvet-black backdrop floated a vertical shaft of raw, white electricity, like a spine carved from lightning. It wasn't flesh or bone, but a luminous axis, as though the essence of existence had been strung into a pulse.

The current rippled in deliberate rhythms, each surge alive with silent thought. On either flank of that lightning backbone, an angel's form blossomed into vast, uneven fields, not delicate feathered wings but great expanses of pure energy that warped the surrounding skin.

The lines didn't just sit there; they throbbed, swelled, and receded like breath beneath my flesh.

Where the ink peaked, reality bent and thinned; where it dimmed, there was only void, no shadow, no residue, pure erasure.

The angel had no face. No features. Only the raw, humming truth of that night was captured in those white-hot lines, forever alive with current on my body.

"I saw this. This image has been in my mind since that night. And it has to be three. One for the spine and two for these," she points to the wings. "I don't know, three just feels right."

She exhales slowly. "Whatever I saw, angel or not, bore no resemblance to those Renaissance paintings hanging in museums. Those are comforting lies we tell ourselves. Real celestial beings aren't soft-winged comforts."

Her voice drops to a whisper. "The number three will mark my end."

Her shoulders cave inward as the words leave her mouth, the weight of prophecy settling between us like dust, but judgment is the last thing on my mind.

My eyes remain locked on the drawing, its electric spine burning into my retinas.

"What do you mean by three?" I manage, throat dry.

She lifts one shoulder in a half-shrug, her face a mask of terrible acceptance, as if she's already glimpsed the hour of her own ending.

"Elli," I say, my voice dropping to a dangerous whisper, "having this etched into your skin would be exquisite, but you can't risk being seen."

I scan the vast loft, suddenly aware of how exposed we are, how the windows could become eyes.

"You've been hiding for a reason."

Her lips curl into that feral smile that makes my blood simmer. She scoots closer, finger jabbing skyward like she's piercing the very air between us.

"Aha, I've already solved that particular problem," she breathes, excitement vibrating through her slender frame.

"Enlighten me," I growl, gripping her wrist and pulling her against me. "Because even with the strongest fucking NDA, the second you walk into that shop, your cover shatters. One photo, one whisper, and everything you've built crumbles."

"They're coming here." She snaps her songbook closed with finality, the sound sharp as a gunshot in the quiet room.

"John drafted two separate agreements. One silences them about seeing me at all. The other..." her lips curve into that smile that's ended careers "...covers everything else. Every whisper, every sketch, every breath they take in my presence. Legally bulletproof."

My voice drops to a lethal whisper. "Does John know about this place?"

"No." Her eyes glitter with dark satisfaction. "He asked, I denied," shrugging her shoulders as if she had done this a thousand times before.

I close the distance between us, seizing her waist and crushing her against me. Her pulse hammers wildly where our bodies connect, a trapped bird beneath my fingertips.

The knowledge that I'm still the only one who can touch her, save for the doctors and August, sends a possessive heat coursing through my veins.

I grip the nape of her neck with calculated pressure. "But make no mistake, I won't be standing behind you. I'll be right there, watching every needle puncture your skin."

Her breath hitches when our eyes lock. “You’re absolutely incredible,” she whispers, voice catching on each syllable.

Color rises across her face as she glances down, but my fingers brush her chin, guiding her attention back to me.

“I think we should christen this room properly,” I murmur against her temple, lifting her effortlessly into my arms.

CHAPTER 34

ELLIA

A week has passed since we arrived in Manchester. Day by day, Jaxon's shoulders have relaxed as he's memorized every exit, studied the club's hierarchy, and cataloged potential security weaknesses throughout the building.

His team touched down shortly after we did. "Put them in those empty flats next door," I suggested, pointing to the building on our left.

Jaxon nodded but still insisted on inspecting the accommodations himself.

"Just making sure it's suitable," he claimed, though the appreciative glint in his eyes as he surveyed my operation told me otherwise.

Jenkins now heads Jaxon's security detail while he shadows me. I catch Jaxon scanning unfamiliar corners of the loft, the club, the city streets, searching for threats he can't yet see.

He doesn't understand that I've disappeared hundreds of times without being discovered. My fortress keeps me invisible when I need to be, and everyone else at a safe distance.

He is studying my security protocols with a hunger that borders on obsession. For all his skill as a hacker, he stands before my system like a man witnessing divine revelation. His fingers hover over the keyboard, trembling slightly.

"How did you conceive of this?" he whispers, voice raw with something between reverence and fear.

I lean in close enough to feel his pulse quicken. "The world isn't just dark, my love. It's a slaughterhouse waiting for the unwary. I built this because I've seen what happens to those who fail."

Jaxon keeps Jenkins and his team at bay, refusing them entry to the loft, and I don't object, but there's irony in how he tries to relay my security protocols to Jenkins from a distance.

Whenever I suggest allowing Jenkins, and only Jenkins, inside, Jaxon's eyes light with that familiar intensity, his hunger for knowledge overriding everything else.

So far, we've spent countless hours in front of my monitors, his fingers tracing code paths across the screens. He absorbs every detail, every security measure, every backdoor I've built. His desperation makes sense.

Michael, finding me in Australia, forced us to run. During my last video call with August, there was no mention of Michael resurfacing.

August has four security men shadowing his every move. I still worry it's not enough, though Jaxon keeps insisting otherwise, his hand squeezing mine when he sees the concern etching lines around my eyes.

Every worry I voice dissolves beneath Jaxon's touch. He's learned to read my tension like code, responding with calculated precision, fingers tracing the curve of my spine, lips brushing against my neck, tongue tasting the salt of my skin until my thoughts scatter like disrupted pixels.

During our security briefings, he'll press against me from behind, one hand guiding his across the keyboard while the other slides beneath my waistband, his rhythm matching the pulse of data across the screen until I shatter, gasping against the desk.

Before him, I kept my body locked down like my systems, impenetrable, cold. Now, when he's across the room, I find myself leaning toward him like a satellite seeking its signal, my skin humming with emptiness until he returns.

Michael waited two years before deciding I was better off dead. Despite sharing his sheets, I never felt with him what courses through me when Jaxon touches my skin.

Now I find myself hungry for even August's territorial nature. A hunger that only intensified after our last video call, when Jaxon made sure August witnessed every intimate moment he couldn't share, trapped as he was by medical appointments and team commitments oceans away.

I watch him on broadcasts sometimes, relegated to the sidelines instead of competing. The athlete in him must be dying, but selfishly, I'm relieved. With Michael hunting me, August's lower profile this season feels like one less vulnerability to manage.

The night August returned from the hospital still haunts me, my composure shattering like glass. Every fear and doubt I'd contained came crashing through defenses I wasn't prepared to reinforce.

So now, Jaxon approaches me differently. He never asks if I'm okay; that question is too simple for what he seeks. Instead, he excavates me layer by layer, fascinated by discoveries his research never revealed.

Once, in a rare moment of vulnerability, he confessed: "I memorized every entrance and exit to your world, but missed how you disappear into yourself when the music starts."

My writing has returned, words flowing after a year of drought. Jaxon watches from across the room, utterly still when my pen moves across paper.

When I play to the tune of my words. He observes everything: my shower songs, the melodies I hum while coding, my concentration when managing investments.

Even when dinner grows cold while he waits for me to finish, he never interrupts. No impatience crosses his face, only that expression I've rarely encountered in my life: someone finding genuine joy in simply witnessing me exist.

The invitation to the members-only masquerade sits hidden in my email. I haven't mentioned it to Jaxon yet. His protective instincts would clash with my newfound courage, the same courage that no longer sends me into panic when my phone chimes or someone knocks at the door.

"Hey, songbird. Where did you fly off to?"

Jaxon's voice pulls me back as he finds me perched in a chair on the balcony rather than my usual spot on the concrete railing where the city sprawls below, a position he's physically removed me from more times than I can count.

"Nowhere important," I answer, which isn't exactly untrue.

After years of suffocation, my thoughts remain hesitant visitors.

In Idaho, my life operated on rails laid by others. Medical appointments scheduled without my input, therapy sessions where I sat mute behind my walls, visitors vetted through an invisible committee.

I remember how Jaxon simply informed me of August's visits rather than requesting permission. August never overstayed, a few weeks at most, yet his presence lingered in every corner of the house.

On my worst nights, he and Jaxon would sleep on the couch nearest my bedroom door like sentinels. I never found the words to acknowledge that kindness.

He settles beside me, his presence drawing my gaze like a magnet. The military fade he typically maintains has grown out, black strands curling slightly at his neckline. It softens him somehow. His stubble shadowing his jaw has become a daily feature rather than an exception, a texture my fingertips seek without conscious thought.

"I think I'll call downstairs," I murmur, resting my head against the chair, its cool surface a counterpoint to the warmth building inside me. "Have them send up their three best artists."

"Songbird," he exhales, the word a raw scrape against the silence between us.

My head snaps to the side, muscles tensing before my eyes even find his. The familiar dread floods my veins like ice water; his jaw already clenched, that dangerous stillness overtaking him that means my wings are about to be clipped. Again.

His voice drops to a whisper that burns like acid. "Now that I know everything there is to know about this place, I want you to be happy, but make no mistake."

He leans in until his breath scorches my ear. "If they touch you in any way beyond putting ink on your skin, I will snap each finger off their dominant hand and feed the pieces to them. One. By. One."

His eyes lock onto mine, pupils blown wide with a darkness I've seen devour men twice his size. "Do you understand me?"

I've watched him hurl two hundred-pound men across rooms like they were made of paper. I've seen bones shatter beneath his grip when strangers' fingers brushed my waist.

The night he found Michael surrounded by those women; I thought I'd witness my first murder. Michael's face was purple, veins bulging as Jaxon's thumbs pressed into his windpipe, that terrifying smile never leaving Jaxon's face.

"Don't be so dramatic." I exhale a soft laugh. He may control my body, my pleasure, even my space, but he'll never control my words.

CHAPTER 35

ELLIA

I pull out my phone and tap the shop's website. The original owner sold me half the business years ago when the place couldn't draw the high-end clientele he'd banked on.

His dream was drowning in empty chairs and red numbers until my capital injection and complete rebrand rescued it from obscurity.

The shop had been a revolving door of walk-ins who never committed to serious pieces. After signing the partnership papers, my first order of business was purging the talent pool, cutting loose the artists I'd spotted getting high behind the dumpsters and showing the door to every so-called friend who mistook my business for their personal clubhouse.

What emerged from the ashes was an elite studio that attracted serious collectors and top-tier professionals.

Now our roster boasts just four artists, each one skilled enough that I'd let them mark me without hesitation.

My eyes drift to Jaxon's sleeve-covered arms.

"For someone wearing that much artwork, I'm surprised you never picked up the machine yourself."

He strokes my cheek. "I never had the time. Work, security details, clients, careers, I was always on the move. But I did make time to be the canvas."

"Funny," I smirk. "You've had plenty of downtime this past year. Sitting here with me must've driven you insane."

His smile cuts like a blade. "Wrong, songbird." His voice drops to a growl that vibrates through my bones. "I was a dead man walking before you. Your tour schedule, weeks here, weeks gone; and I had my team running on fumes while I lived for glimpses of you. Now with Michael out there..."

His fingers curl into fists, knuckles whitening. "If he touches you, I'll tear him apart with my bare hands. There is no reality where you don't exist in my life anymore. None I would permit to exist."

His past remains a mystery. Whispers of classified missions and government contracts, rumors of specialized training beyond standard military. Yet something doesn't add up. What brings a man with those skills to babysit a pop star with mental health issues?

I maintain eye contact with him while dialing, my finger deliberately pressing each number. Two rings later, a polished British accent answers: "Ink Link, how can I help you?"

“Hi,” I say smoothly. “I’d like to book your three best artists.”

“Three? We only have four on staff.”

I hide my grin. She’ll think me mad, but I owe no explanation. “I’m not sure of their rates, but I’m prepared to match that and more.”

I hear rustling papers and hushed voices on the other end. "One moment, please."

When she returns, there's a new eagerness in her tone.

"We could accommodate you as early as tomorrow afternoon, if that works?"

A smile curves my lips as Jaxon stands, moving to the balcony's edge with tension visible in every line of his body.

"I was thinking tonight, actually," I reply, voice honeyed but firm. "And I’d like them to come to me. My head of security can arrange transportation."

The receptionist hesitates. "We rarely travel to clients, but I suppose we could close the shop if privacy is your concern."

When Jaxon reaches for the phone, I swat his hand away.

"Perhaps you didn't catch who's calling," I say, letting my voice drop to that signature timbre my fans would recognize anywhere. "This is Kingston Sage."

The silence breaks with a sharp intake of breath. Then, flustered: "Of course, Ms. Sage. We'll come to you. Would an hour give your security team enough time to prepare?"

"Perfect. And you are?"

"Riley," she manages, voice trembling slightly.

“Thank you, Riley. I’ll ensure you’re properly compensated.” I end the call.

Jaxon's eyes narrow dangerously, pupils dilating like a predator scenting blood. I meet his gaze unflinchingly.

"No one knows I've buried my money in their foundations, but they all whisper about the nightclub, my nightclub, where even celebrities beg for entry."

The truth burns in my throat, desperate to escape. My empire. My labyrinth. A system so intricate that even Jaxon, with all his lethal intelligence, has only glimpsed its shadow.

"You're a goddamn enigma," he growls, yanking me from the chair with enough force to steal my breath.

His fingers twist in my hair, the perfect balance of pain and possession as he crushes me against the hard plane of his chest. His heartbeat hammers against mine, and I surrender instantly, my body liquefying against his heat.

I trace lazy circles over the hard curve of his biceps. "You have one hour until you need to get them."

Jaxon arches an eyebrow. "One hour?"

The words barely leave his lips before he's hoisting me up, one arm curved under me, lifting as if I weigh nothing at all.

I run my fingers along his arms, tracing the contours that haven't softened despite his absence from those brutal training sessions with August back in Sydney. I make a mental note about the private gym just across the elevator.

My legs wrap around him instinctively, a small gasp escaping me. He twists his hand into my hair, pulling just enough to bare my neck as his mouth finds the sensitive skin there.

As Jaxon devours my throat with expert precision, my head falls back, and my vision blurs. Beyond the balcony, I glimpse my unwitting cast of characters, neighbors framed in their windows like living portraits.

They've been my silent companions through sleepless nights: the couple who dance barefoot after midnight, the woman who drinks wine alone, the man who weeps when he thinks no one can see.

Fame has gilded my cage, but watching them taste freedom makes my chest ache with want. My signature hair, raven black with that telltale shock of white behind my ear, makes anonymity impossible.

Jaxon's fingers twist in my hair, sending electric currents racing from scalp to spine. A whimper escapes me as he yanks my head back, his devilish grin hovering just above my parted lips.

When he claims my mouth, a white-hot explosion of pleasure obliterates any thought. His tongue slides against mine, demanding, possessing, and I surrender completely, my body melting into his as waves of ecstasy pulse through me.

The moan that tears from my throat seems to ignite something savage in him.

His answering growl sends violent tremors through my thighs as liquid heat pools between them, my body's immediate surrender to his touch.

As he carries me toward the open window, I tug at my sweatshirt, the armor I've worn to conceal the roadmap of my past.

The scars they've worshipped with reverent lips until I almost believe their whispered devotion. I almost forgot whose hands first carved my skin.

"I need you inside me," I breathe against his mouth, my voice barely recognizable through the haze of desire.

His response is primal, a deep rumble of possession as I chase his whiskey-mint taste, reclaiming his mouth each time he breaks for air, the intoxication more potent than any spirit.

I create just enough space between our bodies to peel away layers, hoodie and shirt discarded in a careless heap. My white lace bra remains the last barrier as he carries me to the massive oak resin table dominating the room's center.

He sets me down, positioning himself between my trembling thighs.

"I'm going to carve my name into your soul," he growls, each syllable vibrating against my pulse. "Until every nerve ending in that brilliant mind screams who you belong to when you wake gasping in the dark."

In one fluid motion, he strips away both joggers and lace, exposing me completely to his hungry gaze.

Jaxon's tongue blazed across my jaw, leaving a slick, burning trail that ignited every nerve ending. He traced a deliberate path to the sensitive hollow beneath my ear, where he lingered, his hot breath making me shudder with anticipation.

When he finally bit down, hard, possessively, marking me, I felt myself unraveling. The exquisite pain radiated through my body like lightning, settling between my thighs where I was already embarrassingly wet.

His muscled thigh pressed against my core, denim rough against my bare, hypersensitive skin, and I ground against him shamelessly, desperately seeking relief.

He laughed, the sound rumbling deep in his chest and vibrating through me like a physical caress.

"So fucking desperate already," he murmured against my skin, his voice dark with promise. "I haven't even started with you."

In one swift movement, he captured both my wrists in his iron grip, wrenching them behind my back until my spine arched, breasts thrust forward in involuntary offering.

His free hand claimed me, calloused fingers tracing the delicate underside of my breast before roughly palming its weight.

When he pinched my nipple between his thumb and forefinger, rolling and tugging until I was gasping and writhing against him, I nearly sobbed with need. The sudden sharp smack that followed sent pleasure-pain spiraling through me so intensely that for a moment I couldn't breathe, couldn't think, could only feel.

I arched wildly against his restraint, but his grip only tightened, reminding me who was in control.

Without releasing my wrist, Jaxon drags a chair across the floor, the scrape of metal against concrete sending shivers down my spine. He sits, spreading his powerful thighs wide, his erection straining against dark denim.

“Worshipping you has become the only religion I'll ever need,” he growls, voice scraping like gravel against the hollow of my knees, his fingers digging into my hips hard enough to bruise.

A desperate sound tears from my throat as I position myself before him, thighs trembling as they fall open, my feet bracing on his thighs. His hungry gaze fixates on the slick evidence of my need, and I watch his pupils dilate with primal hunger.

"Lay back," he commands, his grip tightening to the exquisite edge of pain. When I instinctively try to free myself, his fingers dig deeper.

"No," he growls, a dangerous edge to his voice. "Arms behind you."

The corner of his mouth lifts in that arrogant half-smile that makes my core clench with anticipation. I arch backward slowly, crossing my wrists at the small of my back, completely vulnerable to his mercy.

His breath sears my inner thigh like a brand as he murmurs, "One twitch of those fingers and I walk away, leaving you just like this."

A tremor wracks through me, my plea catching somewhere between my lungs and lips as desire floods every cell.

"They'll be here soon," I challenge, lips curving upward.

The vibration of his growl against my most sensitive flesh is my only answer. I know then he'd relish watching me squirm through professional conversations, desperate for him while pretending I wasn't.

He places both hands on my thighs, his fingers digging into my flesh with possessive hunger. I gasp as he kneads the sensitive skin, working his way from my hips to my knees with agonizing slowness. When his touch suddenly vanishes, I arch desperately toward the emptiness.

"Jaxon, please," I beg, my voice breaking with raw need, my body aching for the return of his touch.

His fingertips reappear at my ankles, tracing electric paths up my calves. When he reaches the sensitive hollows behind my knees, he lingers there, exploiting my weakness until I'm trembling uncontrollably.

With one powerful motion, he drags me forward, skin against table, until my ass barely clings to the table's edge. My crossed arms strain beneath my arched back, muscles burning with the effort to maintain this position of complete surrender.

From this angle, I can't see his face; I can only feel the heat of his breath against my most vulnerable places. His hands slide up my inner thighs, thumbs deliberately grazing my pussy with feather-light pressure that sends violent ripples of pleasure radiating through my core.

His fingers hover just above my center, the promise of touch more excruciating than any pain. My hips strain desperately against his iron grip as I whimper his name, a broken prayer falling from my lips.

"My greedy songbird," he growls, his hot breath caressing my swollen flesh. "Desperate for me, aren't you?"

When he finally lowers his mouth, the first contact of his tongue sends electricity crackling through my veins.

He captures my most sensitive clit between his teeth, applying just enough pressure to make me gasp, hovering in that exquisite space where agony transforms into bliss.

His deep groan vibrates against my core as he devours me with savage intensity, each broad stroke of his tongue collecting my essence. I feel myself dripping, shameless in my need as he works his way lower, teasing the forbidden entrance no man has claimed.

My muscles clench in anticipation, remembering his whispered promises and how he and August compete to be the first to introduce me to that pleasure, each swearing they alone can make me surrender completely.

Without warning, he plunges two thick fingers inside me, curling them against that secret spot that makes stars explode behind my eyelids. My back arches violently, my crossed wrists nearly slipping from their position.

"Uh-uh," he warns, the words vibrating against my throbbing center as his free hand clamps down harder, keeping me prisoner to the pleasure he commands.

His tongue works in devastating rhythm with his fingers as they plunge deeper inside me, the slick sounds of my arousal filling the room.

He devours me like a starving man, his hot mouth capturing my swollen clit and sucking with such perfect pressure that white-hot pleasure explodes through my core.

My entire universe narrows to the exquisite sensation of his skilled mouth worshipping me while his thick fingers stretch and fill me completely.

Their tongues devastate me in different ways, one methodical and precise, the other wild and relentless, both reducing me to trembling surrender, to begging, to that delirious edge where pleasure becomes violence. Some nights, I lie awake imagining them competing for dominance over my body, neither yielding until I'm utterly destroyed between them.

Jaxon's moan vibrates against my throbbing clit as my inner walls spasm violently around his thick fingers. My vision fractures into prismatic light, eyelids fluttering helplessly as a cataclysmic orgasm tears through me.

My legs tremble uncontrollably, threatening to clamp shut entirely if not for his bruising grip on my inner thigh, anchoring me to this exquisite torture.

He mercilessly pumps those skilled fingers deeper, harder, prolonging each wave of ecstasy until I'm sobbing his name. Blinding pleasure explodes behind my closed eyes, my consciousness floating somewhere beyond my sweat-slicked body.

"Jaxon," I gasp, my voice raw and desperate, "I need you inside me."

He releases my thigh, his glistening fingers tailing possessively up my quivering stomach, between the valley of my heaving breasts, leaving a wet path of my arousal across my feverish skin.

Jaxon's hand seizes the nape of my neck, his body blazing like a furnace as he looms over me, yanking me upright. My shoulders shriek in agony from the sudden shift, and my body threatens to slide off the table with the force of his pull.

His lips and chin are slick with my desire, a glistening testament to my need. My gaze is locked onto his mouth, then his ravenous eyes, and back to his lips, a relentless loop of hunger.

I unconsciously wet my parched lips, and his eyes follow the movement, darkening with lust. One hand, still gripping the back of my neck, tangles into my hair, sending electric shivers down my spine. His other hand frees his cock from his jeans, the thick length pulsing with need.

The head of his dick grinds against my swollen clit, drawing a moan from deep within me. Jaxon crushes his lips to mine, swallowing the sound, as he drives into me with a single, brutal thrust.

He fills me completely, stretching every hollow space, satisfying every craving carved out by years of emptiness.

I sob into his mouth, the sensation detonating behind my sternum, radiating out in scorching waves. My wrists burn in his grip, my hips grind against the unforgiving table, and still, I crave more. Always something more.

Tearing his mouth from mine, he drags his tongue along my jaw, biting at my throat, each sharp nip a supernova of pain and pleasure. Then, as if hearing my silent plea, he begins to move, a slow, punishing rhythm that drags his cock almost entirely out before slamming back in, the table scraping beneath us with each thrust.

I hear myself cry out, wild and desperate, my insides clenching around him, frantic to keep him buried deep. He shifts his hips, finding a new spot inside me, and I convulse, almost shattering from the intensity.

"Show me who owns your pleasure," he growls in my ear, and I detonate, my hips bucking to take him deeper.

His thrusts become erratic, his cock swelling inside me. His orgasm hits as I'm still reeling from my own, both of us panting, our bodies slick with sweat.

"Show me who you break for."

It detonates something primal inside me as my hips thrust up, begging for every inch.

Jaxon collapses against me, his ragged breath hot against my sweat-slicked skin. He releases my raw, throbbing wrists from behind my back, and pain shoots through my shoulders as blood rushes back.

My trembling fingers find his damp hair, twisting into the thick strands, holding his face against my heaving breasts.

His powerful arms encircle my waist, fingers digging possessively into my flesh.

When our breathing finally slows, he lifts me with a primal growl, and I wrap my quivering thighs around his narrow hips, still inside me.

I feel his essence mingling with mine, dripping obscenely down my inner thighs as he carries me to the bathroom.

"You are fucking perfect, songbird," he rasps, pupils still blown with lust. "You've ruined me for anyone else. If I ever lose you, I'd put a bullet through my skull. If you die, I die with you." His voice breaks with raw emotion.

He reaches behind me to the massive tile shower, cranking the water until steam billows around us. The scalding heat promises delicious pain against my oversensitive skin.

"And there is no existence without you," I whisper, dragging my teeth down the salt-slick column of his throat before capturing his mouth in a bruising kiss that tastes of desperation and my own arousal.

CHAPTER 36

AUGUST

Two weeks without Ellia in my arms feels like two years. Every hour I wait for travel clearance is pure agony. She calls before our games, her voice breaking when she tells me how much she aches for me.

Something's off. Her words come out measured, guarded. I won't push, not after seeing how Jaxon's interrogations about those mysterious accounts and her hidden billions ended. But her eyes betray everything if you know where to look.

Jaxon parades her in front of me like a trophy, watching me burn as she comes undone beneath his hands. Her screams for him cut through me like knives.

The bastard has no idea what's coming. When I finally claim her, I'll burn the whole world down before letting her go. Again.

He'll have to kill me to take her. I'm counting the seconds until our reckoning, and this brotherhood has become a battlefield of who owns her pleasure.

From the moment I first saw her, I knew she'd destroy everything I thought I was, and she has, and I crave more destruction every day.

I'm haunting the rooms she abandoned. These walls witnessed everything: her screams of pleasure, her breathless laughter, the whispered confessions she trusted only to me and the darkness.

Now they mock me with their silence. I've destroyed my body trying to exhaust my mind, ignoring the doctor's warnings about my injuries. Pain is better than emptiness.

The moment she walked away, something fundamental inside me shattered. I'm a man drowning in memories.

At night, I bury my face in her pillow, desperate for that lingering trace of lavender and vanilla. One breath and I'm on my knees. One more and I'm hard enough to punch through concrete, aching for a body that's no longer here to touch.

I'm a prisoner in my own fucking house. They've got me on lockdown, no coming, no going unless its doctors poking at my injuries or dragging my ass to mandatory team shit.

My own teammates can't even get through the door because of that psychopath, Michael.

The bastard's been spotted slithering around Sydney. I haven't seen him with my own eyes, but Jenkins feeds me updates whenever I'm about to put my fist through another wall.

I need to know where he is. The fucking coward who couldn't walk away like a man, who had to destroy what he couldn't have. I need to find the monster who raped her. Every time I close my eyes, I see what he carved into her back while he, Christ, I can't even think it without tasting blood in my mouth.

The worst fucking part? Those headlines with our faces plastered everywhere like some goddamn tabloid freak show. Reporters swarm me like vultures circling a corpse, not giving a shit about my recovery, just desperate for another sound bite about her.

I can't even breathe without cameras flashing. These desperate girls claw at my car windows, rip at my clothes, scream her name until their voices crack raw, like summoning her ghost might somehow make her appear.

They don't understand I'd trade every single one of them, every headline, every dollar, every fucking breath just to have her back for one minute.

I still don't understand why she chose to go public with our relationship. Not that I'm complaining. Under different circumstances, I'd have proudly displayed her on my arm at every event, standing behind me at games I no longer play, letting everyone see exactly who she belongs to.

Maybe someday she'll explain her reasons. Until then, I'm stuck weathering this storm.

Faith and Jo are fighting to keep the media wolves at bay, but they're fighting a losing battle. New footage keeps surfacing from that night, her tearful escape from the VIP box, mascara streaking down her face as she pushed through the crowd. There's only so much damage control they can do.

She claims she's barely touching her phone, only connecting with her team and checking in with her father. Meanwhile, Jaxon's keeping her occupied. He occasionally messages to say he's "learning so much from her." Whatever the hell that's supposed to mean.

For now, I'm trapped in my own house with four hulking security guards who treat my kitchen like a showdown.

This morning, Briggs nearly took off Rodriguez's hand for the last strip of bacon while Peters and Finn were locked in some asinine competition over who could bench more. The constant dick-measuring over patrol rotations is driving me insane.

We coexist, barely. But every night I lie awake thinking about sharing this space with her instead.

Jenkins pulled a real dick move, taking the guys I knew. I warned Jaxon before they left that surrounding me with strangers was asking for trouble.

After two weeks of interrogating them like prisoners, Briggs is the only one I can stomach. At least he's my age. The others, all south of thirty

Christ. I'm thirty-five, not twenty-two. The way these young bloods throw each other around the yard makes me wonder if I should be worried about keeping up.

CHAPTER 37

ELLIA

I stand motionless under the scalding cascade, letting water sluice over my ravaged body long after Jaxon's fingers have finished tracing every curve, cleaning away the evidence of our savage coupling.

His parting command still burns in my ear: "Don't take too long, songbird. The artists will be here soon, His possessive grip on my ass punctuated each word.

When the water finally runs cold against my flushed skin, I step out, droplets clinging to my hardened nipples as I reach for the plush black towel.

I pad naked through the cavernous walk-in closet that connects to the bathroom, my thighs still trembling, slick with remnants of Jaxon that escaped our cleaning.

My fingers find the drawer containing my matching sweats; black, always black, the color of midnight, of secrets, of bruises that haven't yet bloomed purple.

As I zip the hoodie over my damp skin, I catch my reflection in the full-length mirror and freeze. Raw terror floods my system, my pulse hammering against my throat.

Soon, three strangers will see what lies beneath this fabric, the network of raised pink and white scars crisscrossing my body, the jagged fifteen-inch gash that splits my back from shoulder blade to hip.

My mind slams shut against the memory of how it got there, a steel door clanging against the horror. Jaxon swears it was Michael's blade that carved me open. I've made his explanation my mantra.

His fault. His fucking fault, my skin looks like a roadmap of suffering. His fault, my arms bear surgical scars where doctors pieced shattered bones back together. His fault, I drag my left leg slightly with each step, the hip never quite healing right after what he did.

Jaxon and August insist nobody notices my limp, but I feel it with every goddamn step, the permanent signature Michael left on my body.

I lingered too long in my closet because when I finally pushed open the French doors, four men filled my living space.

Every gaze snapped to me. The blonde one pivoted, his stare boring into mine. The tall one with dark hair paused mid-sentence beside Jaxon, a picture book clutched in his hand. The third man, with light brown waves falling across his forehead, rose from his chair at the table.

The same table where Jaxon had taken me not an hour before. My eyes flicked to its polished end, searching for evidence of our passion.

Jaxon caught my glance and smirked knowingly. He'd cleaned everything while I showered.

My fingers remained frozen on the brass handles. The scene before me belonged in fiction, not in the mundane reality of my life.

Jaxon gestures to each man with a deliberate sweep of his hand. "Ellia, this is Arik, Dakota, and Cedar."

The blonde, Arik, stands a little above my eye level, with sapphire blue eyes, his skin a canvas of intricate tattoos that wind like dark vines up his neck and bloom across his jawline, a constellation of smaller marks dotting his left cheekbone.

Dakota towers beside him, matching Jaxon in height but with a leaner frame, his dark hair falling in a precise cut that accentuates sharp cheekbones.

Cedar, with honey-brown curls that catch the night's light streaming through my windows, watches me with hazel eyes that seem to absorb every detail of my appearance.

My gaze drops to their feet, all bare against my pristine floors, and something softens in me. Jaxon remembered.

A small, private smile touches my lips as warmth blooms in my chest. He catches it, his eyes never leaving my face, and the look he returns makes my pulse quicken.

In that moment, I want nothing more than to cross the room to him, to silently thank him for honoring this one sacred rule of my space.

They acknowledge me with synchronized nods, pulling me from my thoughts, their gazes heavy as anchors. I inch forward on trembling legs, the scent of unfamiliar cologne, sandalwood, citrus, something darker, overwhelming my senses.

"Hi, Ellia." Arik extends a hand adorned with silver rings, his voice unexpectedly gentle.

Before I can speak, Jaxon materializes beside me, his arm snaking around my waist, fingers pressing possessively into the curve of my hip.

Jaxon steps between us, his voice a velvet shield. "Ellia prefers not to touch people she's just met."

I meet Arik's eyes and incline my head slightly. "Hello."

The gesture feels natural now, after years abroad, where I learned the relief of greeting without contact.

I turn to the man with hazel eyes. "Cedar. What an unusual name."

My lips curve into a genuine smile as I nod to him.

Finally, I acknowledge the tallest one. "Dakota. Thank you for being here."

I lower my gaze, fingers twisting together. "Please forgive my awkwardness. New introductions have been difficult for me."

The weight of their stares presses against my skin until Jaxon clears his throat sharply, breaking their trance. I've grown accustomed to being observed, for my hair, under spotlights, or when launching new ventures, but collective attention feels different.

"May I?" I ask, gesturing toward Dakota's book.

He slides it across the table.

"Two years of work," he says, voice trailing off when our eyes meet.

I slide into the chair, leafing through Dakota's portfolio with feigned interest.

"I suppose you're wondering why there are three of you here," I say, watching as they position themselves around me like points on a compass, Dakota settling to my left, Arik claiming the table's end, Cedar taking the seat directly across.

Behind Cedar, Jaxon retreats to the kitchen, the clink of crystal against bottle betraying his whiskey pour. His jealousy radiates across the room in waves of tension. I catch his possessive glare and make a mental note to soothe his territorial instincts later tonight.

I place the book before me and fold my hands in my lap, fingers secretly twisting the hem of my sweatshirt beneath the table's edge.

"For those unfamiliar with my work, I'm Ellia Delvine." The three men exchange glances, a wordless dialogue passing between them that excludes both Jaxon and me.

"I've invited you here because I need a particular design brought to life, something I've created myself that requires three distinct artistic hands."

Cedar, the one with those soft curls, furrows his brow, confusion evident in the tilt of his head. I expected resistance. Yet this design needs to be etched into my skin more desperately than I crave Jaxon's touch against it.

Jaxon wouldn't protest if he understood the depth of it. But he wasn't there in those suspended moments when breath abandoned me, when I glimpsed what waits beyond.

"Let me be direct," I say, my hands punctuating each word with small, precise movements.

"I need three artists for this single design." I nod toward Jaxon, who hasn't looked away from the drawing since I first revealed it.

He places the image at the center of the table. As it passes between their hands, I trace invisible lines in the air.

"One artist for the spine," my finger draws a vertical path, "and two for the wings."

Arik's eyes remained fixed on the design. "Where would this be placed?" he asked, his voice neutral, but the question loaded.

I rose from my chair, my legs carrying me in a restless path around the table.

The NDAs sat before them: one thin document for those who declined, one substantial folder for those who accepted.

My fingers trembled slightly as I explained the legal requirements, knowing what came next. If they agreed, I would need to expose my back, my skin.

Six eyes tracked my movement like predators. Jaxon appeared at my side with a tumbler of amber liquid, somehow sensing my need.

I accepted it gratefully, letting the whiskey's fire trace a burning path down my throat, savoring its warmth. "Thank you," I mouthed against his neck.

One by one, they signed the thick folders. The legal language within the document promised severe consequences should they break confidentiality about what happens here today.

Cedar's pen hesitated above the signature line.

"I've never signed anything this... intense," he murmured. Arik and Dakota exchanged glances, nodding in silent agreement.

Jaxon stayed behind me, his breath warm against my skin. "Well done, songbird," he whispered, lips brushing my temple.

The endearment melted through me, drawing an involuntary smile as my eyelids fluttered. He pressed a kiss to my skin before retreating to the kitchen.

I settled back into my chair and drew a steadying breath. "I stopped breathing for three minutes after an accident."

From the kitchen came the sound of something being set down too forcefully. Jaxon's jaw visibly tightened, though he remained silent.

"After that, I was in a coma for three days. And then..."

"How are you still alive?" Dakota interrupted, leaning forward.

"What do you mean?"

"My girlfriend follows everything you do," he said, voice softening. "She told me you had an accident, and then you just... vanished."

"Yes, well..." I hesitated, weighing my options.

My eyes were fixed on my design in the center of the table.

The story of what I think happened lived behind a wall I'd built carefully, brick by brick. Even those closest to me had only glimpsed what lay beyond it: the pain, the resentment, the anger that still smoldered beneath my skin.

There's something about this, being pinned down, skin exposed, that loosens things I keep buried.

“I don’t know why I am telling you this, but I spent three months in the hospital afterward." I trace the rim of my glass with my fingertip. "Three minutes without breath. Three days unconscious. Three broken ribs. Two broken legs and a broken arm. The number is following me.”

The air thickens as four pairs of eyes bore into me, pupils dilated with hunger for truth. Even Jaxon's gaze has turned predatory.

"Ellia," Arik's voice drops to a dangerous whisper, his knuckles whitening as he leans forward, "why did someone tell Riley this design was for Kingston Sage?"

His jaw tightens. "We know exactly who that is."

Cedar and Dakota close in until I'm drowning in their scents, cigarette smoke clinging to fabric, spiced cologne masking sweat. Their breath mingles with mine.

"Ellia never had an accident," Jaxon announces, stalking toward the metal chair where he once claimed me, each footfall deliberate as a hunter.

"Jaxon!" My voice cracks like glass.

His lips curl into a cruel smile.

"They signed their lives away," he says, eyes never leaving mine. "This one can't even whisper your name to his precious girlfriend without destroying everything he has." His finger jabs toward Dakota like a weapon.

I hold Jaxon's gaze as I say the words: "I am Kingston Sage."

The silence that follows tells me everything, no need to look at their faces to confirm their shock. I turn slowly toward the three artists, these men who now hold pieces of a truth I've guarded fiercely.

I rest my chin on my hand. "I assume you're familiar with Kingston Sage's reputation."

The corner of my mouth lifts without humor. Their eyes tell me everything; they've heard the whispers, the rumors, but the flesh and blood woman before them remains a mystery they cannot fathom.

"Ellia Delvine and Kingston Sage," Arik says, measuring each syllable carefully, his gaze dissecting me. "Two legends occupying the same skin. That's... unexpected."

The name Kingston Sage carries weight in this city, but no one truly comprehends the extent of my influence and I prefer to keep it that way. The last man who believed he understood me ended up stealing what was mine before attempting to end my life.

Cedar runs a hand through his curls. "This is... a lot to process."

Beside him, Dakota leans forward until his knuckles blanch against the table edge. "My girlfriend practically worships you. She's the reason I even recognize your name."

A muscle in his jaw twitches. "She would absolutely freak if she knew I was sitting here right now."

His voice drops to barely above a whisper. "What's with all the cloak and dagger?"

I bite the inside of my cheek, wishing I'd parceled out these revelations more carefully. Before I can respond, Jaxon's voice cuts through the tension.

"She'll share what she chooses, when she chooses," he says, his gaze sweeping across each man like a searchlight.

I tap my finger against the design, drawing everyone's attention back to the paper.

"This piece," I say, my voice cutting through like a silver blade, "will start here."

I turn slightly, pulling the collar of my hoodie down to expose the vulnerable hollow at the nape of my neck where my spine begins its descent.

Dakota's eyes follow my fingertip, his expression shifting from confusion to professional interest.

"The wings will curve around my shoulders, following the architecture of my shoulder blades before hugging my ribs and tapering at my hips."

I trace the imaginary path in the air, my hands dancing to illustrate what words cannot.

"Not solid black, that would be wrong. This force I encountered was luminous, electric white, like lightning captured in human form. I need all three of you working in tandem, your needles synchronized except when we reach the more... intimate areas."

Arik's eyes narrow, calculating. "That's easily seven hours of continuous work. The pain would be..."

He leaves the sentence unfinished, the implication hanging between us.

"Yes," I reply, my voice crystalline with certainty.

The memory of that otherworldly light coursed through me, making my decision absolute. Pain is temporary; this marking will be eternal.

Arik rises from his chair with a slow exhale. "Well, I'm intrigued. This feels like something straight out of a film." His laugh slices through the tension.

When I stand, Jaxon materializes beside me, his palm finding the small of my back.

"There will be no discussion on what you all are about to see," he states, voice hard as granite. "Anyone with objections can leave now."

The threat in his words hangs palpably in the air.

The three artists raise their hands in synchronized surrender.

"Jaxon," I whisper, a plea in my voice.

I pivot to face him and grasp my zipper, drawing it downward with deliberate slowness, trying to hide the tremors.

My gaze locks with his, my anchor in this moment of exposure. The hoodie slides off my shoulders, pooling around my wrists. Jaxon gently frees one arm, then steps aside.

Behind me, someone shifts their weight.

"The design would conceal most of these scars?" Cedar's question floats over my shoulder.

I turn my head just enough to meet his eyes and give a single, definitive nod.

Dakota's gaze shifts to Jaxon before settling back on me. "Would it be all right if I examined the canvas?"

His fingers hover inches from my skin as Jaxon's throat vibrates with a low warning sound. His eyes locked on his.

"Jaxon," I hiss through clenched teeth, "stand down. You're suffocating everyone."

"Yes," I whisper, my permission barely audible.

Three pairs of hands descend on my bare skin, fingertips tracing, mapping, claiming.

My body betrays me with a violent shudder, and Jaxon's jaw locks, a muscle pulsing at his temple as he watches these strangers' hands explore what he considers his.

I fix my gaze on the concrete floor, counting cracks while strange hands brand me with their heat. My pulse hammers in my throat, as Cedar's voice cuts through the fog: "I'll take the spine, you two handle the..."

"Wings." The word tears from my lips with absolute conviction. I whip my head up to face them. "They are wings."

Cedar leans closer, his breath warm against my shoulder. "An angel?"

My laugh is brittle, sharp-edged. "After what you've witnessed today, this will hardly sound insane."

I take a deep breath, still focusing on the cracks in the floor. "It's my guardian, at least I think it is, this force that cradled me when death's icy fingers reached for me. This electricity that showed me everything I'd been blind to."

I lock eyes with Jaxon, watching something raw and primal battle behind his stare.

"This being didn't threaten me. Even as I hovered between worlds, I wasn't afraid." I snatch up my drawing, thrusting it forward like evidence in a trial. "This saved me when nothing else could."

The room falls into a heavy silence, everyone absorbing my words. Jaxon's arms encircle me from behind, a living shield against unseen dangers. The stillness shatters when the massive television screen in the living area suddenly illuminates.

CHAPTER 38

ELLIA

"August" flashes across the display.

It's the middle of the night where he is, but August has never respected time zones when it comes to reaching Jaxon or me.

He'll spring awake at any hour, from restlessness, dreams about me, or just wanting updates. His midnight calls have sparked more than one heated exchange between him and Jenkins.

I slip free from Jaxon's protective embrace and move to the couch. A few taps on my tablet, and August's face fills the screen.

"Hey, baby girl," he says, voice dripping with honeyed affection. "Been missing that voice of yours."

"Hey, August," I respond, feeling heat rise to my cheeks as I perch on the oversized ottoman to meet his gaze.

I'm aware he can see nearly everything, the entire loft except for the bathroom and closet tucked behind walls.

"Must be the middle of the night for you."

His attention shifts to the men behind me, eyes narrowing. "Jaxon, who the hell are these guys?" The question comes sharp as a blade.

Jaxon moves to stand behind the sectional.

"Ellia," August says, my name carrying the weight of demand.

Jaxon rubs his face wearily. "Yes, I'm not thrilled about it either, but when Ellia sets her mind on something..."

He leaves the sentence hanging.

The three artists shift uncomfortably under August's digital glare.

"August," I interject, "meet Cedar, Arik, and Dakota. They're going to tattoo me."

I cross my arms. "And I'd appreciate it if you both stopped talking about me like I'm not standing right here."

The artists drift toward Jaxon like magnets finding their pole. I extend my hand for my hoodie, suddenly conscious of my vulnerability, too much skin on display for comfort.

August's gaze travels the length of my body, his expression hardening with unspoken questions about why I'm standing there in just a sports bra and sweats, adding another layer of tension to an already charged room.

August's face hardens on the screen. "I'll be damned if they touch you, Ellia," he says, his accent thickening with every word.

A small laugh escapes me at his phrasing, another of his peculiar expressions. The way "mate" peppers his speech has become endearing to me, at least when he's not shouting it.

He hasn't realized we're in the UK yet, but with three locals hovering in my personal space, it won't take him long to figure it out.

I sigh and face the screen again. "August, they're professionals from the shop across the street."

His eyes dart between the men, suspiciously. "I own the shop," I add, voice tight. "So I know exactly who they are."

Behind me, I sense the artists shifting uncomfortably at this revelation, and August won't stop until he's satisfied; it's one thing I admire about him.

Beneath his easygoing exterior, the guy who calls everyone "mate" and laughs even in tense moments, lies a mind as sharp as Jaxon's, if less lethal. There's a depth to August that even Jaxon hasn't glimpsed.

Behind me, a voice, Cedar's, I think, asks, "What exactly do you mean by that?"

My chin drops to my chest. Another secret exposed before I'm ready, though at least they've all signed NDAs. Maybe this can stay contained.

"Riley's father is the owner," Cedar clarifies, his tone shifting from confusion to something like respect.

I slide off the ottoman and motion toward the seating area. "Let's all sit down," I suggest quietly.

The men arrange themselves around me, Jaxon pressing close to my side, Cedar and Arik settling across from us, while Dakota positions himself dead center, facing August's digital stare from the screen.

This sectional is enormous, big enough for all five of us to sit comfortably, with extra room to stretch out or add more bodies. I had it custom-made, just like most of my furniture across all my homes.

When you lie down, it feels like floating on a cloud: the plush white fabric, the cushions that swallow you whole. Of course, it's a nightmare to clean if anything spills.

I used to have the same model in my Nashville loft above the other bar I own, only that one was black. Michael managed to ruin it more than once with his food and drinks.

Honestly, Michael wrecked a lot of my stuff and always blamed his clumsiness. That loft, thankfully, doesn't exist anymore.

I scan everyone's faces: August leaning back with his massive, tanned arms crossed; Jaxon beside me, still glaring at the men across from us; and the artist, looking equal parts confused and intrigued.

"I...no," I pause. "Kingston owns half the shop. Years ago, Riley's father reached out because his place was failing."

All eyes stay locked on me, so I keep talking. "I'd opened Obsidian just a couple of years earlier, the spot where the elite gather regularly."

"Yes, we know," Arik says, waving his hand between us. "We've tried to get in on public nights more than once, dressed to code, and still got turned away."

Obsidian is one-of-a-kind. Plenty have tried to replicate it and failed. The membership price alone would leave anyone gasping for air. But I have my reasons.

"Allan was struggling to attract clientele a few years after taking over. His artists were either too high to handle simple tattoos or packed the shop with their friends. Anyone looking for a tattoo would walk away if they saw people standing all around, and that's exactly what was happening. So," I draw a deep breath, "after rebranding most of the businesses on these blocks," I gesture broadly, "Allan wanted the same. I won't bore you with the logistics, but once his rebrand was complete, I stayed on as a silent partner."

They all look like deer in headlights. Mouths wide open, unmoving. Like this other small secret froze them in place. Even with their inked arms crossed over their chests, they look like statues carved from belief.

"Where are you, Ellia?" August snaps, agitated.

"You know we can't tell you that, August," Jaxon says, leaning forward, elbows on his knees.

Hours have passed as I've laid out the full extent of my reach, known only to the men in this room. The three newcomers nod as if they understand, but I can tell they'll go home and chew this over. Once it fully sinks in, they'll realize the power I wield, and now they're part of it, too.

On the screen, August's jaw tightens with each word I exchange with Cedar and the others. His eyes narrow when Arik leans forward to ask a question, and I catch the subtle flex of his forearm muscles when Dakota laughs at something I say.

I know exactly what he's thinking, that I'm collecting men like trading cards. But he's wrong. Once the ink is on my skin, these three will fade from my life like everyone else.

CHAPTER 39

JAXON

The guys finally left, their faces a mixture of confusion and lingering fascination with Ellia. My blood had been boiling with each glance they stole in her direction.

August remained glued to the video call throughout, his predatory gaze tracking Ellia's every movement like a hawk stalking prey.

In all my years knowing August, I've witnessed his territorial nature, but with Ellia, it's different, raw, unfiltered, absolute.

His usual playful demeanor vanished the moment they addressed her, replaced by something cold and calculating.

They bombarded her with questions, invasive, dangerous questions. Every answer she gave made my jaw clench tighter. NDAs are just paper barriers; desperate men will shatter them for the right price.

Later, after I'd claimed her so thoroughly, she collapsed into exhaustion, and I dove into investigating these potential threats.

Her security infrastructure is breathtaking, a digital fortress that makes my own systems seem primitive.

The web of domains, registered under other aliases she constructed, creates an impenetrable shield.

"Kingston Sage can't own everything," she had explained, her voice still husky from our encounter. "It would raise flags."

Flags? She commands a global empire that spans continents. The authorities should tremble at her name, not the other way around.

I tore into the shop's history like a man possessed. Allan, Riley's father, is fifty-something with salt-and-pepper stubble and calloused hands that have built and lost businesses before Ink Link.

His previous ventures thrived until he gambled everything on this godforsaken street where foot traffic evaporated like morning dew.

When Obsidian rose, casting its shadow over the neighborhood and drawing the elite like moths to flame, Ink Link withered. The wealthy wanted their bodies pristine, untouched, canvases for designer clothes, not art.

The rebrand changed everything. My screen blazed with evidence, clients from Tokyo to Berlin suddenly craving their specific style.

I scrutinized Arik, their first hire: Birmingham-bred, early thirties, no siblings to ground him. His rap sheet glowed on my monitor: DUIs that should have landed him behind bars, connections that kept him free.

Cedar came next, Riley's live-in. Four years, one daughter, no ring. Clean record, but reeking of secrets. He'd emerged from Scarce Ink in Birmingham, the same underground den that spawned Arik. Coincidence? Fucking unlikely.

Ellia's facial recognition software made child's play of their digital footprint. Within heartbeats, their lives exploded across the living room display, sweaty nightclubs, chemical-hazed raves, and intimate gatherings where they let their guards down.

Dakota haunted these images like a specter, childhood bonds evident in every casual touch. His stint at Static Ink near Leeds and high school sweetheart notwithstanding, I couldn't shake the primal dread.

Two committed, one single, those weren't odds I liked when Ellia was the prize; they might be eyeing.

My phone vibrates relentlessly with August's messages, each one more demanding than the last. His obsession with Ellia mirrors my own, a visceral need to dissect every detail of her existence.

"Why these three specifically?" he demands. The answer lies locked behind those mesmerizing eyes of hers, a secret I'm determined to extract.

I trust her instincts, but blind faith isn't in my nature.

The whisper of fabric draws my attention as Ellia emerges through the cascading deep blue curtains that separate her sleeping sanctuary from the rest of the loft.

"What are you doing?" she asks, her voice cutting through my thoughts.

The space she's created leaves me breathless, minimalist yet decadent. When I'd questioned the absence of doors, she'd fixed me with that penetrating stare that makes my spine straighten.

"I've never needed walls here," she'd explained, demonstrating how the diaphanous curtains retract completely into the ceiling, transforming the entire floor into one boundless domain.

The massive stained-glass window behind her bed now stands partially open, early morning air carrying the scent of rain and possibility into her lair.

My voice comes out as a low growl. "I needed to know exactly who these men are that can't take their eyes off what's mine."

I track her movement across the room, predatory grace, silent as a shadow. She slides beside me on the sectional, her body heat radiating against my skin. My fingers hover over the tablet, itching for more information, more control.

Her thigh presses against mine as she assumes that defensive position I've memorized, one leg tucked beneath her, the other pulled protectively to her chest like armor. A warrior's stance disguised as casual repose. My lungs constrict at her proximity.

When she places her hand over mine, her touch burns through me. "May I?"

The request ignites something primal in my core.

I surrender the tablet, transfixed as her fingers dance across the screen with lethal precision. The massive display suspended from the industrial rafters floods with their exposed lives, photographs, documents, leases, their existence laid bare before us.

Her voice cuts through the tension. "I selected them for their exceptional talent. Their backgrounds, their choices, irrelevant. I never anticipated becoming the catalyst for their transformation."

Her fingers halt their relentless assault on the screen, and she directs my attention with a deliberate gesture.

"Every one of them is bound by ironclad terms. This is standard procedure for all my investments. They maintain specific personas, attract international clientele, and generate substantial media exposure. And most critically..." her eyes lock with mine, unflinching, "... they cannot violate what they've signed."

I rise to my feet, drawn to the document illuminated on the screen like a moth to flame.

I scan the document, my eyes catching on key phrases. After five years, they must leave the nest and open their own shops.

Kingston Sage, Ellia, doesn't keep them. She launches them. She'll provide startup money, connections, and even branding help if they ask. No ownership unless they specifically want her involved, and even then, she takes the minority position. If they succeed, they buy her out completely. If they fail, she reclaims everything.

The final lines hit like a thunderbolt: "This agreement exists to cultivate excellence, not dependency. Absolute. Non-negotiable. Enforceable without limitation."

Her arms coil around my neck from behind like a serpent claiming territory, her body heat scorching against my skin as she balances atop the ottoman. Towering over me now, like a goddess surveying her domain.

"I salvage the drowning," she whispers, her breath hot against my ear. "Arik was spiraling into oblivion while his mother withered from cancer. He'd mark any flesh that paid, bikers, addicts, teenagers with fake IDs, desperate to fund treatments that were devouring their family whole."

Her fingers trace my collarbone possessively.

"Cedar had raw talent buried beneath poverty. The same filthy streets that forged Arik and Dakota shaped him, too. His needlework was exquisite, but galleries of skin closed their doors to him while Riley's womb swelled and debt collectors circled like vultures."

She presses her lips against my crown, a benediction that brands me and my hands capture her wrists beneath my chin, feeling her pulse hammer against my fingertips.

"And Dakota," her voice drops to something reverent and terrible, "watched the love of his life fade in sterile hospital rooms, tethered to machines while her family crumbled under mountains of medical debt. He refused to abandon her, even as it destroyed everything else he'd built."

I am in awe of this woman. She's a revelation, a force of nature disguised in human form. The way she elevates everyone in her orbit, as if their success were oxygen to her lungs.

"Let me show you something," she whispers, extending her hand.

I help her down as she throws open the massive stained glass windows, jewel-toned light fracturing across her skin as we step onto the secluded balcony.

"You see those apartments?"

She gestures toward the buildings I've scrutinized countless times, memorizing every entrance, exit, and shadow. The same structures where her artists create their lives like canvases.

"Yes," I murmur, drawing her against me until I feel her heartbeat echoing through my chest.

She tilts her face upward, vulnerability softening her usually impenetrable gaze.

"They all live above the shop. Completely rent-free."

My brow knits together, confusion tugging at me.

"Within months, their crushing debts vanished. Every last cent."

I tuck a strand of hair behind her ear.

"I watch them because their beginnings were barren, where mine was abundant," she continues, her voice taking on a reverent quality. "I witnessed Dakota's woman bloom again, illness retreating from her body until her skin glowed with life."

She indicates windows several units down. "I saw Arik with his mother, through her good days and her awful ones. When her body began its ultimate surrender, he brought her here, hired round-the-clock care so she could die with dignity."

"Ellia..." Her name catches in my throat like a prayer too sacred to complete.

This woman has infiltrated my defenses, colonized my heart with surgical precision. The way she orchestrates miracles from shadows, never once stepping into the light to claim credit.

"And Cedar," she continues, "has claimed the back apartment, though he's rarely there. Most nights, he's battling virtual worlds with Arik and Dakota, building the brotherhood he never had."

She just answered every question I never voiced about these three men, yet something primal and possessive still coils inside me like a viper. The mere thought of their hands on her skin, even professionally, sends white-hot rage coursing through my veins.

I would shatter each knuckle, snap every finger joint if I caught even a hint of inappropriate contact. I'd make them regret the day they first held a tattoo gun.

"Are you and August going to calm down now?" she asks, her voice slicing through my violent fantasy like a blade through flesh.

My gaze burns into the apartment, cataloging every shadow, every potential threat. When I turn back to her, exhaustion claims her, a yawn that reveals the vulnerability I've wrung from her body hours earlier.

The memory of her beneath me ignites my blood all over again, her skin marked, claimed, conquered. Mine. The scent of her surrender still clings to my senses, driving me half-mad with possessive hunger.

"Come on, let's get you to bed." I capture the corner of her mouth as another yawn breaks free.

For weeks now, she only sleeps peacefully when caged within my arms. The instant I withdraw, terror finds her again.

Twice this week alone, while hunting Michael and Robyn through digital shadows, I've had to wrench her from nightmares that leave her drenched in cold sweat, her screams tearing through the darkness, her mind trapped in horrors I cannot reach.

Her nightmares have infected me. They stalk my thoughts even in daylight. I've demanded she share them, but some terrors she guards like precious wounds. She permits only this, my arms as fortress walls until the trembling subsides.

I guide her through the bedroom's towering windows, nineteen feet of architectural defiance.

Someday she'll design our fortress, our sanctuary. August can protest, but his aesthetic sensibilities are as barren as that Australian compound he occupies, my design that Ellia correctly identified as soulless, desperately needing her touch.

CHAPTER 40

JAXON

By morning's first light, she's still tangled in my arms, her head nestled against my chest, one leg thrown over mine, the thin fabric of my boxers stretched tight around my hardened cock, begging to be freed.

Her breathing is slow but deliberate, a reminder that she's still deep in sleep, so I lie perfectly still, eyes tracing the dark lattice of industrial rafters overhead as I steel myself for the day's battles.

Jenkins will be calling in any second. Last night, he and his team swept every inch of her apartment's exterior when three strangers slipped in.

He was furious at first, all sharp edges and instinct. Delta Force never really leaves you. I could see it in the way his body locked, the way his eyes tracked exits before faces. Breach, clear, eliminate.

It was written into him deeper than bone. But once I told him who had come through and why, the tension bled out slowly, controlled. Not gone. Just leashed.

High alert is why he's still here.

We met before the world got quiet. Before sleep turned into something you had to survive. I'd been pulled out of nowhere—no warning, no choice—and dropped into a unit that was supposed to feel like family. It didn't. It felt like a countdown. Men in, men out. Some transferred. Most didn't make it that far.

I thought I'd spend my life behind a screen, chasing ghosts through code, working in the shadows where damage could be contained.

Instead, I learned how to kick in doors and pull people from the fire while leaving others behind in pieces. Eight years of it. Missions that didn't exist. Names we weren't allowed to remember.

Jenkins was the only thing that stayed the same.

When the nightmares started, we made a deal—no disappearing, no pretending we were fine. No matter where we ended up, we checked in.

Because we both knew how easy it was to slip. To stop answering. To become one of the ghosts we used to hunt.

I got out thinking I'd finally be done with it. I was wrong.

Turns out the world doesn't stop needing men like us. It just changes the rules. No flag. No chain of command. Just a list of names and the kind of money that makes people look the other way. Same work. Different justification.

A soft rustle beneath me: she's waking. Her lips brush over my chest in a lazy, possessive kiss, yanking my mind back to the here and now.

"Good morning," she murmurs, voice rough like gravel, the kind of voice that could reduce the toughest man to jelly.

I press a gentle kiss to her temple, then reach for the laptop as it springs to life, Jenkins, right on cue.

"Everything was clear last night," Jenkins says, his tone clipped, no room for fluff. "No unexpected guests after the initial sweep."

"Appreciate it," I reply, throat tight. "What about Michael? Any trace? And how's August holding up? I know he's brewing trouble."

"Michael's gone dark. As for Robyn, she was spotted at Sydney Airport but vanished in the underground lot. The camera's been sabotaged; someone snipped the wires. We're combing every outbound vehicle, but she could be hiding in a trunk."

I let the silence stretch. Jenkins doesn't sugarcoat.

"We need August cleared to travel. Get into his doctor's files, erase any sign of instability."

"Already on it, Jaxon."

Only Jenkins calls me by my first name. After nearly dying together too many times, he earned that right. The rest stick to "sir" or "Mr. Carver" until they prove they'd shield her or me from a bullet as without question as Jenkins would.

"What about his team obligations?" I demand.

Jenkins' mouth twists into a grim smile. "Peters is 'rearranging' some things," he says, fingers carving air quotes. "August hasn't been made aware of the changes."

"Good. Keep it that way. He'd break free before we could get him cleared. Alert me the moment everything's in order; we'll need to manipulate his flight path."

"Consider it done," Jenkins replies, then the screen goes black.

Through the gossamer curtains veiling her sanctuary, I watch Ellia in the kitchen. Steam rises from the coffeemaker as she stretches for mugs, her movements liquid grace despite everything.

My shirt hangs from her shoulders like a flag of conquest, and insists my scent anchors her when I leave to hunt.

Beneath, she wears thin sweatpants that conceal the battlefield of scars mapping her legs. Scars I've claimed with my lips, my hands, my worship.

Michael will never have the satisfaction of knowing he marked her first; those scars belong to me now.

Observing her has become my obsession. The way she moves through space is as if reclaiming territory.

The determined set her jaw as she reclaimed her mind from the past year's torture. The almost imperceptible hitch in her left hip, invisible to anyone who hasn't memorized every millimeter of her body as I have.

I remember her face when Doc Kirkland delivered his verdict: permanent damage, learn to live with it. I'd cornered that same surgeon against a wall later, my forearm crushing his windpipe as I demanded he fix what she wanted fixed.

She refused to let white coats dictate her limitations. Not once did she surrender to tears over her broken body. Instead, she attacked physical therapy with military precision, shattering every timeline they set.

Where they prescribed management, she demanded recovery. When the three casts finally came off, what emerged wasn't a victim; it was a warrior queen rising from the ashes of her own destruction.

Morning light slices through the stained-glass window like fractured rainbows. I haul myself out of bed and head into the stainless-steel kitchen. She's already there, pouring coffee into two black mugs, every movement precise. She hands me one, serene as a sniper.

"You look calm this morning," I say, tilting my head.

A smirk curves her lips. A soft laugh, and her cheeks flushed rose. "Thank you. I have something for you." She turns toward the closet, mug in hand. I follow without question.

The closet spans the loft's back wall, racks overflowing with clothes, shoes, glinting jewelry, pure Ellia style. She slides the edge of a shelf; the wall groans open.

I suck in air. "You're full of secrets."

Without a word, she guides me inside a hidden safe room. She hands me a USB drive.

"Everything I have on Robyn and Michael," she whispers. "My system couldn't trace them past their early twenties. Robyn went to school with me; you knew that. Michael's records vanish the same way. It's like they never existed."

She stares at her feet, gripping her mug, her other hand clenched behind her back.

I seize her chin with bruising tenderness. "We'll find them. And when we do, they won't know what hit them. Understood?"

She nods, eyes fierce.

"That's my girl." I crush my lips to hers. Her mouth parts, coffee and morning on her tongue.

I pull back and survey the room. Fifteen feet of secrets.

To my right, velvet boxes in neat towers, thirty at least, in black, blue, red. Straight ahead, stacks of cash: dollars, euros, Australian notes, enough to drown in.

She lingers in the doorway, watching.

To my left, supercomputers hum. Screens flicker with live security footage. Lines of code scroll in fluorescent streams, hard drives blink in syncopated rhythm.

"This is Solace," she whispers. "At least that's what I call it." My gaze is glued to the pulsating lights.

She pushes off the door frame, crosses the room in two swift strides, lifts her mug to her lips, then slams a hidden switch.

Alarms scream, red lights stab the darkness, a digital timer counts down from twenty.

"What the hell is this?" I demand.

Her eyes blaze. “If I detect a threat, every line of code, every secret, will be wiped clean. Irreversible.”

She slams another button; alarms die, lights shift to green. “I keep backups somewhere that’s not here. But if the firewalls fall, this whole system self-destructs. I’m untraceable here.”

She leans in, voice cold steel. “I know what you’re thinking, Jaxon. Why would I sabotage my empire from anywhere on the planet?”

I follow her out of the safe room into the living space without looking back.

“I found out Michael had been stealing from me for months,” she says, stopping in her tracks.

She lowers herself into a chair and adds, “Then I learned he was seeing Robyn behind my back.”

“You knew?” I burst out, rounding the table to stand before her. “Why the hell didn’t you tell me? If you’d warned me sooner, none of this would’ve happened.”

I start pacing, my mind racing through all the things I should have done, things she kept quiet. I halt, hands gripping the back of a metal chair as I lean in. I shouldn’t be furious, but I am.

She sips her coffee and continues, “At first, it was small, cash lying around, a piece of jewelry gone. Just enough that anyone would blame it on misplacing.”

I circle the table and sit down. “Ellia.”

She snaps, “Don’t call me that. You only use it when you’re mad.”

She’s right, I hate her name on my lips like this.

“It was simple,” she says more softly. “I left one of my accounts open on my studio laptop. Michael knew I stored digital lyrics and unreleased songs there.”

“Your secret songbook?” I rest my hands on the table, bracing for another secret to blow.

She stabs the air with her index finger. "That's it exactly. I started storing my drafts there, and suddenly, funds began disappearing. The account was so small I didn't catch it until you pointed out those discrepancies in Australia. He emptied it, probably planning his escape, but..." She stops abruptly.

There's more she isn't telling me. I can sense it like a storm front approaching. She pulls one leg beneath her, shoulders rigid with unspoken tension. I rise to top off her coffee.

While I pour, she continues. "That night on the mountain, I was ready to call him out. But he flipped the script, confessing while he pinned everything on Robyn. Said she was the mastermind behind targeting that specific account."

I set the pot on the stainless-steel bar. "What do you mean?"

She sighs, lifting the mug to her lips. "I intended to confront Robyn when we got back. I even wanted you there, in case she got hostile. But I never made it that far."

She laughs, but it sounds empty. "Everything's on that drive. You'll see it all. Yet I still can't figure out why Michael came after me. He got forty million, and Robyn. She has him and the money now. I thought I knew her. We were best friends in high school."

She shakes her head, as if trying to shake off the pain of their betrayal.

This woman and her goddamn secrets, they're a labyrinth with no exit. I drag my fingers through my hair, yanking until pain sparks across my scalp.

My blood thunders in my ears. Every revelation she drops is another piece of a puzzle I can't solve, expanding in all directions. This isn't just about stolen money or betrayal. Robyn hunted her specifically, knew something about her, something I might still be blind to.

"I need a shower," I mutter, already stalking back through her closet, my jaw clenched so tight my teeth might shatter.

My thoughts race like bullets. I should be out there hunting them down myself. They'll extract whatever information they need from her, then discard her like trash. The image of her body, broken and abandoned, slams into me with physical force.

I'll die before I let that happen. She's the oxygen in my lungs, the reason I didn't put a gun in my mouth after Dave, my former team leader and her ex-bodyguard, retired.

CHAPTER 41

ELLIA

The scene unfolded much as I had anticipated. After Jaxon retreated to the shower, the loft filled with the pulsating rhythm of music blasting from the surround speakers, as I began to clean up the remnants of our coffee conversation.

The mugs clinked softly as I gathered them, and the coffee pot gurgled gently as I rinsed it, before placing it back under the stainless steel open cabinets.

The open design allowed the appliances to be both aesthetically pleasing and easily accessible, a look I truly loved.

This space had transformed into Jaxon's culinary domain, where he reigned supreme over lunch and dinner. I possessed the ability to cook, yet he insisted on shouldering the responsibility alone, a desperate grasp at control in a world where he felt it slipping away.

Jaxon, my steadfast protector long before our mountain refuge, had replaced Dave with a palpable sadness clinging to him. I never dared to pry, only stealing glances when he wasn't aware, witnessing the silent battle he waged with his demons.

But gradually, like the first rays of dawn breaking through the darkest night, life returned to Jaxon's eyes. His deep green irises lightened, as if death itself had retreated from his doorstep.

Those once haunted eyes became an object of my fascination. Jaxon was a fortress, his emotions locked away, inaccessible. He moved with the predatory grace of a hunter, his feelings as elusive as his prey.

Before that fateful night, I wore a permanent smile, a mask to conceal the tumultuous emotions roiling beneath. The world saw me as a golden-hearted sweetheart, ready to give the very shoes off my feet. Literally.

My team, exasperated by my impulsive generosity, learned to keep sensible replacements at the ready. Their glares and snarky comments in private dressing rooms were battles they often lost.

Pushing off the cool counter, I made my way toward the shower. The music grew louder with each step, the beat pulsating through the air like a living entity. I shed my clothes piece by piece, the steam from the bathroom billowing out like a welcoming embrace.

I opened the door silently, revealing Jaxon in all his glory. Leaning against the door frame, I admired the sight before me. The song "One Way or Another" by Giorgio Moroder played overhead, the rhythmic beat echoing off the tiles.

His perfectly chiseled back was to me, one hand braced against the tile as water cascaded down his muscular frame. I felt an instant heat between my thighs, a primal response to the raw masculinity on display. His other hand moved rhythmically along his length, a growl escaping his lips as his head bowed forward.

My hand traced a path across my waist, descending to the aching need between my legs. My index finger circled my swollen clit, matching the tempo of his strokes.

A primal moan escaped him before he rasped, “Elli.”

Propelled by desire, I crossed the bathroom in urgent strides as I shed my panties. His back still faced me, rivulets of water tracing paths down his tattooed skin. I slid open the glass door, the steam enveloping me like a lover's embrace.

He didn't falter, his hand still moving with deliberate precision. Turning his head slightly, his eyes met mine, wide and burning with a heat that mirrored my own.

My hands find his perfectly inked back, tracing the dark patterns that disappear beneath rivulets of water. His eyes stay locked with mine over his shoulder, heavy-lidded and hungry, following my every touch as if memorizing the sensation.

A primal growl escapes his lips when my fingernails rake lightly down his slick skin. My hands stroke from his sides to his taut abdomen, feeling every perfect muscle clench beneath my exploring touch, his body responding to mine like an instrument tuned only for my fingers.

I trace my lips across his shoulder blade, tasting salt and steam on his skin. My hands explore the hard planes of his back, fingertips memorizing each ridge of muscle.

As I slide around him, my breasts brush against his wet skin, sending electricity through my core. His dark green eyes, heavy with desire, lock onto mine as I bite my lower lip, barely containing the sounds threatening to escape my throat.

I guide my fingers along the sculpted curve of his side, up his shoulder, then down his tensed arm. Tangling my other hand in his wet hair, I pull his mouth to mine, our tongues meeting in a desperate dance.

His groan vibrates against my lips as my hand trails down his neck, following the dark lines of his tattoos.

My fingers find his hand wrapped around his thick, throbbing cock. I join him, our fingers intertwining as we stroke together, feeling him pulse and swell against my palm.

His breath hitches, a primal sound of pleasure escaping into my mouth as I feel him growing harder, the veins prominent beneath my touch.

With a soft motion, Jaxon backs me against the shower wall, the cool tiles sending a shiver across my feverish skin. As his grip loosens, I take control, my fingers encircling his rigid arousal with deliberate pressure.

His cock throbs against my palm, slick droplets forming at the tip with each beat of his pulse. I collect this liquid proof of his need on my thumb, then raise it to my lips unhurriedly.

When my tongue flicks out for a taste, his eyes grow hooded and intense, watching me sample the salt-sweet evidence of what I do to him.

"You are perfect for me," he growls against the sensitive shell of my ear, his voice vibrating through my body like a physical caress.

His powerful hands grip my hips, pressing me harder against the tile as water cascades between our bodies.

I close the last inch between us, my hand firmly stilling his movements.

"I need to feel every inch of you," I whisper, my lips brushing against the rough stubble of his jaw. "Right now."

His breath catches as I take a half-step forward, just enough to let my fingers encircle him again, my thumb tracing the sensitive ridge beneath.

"Tell me what you want," he demands, voice ragged with desire.

"Everything," I breathe against his mouth. "I want everything."

His hands braced on either side of my head, trapping me against the slick wall. Still stroking his length. The pressure of his gaze made me dizzy.

"You like making me crazy?" he whispered, the words so low and hoarse they were almost a snarl.

Never releasing his throbbing shaft, I surrender to my knees, the shower's cascade drenching my skin. His eyes, dark with primal hunger, claim me as his own while he positions himself above me, one powerful forearm braced against the tile to shield my face from the torrent.

My tongue traces the swollen head, savoring his salt and musk like a sacrament.

"Perfect," he growls, fingers twisting in my soaked hair, commanding my mouth to take him deeper.

His hips thrust forward, possessive and demanding, as he claims my throat. I yield completely to his dominance, my body existing solely for his pleasure, craving the sweet surrender of being utterly, completely owned.

He claims my throat inch by relentless inch, each thrust deeper than the last until I'm choking around his length.

Tears stream down my cheeks as my throat stretches to accommodate him, this magnificent invasion I've surrendered to completely.

My tongue traces the throbbing vein underneath as he fists my hair tighter, marking me as his property.

"That fucking mouth belongs to me," he growls, his voice primal with possession.

His hips jerk forward when I hollow my cheeks and suck harder, drinking down the salty evidence of his arousal.

The knowledge that I alone can reduce him to this savage state of need makes me dizzy with power even as I submit.

"Touch that pussy, my pussy," he commands, voice rough as gravel. "Show me how wet you get choking on my cock."

My fingers find my drenched folds instantly.

"Eyes locked on mine while you pleasure what's mine."

His gaze devours me, branding both my stare and the dripping heat between my thighs as his property alone.

My sex clenches violently at his possession, drenching my fingers with the evidence of my absolute submission.

"Feed me what belongs to me," he demands, voice thick with ownership.

I gather the slick evidence of my need, fingertips glistening as I reluctantly abandon my swollen clit that aches for release.

He seizes my wrist, his grip possessive enough to leave tomorrow's bruises, and draws my fingers between his parted lips.

The wet heat of his mouth engulfs me as his tongue slides between each digit, his eyes never leaving mine as he tastes my essence.

His throat vibrates with a primal sound as he sucks harder, drawing my fingers deeper, claiming even this small part of me with devastating intimacy.

He releases my fingers with a primal sound, saliva and arousal connecting us momentarily.

"Your cunt will surrender to me, you will come only when I flood your throat," he growls against my palm.

His grip in my hair becomes painful perfection, immobilizing me completely. I can only flutter my lashes in desperate submission, silently begging him to use me harder.

"My little songbird," he moans. "Look what you do to me."

My consciousness narrows to his possession, his voice claiming my mind, his cock owning my throat, his dominance conquering my will. I exist only to be filled by him, consumed by him, destroyed and remade by him.

He brutalizes my throat with savage thrusts, claiming my mouth as his personal fuck-toy while my fingers desperately work my dripping cunt at his commanded pace.

My jaw aches deliciously as his cock swells impossibly larger, the veins pulsing against my tongue as his rhythm fractures into animal need. My pussy clenches violently, hovering at the precipice of oblivion.

"Cum for me while I mark your throat as mine," he snarls, voice raw with dominance.

My entire body convulses in violent surrender, my consciousness fragmenting as my cunt spasms uncontrollably. I choke and gag around his massive intrusion as he roars his triumph, flooding my throat with hot, thick spurts that brand me from within.

"Take every fucking drop," he growls, holding my head immobile as his essence overflows my mouth, marking me as thoroughly used property.

His possessive hands cradle my skull as aftershocks ripple through my conquered body, my existence reduced to nothing but his vessel of pleasure.

Just as the last shock wave ravages my conquered body, he withdraws his length with deliberate slowness, leaving me hollow and desperate.

He yanks me to my feet by my hair, claiming my mouth with savage possession, his tongue invading the same throat he just defiled.

He devours every trace of his seed from my lips and chin, growling against my mouth like a predator reclaiming its kill.

"I can't believe you're mine," he snarls between brutal kisses, his hands branding ownership into my flesh. "Your body and soul was made for me."

I claw at his shoulders, trying to crawl inside him, to surrender the last fragments of my separate existence.

"Please," I whimper, "mark me everywhere."

His eyes darken with primal.

"By morning, your body won't remember belonging to anyone but me," he promises, voice thick with violent intent. "I'm going to claim and ruin every hole you have before those men arrive tomorrow. They'll smell my ownership all over you."

His hands claim my hair, fingers digging into my scalp as he works shampoo through the strands. I clean him with reverent strokes of the sponge while he turns me roughly to face the tile, pressing his hardening cock against the curve of my ass.

"Do you know how beautiful you are?" he growls, his palms possessing my breasts, my hips, between my thighs.

This force of a man who threatened violence to others now brands me with his touch.

"I'll kill any man who looks at what's mine," he whispers, his teeth grazing my earlobe as the sponge glides between my legs, lingering where I'm still sensitive and swollen.

"This cunt is mine to pleasure, mine to punish." His fingers replace the sponge, probing deeper.

There is no warning when he claims what belongs to him, his cock gathering my slickness as he positions himself at my entrance.

Blood wells from my lip as I bite down, desperate whimpers escaping my throat as I feel the brutal heat of him preparing to invade me.

One hand fists my hair, slamming my cheek against the cold tile, marking me as prey. His other hand spreads me open, his thumb circling my entrance with cruel precision.

I arch my ass back shamelessly, silently begging him to fill the aching void he's created within me, to stake his ownership in my most intimate flesh.

"Please," I sob, pride annihilated by need. "Please claim me...mark me...own me..."

With savage possession, he impales me completely, stretching me beyond capacity as he brands me from within. My entire body convulses around his invasion, trembling in violent surrender as he stakes his claim on territory that will forever bear his mark.

My knees threaten to buckle as he pounds into me with brutal force, his massive cock hammering that secret spot deep inside that makes my vision blur with pleasure.

"You will carry my baby one day," he growls against my ear, his teeth grazing the sensitive skin. "Your belly swollen with my seed, your tits heavy with milk, a temple built to worship my legacy."

He hooks my knee over his forearm, spreading me open wider, my glistening sex exposed completely to his hungry gaze.

The haze of approaching orgasm clouds my mind as his thick cock drives deeper, hitting that spot that makes my walls clench violently around him.

The contraceptive hidden inside me feels like a secret weapon against my past as his body fills mine completely. For three years, I've carried this invisible barrier, this guarantee that no part of Michael would ever grow within me, binding us together beyond escape.

Now a cold realization crawls through me, paralyzing my thoughts even as my body responds to Jaxon with undeniable heat.

My pussy convulses violently, clamping down on his throbbing length as a scream tears from my throat. My orgasm rips through me with savage intensity, every muscle seizing as he continues his relentless assault.

His rhythm fractures, becoming desperate and primal as he drives deeper than ever before. His hot breath scorches my neck, his guttural roar vibrating against my skin as his cock pulses, flooding my insides with hot spurts of cum that seem endless.

Our ragged breathing mingles as we collapse against each other, my body still trembling with aftershocks.

We lingered in the shower, hands gentle on each other's skin, neither rushing to break the spell between us. I told him about my first broken bone, my father's garden, the tree house he had built.

Jaxon listened, offered small smiles, but volunteered nothing of his own. The fragments I've collected about him, empty liquor bottles lining his childhood home, split knuckles from fights that weren't worth remembering, a duffel bag packed on his seventeenth birthday, I've preserved each one carefully, precious as rare coins.

The rest remains locked away, classified information from years spent making people disappear for whoever could afford his services.

CHAPTER 42

ELLIA

Jaxon meticulously erased every trace of our shower encounter, wiping down the fogged glass and gathering discarded towels with practiced efficiency.

Steam still clung to the mirrors when the water ran ice-cold against my flushed skin. I stepped out with a shiver while he remained unfazed; the man could shower in Antarctic waters without flinching.

Jaxon hunched over his laptop, decrypting the USB I'd handed him earlier, while I drifted through my loft, fingertips trailing across instruments that gleamed in the afternoon light filtering through dust motes. Just left of my hidden closet entrance, my collection waited like old friends.

The honey-gold curves of my Martin D28 caught the light, its spruce top worn to a silken patina from thousands of strikes by my pick.

Beside it hung my Kingfish Delta Telecaster, electric blue with a lightning bolt scratch plate, bearing witness to countless three a.m. sessions.

I examined my hands. Calloused fingertips crisscrossed with thin white scars where steel strings had sliced through tender skin during marathon practices when emotion mattered more than physical pain.

My Kawai Casio digital piano commanded in front of a window that fractured sunlight into jewel-toned patterns across its polished ebony surface.

During sleepless nights, I'd sit there translating the symphony of the streets, taxi horns, drunken laughter from Obsidian's music, occasional sobs from the alley, into melodies that flowed from my fingers like confessions.

In the corner where exposed brick meets floor-to-ceiling windows sits my drum kit, its fire-engine red shells gleaming like a warning. Though my fingers itch to strike those taut skins, I resist.

Even the softest tap might carry through these windows, betraying the existence of my sanctuary, this hidden loft where I can disappear from the world below.

My memories spiral back to the nights I would scream every lyric, pour out every wound I carried.

"I'd kill to hear your voice," Jaxon calls from the oak table. His words sliced through my head like a fiery blade.

"You hear me every day," I murmur without turning around, though it isn't true.

Months passed without a single word from me. I was trapped in a prison of my own vicious thoughts, plotting revenge while my tongue lay useless.

Doctors seethed at my silence. My team's soft voices drifted over me unanswered. Even Jaxon, I ignored, though he was the only soul I longed to feel near.

In that hospital room, I was nothing but an observer: tubes in my arms, casts on my limbs, machines clattering like uncaring judges. I heard every diagnosis, every "best case" scenario as if I were a ghost haunting the bed.

Jaxon and August sat vigil, hour after heavy hour, shadows by my window. When August flew back to Australia, Jaxon never budged.

He slept in that chair, threatened violence if any nurse touched me again after the first time she flinched at my scars. His iron jaw softened only for me: wiping my hair from my face, pressing cool towels to my fevered skin.

He insisted on tending to my back wound himself, his hands gentle but his expression brooking no debate. I suspected it wasn't just about proper medical care; something possessive flickered in his eyes whenever the nurses approached me.

On the days Jaxon couldn't stay, August filled the silence with tales of home. His voice trembled like a cello's low note, and I clung to every word, anything to drown out the machines.

I fell in love with the shape of his stories, the way his words tremored with devotion for his family, his teammates, his friends.

"I haven't heard that singing in over a year," Jaxon murmurs now, stalking across the room in three long strides. "Only low hums as you write."

My chest tightens with the urge to answer him, but the shrill ping of the laptop cuts through the air.

"Jenkins?" Jaxon snarls, leaning in.

"Jaxon, we've got a situation. Robyn was spotted in August's neighborhood."

I'm across the room before I realize I've moved, each heartbeat a thunderclap in my ears. My fingers find my mouth, pressing hard enough to bruise as I crowd against Jaxon's back.

I make myself small behind his broad shoulders, straining to hear news that August remains untouched, beyond her reach.

"Ellia." Jenkins' tone is brittle steel.

"Tell me," Jaxon demands.

"There was a letter slipped into August's mail slot. It never went through the post; it must've been inserted with the daily delivery. No record, no postage. We suspect the mailman knows something, but..."

"The letter reads: 'I didn't mean to. You have to believe me. I'm sorry. I never meant to hurt you.' That's it. We have a team working the cipher, but..."

My blood runs cold. Jaxon rubs his face, glaring anywhere but at me. I know that look, his murderous calm.

Jaxon's hand slams onto the table, rattling cups like fallen soldiers. He still hasn't looked at me, his trademark fury. When he's murderous, he refuses my eyes; I've seen that cold war all year long.

"Extract August now," Jaxon snaps. "Handle his agent, clear his medical hold. He boards that plane." He rubs his face, fingers curling into fists.

Jenkins clears his throat. "The plane will be local by six A.M. He's packing now. I will get to work on his manifests."

"I need to talk to him," I choke out.

But Jaxon's glare severs me. "Not now, Ellia." His voice is final, like a guillotine dropping.

"Wait, why?" I say with an unsteady voice. "I need to know he is ok," my chin trembling faster under my hand.

"No, ma'am," Jenkins interrupts.

Jaxon stands silent, his eyes burning with an intensity that scorches the air between us, and the realization hits me like a physical blow.

This letter isn't just a message; it's a declaration. Robyn claims innocence? After she sabotaged my motorcycle, then stood watching from the shadows as metal twisted and my body broke against unforgiving pavement? After she walked away while I lay bleeding, my consciousness faded to black.

I spin away from them, a curse escaping through clenched teeth. Their voices dissolve into a distant hum as my pulse hammers against my temples.

I press my palms against my ears, desperate to silence the roaring tide of my blood. "Focus, Ellia," I whisper to myself, a mantra repeated with diminishing conviction.

The question lingers, unanswered: am I truly capable of handling this?

I find myself in my closet without remembering the decision to retreat there. The silence wraps around me like a shield against the chaos. Through the open doors, Jaxon's irritated voice rumbles, but I've already turned to Solace, my fingers dancing across multiple keyboards.

"Come on, girl, speak to me," I whisper as I access every CCTV feed around August's neighborhood, eyes scanning for any anomaly, any clue.

If Robyn is there, a camera had to have picked her up somewhere. She is working with Michael. She was up on that mountain in the selfie I took of Michael and me.

Minutes pass as Solace sifts through countless images until a match flashes on screen.

I bolt from the closet, information tumbling from my lips before I've fully processed it. "Silver BMW, plates NMT-78G!" Jaxon catches me mid-stride, steadying me against his chest.

"What?" His eyes dart to the open closet doors. "Elli, can you verify that?"

I nod rapidly, then hesitate, glancing at Jenkins on the video call. "My..." I stop myself.

Jenkins doesn't know about Solace, and Jaxon seems to understand immediately, muting the laptop and positioning himself to block the camera's view.

"He can't hear you now," he assures me.

I exhale slowly. "Silver BMW, four-door, plates NMT-78G. She was caught on camera returning to Crown Towers Sydney yesterday."

My hands steady on his biceps. "Solace found images of Robyn. I still can't find anything on Michael. Do you think she placed the note?" My question hangs in the air.

Jaxon's eyes soften momentarily. "That brilliant mind of yours," he murmurs, then his tone hardens. "You're going to show me everything, understand? No more secrets, Elli," he presses a kiss to my forehead before turning back to unmute the call.

As Jaxon relays the information to Jenkins, he demands to know the source, but Jaxon sidesteps the question expertly, his way of preserving this one thing that remains solely mine.

Jaxon terminates the call with a tap.

"Jenkins has dispatched a team to the hotel," he says, then fixes me with that steel-eyed stare. "Show me."

His voice is a controlled burn, the careful containment of a wildfire.

I lead him to Solace, my system still churning through feeds, traffic cameras, ATMs, security monitors, digital billboards.

The screens flicker with faces and license plates, each frame analyzed and discarded in milliseconds. My fingers hover over the keyboard.

"I can access almost anything with an internet connection," I explain, "except smartphones. That was my next project."

My fingers dance across the main keyboard in front of me. "Watch," I say, nodding toward the secondary console. "Take that one. Any demand you plug into the software, it will translate, even if it's a jumbled mess. I created that in case I need fast action with unsteady hands."

Time dissolves as I guide Jaxon through Solace's architecture, teaching him extraction protocols, access points, and command sequences. We fall into rhythm, four hands orchestrating a digital symphony across twin keyboards.

While Jaxon monitors his team sweeping the hotel, pulling security feeds from every angle, I tunnel deeper, tracing the letter's journey.

Something about the timing, the placement, Robyn had to be the one who slipped it into August's daily mail. I just need to prove it.

CHAPTER 43

JAXON

Dawn broke as Ellia finished combing through every algorithm in her arsenal, ensuring we'd left no corner of Sydney not surveilled.

The system pinged when it caught Robyn checking into a penthouse suite, but she'd vanished before our team could mobilize.

We tracked her through the city in fragments, losing her in blind spots, finding her again, until airport surveillance captured her boarding a private aircraft.

After slipping into the flight database, we traced her trip: Denver, Colorado, landing at first light. The Gulfstream G800 waited in the shadows, its sleek white hull visible on camera and in runway feeds, her name stood plain on the manifest, an encrypted truth hidden among layers of locked files.

As I make my way to my laptop on the center oak table, I look back over my shoulder to make sure she is still sound asleep.

This morning, I had to wrestle Ellia into our bed. Her mind teetered on the edge after August's confrontation over that letter; she blamed herself for never mentioning Solace and refused to let it go.

I found her pacing the loft at dawn, fingers shaking, eyes flickering like trapped birds. I coaxed her down with soft words, but she fought back tears I've only seen for the other man she loves.

She'd downed cup after cup of bitter black coffee until her body felt as hollow as her racing thoughts. Carrying her to the mattress was like hefting all her anxiety at once; I shouldered her gently and laid her down, then slipped back to the control station to triple-check our servers.

Every line she'd written had to perform perfectly; only her custom protocols could guide that system to every camera feed in and around that airport.

Even flat on her back, her brain kept tallying codes and coordinates. Ellia has never slept deeply; she writes through the night, chases bugs in her head, and ever since she fell on that summit, insomnia has been her closest companion.

The only remedy I've found is to anchor her with my arms: her head resting on my chest, my lips brushing her forehead, fingertips tracing lazy spirals across her ribs until her breathing eases.

When exhaustion hasn't claimed her entirely, she stays awake beside me, her thoughts gradually settling like dust after a storm.

In these quiet moments, she whispers about transforming the loft, about Obsidian's future, about her longing for peace when this mission ends. Sometimes I feel the curve of her lips against my chest, a brief warmth that vanishes too quickly.

Having her scent, lavender petals dusted with vanilla, so close each night feeds an obsession I can't deny. The woman sleeping in my arms doesn't know I plan to make her my wife and the mother of my child someday soon.

When August arrives, we'll compete to be the one holding her until sleep finally claims her. He's already declared that if anyone "wins" her hand, it'll be him. A soft laugh rises in my throat because if I haven't knocked her up already, I will soon enough.

I've grown used to sharing a bed with the two of them. Both of us were playing tug of war with her while she slept. Tangled arms and legs, and nothing has ever felt so right.

Outside of covert ops, I've never bunked with another man, let alone another man who's in love with the same woman. I remember the first time Ellia met August: she observed him over the rim of her whiskey glass, curiosity bright in her eyes, stealing glances whenever he looked away.

He showed up innocently enough at one of her performances, then lingered backstage for hours, offering help, cracking jokes, until she gently sent him on his way.

Ellia loves her touring family and insists every member feels valued. But Michael and her so-called best friend are absolute poison—neither has earned her kindness. Because she wants her flock to feel whole, she encourages them to bring loved ones on the road.

In the years before her injuries, we stopped asking permission, just let friends and family tag along. Her crew worships her in return.

When Dave announced his retirement, Ellia chartered a private jet to fly his nearest and dearest to the next show, covering every expense.

Dave came home in tears with a bank balance he never dreamed of, then told me he hoped I'd inherit that legacy, so he recommended me as his successor.

At first, I hesitated to join her security detail; she already had four bodyguards. I didn't see a place for number five until the day I met Michael.

Jenkins was Dave's choice for lead guard; I'd been brought on as backup whenever Jenkins had other duties. But the moment I stepped up, steadily, without question, to protect her, I quietly assumed the lead role. No title needed beyond "keep her safe."

Jenkins didn't object. He has a wife and two kids; being her primary guard demands you're on call twenty-four-seven. I, on the other hand, had no one special waiting at home; my life was in ruins long before Dave called me.

Months earlier, I'd lost an operative and an entire case I'd poured myself into. The mission went sideways, and I was left standing there, barely holding it together.

Ellia begins stirring in her sleep now, a soft moan telling me she's dreaming. I hold her close, silently praying it's not a nightmare. She only finished the last sequences a few hours ago, so I know her rest will be fractured today.

I need to monitor August through her system, though I trust my team to extract him flawlessly; I trust no one completely.

Years ago, one of our teammates went rogue, bought by the highest bidder, and I was the one who had to put him down. The darkness won in his mind, just as it swallowed so many others who couldn't handle the outside world.

Some succumbed to voices in their heads; others took their own lives. I nearly did myself in, overtaken by PTSD.

Maybe that's why Dave reached out to me; I'll never know. He was unrelenting, and I'll be forever grateful, but no one's heard from him since he vanished to some tropical haven.

Once I'm sure Ellia has slipped past nightmares into a deep, dreamless sleep, I cocoon her in the down comforter and prop pillows around her like a barricade. If the darkness finds her, it has to face my decoys first.

Only then do I tap Jenkins: "August update?"

His reply burns on my screen. August boarded hours ago after premaintenance delays. Jenkins welded the manifest, so it looks like a random weekend flight, not a direct plunge into Ellia's arms.

I rake a hand through my hair. I pray she sleeps until he arrives. Tonight, the tattoo artists come to ink her skin in the quiet. And that will keep her mind occupied until he is safe.

Too many strangers on the street for me to show face, but Jenkins swears he's wiped every camera feed. I hate the thought of anyone touching her, but after her careful explanations of why she chose these men, I can almost relax.

Still, I'll keep my gun within reach. If they slip up, I won't hesitate. August would have faced murder charges, lost everything, but I have a little more self-control than he does.

By late afternoon sunlight fractures through the curtains. Ellia stirs: low moans, legs lashing, sweat glinting like hot metal on her ribs. Shit. I hover by the bed, hands poised.

Every wrong move yanks her further from me. When her pulse thunders too hard, I lean in: "Songbird, you're safe. Come back to me."

I repeat it like a prayer, feel her breathing slow. Her eyelids flutter open, confusion, fear, relief.

"You left again," she whispers, her voice raw.

"I was at the table, love. Working." If she'd only believe me. Doubt is a blade between us.

As she shifts free. "I need a shower."

Music streaks through the hall, a good sign. When she blares tunes, she fights the dark. Someday I'll bury Michael and end these nightmares forever.

Towel-wrapped, hair dark and wet, hoodie hanging off one shoulder, joggers hanging low on her hips, Ellia is beauty and chaos. Every inch of her takes my breath away.

I want to bend her over the table and claim her raw before those three tattoo guys arrive and defile what's mine.

"Can one of the guys pick up everything for when they arrive?" She asks, toweling her raven waves streaked with ash, before throwing it in a messy bun.

"Jenkins is already on it," I lie easily. She gives me a look like I sprouted two heads. "He wants to oversee the setup personally."

She bites her lip, anxiety etching her features. "When do they get here?"

I close the distance in three strides and cup her chin. Even this small contact sends a bolt through me.

"Jenkins will be here in forty-five minutes. The artists shortly after. He's volunteered to round them up himself."

She leans back against me, wary. "Let me guess, he wants his own look at them first."

I don't bother answering. Ellia rarely asks questions for new information; she just needs confirmation. I press a kiss to the corner of her mouth, tasting mint, and step back as she smiles.

Fuck, she does that to me every time.

CHAPTER 44

JAXON

Jenkins shows up with food and drinks, far more than three people could consume. I resist rolling my eyes.

Financing this? Feeding their asses? The only thing left would be letting them fuck her. Over my dead body. And yet, I have to share her with my best friend.

We spread everything out on the stainless-steel kitchen bar. Jenkins dashes off to fetch the artists, and Ellia paces, dark thoughts trying to worm back in through her cracks.

A little while later, a text buzzes: 'Meet in the garage.' Jenkins, never one to trust danger, wants an escort. No argument there.

Working for Ellia brought him back from his own brink. Like me, he was hired for a special set of skills. Now he fights to keep her alive every damn day.

His wife, Alma, saw the miracle in him, and their life bloomed with laughter. They even tour with him, a whirlwind of two little kids running wild, tearing through tour buses, and number threes on the way.

Every tear of joy Alma sheds goes straight to Ellia. He's her brother; I'm her shadow. Together, we're her fortress.

In the garage elevator, I see Jenkins looming over three tattoo guys, arms crossed, face thunderous. I snort a laugh into a cough.

"Hungry?" I murmur. "Ellia ordered enough for an army."

"Yeah, about these guys..." Jenkins says, who never shifts his glare from the trio. "You sure?"

I wave him silent, his dark fade catching the light. He's broad-shouldered and inked, though he hides most of it beneath tailored suits he despises.

We arrive at Ellia's loft; the biometric locks refuse any entry except ours and a handful of trusted.

Jenkins doesn't blink. He is amazed at the fortress Ellia had built before all of this like she was waiting to be hunted.

I wave the artists inside. Ellia greets them, arms open like a general: "Excuse my guard dogs...they're still untrained."

Cedar and Arik offer polite, nervous laughs. Dakota's face ghosts white. Jenkins nods, mission accomplished: intimidation.

Cedar scans the stainless-steel bar, still piled with trays. "Where to set up?"

"At the table," Ellia says. "Also, help yourselves, I know you all will be here for a while." Motioning to the kitchen bar piled high with appetizers, entrées, and every sort of drink.

Jenkins shadow makes Ellia look fragile, though she towers at 5'11".

I lean against the wall, arms folded, biting back a grin. Jenkins is the iron fist behind her velvet throne, gentle with her, lethal to anyone else. This trio is just another job to him.

Arik lays out a stencil. "We'll start here, front of the collarbone and shoulders, then across the back. Sides we tackle solo, Cedar jumps in on the back panel."

Ellia nods, bracing herself. I watch her steel herself against the needle's bite. Arik spreads the scaled design across the table.

Jenkins snatches it up. "She can't sit that long. Zero tattoos, this looks like a marathon. What's next, a full sleeve?"

Ellia yanks the drawing away in one fluid motion. "Don't." Her voice is steel.

I clear my throat.

"Brother, get me August's ETA." I clap him on the back, guiding him like a shepherd.

He glowers, then storms toward the garage controls. I trail him, blood pounding, because for Ellia, I'll gladly take these three out myself.

Ellia meets my eyes, and for a heartbeat, I see the fear flicker there. Then she squares her shoulders and faces her mark. And I know: no matter how dark her nightmares, she'll wield this pain as art. And I'll be here, every bloody second, to hold her when it all falls apart.

I press my spine against the edge of the kitchen bar, eyes locked on the trio hustling around Elli, Cedar stretching cling wrap over the table, Dakota arranging inks, and Arik chatting her up with that easy grin.

My pulse throbs as he leans in too close; I can almost taste the bile rising in my throat. I want to carve out his silver-tongued trap and remind him who owns this woman.

Ellia glances back at me, her gaze soft but alight with that fierce tremor of courage braided with fear. I lift my glass of neat whiskey, amber fire in my hand, and give her a slow, steady nod. Every inch of me screams to protect her, to warn her that I'm here.

"You'll need to be in a bra or a bikini top," Cedar says without looking up, wrapping the table like he's sealing a vault.

"Fuck that," I snap, shoving away from the bar so hard the glass jumps.

Ellia presses her palms to my chest, halting me before I storm the room. "Jaxon, it's fine. They've seen more skin than this."

She leans up to me, voice low. My ears hum; I let out a guttural growl and tilt my head toward the artist.

"Please," she whispers.

I drop my hands to my sides, surrendering, reluctantly. She closes the gap and brushes a kiss to my cheek. My glare never leaves Arik's back.

"Let me know the moment you're uncomfortable," I murmur in Ellia's ear, voice a blade disguised as silk.

She wants this tattoo because she feels it's a bridge to something beyond, something she won't fully explain. She won't say more; every time I pry, she shuts down, but she's opened up a mile since this all started.

A few months ago, she couldn't string two words together. Now she lectures me on esoteric symbols I still have to Google. Her mind is cracking open, and I've never been prouder. She's teaching herself new abilities and letting them bloom.

My heart hammers in my ears so loud I can't focus on their chatter. Today, she sheds every layer of clothing that's been her armor. Her walls will rise again afterward.

Fuck, why did I ever think this was a good idea? It's too soon.

As Ellia slips off toward her closet, I force myself to relax and try small talk before I lose my mind entirely. "So...how long have you three been at Ink Link?"

Cedar saunters over, tearing off plastic wrap and snagging a sandwich. "Four years for me. Arik and Dakota joined a few months later. We're looking to open our own shop soon."

Arik and Dakota exchange a glance. In five years, the contract says, they have to strike out on their own. I cross my arms, acting intrigued.

Ellia owns most of these blocks; the rebrand is all due to her.

"And where would you put this new shop?" I wave toward them, my tone casual but my eyes cold.

"Two vacant lots down the block are up for sale," Dakota says. "We want more space. By the end of..." He clears his throat as if fishing for the finish.

I finish for him with a slow, knowing raise of my brow: "Five years."

They all shut up, swallowed by the hum of silence, until Ellia's French doors click open.

My breath hitches. She stands there in low-slung sweatpants rolled at the waistband and a thin black bra, shadows and curves in perfect relief.

Every second she held back comes bursting forward: raw beauty, fierce vulnerability.

I'm across the room in a heartbeat, arm sliding around her waist, drawing her in tight. My lips brush her temple. "You're a goddess," I growl, slapping her ass gently. "And I'm your servant. Now go show them that unstoppable force you carry."

One of them clears his throat.

"You'll need to hold perfectly still if we're to place this stencil correctly," Dakota says as Ellia straightens like a warrior stepping into the arena and walks to the tattoo station.

I materialize beside her. "I've got you," I murmur against her ear.

Her fingers tremble as she unhooks her bra, exposing warm, vulnerable skin. Before it even falls, I yank off my shirt and drape it over her chest. The cotton presses warm and soft against her skin.

"You know," she murmurs, that playful curve blooming in her eyes, "I'm not sure a bra was ever the real solution."

My breath catches. I lean down and press a gentle kiss to her forehead as Arik, Cedar, and Dakota shift behind her, positioning the giant stencil.

Arik's finger arcs in a swift, swirling motion. "Turn around."

In perfect sync, we grip the shirt's edge, muscle and fabric taut, as she pivots. She drops her hands to her sides. Her back goes rigid as they place the remaining stencil over he shoulders and around her ribs.

I lean close enough to feel her breath. My heart hammers as the stencil's adhesive kisses her skin, cold, precise.

"How're you feeling?" I murmur against her ear.

A tremor ripples through her, fear and adrenaline dancing beneath her skin. She sucks in a breath, slow and deliberate, forcing calm into her lungs as she nods.

I watch Dakota press the stencil to her shoulders, dangerously close to that soft hollow at her neck. Cedar and Arik glide the wings around her ribs and hips, each placement precise, as if sculpting her flesh. When the last edge clicks into place, they step back.

"Tell us what you think," Cedar says, voice low.

Ellia slides my hands from her shirt and wraps her own around the cotton. She moves to the mirrored closet doors, angles them until she can see both front and back in a single reflection.

Her breath hitches the moment she takes it in. We all lean forward, the scent of green soap sharp in the air.

"What is it?" I murmur.

She lifts her head, glossy-eyed, and strokes the stencil's curves across her body.

"It's perfect," she breathes.

A tear pools at the corner of her eye. I brush it away with my thumb.

Then she turns, eyes searching the mirror as if it might offer a different reflection. "Thank you," she whispers, her fingertips hovering an inch from Cedar's forearm before finally making contact.

The air between them seems to shimmer for a heartbeat—a blue-white flicker like static in dry air. Cedar's pupils dilate. My mouth goes dry, and I find myself rubbing my thumb against my fingertips, remembering August's words: "Like touching a live wire, but pleasant somehow." The hair on my arms stands up despite the room's warmth.

A faint, triumphant smile curves her lips. "Shall we?"

She releases Cedar and strides toward the tattoo table, her steps confident, commanding.

The three of them trail after her like eager pups, adorable, but I'd gladly put them down.

She climbs onto the table, positioning her head where I once marked her skin. As she lies back, our eyes lock. She offers me a wicked smile, and I know she's thinking the exact same thing I am.

Arik and Dakota lean on her shoulders. "You ready?" Arik's voice is a low hum against the buzz of the tattoo machine.

I'm crouched by her feet, fingers tracing small, circular patterns over her freshly shaved ankles. Her skin's warm, almost trembling under my touch; every time, the same electric jolt shoots up my arm.

August swore it felt like his skin threatened to burst the first time he brushed her, heat and cold detonating in his veins, too much and yet not nearly enough.

His body fought between burning up and shutting down. That's what Ellia does: she hacks your senses, leaves you exposed just by breathing in her orbit.

Cedar's silent too, locked up since she grasped his arm. I caught it in his eyes, the instant his breath snagged, focus narrowing as though reality tore open and he tumbled through.

And the first time you touch her, you understand something immediately, and without comfort, you won't forget it. And you won't be untouched again.

I move to her head, gripping her hand to keep her steady. Time warps as electricity peeled open every nerve ending in my arm, sharp and alive.

Ellia alters people. Leaves a residue you can't wash off. Touch her once, and your world tilts forever.

Now two of the three artists have already blazed ink across her collarbone and shoulders, wiping her down with green soap.

Ellia's eyes are closed; she looks serenely untethered. Tattoo needles hum, but she betrays no flinch.

Arik straightens, brushes a stray hair back. "Sides or back next?" His question pulls her from that calm place.

“The back,” she says, voice soft but sure. She sits up, regarding the three of us without a flicker of doubt. “Jaxon, help me flip over.”

I snatch the shirt, stretching it tight across her spine. She holds the front, and I pull the back, careful not to expose more than we must.

“You comfortable?”

“Mm-hmm.” She settles onto her side, head resting on her left cheek, facing Dakota.

The needles start to roar to life, machines buzzing in unison.

Cedar slips on his gloves and moves to her head, tattoo gun poised at her spine. I’ve been watching him since that first brush; he is careful not to crowd over her.

“You good, Cedar?” I tease, voice a little too loud.

His cheeks flare red, and calling him out has him twitchy. I grin, voice softer. “Relax. She has that effect. I’m not gonna kill you...yet.”

In perfect sync, they begin: Cedar tracing white ink down the crown of her spine, Arik carving art into her hip, Dakota etching lines across her shoulder blade.

The hum of needles, the smell of ink, the taut skin under their hands, it all crackles with a fierce, unbreakable energy. And as Ellia breathes steadily beneath the assault of needles, I know none of us will ever recover from her touch.

The artists' needles bite into Ellia's flesh, devouring scar after scar. That jagged lightning bolt carved across her back, the one that's kept her shrouded in fabric fortresses, disappears beneath electric ink like a body sinking into clouds.

The machine's buzz drowns out everything but the memory of what put that mark there.

"My ex tried to kill me. He succeeded." Ellia's voice slices through the room.

The machines fall silent. Blood beads along fresh lines of ink.

“He cut my brake lines at the summit. When I crashed, while I lay unconscious and broken on the rocks," her voice doesn't waver, “he carved this into my back to mark me forever."

Three pairs of eyes drill into me. I stand frozen, one arm barricading my chest, fist pressed against my mouth so hard I taste copper.

The shock must be radiating off me in waves. She's never told anyone. Not even me, not really. Not the full horror of how she feels.

I jerk my hand forward, commanding them to continue, needing the needles to drown out her words.

This isn't Ellia emerging from her shell; this is Ellia shattering it with a sledgehammer.

The night she collapsed in the shower, sobbing against the tiles, fragments of that night spilled out between gasps but never like this.

Her tears had soaked through her pillowcase, through the mattress, straight into my soul. But what Michael did while she lay there dying, the violation August and I never speak of, hangs between us like a blade.

"Don't pity me," she commands, her breath hissing between clenched teeth. "I saw your eyes when you traced those scars. The questions burning behind your professional masks. This is why I have security. Why Jaxon keeps me hidden until that monster is found."

I step forward, arms locked across my chest like iron bars. "Yes," I growl, "that's the accident that made her disappear. And why I'll kill him when we find him."

CHAPTER 45

ELLIA

The artists keep etching ink into my skin. Maybe that's when the gravity of my confession finally hits them; everyone has fallen into an uneasy silence.

Normally, people pepper me with questions about the accident that forced me into hiding for over a year. Granted, Jaxon usually stops them before they become intrusive.

Jaxon stands to my right; concern etched across his face. I turn my head to my other cheek and meet his gaze.

His expression softens; I know he wants to shield me from any more pain, but I had to explain why these men are here at all, why they came under the cover of darkness, and what really happened when my guards threatened to rip their hands off.

"Your tattoo will cover most of your scars," Arik says, exhaling softly.

He holds my eye with pity in his expression. I don't want pity. I want to heal.

Jaxon and August pulled me out of seclusion simply by being themselves. They never pitied me, though their guarded looks sometimes betrayed their uncertainty.

"Thank you," I whisper. "And thank you for agreeing to this. You could have said no, but this means more than you'll ever know."

I pause; his eyes say it all.

"When does August arrive, Jaxon?" I ask, desperate for him to think about something other than all these hands on me.

"By first light. His plane lands in London. Jenkins is assembling his team for the extraction," he replies, still watching the tattoo artists.

I wish Jaxon could fetch August himself and bring him straight home, but I know he'd veto that idea before I could finish the sentence.

He should be the one to pick him up. To tell him about my loft, my club, and of course, about my program. Jenkins will give August the watered-down version, and then August will ask all the questions Jaxon has.

Jaxon interrupts my thoughts: "If there's a problem, I'll help. But I'm not leaving you unless I have to."

It's like he reads my mind, because maybe he does.

"I'll be safe here for a few hours," I remind him. "No one knows I'm here."

Yet Jaxon's gaze flicks to the men tattooing me; he still sees them as threats, though they've kept my secret.

I push up on my elbows. "Jaxon, look at me. They haven't said a word, and they won't even be here. You have to trust that."

He lowers himself until we're eye to eye. "Songbird, I don't trust you being alone that long."

Relentless. Jaxon's devotion to me brooks no compromise. He settles back against the cold metal chair, eyes never leaving mine as his thumb drags across my cheek.

"If anything ever happens to you," he breathes, voice raw enough to crack glass, "I couldn't live."

That stare of his, the iron-forged promise that he'll command the universe to bend if it means keeping me safe, sends a thrill of both comfort and fierce longing through my veins.

When he steps onto the balcony to take a call, I pivot the conversation toward the three artists clustered around the oak tattoo table.

"So you guys still can't get into Obsidian?" I ask, and Cedar laughs, a low rumble that contrasts with Arik's quiet breaths as he lines in the last of the jagged scar cover-up.

Dakota shakes his head, exhaustion and hunger flickering in his dark eyes. "Public nights aren't very public if no one makes it inside."

"How many times have you tried?" I press.

Cedar shrugs. "Three, maybe four."

I draw in a breath. "That's unacceptable." My tone brooks no argument. "I have entry rules, but loyalty deserves its own reward."

Dakota sets down his machine and rubs his fingers together, a concession. "After a while, we just stopped trying."

"I intend to compensate," I murmur.

The silence that follows is heavy with anticipation. Arik peels off his gloves, voice thick: "Where's your restroom?"

I point into my closet, "Through there, right side."

I've tucked the only bathroom into my wardrobe because, until Jaxon arrived, I was the building's sole occupant.

I mentally map out a new door through the living room wall; there's nothing irreplaceable in that closet, only ghosts of my solitude.

Cedar switches off his tattoo machine and steps back. Dakota tosses his gloves into the trash can, already heading for the kitchen to scavenge cold sandwiches and water.

Knowing Jaxon would dismember us if he could, I clutch the front of my loose shirt as Cedar clamps the back around my spine.

"Jaxon may look like a god of war," I whisper, "but he's all heart."

Cedar cracks a half–smile.

"He looks fierce," I whisper, nodding toward Jaxon's shadowed figure leaning over the balcony rail, "but he's a big softy."

Cedar's tension eases in a single exhale.

Dakota disappears for snacks. I turn to the open window. Jaxon, a shadow backlit by city lights, shouts down his phone: "I won't risk it!"

Cedar drops his hands and steps back, palms raised.

I seize the moment and rise, sliding to the double mirrors. Goosebumps spike across my skin as I glimpse the masterpiece on my back.

Five hours of buzzing needles have carved mythic wings across my flesh. I slip off to the full-length mirrors: my spine, once marred by a jagged scar, now slices clean through fields of electricity that arc to my shoulders and ignite in blinding threads of pale gray power.

The wings don't touch my spine, just as I envisioned, and their currents hum against my sides. Most of the old scars vanish beneath the ink; only the longest ridge remains faintly visible, a testament to how close I came to losing myself.

Behind me, Arik emerges, breath catching at the sight. His sapphire eyes flare, and he steps forward. I taste the tang of leather, spice, and something raw in his proximity.

"It's more than I ever dreamed," I breathe, fingertips tracing the thunderbolt edges of the wings.

He steps closer, so close I can feel his breath: "Your vision breathes, unlike anything we've done. You made it alive."

A cool hand settles on my shoulder, and I whirl to find Jaxon's chest against my back, his voice low in my ear. "Songbird, your vision is breathtaking. I can't wait to trace these lines with my fingers once it's healed."

His gaze flicks to Arik, challengingly possessive. I laugh, letting his stubble graze my cheek. "Is that all you think about?"

He presses closer. "Not at all," he growls so Arik can hear, "I also dream of ways for you to ruin me."

Arik slides past us, heading back to the oak center table, voice tight with reluctant admiration, "Just a few more hours."

Jaxon nods, a silent pact sealed between them.

"Let's finish up so I can carry you to bed," he whispers, guiding me back to the table. He tugs my shirt taut as the others file back in.

Their machines come to life again, buzzing to fill the final margins of my ribs. I lie still, arms folded beneath my cheek, while Cedar and Dakota devour cold food at the bar, before joining Arik.

Thirty minutes later, they wipe cleaning soap over my newly inked skin.

Jaxon hovers, phone pressed to his ear, checking in on me between terse whispers.

None of them understands why I hold perfectly still, why every sting of the needle feels like mercy.

Maybe it's the energy coursing through this sacred ink, an imprint of my own resilience, calming the tremors in my bones. Or maybe it's because I've survived agony far deeper than any tattoo.

The nights when I held my breath until my lungs begged for air. The silent sobs into a pillow hidden in my closet. In the mornings, I prayed for the sun to never rise again.

I tell myself it's the ink. But the truth is, I've felt pain so deep that these needles are a whisper against the scream inside me. And now that scream has wings.

Dakota chooses to ink my right side first while Arik and Cedar gather around the bar.

Jaxon offers Cedar a glass of whiskey, a gesture that feels more like the beginning of an interrogation than a celebration of completed work.

Cedar accepts with wary eyes, clearly sensing the threat beneath the hospitality.

"For someone getting this much work done, you barely flinch," Dakota murmurs, his machine buzzing as he adds electricity currents along my lower ribs.

I shift slightly to meet his gaze. "After a year of piecing myself back together, this is nothing."

His body tells its own story, ink crawling up his neck, disappearing into his hairline, curling around his ears. Only his face remains a blank canvas in a sea of color.

"My girlfriend had tickets to your London show," he says, not looking up from his work. "She was devastated when the news broke about your accident."

"I'm sorry I disappointed her and everyone else." The words feel hollow in my mouth. "Someday, when this is over..."

"It wasn't about the refund." His voice drops lower. "She checked the news obsessively for weeks, praying it was all some mistake. And now here you are, alive, and I can't even tell her."

The raw hurt in his eyes as he works on my hip makes me prop myself up on one elbow, my other hand still clutching my shirt closed. I need to find a way to let his girlfriend and the world know I survived without putting myself in danger again.

"She saw you come back when you and August Tate went public," he says.

"When I make my official return, I promise, your girlfriend will get a personal message," I say. "Assuming I survive that long."

"Ellia," Dakota's machine pauses. "What you've been through... I've only known you briefly, but I can tell you're a fighter."

"Like Lyric." I meet his gaze, those dark eyes widening at the name. "Yes, I know about her. And I admire her strength."

Dakota sits back, respect flickering across his features. I've seen the same devotion in Jaxon's eyes, that rare loyalty that stays when everything falls apart.

When Lyric received her diagnosis, Dakota remained while other men would have fled. Just as my team stood by me when I wanted the world to burn.

"Hey," I whisper. "Thank you."

He nods, standing.

"Arik, your turn." Then to me: "I never doubted Lyric would survive. I'd do it all again to give her more time. You helped her without even knowing it."

As Dakota heads to the kitchen, I notice Jaxon at the bar, one hand braced against the counter, the other cradling his whiskey.

Shirtless, his tattoos map stories across his skin. Cedar points to his own ink beside him, explaining each piece's significance.

I clutch my shirt closed and carefully turn toward the kitchen, easing onto my freshly tattooed side.

The needle's buzz fades as Arik completes the final electric currents of my wings. Across the room, Jaxon leans against the bar, whiskey glass dangling between his fingers, actually laughing at something Cedar said.

The three men share an amber bottle between them, shoulders relaxed, guards temporarily lowered.

"Where would you even put another tattoo?" Cedar asks Jaxon, gesturing with his glass.

I smile to myself, knowing every inch of Jaxon's inked skin by heart: the meaningless tribal bands from drunken nights with his unit, the coordinates he never explains, the symbols whose stories change with each telling. His entire body is a map of stories to be told when he is ready.

"Ready to see the finished piece?" Arik asks, wiping away the last traces of green soap.

I nod and rise, Arik pulling the shirt tight, skin stiff and pulsing as I approach the mirrored closet doors.

Behind me, glass clinks against steel as Jaxon abandons his drink. His reflection appears behind mine, eyes darkening as they travel across my newly marked flesh.

I face the mirror. Electricity cocoons my front in delicate patterns. I turn slowly, currents of power flow along my sides, forming wings exactly as

I'd imagined. When I finally glimpse my back, language abandons me, my mouth falling open.

Tears spill before I can stop them. Jaxon steps closer, his gaze following my fingers as they hover over the outlines.

"Elli," he whispers, nothing more.

He says nothing more, just witnesses as years of carefully contained emotion spill down my cheeks.

I turn toward him, but my eyes keep returning to the living art now permanently etched into my skin.

"When I was dying, it came for me," I whisper, my voice trembling as I press my palm flat against the mirror. "I etched it into my skin so it could never leave again. I didn't want it to leave."

I swipe at the tears streaking down my cheeks, close my eyes, and inhale slow, shaky breaths. When I open them, four pairs of eyes are locked on my reflection.

"Thank you," I murmur, first to the tattooists and then to Jaxon, who's finally unclenched his fists and stopped pacing.

Arik steps forward, his gloved hands steady. "This is called second skin. Leave it on for five days, then peel under water."

Cedar and Dakota join him, precision scissors in hand, cutting the material into panels that mold to every curve of my body.

They work in a synchronized dance: Cedar trimming the edge by my shoulder, Dakota aligning a seam at my hip, Arik smoothing the last piece across my spine and ribs.

Jaxon's hands drift back to my chest, cradling the armor over my breasts. His green eyes burn with hungry pride.

Heat pools between my thighs, fuck, not now, I tell myself, but the ache only intensifies when Jaxon's gaze darkens. My knees threaten to buckle; I clamp them together, hunting for friction.

"It comes off easy in the shower," Dakota adds softly.

I study the mirrored masterpiece one last time before retreating to my closet. Jaxon follows, breathing soft behind me; his shirt, I've been clutching for hours, finally slips from my fingers and hits the floor. He leans against the closed door, arms crossed.

"I couldn't have imagined you more breathtaking, songbird," he rasps.

My wardrobe blooms, layers of black with sprinkles of deep crimson and steel gray. I reach for a zip-up hoodie. Jaxon's gaze tracks every motion. I slip into the soft fabric, backing into him.

"You and Cedar seem to be hitting it off," I say, tugging the zipper.

He rakes a hand through his hair, the flicker of a smile ghosting his lips. "They're not so bad once the whiskey hits."

There's a tenderness there, a crack in his armor, reserved for this moment.

Hoodie zipped, I turn to him, my palms finding the warmth of his exposed sides. Rising to my toes, I capture his mouth with mine.

He tastes like whiskey and embers, his tongue exploring as his arms encircle me. The heat between us builds until we separate, both breathless.

He traces my cheekbone with his lips before finding the edge of my mouth. "You amaze me," he whispers.

"I couldn't have done this without you." My arms encircle his waist, emotion tightening my throat.

His fingers thread through my disheveled hair as he inhales against my skin. I rest my lips against his chest, feeling his heartbeat quicken beneath them.

A deep, possessive sound vibrates through him. "Don't give me credit for your strength, Elli."

I smile against his skin.

"Whatever you say," I murmur, brushing my lips across his chest before stepping back. "After all that, I could use something stronger than water."

CHAPTER 46

ELLIA

The guys pack their gear while Jaxon guides me to the massive oak table that runs like a river through the center of the loft.

He pours amber whiskey into crystal tumblers, then slides onto the bench beside me, drawing me between his thighs.

His fingertips find bare skin at my shoulder, tracing patterns that make my breath catch. He can read my body like a favorite book.

The artists rejoin us, drinks in hand. I lift my glass in their direction. "Your talent deserves proper recognition. Give me just a second."

I disappear into my walk-in closet, where my heartbeat quickens. I slide open a concealed panel, revealing my private collection, neat rows of velvet boxes in three colors: midnight blue, onyx black, and deep crimson.

I select three black boxes and three blue ones.

I return to the table and set down a black velvet box in front of each artist, then arrange the blue ones in a neat row between us.

The three men trade hesitant looks, fingers hovering momentarily before they open their gifts. Inside each box nestles a polished black VIP bracelet, the word 'Obsidian' etched into its gleaming surface.

Arik stares, open-mouthed. "These must cost..."

"No," Dakota interrupts, his hand suspended above his box. "I...I can't take something this valuable."

"You can and you will," I say firmly, leaning closer. "I won't take no for an answer. Money doesn't matter to me; quality does. Obsidian is the hardest club to enter for a reason. And you each earned a spot."

The artists' eyes widen, their fingers hovering over the boxes as if touching something sacred or forbidden. I clear my throat and begin explaining the membership hierarchy.

"Onyx black signifies the highest level of exclusivity, not only for Obsidian, but for all my bars and clubs worldwide. It works in any country," I explain, settling back into Jaxon.

"On the back, you'll find a unique barcode for each one."

Leaning forward with my elbows on the table and my chin in my hands, as they turn the bracelets over. One by one, they snap them around their wrists.

Next, I point to the blue boxes.

"These are for a partner of your choice," I say, opening one of them. "Once you both register, no one else can use your bracelets. You'll need to sign up on the official Obsidian club site. It might be a little confusing at first, so take your time," glancing at the three artists.

"You'll enter the code inside the box when prompted," I continue.

Jaxon leans in, his fingers grazing my hair as he kisses me behind the ear. His emerald eyes blaze with pride and a fiercer, protective possessiveness.

I lean into his embrace, my pulse spiking with triumph and heat. The night crackles around us, every heartbeat a testament to how far I've come, and to the loyalty I've earned.

"The silver bracelets are a step down," I add. "They offer more perks than gold, but not as many as black."

"What do you mean, no one else can use the bracelet?" Cedar asks.

"At the door, security scans the bracelet and pulls up your profile—face, name, everything. If it doesn't match, you're not getting in." I extend my hand. "May I?"

Jaxon straightens behind me, his attention snapping back to the conversation as Cedar extends his arm, and I take his wrist gently, turning the bracelet to catch the light.

"Notice these micro-engravings?"

I trace the marks with my fingertip as they lean in, and Cedar nods.

I release Cedar's hand and settle back against Jaxon's chest, his arms encircling me while his lips brush my temple.

"Each bracelet is completely unique. It can't be copied or duplicated. On the site, you'll upload a clear photo, your full name, any info you provided, plus any club nickname you'd prefer. Once registered, you can explore all the perks and offers Obsidian provides. Each bracelet is also engraved with the name of the club where it was purchased."

"All the same process applies to silver," I clarify, "except silver members are blocked from many site features reserved for black."

Arik pulls out his phone, and Dakota and Cedar follow suit. I lean back into Jaxon's chest, rubbing my forehead along his jawline. Jaxon chuckles softly.

"So...where's mine?"

"You don't need one, one day it will be yours." Nuzzling in the crook of his neck.

"Absolutely not, Ellia."

Jaxon launches to his feet, putting distance between us. His fingers rake through his dark hair, knuckles white with tension.

The sudden shift in his energy hits me like a physical blow, the warmth in his eyes replaced by something stormy and unreadable. How can he go from tender to thunderous in the space of a heartbeat?

We're tethered to each other now, and I've never questioned this certainty. To me, it's always been straightforward: what's mine becomes his, becomes August's too.

Love isn't a resource that depletes with sharing. I didn't create this empire to perch alone, clutching it like something that might bleed if touched.

My father followed the same blueprint. He stood beside my mother until I came along. Then she vanished while I was still in diapers.

Throughout my childhood, he would remind me that the spotlight burns too bright for certain souls. I gathered my courage just once to ask why she disappeared, whether their love had been real.

His eyes clouded over as he answered: "Sometimes loving someone means watching them walk away."

After Mom vanished, Dad built walls around his heart as tall as his skyscrapers. I'd find him at dawn, already hunched over spreadsheets, teaching me to spot patterns in the market chaos.

"Watch for the dip before you strike," he'd murmur, his coffee going cold beside stock projections.

I blink the ghosts away.

"What's wrong?" I ask, following Jaxon's restless path across the floor. His palm scrubs down his face, that gesture I've come to recognize as his prelude to stubborn resistance.

"This belongs to you alone, Ellia. Not to me, not to anyone. You built this empire."

My voice cracks through the room like a whip. "Goddammit, Jaxon, enough."

The guys rise from the table with deliberate slowness, exchanging glances. Jaxon drops his eyes to the floor, jaw clenched.

He doesn't want this partnership, but I'm not giving him a goddamn choice.

"This," I sweep my arms wide, voice trembling as I back away, "isn't just mine anymore. You are here. You demolished my walls, Jaxon. You can't just hand back the rubble and not be with me all the way."

He takes a half-step toward me. "I didn't help build your empire."

“But you did," I cut him off, slamming my palm against the table hard enough to rattle the crystal tumblers. My pulse hammers against my throat as I close the distance between us.

"You kept me breathing. You saw me, the real me, when everyone else just saw dollar signs. It was always you," I hiss through gritted teeth, my fingers digging into my palms, " from the very fucking second I met you."

The artists edge toward the balcony, faces frozen in shock. I let out a laugh that sounds more like glass breaking.

"And too fucking bad," I spit.

“Absolutely not, Ellia.” He steps forward again, every vein standing at attention.

I reach for his hand, voice barely audible.

"Everything I built... it means nothing if I can't share it with you." My throat constricts around the words. "You promised you wouldn't hurt me. Is that what's happening right now?"

The silence between us stretches, becomes its own presence.

I dig my fingertips into my hairline, trying to steady myself.

"Do you think I want this empire if I have to stand at its summit alone? When I was falling apart, you were there. You and August..." My voice catches. "You see all my sharp edges, my fractures, and you stay anyway. I need that. I need you beside me through everything that comes."

My eyes lock onto his. "It was never Michael. Not once."

CHAPTER 47

ELLIA

The pale morning light shredded the skyline. Inside, Jaxon stood in the kitchen, shoulders rigid, worry pulsing through every muscle.

When I whispered forever, he didn't respond; he just backed away, sorrow etched on his face. He didn't just crack my walls; he obliterated them.

Shards of my defenses lay scattered at his feet. The moment his weight settled on me, I abandoned the charade of control.

The men slipped out after stiff goodbyes. I handed them my cell for club-site questions, voice steady.

Jaxon and I cleared the last plates in silence, the scrape of dishes echoing like a heartbeat.

Every time our eyes met, my cheeks flamed. But neither of us backed down.

Finally, I forced out, "When will August be here?"

He exhaled, pale in the dawn.

"Not sure. His flight was diverted to Amsterdam." His voice tightened. "Jenkins rerouted him; they found a bug on the plane. A team's en route to sweep the jet down."

He cupped my face, his thumbs brushing tears already burning behind my lids. He slid my jaw in his palms. The warmth steadied me, because I am anything but steady right now.

"What does that mean? Does Michael or Robyn know?" My voice was brittle.

"Songbird, they found it quickly. Peters scanned the plane mid-air instead of on the ground. Still, I'm going to carve Jenkins's eyes out for letting this happen."

He forced a wry smile and brushed a stray black lock behind my ear.

Tears forced me to look away. I couldn't meet his gaze when everything inside me threatened to shatter. I drew a rigid breath: one...two...three, no relief.

"Is August safe?" I swallowed the tremor in my voice.

He pulled me into his chest.

"Let's get you rested. You looked wrecked from last night."

He led me behind azure curtains to the king-size canopy, its metal frame regal in the morning glow.

That evening, Jaxon rose like a dark avenger when his laptop chimed. I curled around the pillow he'd just abandoned, craving the quiet sanctity of his arms. No dreams when he held me, no nightmares.

I caught, "ETA on August?" in his low voice to Jenkins.

"Compromised," Jenkins answered. "We're rerouting a team by vehicle. Once we hacked the implant, we saw it was placed while the plane was parked in London."

I bolted upright, terror searing my face. Jaxon didn't look at me; he paced, fingers raking his dark hair.

"I'm coming with you," he said, voice low and determined, glancing at me through the curtains.

Jenkins protested: "Jaxon, stay with Ellia. I'm point on this..."

I slid off the bed, Jaxon's oversized shirt slipping from my shoulders. Jaxon's eyes locked on me, then back to the screen.

"No," he said, flat. "I'm bringing August home to her. I don't trust your hires."

I rounded the oak table.

"Jenkins, every detail. No lies."

He inhaled, voice grim, exhaled hard. "We suspect a mole. Our guys sweep the jet before departure and after. No device when you left Sydney, or when you landed, but someone planted it in London."

My blood boiled. "So one of your hires betrayed us, feeding Michael intel?"

Tears stung my cheeks as I screamed at the video feed.

Jaxon's calm voice cut through: "Gather everyone. I want names and answers. I'll be there within the hour." Jaxon's voice dropped to a dangerous whisper before he cut the call.

"Jaxon, please don't go," I whispered as he pulled me into a fierce embrace.

He pressed his forehead to mine.

"I have to. If there's a spy on our team, I can't leave you vulnerable." He tilted my chin so I met his stormy eyes. "This place is a fortress. You built it perfectly, and I've got the codes..."

I nodded mechanically, my chest hollowing out with each passing second. Just hours ago, I'd imagined us together; Jaxon beside me, August safe in my arms. Now that vision crumbled like ash.

"I'll bring him back to you," he whispered, his thumb catching the wetness on my cheek before it could fall.

I clung to him, feeling the weight in my chest. August and Jaxon are my anchors, and now both are at risk.

"What will you do?" My voice cracked.

"Extract confessions," he whispered, his heart pounding like mine.

I nod. "Bring him home," I whisper.

I peeled off my shirt for a hoodie, sweatpants, and combat boots.

By the time I arrived in the garage, Jaxon had laid out his gear: black metal cases bursting with handguns, fixed-blade knives, and automatic rifles.

I watched him load a duffel bag with lethal precision, holsters clipped to his thighs, a micro-pistol strapped to his ankle, two combat knives sheathed against his calf.

His movements were surgical, as if he'd done this nightly for a decade.

I flashed back to that night I'd found his file in Dave's office, pages of redacted text and commendations with presidential seals. The languages listed under his name are Russian (native), German (fluent), and Spanish (operational).

Mission photos: Jaxon with different haircuts, different scars, always those same vigilant eyes.

Once, driving through the midnight desert, headlights carving the only path through darkness, he'd confessed why he lived alone.

"Can't give someone nightmares they never asked for," he'd said, knuckles white on the steering wheel.

When he finally told me some things, years later, the confession seemed to physically lift from his shoulders. I watched the weight dissolve, like witnessing rain clouds break after weeks of storms.

"Hey," Jaxon interrupted, lifting my chin from my whirlwind of memories.

"Kill whoever did this," I said. Cold certainty settled in my bones. No mercy. No retreat. Not this time. I wrapped my arms around his neck. "Make it hurt."

He kissed me like he was devouring every last drop of my fear.

"Go upstairs. You will know every truth. I'll make it hurt." His lips were fire, a defiant vow.

I let him guide me toward the elevator, my fingers laced through his until the last possible second.

As the doors begin to slide shut between us, I turn. "Jaxon, possibly check for camera breaches on the jet. I wrote a detection program."

The metal panels close with finality, his face vanishing like a premonition of loss.

CHAPTER 48

ELLIA

Night bled into my loft as cameras flickered across the massive dropdown screen. Jaxon had been gone for hours, and I wrapped myself tighter in a heavy blanket, eyes glued to every angle.

The alley behind the garage lay in blue-gray shadows, punctuated by distant streetlights.

Club Obsidian's façade gleamed from the camera farther down the block. I watched tuxedos and evening gowns fade into the black-suited crowd, each guest clutching their ebony envelope like a ticket to forbidden secrets.

My pulse hummed with tension. I could pick out the members, perfect posture, confident strides, and the interlopers trembling for a glimpse before slipping away.

Victoria, the club's promoter and manager, flitted among the guards without pausing. She knew who owned this place, and she knew I claimed the loft above it as my sanctuary.

Jaxon didn't, yet, and teaching him my security matrix had overshadowed every other confession I meant to share.

I sank deeper into the cushions, thoughts spiraling.

Obsidian's upcoming masquerade loomed just fourteen days away, black ties, covered skin, and those mandatory masks that revealed nothing but eyes. Hoping for anonymity, I might pursue Jaxon for a night of fun.

I tore myself from the couch. Amsterdam's nine-hour trek loomed; I wouldn't see Jaxon or August until tomorrow night.

Silence usually soothed me, but tonight it twisted the ache in my chest. Jaxon knew me too well: when I needed quiet, he dove into code-breaking or trailed Michael and Robyn's last known coordinates. But I needed him now.

I stride to my closet and fling open the doors. The contents stare back at me: rows of black fitted suits, corsets, Louboutin boots, and loafers.

At 5'11", I've always avoided heels; not from shame, but practicality. I already tower over most people.

Michael, barely 5'9" on his best day, used to bristle when I wore them. Though I tell myself it wasn't because of him, I simply hate discomfort.

On the rare occasions I wear dresses, they're floor-length and fitted to minimize movement.

Everything changed when I discovered an Italian tailor who specializes in women's custom suits. Her work fits like a second skin, rendering other designers obsolete. She even crafts most of my stage outfits.

My fingers drift across boots, blazers, and corsets, and now it's time for a change.

These past weeks, I've dressed like a stay-at-home mom with nowhere to go.

I select a long-sleeved black button-up that hugs every curve, paired with black slacks. After adding a black vest, buttoned, with sleeves rolled just below my elbows, I slip on my favorite Marinetta Pyraclou shoes.

The full-length mirror reflects someone I've missed: myself.

My hair falls in loose waves, the distinctive white streak visible behind my ear, the one critic accused me of dying, the one fans imitate.

I've contemplated coloring it to blend in public, but never could. Instead, I gather it into a low, loose side-braid before pressing the elevator button for the garage.

No sensible person climbs back on a motorcycle after a fatal crash, but I count myself above "sensible."

My black Ninja waited, dust gathering on its tank. Jaxon would kill me for this, but the craving was irresistible, especially now.

I tugged on a black balaclava, twisted my braid into my helmet, and checked the feeds on my phone. I straddled the bike, thumbed the starter, the engine roared like a lion unleashed, and heat bloomed through me.

The vibration thrummed between my legs, and my head snapped back as if I'd tasted pure bliss. I scrolled through my phone one-handed, finding the playlist that would complete this escape.

There was nothing like Crucifix thundering through my helmet speakers while the asphalt ribbon unwound endlessly before me.

The alley was empty; Jenkins was hidden somewhere in the factory building across the street, scanning surveillance. Making my escape only seconds before being seen.

I cracked the garage door, slipped into the night, and it sealed shut behind me. Rolling left out of the club's private driveway, merging into the stream of headlights.

Each red light feels like a hand trying to hold me back. I glance skyward, making bargains with a deity I've never believed in, just let me have this freedom.

With Jaxon and August gone to Amsterdam for nine hours, I have until tomorrow. I need this: the warmth of the engine beneath me, the wind carving paths across my body, before Jaxon returns to seal me inside protective walls again.

The last block before the highway stretched ahead as Crucifix's "My Way" filled my helmet speakers.

Through my visor, I spotted them, the three tattoo artists huddled with friends outside the bar. I slowed, raised my hand, and offered a small wave. The group fell silent.

Arik detached himself, approaching cautiously while the others watched. I pressed my gloved finger against where my lips would be beneath the helmet: don't speak.

His head cocked to one side, those blue eyes traveling from my fitted suit torso to the sleek machine beneath me. When I flipped up my visor, recognition hit him like a physical blow.

"What, what are you doing out here, Ellia?" His voice trembles as a car honks behind me; I wave it through, then pivot back.

"I needed air," I whispered. "Jaxon went to fetch August, and I had to clear my head."

Looking away.

He frowned. "Where are you headed?"

"Anywhere," I said, my throat tight with need. "Want to come?"

He shot a look at his friends, jaw tightening. I jabbed my finger toward the spare helmet gleaming on the seat.

Michael used to rage about those extra helmets, hurling accusations across our bedroom at 3 AM, veins throbbing at his temples as he swore, I was fucking someone else. Truth was, I'd survived too many emergencies to be caught unprepared again.

Tonight, I simply wanted company.

“If you don’t want to leave them...”

“It’s not them,” Arik ran an inked hand through his blonde hair.

“But Jaxon will skin me alive if I...”

“I won’t tell him if you won’t,” I gestured toward the handlebars. "Want to take control instead?"

His Adam's apple bobbed as he glanced at the motorcycle. "Never learned how."

"No worries." I shifted into gear and lowered my visor, ready to leave him behind. "Enjoy your night."

"Hold on." Something urgent edged into his voice. "I'll come. Just... Jaxon doesn't need to know about this, okay?"

A laugh escaped me, hollow inside my helmet. As if secrets from Jaxon ever stayed buried, especially ones involving me on a motorcycle with another man.

Arik turns and raises his hand in farewell to his friends, who remain fixated on me, their gazes burning with curiosity.

Behind the shield of my visor, I lift my gloved hand in acknowledgment, secretly savoring how he'll squirm later under their inevitable interrogation about tonight's unexpected rider.

I passed him the spare helmet, then guided his arms to encircle my waist.

"Closer," I instructed, not satisfied until his chest pressed against my back and I could feel the rhythm of his heart.

After connecting our helmet comms, I revved the engine as the light turned green and left the city behind us.

The road stretched before us like a black ribbon unwinding into darkness as music poured through the comms.

Nearly an hour into our ride, I felt Arik’s fingers suddenly dig into my sides, urgently tapping.

His voice crackled through the comms, sharp and clear despite the engine’s roar, pulling a laugh from me. He pointed toward a narrow turnoff to the right, an unlit path where tall grass swayed at the edges like ancient guardians.

I slowed enough to lift my visor a crack.

Wind rushed against my exposed skin as Arik shouted over the engine's growl, his helmet knocking against mine: "Take this way, it leads to an overlook above the Loch!"

Minutes later, Arik stabbed his finger toward a crumbled stone wall. Killing the engine, the sudden silence was violent in my ears. He dismounted, his legs unsteady.

"Are," my laughter in my throat. "Are you good?"

I swung off in one fluid motion, ripping my helmet free. Behind my balaclava, my eyes burned with adrenaline.

"Ellia," he demanded, voice raw, "why the hell are you out here alone?"

I yanked the covering off, my braid whipping loose down my back.

Arik's eyes locked onto me with such hunger I could almost taste it, like he'd glimpsed something forbidden and couldn't look away.

This may be the reason Jaxon rips his hands off, but I sigh; that is not my place to tell.

"My jet was compromised by the same bastard who carved that scar into my back," I say softly, stuffing the face covering into my helmet. "Jaxon's hunting blood because he's convinced there's a traitor on his security team."

"Ellia," he says gently, gesturing toward the crumbling stone barrier that once enclosed the Loch.

I settled against the rough stone, and he joined me, our shoulders nearly touching.

The silence between us felt charged, yet comfortable. I wondered if his companionship was genuine or merely a contractual obligation.

I twisted a blade of grass between my fingers until it frayed.

"Funny how life turns out," I said, eyes fixed on the dark water. "Nothing as I imagined."

He remained quiet, his gaze patient and steady.

"Michael was..." My voice caught.

Why was I telling him this? Arik existed outside my dangerous orbit, though that line was blurring by the minute.

"You don't need to," he said, leaning forward.

I let the conversation hang in the air, meeting his eyes. He probably thinks the whole situation is crazy, with me at the center of it, and he wouldn't be wrong.

My fingers twist the grass stem until it snaps. Arik shifts beside me, his attention drifting to the dark water.

"We signed up on the club's website today," he says, clearly steering us to safer ground.

"Did you?" I ask, genuinely curious.

I've only seen the administrative side, never experienced it as a member.

"Have you seen all the perks your bracelet gets as top tier?"

"I think we just scratched the surface," he says, scratching his head, with an arched brow.

"It's a lot, but I wanted something different than most clubs." Smiling, I say, bowing my head to avert my eyes from his glare.

"Yeah." He tears a blade of grass into precise strips. "I'm still holding onto my silver bracelet, but Cedar gave his to Riley, and Dakota's went to Lyric."

I smile.

"Finding someone worthy doesn't come with a deadline, Arik. It either happens or it doesn't." I lift one shoulder in a half-shrug. "Jaxon is the only person I'll share Obsidian with. Well, and August, of course."

The moon sits high tonight, making the lake reflect and lighting up the night sky.

"You go alone?" he asks shockingly.

"I mean, yeah." My hands dance with every word. "It takes someone special for me to share my secrets with. And Obsidian is one of my biggest secrets."

Everyone in this industry has something to hide," I say, watching his face. "Secrets are our currency."

Arik nods slowly, acknowledging the truth in my words. He stands, brushes grass from his jeans, and searches the ground until he finds a smooth stone. With practiced ease, he sends it skipping across the dark surface of the loch.

"What's your favorite flower?" Arik's question floats across the darkness between us.

I blink twice, caught off-guard by such ordinary curiosity. The moonlight catches his face as I meet his gaze, tiny stars reflecting in his eyes.

"No one's ever asked me that before," I admit, the words feeling strange and vulnerable to my tongue.

"No?" His eyebrow lifts as he sends another stone skipping across the black mirror of the loch.

Five perfect bounces before it disappears. Silver ripples spread outward, catching moonlight.

"Just trying to give you something else to think about for a minute."

It's been over a year since I've had a conversation that wasn't about security protocols or threats. No cameras track me here. No earpieces, no hovering personnel cataloging my every movement. Just the cool European air filling my lungs.

"Purple tiger lilies," I say, the answer coming with unexpected certainty. "And black roses."

I smile, tucking a strand of hair behind my ear.

I can see my father's garden again, those speckled tiger lilies bobbing in summer breezes while he sat inside, hunched over market projections.

I'd escape there whenever I could, losing myself among the blooms while everything inside our house remained sterile, controlled, and cold.

Season after season, I'd whisper requests to the weathered gardeners, watching their calloused hands coax my wishes from the soil.

The day the black roses, deep burgundy but midnight dark against their emerald leaves, unfurled beside the purple tiger lilies, something inside me unfurled too.

Their unlikely beauty together, defiant and striking, spoke to something I couldn't yet name.

“And I can guess your favorite color is black." His words aren't a question but a statement of fact, his lips curving knowingly.

I duck my head, feeling an unfamiliar warmth spread across my cheeks as a genuine laugh escapes me.

"Yes," I admit, the sound of my giggle strange in my ears.

"And dark purple," I add, remembering the lilies, their petals like velvet midnight touched by storm, watching how the admission makes his eyes crinkle at the corners.

Time slips away as Arik and I trade questions and answers about nothing consequential. There's something freeing about conversation without an agenda or ulterior motive.

When he tells me his favorite color is blue, I can't help but ask, "Like your eyes?"

Those sapphire irises belong to him alone.

He teaches me to skip stones across the water's surface, my wrist finally finding the right angle after several stones sank immediately. Now I watch my pebbles dance four, five times before disappearing beneath the dark surface.

Cars whisper in the distance, their sounds carried on the night air. I breathe in deeply, savoring the earthy scent of wild grass.

I'd become my own jailer at the Idaho house, venturing out only for occasional circuits around the back lake, always with someone's gaze tracking my movements.

My injuries had kept me bedridden at first; perhaps that's when the walls started closing in, when I began to prefer the shadows of the house to the vastness beyond.

A slight vibration catches my attention. I cross back to the bike and grab my phone, my gut twisting at the name on the screen: Jenkins.

I swipe to dismiss the call and tuck the device away.

The knot in my stomach tightens. Jenkins only reaches out when there's trouble, which means my absence from the loft hasn't gone unnoticed.

Arik flashes a mischievous grin. "You're in serious trouble. Ready to head back?"

"No," I say without hesitation. "Once I return, my freedom ends. Jaxon will be livid, but I'll face that storm when I get there."

I reclaim my perch on the crumbled stone while Arik collects pebbles, sending them skipping across the dark water. He maintains a companionable silence, allowing me this stolen moment before Jaxon tears into me.

The distant growl of an engine shatters our peace as it grows closer, making my muscles tense.

"Who uses this road, Arik?" I demand, springing to my feet.

"Nobody I know of." He raises his palms defensively. "I come here because it's always deserted."

If it's Jenkins, I'm finished. If it's Michael, I'm worse than finished. I stand my ground as headlights slice through darkness, growing brighter with each heartbeat.

The vehicle screeches to a halt yards from my bike. A car door slams open.

"What the fuck were you thinking?" Jenkins roars, slamming it shut behind him. "Have you lost your goddamn mind?"

One hand gestures wildly toward my motorcycle while the other grips a pistol, pointed at Arik's skull.

I lunge between Jenkins and Arik, my hand slamming against Jenkins' chest.

"Back off. This was my call, not his."

Jenkins' nostrils flare like a bull's. His knuckles whiten around the pistol.

"Please," I whisper, voice cracking. "Don't tell Jaxon."

"Tell him?" Jenkins' laugh is razor-sharp. "Who the fuck do you think sent me? He's tracking your bike, Ellia."

The ground seems to tilt beneath me. I should have known Jaxon's surveillance is absolute, his digital fingers wrapped around every engine, every wheel, every machine I've ever claimed as mine.

"Arik. Tahoe. Now." Jenkins barks, gun still trained on him. "I'm right behind you."

Jaxon will eviscerate me for this. Jenkins, too, for failing to keep me caged.

I mouth 'I'm sorry' as Arik passes, his face drained of color. Jenkins tosses my spare helmet into his passenger seat like it's contaminated.

I straddle my bike, bracing for the execution march back to the loft.

"It's Jaxon," Jenkins thrusts his phone at me.

"Hey," I manage, my voice hollow.

"Ellia." My name in his mouth sounds like a death sentence. "Why the FUCK did you think you could leave?"

Silence stretches between us. My head bows in defeat.

"Are you trying to get yourself killed?" His voice drops to something worse than shouting.

"I just needed..." My throat closes.

He'll never understand what it's like being locked away while he moves freely through the world.

"I'm sorry," I choke out, shoving the phone back at Jenkins.

With trembling fingers, I pull the balaclava over my face until only my eyes remain visible, tucking away every strand of hair.

The helmet clicks into place as I twist the key, and beneath me, the engine roars awake like a beast unleashed from its cage.

I don't wait, I stomp down, wrench the throttle, and the back tire shrieks against gravel. The bike whips into a tight, violent donut, stones exploding outward like shrapnel.

Jenkins stumbles backward, spitting profanities as pebbles spray across his tailored jacket.

Satisfaction burns through me, a minor rebellion in a life of compliance.

Through the SUV window, I catch Arik's gaze, the corners of his mouth lifting in silent approval. I slam the bike into gear and launch forward, tasting freedom in the rush of night air against what little skin my helmet leaves exposed.

CHAPTER 49

AUGUST

Jaxon's first words when he met me in Amsterdam: "Our woman went rogue." Not "hey brother" or "How was your flight?" Just the gut-punch I didn't need.

This whole fucking trip's been a nightmare since Ellia vanished from Sydney. Now my blood pressure's spiking again.

Jaxon swears Jenkins is glued to her side until we reach them, wherever the hell that is. He won't tell me. Says it's safer that way. Maybe he's right.

Finding that bug on the plane wasn't in anyone's playbook. Neither was watching three grown men, two pilots, and a steward, on their knees, trembling like children while we interrogate them.

"I'm going to ask you one more FUCKING TIME!" Jaxon's voice explodes, veins bulging at his temples.

"We don't know, sir," the co-pilot whimpers, eyes wet, faces bloody and broken.

These men have served Ellia for years. Now they've compromised everything by letting this happen. Bug planted or not, they should have had this aircraft sealed tighter than a goddamn vault.

Jaxon jams his pistol against the pilot's temple. The man's face is a mess of tears and snot, his dignity gone.

I've seen Jaxon execute men for less than this betrayal. These poor bastards are already dead.

"What about you?" Jaxon whips around, driving the gun barrel into the steward's forehead hard enough to snap his head back.

The man crumples to his hands, a red circle forming where metal met flesh.

"Every fucking one of you signed her death warrant," Peters hisses through clenched teeth, looming over them like the reaper himself. "Did Ellia's trust mean nothing?"

I lean against the SUV's hood, close enough that I'll catch arterial spray when Jaxon finally ends this.

The bastards who planted the bug were professionals, tucked it into the luggage compartment where it mimicked a bolt head perfectly. But our sweep teams don't miss shit like that. Ever.

"Alright," Jaxon doesn't even blink.

The pistol cracks, punching a neat hole between the pilot's eyes before the man can even process his death. His body crumples like wet cardboard.

Our men drag the corpse away, boots leaving red smears across concrete. The remaining pilot and steward dissolve into animal sounds, pleading, sobbing, pissing themselves. Still denying everything.

The pilot's voice fractures. "Nobody, nobody touched that plane except your security team and us."

Jaxon crouches, bringing his face inches from the man's. "Tell me something useful before I paint this hangar with your fucking brains."

"Had to be an inside job." The pilot's bloodshot eyes lock with Jaxon's. "One of your own men."

The pistol's report echoes like a thunderclap. The pilot's head snaps back, a perfect crimson hole appearing between his eyes, matching his colleague's.

The steward bolts, three desperate strides before Peters' boot catches his ankle. He crashes face-first onto concrete.

Peters looms over him, weapon trained on the sobbing man's skull. One glance at Jaxon, and a slight nod.

The steward's hand flies up in desperate protection. The bullet punches through flesh, bone, and brain matter in one brutal trajectory.

Jaxon doesn't even glance at the bodies.

"Clean this mess up," he commands, striding toward me while checking his 9mm with blood-slicked fingers before jamming it into his waistband. The metal disappears into black fabric, still warm from killing.

"Time to collect our little runaway," he says, his voice dropping to something primal. "Ellia needs to learn what happens when she breaks the rules."

I watch him, relaxed, focused, alive in ways most men never experience. The three executions didn't satisfy him. They were just appetizers. His genuine hunger waits elsewhere.

I push off the hood. "Was she compromised?"

Blood still dots my sleeve as I slide into the passenger seat. Jaxon slams his door shut, knuckles whitening around the steering wheel.

"Jenkins says she kept covered. Face, hair, everything. But that fucking tattoo artist was with her." His jaw muscles pulse beneath his skin like something alive and hungry.

"Then eliminate him." The words leave my mouth with terrifying ease.

Yesterday I'd never seen a man executed like that. I'd seen him kill, but not like this. Now I've watched three executions without blinking, their blood still warm on the concrete behind us.

He shakes his head as he pulls away from the private hangar. Nine grueling hours ahead, and he still won't tell me where we're keeping her.

The cityscape gradually gives way to desolate back roads. Jaxon's shoulders finally drop an inch as he reveals our destination, Ellia's secret loft in Manchester.

A sanctuary untouched by anyone until him. Now three random tattoo artists know about her existence, about the danger circling her like sharks.

"She made them sign NDAs," he says, but that doesn't settle the acid in my stomach.

Ellia's too calculating for such a reckless move. Even as Jaxon recounts their alibis, my jaw remains clenched.

"You have no idea how fucking brilliant that woman is," Jaxon says when I voice my concerns. His knuckles whiten around the wheel. "This life she built years ago, I didn't even know about it. And that fucking piece of shit Michael has no clue."

I nod, but something about this feels wrong, sending cold ripples of warning up my spine. Whatever's happening, we're not driving toward another sterile safehouse designed to keep her docile and controlled. Sydney changed her.

Those walls she built around herself have started to crack. And if what Jaxon says is true, this loft, her private sanctuary, means she's becoming someone I haven't seen in years. The Ellia from before the mountain incident.

I jolt awake after a few hours of dead sleep. Jaxon's voice cuts through my fog; he's on comms with Jenkins.

In the background, Ellia's fury crackles through the speaker like electrical current. Something about Jenkins forcing her motorcycle back to base.

"Sounds like our girl found her fangs again," I mutter, rubbing life back into my face as Manchester's gray outskirts blur past the window.

CHAPTER 50

ELLIA

I finally crashed on the couch sometime after Jenkins tore into me, my sleep fitful and shallow. He had confined me to the loft like some overprotective dad.

Now he sat at the far end of the sectional, his eyes flicking between me and the massive screen where he scrolled through data feeds. He'd made it clear that I wouldn't be out of his sight again.

"The nightmares," he says as I stir awake, pulling the weighted blanket tighter around my shoulders. "How bad?"

The question catches me off guard. I blink, trying to organize the fog in my head.

"Bad enough," I finally mumble.

Jenkins lowers his voice.

"I'm sorry," he says, as though he's personally responsible for the nightmares that haunt me.

"Don't be," I reply, watching data streams flash across the screen, knowing Jaxon and August will arrive soon.

Silence falls between us, each second ticking by like a countdown to whatever creative punishment Jaxon has planned for me.

My face warms at the thought of his particular brand of "discipline", the way he and August introduced me to pleasures I'd never imagined.

I wasn't inexperienced before them, but they've shown me desires I never knew existed within me.

"I should have seen it coming," Jenkins interrupts my thoughts flatly. "I'd have put bullets in their heads if I had."

I changed the subject. "How's Alma doing? And the little ones?"

Jenkins' face transforms instantly, the hard edges softening into something almost boyish.

"They're good. Missing me. Alma tells them that Daddy is on a special mission." He makes air quotes, but there's no irony in his smile.

It twists something in my chest, knowing he's here instead of with them. I understand that particular ache too well.

My father and I existed in the same space for years without really seeing each other. Only when I grew independent did we finally become friends.

He showed me how to navigate boardrooms and balance sheets; I showed him the emptiness of hoarding wealth. People call me philanthropic, but they should see my father's work; the foundations he's quietly built and funded without fanfare.

Between us, we command billions, though these days he's content to redirect potential investments to me instead of chasing more himself. And I miss him every damn day.

"She's pregnant," he adds, his face lighting up with genuine joy.

"Go home, Jenkins," I whisper. "Your family needs you more than I do."

Without looking away from his screen, he shakes his head.

"Not until we're secure, ma'am." His voice carries the practiced formality of his military days.

"You're too loyal for your own good," I murmur, meaning every word.

Jenkins has been my shadow longer than anyone. He stepped in before Dave, my previous head of security, retired to some nameless beach with his wife.

Some days I envy that escape, trading spotlights for anonymity, trading fame for peace.

Jenkins rises from the couch, tablet gripped in one hand as he approaches the wall-mounted display, and a black vehicle appears on screen.

"I have eyes on target," crackles a voice through the comms.

"Any tails?" Jenkins asks, shoulders tensing.

"Negative. The rest of the security team is approximately sixty minutes out."

"Copy that."

He turns to me, his professional mask slipping for a moment.

"About last night... had to bring you back. Jaxon would've buried me if anything had happened. Besides," he adds with a hint of a smile, "I've grown rather attached to you."

My stomach drops as I spot the SUV pulling into the alley on the security feed. Jaxon and August, knowing my punishment draws near.

I acknowledge Jenkins with a silent nod as he moves to the foyer, bending to lace up his tactical boots.

At least when he'd lectured me earlier, after depositing Arik God-knows-where, he'd had the decency to kick his boots off first.

The elevator doors burst open, and August strides through, alone, Jaxon nowhere in sight. Before I can stand, August lifts me with one powerful arm, his mouth claiming mine in a hungry kiss as he spins us in a slow circle.

"God, I've missed you," he murmurs against my lips, his breath ragged.

I thread my fingers through his hair, drawing his face to my chest, when something catches my eye: tiny crimson speckles dotting the sleeve of his pristine white shirt.

My hands freeze. I pull back and tug at the fabric, questioning.

August's laugh is casual, chilling.

"Don't worry. We'll find you a new flight crew," he says, as if he hadn't just eliminated people who'd been with me for years.

The hair on my neck rises at Jaxon's voice behind me. "Seems our caged bird tried testing her wings."

August lowers me to the floor with deliberate slowness, his palm delivering a sharp sting to my backside.

"You're on your own for this one, sweetheart."

"Jaxon, please... I can explain everything," I say, circling the sectional with my palms raised in supplication.

He ignores me completely, directing August to the bathroom while suggesting he make himself comfortable.

August's eyes meet mine with feigned sympathy, but I catch the anticipation lurking beneath; he's already imagining how he'll participate in whatever correction Jaxon has planned for me.

Once August disappeared, Jaxon's gaze locked onto me like a predator scenting blood. Each deliberate step he took toward me sent heat spiraling down my spine.

I retreated, pulse hammering in my throat, until the sectional pressed against the backs of my thighs, trapping me between leather upholstery and the hard promise in his eyes.

My voice catches in my throat. "No one saw me."

The plea dies on my lips as his eyes darken.

Jaxon towers over me, his body so close I can feel the heat radiating between us. I crane my neck to meet his gaze, feeling impossibly small beneath him.

The cologne clinging to his skin, leather and spice, makes my core throb with a shameful, delicious ache. I press my thighs together, desperate to hide the evidence of how thoroughly he affects me.

His voice drops to a primal growl. "Do you have any idea what I imagined when your tracker activated?"

I shake my head, transfixed by his eyes darkening from emerald to midnight.

My throat tightens as I swallow, pretending I want mercy while my body betrays me, already wet with anticipation of his punishment.

"And finding Arik there..." He cracks his neck, his lips grazing my ear as he whispers, "I'll make him beg before I end him."

"You won't," I protest, hands pressing against his chest like pushing stone.

His muscles flex beneath my fingertips, reminding me how easily he could break me, and how much I want him to.

"I saw him on the street. Asked him if he wanted to ride."

His blood-stained knuckles trace my cheek, trailing down to my collarbone.

"Jenkins told me," he says, thumb pressing against my pulse.

"Then leave him alone," I demand, gasping as he lifts me with such force my core clenches in desperate need.

CHAPTER 51

JAXON

I land a firm smack on Ellia's ass as I carry her over my shoulder toward the bed, the curtains billowing by the stained-glass windows.

I toss her onto the mattress, watching her body bounce as she gasps.

"Jaxon!" she cries out, her voice husky with desire.

I give her a knowing smirk as I move to her nightstand, feeling her hungry eyes track my every movement while I search for what we both want.

"How did you know about those?" she asks breathlessly.

I say nothing, recalling the moment her drawer revealed silicone treasures when she'd carelessly tossed her phone inside.

Each curve and contour of her private collection told me everything, this woman who'd kept men from her sanctuary, had been pleasuring herself all along, craving what I'm about to give her.

"Strip," I command, tossing a sleek vibrator onto the bed beside her trembling thighs.

She shakes her head, defiance in her eyes that only makes me harder, knowing I'll soon break that resistance into moans.

"That wasn't a question, Ellia." Her full name falls from my lips like a promise of what's coming.

Her gaze never leaves mine as she peels away her hoodie, revealing her fresh tattoo against flushed skin. Her sweatpants follow, leaving only those black lace panties clinging to her hips.

Her eyes darken with hunger, fixing on my cock straining painfully against my zipper, then lift to meet mine.

When she bites her lower lip, dragging her teeth slowly across it before looking back at my throbbing erection, I know I won't last long before claiming what's mine.

I seize her ankles and drag her to the edge of the bed.

"Jaxon, I'm sorry," she gasps, chest rising and falling with each ragged breath.

"Not sorry enough," I growl, ripping her delicate panties away in one savage motion.

Her sex glistens, already slick with need. The sight of her arousal makes something feral twist inside me.

I grasp her wrist and pull her up to her knees, bringing the soaked fabric to my face as I inhale deeply, her musky scent flooding my senses, itching to devour her.

I wrap the torn lace around her wrist and guide her to stand, securing her to the metal bar of our canopy bed before binding her other wrist.

I step back, drinking in the sight of my woman displayed before me, vulnerable and waiting.

I deliver a stinging slap to her ass, watching the flesh redden beneath my palm.

"I need to clean up," I growl, my voice thick with promise rather than goodbye.

"You can't just leave me," she protests, her voice breaking with frustration as I stride away from her bound form. Only turning to watch her struggle to keep her thighs together.

August emerges from the bathroom, steam clinging to his muscled torso as I strip off my clothes, still marked with evidence of our earlier violence.

As he secures the towel low on his hips, I catch his eye.

"She's primed and ready for you," I murmur, stepping into the scalding spray.

The predatory hunger in his smile tells me he'll make her scream louder than I ever could.

Clean, I towel off, muscles still twitching with anticipation, and pull on low-hanging sweats that do nothing to hide my renewed arousal.

When I enter the loft, the sight nearly brings me to my knees. August lounges in the chair like a king while Ellia's spread-eagled body glistens with sweat, her pussy dripping wet, creating a slick trail down her trembling thighs.

August catches my eye, his teeth dragging across his bottom lip as he gestures to her collection of toys arranged meticulously before him, dildos, plugs, and vibrators lined up like instruments of exquisite torture.

"Jaxon," Ellia whimpers, her voice cracking as she strains against her restraints, "I can't take it anymore."

I tap the tablet until music plays over the ceiling speakers. “Hands on Me” by RHYXA feels the space.

With a single nod from me, August's expression darkens with carnal intent. His fingers close around a silicone feather vibrator, thumb hovering over the button that will make her scream.

I watch him stalk around her trembling body like a predator savoring the moment before the kill, while I position myself behind her, my breath hot against her neck, my cock throbbing against the small of her back.

CHAPTER 52

ELLIA

Jaxon and August stalk around me with predatory focus, their eyes devouring every inch of my exposed skin.

Between Jaxon's fingers gleams the silver plug, catching the light as he turns it slowly, deliberately. August trails the soft feather across his palm, testing its delicacy, a toy I'd dismissed as too gentle for my usual cravings.

"August," I moan as the feather's first whisper-light touch traces from my bound wrists down my inner arms, igniting nerve endings I never knew existed.

My thighs tremble, slick with need. When Jaxon presses the cool metal between my folds, teasing my entrance with agonizing patience, my spine arches involuntarily, surrendering to their shared control.

I arch my back, desperate for Jaxon to fill me completely. Each time I chase his thick length, he withdraws just enough to leave me whimpering with frustration.

"This is exactly how I like you," he growls against my neck, his breath hot on my skin.

My eyes lock with August's, silently begging for mercy, but he only smirks as he tortures my swollen clit with featherlight circles.

Jaxon's strong arm anchors around my waist as the cool metal plug presses insistently against my virgin entrance, demanding access to my most forbidden place.

My muscles clench instinctively against the intrusion.

August and Jaxon exchange a knowing glance before August captures my face between his hands and devours my mouth with a kiss so consuming that my resistance crumbles.

As Jaxon's grip tightens possessively around me, I surrender completely. They've mastered the art of breaking me apart.

"That's it," Jaxon hisses as I yield. "God, you're so fucking tight."

I moan into August's mouth as Jaxon drives the jeweled plug deep inside me, stretching me open.

When they both release me simultaneously, the sudden absence of their touch is excruciating. A desperate, needy whimper escapes my throat as my body aches for contact.

Jaxon prowls to August's side, their ravenous gazes devouring my exposed, trembling body.

My cunt clenches around emptiness, wetness sliding down my inner thighs.

"Fuck, look at her dripping," August growls. "Bad girls who can't control themselves get punished, don't they?"

Approaching me again, Jaxon watches intently as August coats the vibrator with my slick arousal before pushing it inside my swollen, sensitive pussy.

My head falls back, a guttural cry tearing from my throat as pleasure crashes through me, only for August to step away, leaving me quivering on the edge.

These merciless men will torture me with denied release until I break.

My head snaps up to find August smirking, remote dangling between his fingers like a taunt.

Jaxon's palm cracks against my ass, a stinging blow that coincides perfectly with August reactivating the toy.

My inner walls grip it hungrily, desperate for what they're denying me.

The vibrations ravage me from within, my body folding forward against my restraints.

You think you deserve to come?" Jaxon's fingers twist savagely in my hair, yanking my head back until tears spring to my eyes. The vibrator inside me dies without warning, again.

"Please," I beg, voice fracturing as August cranks the intensity to maximum.

The vibrations ricochet through my swollen flesh, my spine arching involuntarily.

I gasp for breath as my body betrays me, convulsions ripple outward from my core, unstoppable waves of pleasure-pain. The jeweled plug stretches me obscenely, making each pulse feel deliciously filthy.

"You're going to come so hard you'll forget your own name, songbird," Jaxon growls against my ear, his voice dark whiskey and sin. "This is what happens when you disobey."

I hover at the precipice, lungs burning for air, but August's grip on my hips is unrelenting. His teeth sink into the tender flesh of my lower back—claiming, marking.

Ecstasy and agony fuse into something primal as my scream echoes off the walls.

Jaxon releases my hair, dropping to his knees before me. His fingers dig mercilessly into my inner thighs, branding me with tomorrow's bruises while his breath scorches my dripping sex.

His eyes lock with mine, dark with possession, before he claims my swollen clit between his teeth.

The exquisite pressure sends lightning through my veins as I arch helplessly backward. August's firm hands spread me wider from behind, offering my most intimate flesh to Jaxon's relentless tongue.

August's mouth blazes a torturous path down my neck, across each vertebra, until he reaches the curve of my ass. He kneels behind me, his grip unyielding as he exposes me completely to Jaxon's devastating assault.

The orgasm detonates through me with such violence that my vision fractures into white-hot fragments. My screams are raw, animal, and drown out the music throbbing above us.

Jaxon's merciless mouth refuses to relent as my cunt spasms wildly around the vibrator he's cranked beyond bearable limits.

Behind me, August extracts the jeweled plug with excruciating deliberation, leaving me empty for only the heartbeat it takes him to press his thick cockhead against my forbidden entrance, slick with my arousal.

"Jax... Aug... fuck..." The words disintegrate into desperate, broken sounds.

August's massive cock breaches me, stretching tissue never meant to accommodate such invasion. The burn transforms into molten pleasure as he feeds his length into me with ruthless precision, each inch claiming territory no man has possessed before.

Jaxon's eyes lock with mine, predatory satisfaction in his gaze as he deliberately, torturously circles my swollen clit with the flat of his tongue.

"Take every fucking inch," August commands against my sweat-slicked spine, his hips finally flush against my ass.

When August establishes his punishing rhythm, Jaxon drags his tongue from where August's cock splits me open all the way to my throbbing clit.

His fingers find my nipple, twisting cruelly in perfect synchronization with August's matching assault on the other, turning me into nothing but nerve endings and surrender.

Jaxon rises, freeing my wrists from their bonds. My knees buckle instantly, but August catches me, his powerful hands digging into my hips as he guides me down onto him.

The impossible fullness of his cock stretching my ass makes me cry out as I straddle him, my thighs trembling uncontrollably on either side of his muscular frame.

My gaze locks on Jaxon's cock as he palms his length, glistening bead of pre-cum. My mouth waters, tongue darting across my lower lip without conscious thought.

His knowing smirk tells me he sees the hunger in my eyes, the desperate need to taste him, consuming me.

I reach forward, gathering that salty essence on my thumb before bringing it to my mouth. The primal taste of him floods my senses, my eyelids fluttering closed in shameless pleasure.

August bends me forward at the waist while Jaxon grips the canopy bar above, steadying himself on the mattress.

The moment August loosens his iron grip, I lunge for Jaxon's cock, swallowing him to the root in one greedy motion.

Jaxon's head snaps back, a feral sound tearing from his throat.

"That fucking mouth," he snarls, while August's hot breath scorches my ear with his own guttural moan.

I surrender completely to their rhythm, taking Jaxon's thick length down my throat as August impales me from behind.

Jaxon's fingers twist viciously in my hair, controlling every movement while the relentless vibrator inside my cunt pushes me toward madness.

August's calloused palm circles my swollen clit as he forces two thick fingers alongside the vibrator, stretching me beyond capacity.

Utterly filled, mouth, cunt, ass, and I fracture. My orgasm detonates through me with such violence that tears stream down my face, my screams muffled around Jaxon's pulsing shaft.

They fuck me through the endless waves, August's thrusts growing erratic, his groans deepening.

"Fuck," he roars against my spine, triggering another devastating climax that shatters my consciousness into blinding fragments.

Jaxon and August erupt simultaneously, marking me as theirs from both ends as my body convulses between them.

Steam still rises from my freshly showered skin as I settle between my two men. August's arms claim me first, though not without Jaxon's momentary resistance.

I catch Jaxon's understanding nod; he needs to work anyway after spending half the night guarding my sleep from nightmares while I was wrapped in August's protective embrace.

CHAPTER 53

ELLIA

"But Jaxon..." I tug at his rolled sleeve, the morning light slanting through the loft's steel-framed windows.

Days have blurred into each other these past weeks, each one pressing me closer to the glass. He stands by the balcony window, dressed head to toe in black, refusing even a moment of fresh air.

"No. And that's final." His voice grinds like gravel. This is ridiculous.

I sidestep a chrome lamp and a driftwood side table to cut him off. When he's angry, his strides become a gallop; the faint hum of traffic below ratchets tension through my veins.

"Jaxon, it's invite-only, and I'll wear a mask," I plead, arms flailing like a windblown sapling. "Please, August, help me out."

I glance at August, lounging like a sunlit statue on the white sectional, hair still wet from his shower. He's watching us, amusement dancing in his bright chestnut eyes.

"Come on," I add, voice near a whimper. I'd drop to my knees if it meant a yes.

This gala, Obsidian's annual affair, is life itself, and they're shutting me out of my own club.

"Listen," Jaxon steps closer, seizing my hands and bringing them to his lips. "I don't trust you'll be safe. If anything happened to you, I won't survive."

My heart clenches. I yank free.

"Victoria knows I'm here. There's a private elevator; no one will see us. They still think I'm in Australia. Solace hasn't seen them leave the country. August..." I swivel to my lover.

August scrubs at his stubbled jaw, his grin widening.

"Yeah, mate, it'll be fun."

Relief catapults me upright; I clap like I did when summer vacation was announced as a kid. "See?"

I race to the couch, hurling myself over its back. He catches me midair, hands firm around my waist, cedarwood and fresh cologne swirling around us.

"Thank you," I murmur, straddling him, bliss blooming in my chest.

"Whoa, whoa," Jaxon protests, waving a hand. "Just because he wants to go doesn't mean I'm changing my mind."

August's eyes glitter with delight, and my heart stutters against my ribs. God, this man is breathtaking with his dark lashes, the curve of his smile, the way his hair falls in a careless wave over his forehead.

I press a kiss to his temple.

"Two," I murmur, then another to his jaw. "Against," another kiss to his warm throat. "One." My lips linger, tasting him.

Jaxon's jaw clenches as he surrenders. "Fine," he growls, eyes flashing dangerously. "We'll get suits, and Jenkins will be armed. He doesn't take his eyes off you for a second, understand? My little bird stays caged."

I sink my teeth into the hollow of August's neck, drawing a sharp hiss from him as I inhale the intoxicating scent of his skin.

Victory pulses between us like a living thing. And now I want my prize.

"I only flew away once," I breathe, gasping when August's fingers dig into my hips, hard enough to bruise.

His touch borders on pain, exactly how I need it.

"I swear I'll be good this time." My teeth graze his jaw, tasting salt.

His growl vibrates through my bones. Heaven has never felt this much like hell, and I'd burn alive to stay here forever.

"You, songbird, are going to be the death of me," Jaxon says, putting a kiss on the top of my head.

Fuck, to be loved by two men at once has filled a void I never knew I had. And I don't ever want to look back.

Jaxon retreats to his makeshift command center, his shoulders rigid as he hunches over surveillance footage. The blue glow from his monitors illuminates his face in harsh angles, casting shadows that deepen when his eyes flick to August and me.

My fingernails carve desperate crescents into the taut canvas of August's neck, as I rock my hips against his restrained, throbbing length.

The friction kindles electric wildfires up my spine, each deliberate roll eliciting gasps from my lips, my throbbing clit pulsating against the denim-encased ridge.

His hands, strong and sure, grip my waist with a force that promises bruises, guiding me in a frenzied rhythm, pulling me down against him with an urgency that leaves me breathless.

He tugs at the waistband of my sweatpants, just enough to allow his hand to slip inside, finding me bare and ready.

"Mmm, already drenched, baby girl," he growls, his voice a low rumble as he slides one finger into my slick heat.

A symphony of moans escapes my lips as he curves his finger, hitting that sweet, secret spot that detonates stars behind my eyelids.

"August, please," I beg, my arms wrapped around his neck like a lifeline, and in this moment, he is exactly that.

I need this man like I need air, like I need the blood in my veins.

"Fuck, my name on your lips," he murmurs, pressing a hot, open-mouthed kiss to my exposed throat.

I flutter my eyes open, just enough to see Jaxon watching, his green eyes a caress, a flame, a sinful promise that sets my body on fire.

August slips another finger inside me, thrusting in and out, pulling his fingers away just enough to make me chase them, to grind harder, deeper.

"Ride until you come," he commands, his breath hot against my ear, and I crave more; I need his fingers buried deep within me.

"That's it, songbird, come on his hand," Jaxon urges, his own hand stroking his length.

He's fully turned his chair, his eyes never leaving the scene of me unraveling at the hands of his best friend. My eyes stay locked on his hand, stroking, squeezing, promising.

August fists my hair with his free hand, sending pinpricks of pain and pleasure across my scalp.

My hips move in a dance of desperation, back and forth, chasing the orgasm that hovers just out of reach. My eyes never stray from Jaxon, even as August devours my throat, his stubble a delicious burn against my skin.

August thrusts deeper, hitting the exact spot my body craves, and my head snaps back.

The two men I love know exactly how to shatter me and piece me back together with their touch.

"There it is, baby girl. Get yourself off," August growls, and on cue, my body detonates.

My walls clench around his fingers, riding out the aftershocks on his hand.

Jaxon has freed his cock, stroking the precum down his length, his eyes a fiery brand on my skin.

I never imagined this would be my life. My body aches for their eyes on me while I come undone just for them.

"Please," I whimper, my eyes still trained on Jaxon.

Releasing my grip on August's neck, I peel off my hoodie and shirt in one fluid motion. August releases his grip on my hair to palm my already peaked nipple.

His moan against my skin sends my body jerking, hoping for another orgasm.

"Jaxon," I whimper.

His strokes become rigid, erratic. He's close, and my body is straining to hold on until he comes. His eyes never leave mine as his orgasm builds, a storm ready to break.

"Come again, songbird," Jaxon breathes from across the room.

My body begins to stutter, chasing my own release. Leaning back for a better angle, the sensation wreaks havoc as August pumps his fingers inside me one last time.

I shatter in his arms, my body trembling as he thrusts through my orgasm, the aftershocks of my second climax leaving me collapsing in his arms.

My erratic breaths are hot on his ear, and Jaxon's hand smears his orgasm along his length, his body convulsing as he comes down from his high.

Only when his eyes finally leave mine, his head snapping back, do I close my eyes, letting my body feel the euphoric tingles coursing through every nerve ending.

"You are so beautiful when you make yourself come," August murmurs against my neck, his hot breath sending tiny shivers down my spine.

He slips his fingers from deep within me, and I ache at the sudden void, my walls clenching around nothing.

August brings those damp fingertips to his lips, tasting my release, and closes his mouth with a low groan, eyes rolling back as if he's sampled the most exquisite delicacy.

"God, you taste incredible," he rasps, offering me his finger. "Open. You need to savor what only we create together."

In my thirty-plus years, I've never allowed myself to taste my own sweetness until these two showed me the joy of it. Now I revel in every drop, every quiver under their touch.

"Mmm," I moan, drawing each finger clean with a slow, deliberate suction.

Then I deepen our kiss, devouring his mouth as though it's been too long since I last tasted him.

When we finally break, gasping for shared air, he straightens, and I instinctively wrap my legs around his waist.

"Let's get you cleaned up," he says softly.

Jaxon watches us through the closet door, eyes dark with anticipation, but he knows August claims me next. The last time, in a fit of reckless passion, we flooded the bathroom by making love in the tub, soaking towels and tears of laughter everywhere.

The claw-foot tub stands vast and gleaming, porcelain bright beneath the soft overhead light. It's spacious enough for three but too small for the way August and Jaxon devour me, unravel me, until I'm laid bare in every sense.

August stayed behind in Sydney for so long, missing this fierce intimacy, and I missed him.

Jaxon captured every gasp and moan on his phone, an intimate record of desires I never knew existed. Michael's adventures now feel tame, almost vanilla, by comparison.

August sets me down before the tub, kisses my forehead, then cues the music, "Dirty Mind" by Boy Epic on the overhead speakers.

Steam coils around us in lazy tendrils, and I slip out of my damp sweatpants and step into the warmth.

August's eyes roam me hungrily from crown to thighs. He licks his lips when I approach, peeling off his snug black tee to reveal lean, tattooed muscles rippling beneath.

They both love it when I take charge, though not always. I'm no helpless victim; their pleasure comes in equal measure to my own. And yet, missteps, like when I snuck away for that bike ride with Arik, earn me punishments as exquisite as they are strict.

My fingers hover over the button of his dark jeans. August breathes patience into my ear as I unbutton each stud and slide down the zipper.

He captures my lips as his tongue chases mine, then hoists me so my legs coil around his waist. His cock, rock-hard against my thighs, teases my entrance with every eager step.

The hot water swirls around us as he lowers us into the tub, pulsing beat of "Lady, Touch Yourself" by Nikki Idol, filling the foggy air.

He settles against the marble, arms stretched wide along the rim, watching every inch of me with lust-darkened eyes.

"I won't touch you," he vows, voice thick with need. "You're going to ride me until I say stop. Do you understand?"

My fingertips glide up his forearms to his shoulders, tracing the bold ink of his tattoos. Goosebumps rise along his skin as I follow the path from collarbone to biceps.

I shift until the slick tip of his cock brushes the velvet folds of my entrance. My other hand caresses the planes of his chest, down to the defined V of his lower abs.

He never averts his gaze as I stroke him, wrapping my hand around his length.

"Yes, sir," I whisper, a soft moan riding the words.

His pupils darken, feral with anticipation.

One palm pressed to his firm chest, the other guiding his cock slick with my wetness, I coat the tip before slowly sinking. Inch by inch, he fills me, every fiber of my being igniting under his girth.

His muscles bunch with each deepening thrust. My head tilts back as I settle fully around him.

"I love when you ride me," he growls, low and rough, sending fresh waves of heat through me.

"August," I breathe, rocking my hips back and forth. The marble edge presses into his fingers as he fights the urge to claim me.

I circle my hips, pulling him out just enough for the head to stay buried inside me, just enough to keep that delicious stretch.

"Fuck," he moans, cock pressing against a spot that sends sparks straight to my core.

My release hangs just out of reach as he commands, "Eyes on me," and I lift my gaze as his body tenses, matching my impending shudder.

My nails score tiny crescents into his chest.

"August," I gasp. "I'm so close."

I bite my lower lip, tasting copper bliss, determined not to break until he grants permission.

My hand drifts down to circle my swollen clit as I brace against his strong thighs. He watches, breath hitching, as I palm my breast, my arousal shining in his gaze.

"Ellia, damn, you're beautiful," he breathes.

His praise tightens the coil of my desire.

I thrust on him once more, and the world narrows to heat and friction.

"Come for me," he groans, and I obey, tearing past the edge in blissful convulsions.

August answers with his own release, pulsing deep inside me. His seed warms me, spiraling toward another crescendo.

His breath rattles as we climax together, but I'm not done; I find another edge.

"It. Feels. So..." A fourth orgasm shatters me, leaving me trembling and collapsing into his arms like a spent goddess. My vision swims with sparkling stars.

"I love watching you use my cock like this," he whispers, pulling me close as our chests rise and fall in unison.

After a moment of tangled limbs and ragged breaths, August shifts beneath me.

"Now, let me clean you up," he murmurs, planting tender kisses into my damp hair as he reaches for a soft washcloth, devoted to caring for the woman he's just undone in every perfect way.

His breath scorches my ear as he whispers, "I love you, Ellia Mae Delvine," each syllable vibrating through me like an electric current.

My body tenses around him, still impaled on his throbbing length. Those three words, never before directed at me despite overhearing them between him and Jaxon, ignite something primal inside me.

I arch my spine, grinding down harder on him, feeling him pulse deeper.

"What did you say?" My voice emerges ragged, disbelieving.

His muscular hands capture my face, thumbs pressing into my cheekbones. He drags me close enough that I can taste the lingering sweetness of my own arousal on his hot breath.

"I. Love. You."

Each word is punctuated by a subtle upward thrust that makes my vision blur. Something breaks open inside me; raw, vulnerable. Tears burn behind my eyes as pleasure and emotion collide in violent waves.

My walls clench around him involuntarily, drawing a guttural moan from his throat.

I crush my mouth against his, tongue seeking, teeth grazing his lower lip.

My hips roll in desperate circles, seeking the friction that might drown out the terrifying vulnerability. His hands slide down to grip my ass, fingers digging into flesh as he guides my movements.

"I..." The word catches in my throat, strangled by fear and desire.

His lips hover a breath away from mine, our shared air thick with sex and confession.

"You don't need to say it back. Say it when you're ready."

His cock twitches inside me as if emphasizing his patience, and I feel myself clenching around him again, my body speaking what my voice cannot.

My body surrendered to August twice more, each climax ripping through me, whether from my stubborn silence or from the torturous moments he stayed away.

The way he reduces me to nothing but raw sensation makes me feel utterly claimed, completely his.

CHAPTER 54

ELLIA

The blue light of the laptop screen illuminates August's furrowed brow as he hunches over the device.

"Ellia, have you seen the contract for the event?"

His voice carries an edge of suspicion that makes my skin prickle.

The document glows on the screen, white text on black, spelling out rules, obligations, the minimum bid of $10 thousand dollars, and those damning full consent clauses that might as well be written in blood.

"Yes, I helped build this event," I reply, crossing the room with measured steps.

The concrete is cool under my bare feet as I reach him.

I place my hand on his shoulder, feeling his muscles coil like a snake about to strike. His cologne, sandalwood, and something darker fill my nostrils.

I could have let them walk in blind, but Jaxon would have hauled me out of there, thrown me over his shoulder like a caveman the moment the auctioneer's gavel struck.

It's for charity, but they won't see it that way. To them, everything outside these walls is a threat, a danger to be neutralized, and I understand their paranoia, but after weeks trapped in this loft, the walls are closing in, suffocating me.

Usually, I'd be attending galas, charity events, slipping through crowds with my signature white streak carefully concealed, the one feature fans instantly recognize.

"Jaxon," August calls, his voice cutting through the tension.

Across the room, Jaxon stands in the kitchen's half-shadow, amber whiskey swirling in his crystal tumbler, ice clinking like tiny warning bells.

"Read the contract," Jaxon commands, his deep voice rumbling as he approaches.

His footsteps are heavy, deliberate, each one bringing the scent of expensive liquor and barely contained anger closer.

Here we go. These two are looking for any excuse to lock me away from the world.

August clears his throat, the sound like sandpaper in the tense silence, and begins to read aloud: "Members-only access," August reads, each syllable dropping like ice into still water.

"Black and silver bracelets verified at entry. Gold prohibited. Masks mandatory." His voice lowers to a dangerous whisper. "Names prohibited. Asking for them gets you removed."

His jaw tightens with an audible click that sends a chill down my spine.

"Minimum bid $10 thousand. Consent assumed upon RSVP." He exhales sharply through his nose, nostrils flaring. "Auctioned privileges include immediate summons, private access, and..." he pauses, eyes flicking to me, dark and penetrating, "...temporary unmasking."

Jaxon stops beside him, so close I can feel the heat radiating from his body, smell the whiskey on his breath mingling with the metallic scent of his cologne.

"Consent can be withdrawn," August continues, each word like a blade being sharpened. "But until then, the house enforces compliance."

His knuckles whiten around the laptop edge.

"No recording. No phones. No witnesses." He looks up now, pupils dilated, suspicion crystallizing into something feral. "And Obsidian reserves the right to remove anyone, anytime, without explanation."

Silence drops between us like a guillotine blade.

August closes the laptop with a snap that makes me flinch.

"This isn't an event," he says, voice vibrating with barely contained rage. "It's a controlled risk."

"Elli, I don't like this." Jaxon's voice comes low and controlled, but I can see the muscle jumping in his jaw.

He takes a deliberate sip of whiskey, amber liquid catching the light as it disappears between his lips. His gaze burns between August and me, scorching in its intensity.

I wet my lips, feeling each heartbeat like a hammer against my sternum.

"Security is always tripled for these events," I manage, though my voice threatens to crack. "The complete system is designed to protect everyone involved."

I move toward them until the heat from their bodies mingles with mine.

"Besides, only the highest bidder gets private access, and who better than you two?"

My finger traces a line between them, the tremor betraying me. "You'd outbid anyone who showed interest."

My chest rises and falls too rapidly now. "And remember, I'm only up for auction if someone specifically requests me. Even then, every person there received a personal invitation."

The metallic taste of adrenaline floods my mouth as I swallow.

"You might find yourselves on the block, too. Not everyone gets bid on, but if someone chooses you, they'll pay at least the minimum to claim their prize for the night."

My hands twist together, betraying me. The silence stretches, taut as a garrote wire, as I wait for their verdict.

Jaxon takes one step toward me, his jaw clenching so hard, I think he might break a molar. The space between us collapses to nothing but breath and heat.

Simultaneously, August rises from his seat, the scrape of the chair legs against concrete making my nerves jangle like loose piano strings.

"How often have you joined these events, songbird?" Jaxon's question slides between us like a blade.

His pupils dilate until his eyes are almost black, his nostrils flaring with each controlled breath. The question I've been dreading since I showed them the contract.

"A few times," I whisper, my fingers twisting the hem of my shirt until my knuckles blanch white.

My mouth goes desert-dry, pulse hammering so hard I can feel it in my throat, and behind my eyes. I can taste copper on my tongue.

My face instinctively contracts, muscles tightening as though preparing for impact, a defensive reflex I thought I'd buried years ago.

Please, please don't ask me anything more. The silent plea screams in my mind as their shadows stretch across me, tall and unforgiving.

August closes what little space remains between us, his solid chest pressing against my back with deliberate pressure. He leans in until his lips nearly graze the shell of my ear, each exhale sending hot currents down my spine. My stray hairs dance with his breath, tickling my hypersensitive skin.

"Anything else you're hiding?" he whispers, voice like gravel wrapped in velvet.

Jaxon sets his glass down with a sharp clink that makes me flinch. The amber liquid sloshes dangerously close to the rim as he stalks forward, predatory and focused.

His fingers brush my cheek before capturing a strand of hair, tucking it behind my ear with deceptive tenderness that makes my pulse skitter.

"Have you been bought, Ellia?" Jaxon enunciates my full name with such precise control that ice floods my veins. His forest-green eyes narrow, pupils contracting to pinpoints of pure intent. "Answer me."

"Once," I whisper, throat constricting. "The others, I stayed mostly out of sight."

My voice sounds foreign to my own ears, small and brittle. A fleeting thought, maybe I was worried for nothing, dies as August's hand slides around my throat.

"Did you fuck, Ellia?" August's question slithers into my ear as his lips brush against my throat, the contact electric and terrifying.

Fingers splaying across my windpipe, thumb pressing into the hollow beneath my jaw. I try to lower my head, to escape his grip, but he holds me firmly in place, forcing my gaze to meet Jaxon's.

His lock onto mine, pupils dilated to black pools rimmed with emerald fire, boring into me as if they could extract the truth directly from my soul.

A pathetic whimper escapes my throat, the sound hanging between us like a confession.

"I didn't fuck him," I whisper, each word scraping my throat raw. "But I came close."

The memory floods back, Michael sprawled across hotel sheets, nostrils rimmed white, glass coffee table dusted with fine lines of powder like fresh snow.

I try shaking my head violently, hair whipping across my face, silently begging them to let this die.

August's free hand snakes around my waist, fingers digging into the soft flesh above my hip bone, pulling me flush against him until I can feel every hard plane of his body.

His breath scorches the sensitive skin behind my ear. Jaxon's predatory gaze holds mine captive.

"What are you hiding, Ellia?" My name slithers from his lips like venom, burning everywhere it touches.

"I..." The word chokes off as August's grip tightens around my throat, the pressure making stars dance at the edges of my vision.

My hands fly up instinctively, pressing against his chest, feeling the thunderous rhythm of his heartbeat beneath my trembling fingers. Each muscle beneath his shirt feels like carved stone, unyielding and dangerous.

"I was close," I gasp when he allows me just enough air, "but I never did. When my mask came off, the bidder recognized me. His eyes... the way they changed... he started touching me, as if he owned me. I called security."

The last words tumble out in a desperate rush. I hold my breath, waiting for punishment to fall.

The words fracture in my mouth like broken glass. "Michael was...I was trying to forget..." Each syllable feels like swallowing thorns.

"What happened with Michael?" Jaxon's shadow falls across me like a shroud.

My secrets press against my ribs, desperate to escape, but I lock them tighter.

Someday they'll pry the whole story from me, the one I've buried beneath layers of shame, but not tonight. Not yet.

CHAPTER 55

AUGUST

If this auction doesn't proceed flawlessly, there'll be hell to pay. Jaxon's already prowling like a caged predator because Ellia refuses to back down.

I want her happiness; she's endured her captivity with surprising grace. Most would have shattered under such isolation, but now that she's emerging from the shadows, restlessness consumes her like a fever.

When Jaxon discovered she'd slipped away for a bike ride during my extraction from Amsterdam, his eyes went cold in that way that makes my spine turn to ice.

I found her rebellion darkly amusing; he responded by putting a bullet through the flight crew's head.

Ellia's been floating through the loft today, her smile genuine for once. Who am I to extinguish this rare spark? Even after I punished that pretty mouth and pussy this morning for her reckless decision to auction herself off like merchandise.

She keeps reminding us that this is Obsidian's crown jewel event, generating millions.

This year, benefits the Afterlight Foundation, the charity that extends support to victims long after the headlines fade and the world forgets.

The organization nobody wants to fund because it forces them to acknowledge that trauma doesn't end when the news cycle does.

Her generosity still cuts through my cynicism. Last year, she funded trauma-focused mental health programs, bringing in over $90 million.

The elite flock to Obsidian for these events, hiding their depravity behind philanthropy.

Everything's "consensual" with safe words in place, but watching her surrounded by hungry eyes makes my trigger finger itch.

Jaxon's been stalking through the club, terrorizing staff with security protocols. Victoria's called three times already, complaining about the "dangerous shadow" making everyone nervous. If only she knew what he's capable of when protecting what's his.

The contract glows on the screen, each clause a potential trapdoor. I scrutinize every word, searching for the hidden knife that could slice through her fragile security.

The language seems airtight for ordinary participants, but not for a woman whose existence depends on remaining a ghost.

"August." Her voice brushes against my neck. "You won't find some legal loophole that predicts my doom."

Her smile is patient but hollow.

I pull her onto my lap, feeling the moisture of her shower-fresh skin through the thin barrier of the towel.

When my mouth finds the curve where her neck meets her shoulder, right where that tattoo blooms across her skin like it was born there, I feel her heartbeat accelerate against my lips.

"Tell me how this works again," I whisper, my words disappearing into the hollow of her throat.

She shifts, angling toward the screen where "House Invite" glows in elegant script. Her face transforms, danger forgotten in her excitement.

"Every guest is automatically in the pool," she explains, voice steady. "No public announcements. If someone catches another guest's interest, they submit through the house."

Her finger traces the line on the screen.

"$10 thousand per nomination card. They can select as many as they want, but payment is immediate."

I meet her gaze, searching for doubt.

"The staff delivers a black card on a silver tray," she continues. "Refuse it, hand it back, no questions, no consequences."

"And acceptance?" The question feels heavy on my tongue.

"Opens bidding at $20 thousand," she says, voice light. "Only after consent. The house manages everything else."

The laptop snaps closed beneath her fingertips.

"Discreet. Regulated. Untraceable."

She frames my face between her palms, and I surrender to her touch, capturing one hand against my cheek.

"Trust me, August. It's just a game." Her eyes darken. "Though I should worry about you and Jaxon being claimed instead, you're both on the block the moment I RSVP'd."

She claims my mouth with hers, a kiss that borders on ownership. The kind that brands itself into memory, that makes my pulse hammer against my ribs like a prisoner desperate for escape.

She withdraws, trailing fingertips along my jawline as she retreats toward the closet.

Water beads trace forbidden paths down her spine, disappearing beneath the precarious edge of her towel. The fabric shifts with each step, threatening to surrender to gravity. My throat tightens.

Such a dangerous creature, lethal and magnificent, and somehow, impossibly mine.

The bass line throbs through the loft speakers, vibrating beneath my skin like a second heartbeat.

Ellia's resurrection through music, a woman who once stared at her own instruments like they were instruments of torture.

She moves differently now, her body fluid where it was once brittle. I watch her breathe, each inhale deeper than the last week's, and something possessive coils in my chest.

She's mine, not because I own her, but because I witnessed her crawl back from the abyss.

The elevator doors slide open with a metallic hiss.

Jaxon emerges, jaw tight, shoulders rigid with tension. His fingers rake through his hair as he approaches, leaving furrows like battle scars. He collapses into the chair across from me, the oak table between us suddenly feeling like insufficient cover.

"This auction..." he mutters, raking his hands down his face. "Everything's in place, but my instincts are screaming. And my instincts..."

"...have kept us alive," I finish. "But who's going to tell her? You want to be the one to extinguish that spark we've spent months trying to ignite back," maintaining the careful distance between us.

"Because I won't." My words hang between us like smoke. "She knows the rules. First sign of danger, we extract her and consent be damned."

I tilt my chin towards the ceiling. "Listen."

"Nothing's Gonna Stop Us Now," by Starship is playing overhead, and Ellia's voice twines with the music, raw and unpracticed but alive.

The sound hooks into something primal in me, and I close my eyes against the wave of relief.

Jaxon's expression softens, the predator momentarily caged by something dangerously close to hope.

His eyes track the sound like a man dying of thirst. We both know tonight's risks, but we've tasted her silence for too long to deny her this moment of flight.

Ellia's voice cuts through the tension. "Get dressed." The command slices from behind the closet door. "And don't look until I'm ready."

The heavy doors close with a decisive click, leaving just a sliver of light escaping through the crack.

I catch Jaxon's eyes, witnessing that rare, unguarded smile that only she can summon from him.

The first night I met him, his hands were still stained with someone else's blood, and he never revealed whose.

Over bottles of whiskey that couldn't wash away whatever haunted him, he shared fragments of war zones I couldn't imagine while I offered trivial stories of rugby scrums.

By dawn, he'd killed two men who tried to rob us. I never saw the bodies. Just the cold efficiency in his movements and the way he cleaned his blade on their clothes before walking away.

Jaxon's jaw tightens as he stalks to the kitchen. The whiskey bottle trembles slightly in his grip as he pours a double. His knuckles, scarred from countless fights, whiten around the glass.

I recognize the ritual, the calm before violence.

Tonight, his vigilance has an edge I've never witnessed, something untamed and desperate. He's kept her breathing through situations that should have left her a nameless corpse.

I'm grateful for his lessons in killing, the precise pressure points, the angle of entry for a blade, the cold mathematics of a clean shot, though I pray I don't need them tonight.

The custom suits Ellia commissioned cling like a second skin, midnight armor tailored to kill.

Mine: black on black with a silk tie that feels like a garrote against my throat—a beautiful noose I'll gladly wear because her fingers selected it.

Jaxon's matches but without the tie, the assassin's concession to vanity without sacrificing the ability to breathe when violence erupts.

Jaxon stands before the mirror, fingers trembling against French cuffs that refuse to submit. Blood has drained in his fingertips, and the tremor betrays what his face never will.

I approach, reaching for his wrist. "Here."

"I'm good." The words slice between us, sharp as the blade I know is strapped to his ankle.

His eyes meet mine in the reflection, glacial, haunted, before returning to the task. The man who's slaughtered without hesitation is now undone by waiting for her.

"I'm ready." Her voice floats over the music from behind the closet doors, soft as a death whisper.

The doors part with excruciating slowness. My lungs seize, oxygen becoming a luxury I can no longer afford.

Beside me, Jaxon's breath catches—the sound a man makes when taking a bullet.

She emerges like a beautiful specter, draped in darkness. "What do you think?"

The gown is a weapon, midnight-black lace revealing tantalizing glimpses of alabaster skin beneath, the faint silvery lines of her angel tattoo visible then vanishing with each breath, like forbidden secrets offered then cruelly withdrawn.

The lace drapes from her collarbones, cascading over the rigid structure beneath, hooked delicately on her middle fingers as if the material were spun specifically for her hands to command.

The corset cinches her waist with brutal precision, whalebone architecture creating an hourglass silhouette that defies nature.

Embroidered black roses with bloodred centers and deep Amethyst accents bloom across the satin like elegant bruises, catching the light with each inhale.

The skirt splits high on her right thigh, a calculated vulnerability that makes my mouth go desert-dry, the hemline pooling at her feet where it meets stilettos sharp enough to pierce flesh.

We move toward her in unison, predators answering a siren call. Her scent, lavender and vanilla with something darker beneath, floods my senses.

My body responds with violent need, straining painfully against the expensive suit, the physical ache nothing compared to the desperate hunger clawing through my chest.

Jaxon's exhale is almost inaudible. "Fuck." He growls.

The single syllable hangs between us, raw and reverent. She turns slowly, the fabric catching light like oil on water, revealing glimpses of thigh that make my mouth go dry.

Her eyes, lined dark, that make the amber almost phosphorescent, drink in our reactions, hungry for the power she wields.

"You've rendered him speechless," I say, my voice rougher than intended. "What he means is you're devastating."

My fingers itch to touch the hollow of her throat, the elegant curve now exposed without her usual streak of colored hair swept into that low side bun she sometimes wears.

"Your hair..." I say, reaching where her famous white streak was.

"Temporary," she interrupts, eyes dropping to the floor. Her tongue darts across her ruby red lips.

The music shifts, "This Year's Love" by David Gray, a haunting melody spilling from hidden speakers.

I extend my hand. "Come to me," I command, voice like gravel over velvet.

She crosses the distance between us, her movements liquid, and I pull her against me with possessive urgency, one hand splayed across the small of her back.

"You're trembling," I murmur against her temple as we slow dance to the music

"You're the reason," she whispers back, pressing closer.

Jaxon retreats a step, watching us sway to the music. His eyes meet mine over her head, a silent communication, predatory and protective.

We both know the truth: she's been caged too long, and tonight's freedom might destroy us all.

I twirl her once in Jaxon's direction as he catches her mid-spin. He pulls her into his embrace, swaying to the music while whispering confessions in her ear.

As the song fades into "Seven Devils" by Florence and the Machine, the vocals fill the space between us.

Ellia's pupils dilate as the first notes hit, her body swaying almost imperceptibly.

They break apart, but not before his lips brush her knuckles, lingering a half-second too long.

Her gaze finds mine over Jaxon's shoulder, something dark and possessive flashing across her face as she releases his hands.

The smile she gives me is deliberate, calculated; she knows exactly what she's doing to my body.

"Christ, Ellia," Jaxon breathed, pulling her in tighter. "You're not just beautiful tonight. You're lethal."

"Wait until you see what else I've prepared," she whispers, her breath hot against my ear.

She pulls away, fingertips trailing down my chest as she turns toward the table. "I had something made for us."

The velvet box sits like a dark promise, its presence commanding attention. Her fingers caress the lid before lifting it with theatrical slowness.

"When exactly did you arrange this?" Jaxon's voice cuts through the room, sharp with suspicion.

"The moment we landed in London." Her laugh is low, throaty. "Weeks before you even knew about the auction."

"That was reckless," Jaxon says, his voice low and lethal.

"Careful," she interrupts, eyes flashing.

The lid lifts with a whisper of resistance, revealing three masks nestled in black silk that absorbs all light except where it catches on their edges.

"Obsidian Twilight," she murmurs, her fingertip tracing the contour with such delicate precision it's almost obscene.

The twin masks gleam with malevolent beauty, obsidian black bleeding into bruise-purple at their edges, like violence captured in porcelain.

Between them lies something that makes my throat constrict: a metal creation of razor-sharp filigree, tiny diamonds catching light like frozen tears about to fall.

The cut-work patterns pulse with meaning, the design twisting into feathered edges—raven-like, predatory, as if it might move if I look away.

From the temple, where dark metal transitions to royal purple, a single raven feather curves upward, its barbs gleaming with an oily iridescence that seems to drink in the surrounding darkness.

CHAPTER 56

ELLIA

Our masks glint in the dim light as we enter the private elevator that descends to Obsidian's hidden hall, a passageway known only to us.

Victoria has cleared the back area of other guests in anticipation of our arrival.

Jaxon's fingers press possessively against my spine, his touch burning through the thin fabric of my dress while I curl my hand around August's arm.

The elevator's polished metal doors reflect our trinity: dangerous, beautiful, untouchable.

I lean into their bodies, savoring their heat like it might be our last embrace. The air between us thins, my lungs fighting for breath, not because they're too close, but because they're not close enough.

Their beauty is a knife-edge against my self-control. By midnight, I'll be crawling across the velvet seats, mounting them before everyone, marking territory with lipstick and fingernails.

August's lips brush my palm, reading my thoughts through skin, while Jaxon's grip tightens, promising violet shadows on my hips by morning, shadows I now crave like addiction.

As the elevator descends, I press closer still. What consequences could possibly matter in a world where the doors open only for those I permit?

Obsidian's exclusive gatherings draw wealthy couples hunting for their perfect addition. Many such arrangements have flourished over the years, returning season after season.

We've cultivated a sanctuary for the elite with particular appetites.

The black bracelet auctions were initially selective, but after expanding to silver-tier memberships, we now turn away latecomers.

First response, first served. Perhaps I'll extend these events to my other establishments, but for now, the revenue flows generously into a city desperate for such infusions.

As we step into the club, "Bad Angel" by Nikki Idol echoes through the speakers, and desire crackles in the air like static electricity.

I've hungered for this; perched in the shadows, observing the beautiful and damned as they surrender to private performances where artists bare their souls to the precious few rather than the faceless many.

Victoria stands sentinel by the obsidian bar, her black fitted suit a second skin, blonde waves cascading around her face like a halo for the wicked.

Around us, security personnel and staff move like wraiths, their black satin masks both uniform and shield, granting them the same anonymous power we all crave in this sanctuary of secrets.

Victoria glides toward us, her ever-present clipboard clutched against her chest like a talisman.

"Welcome," she purrs, her crimson lips barely moving as she beckons us toward a secluded circular booth.

A perfect positioning, close enough to witness every delicious moment on stage, yet shrouded in shadows where prying eyes can't follow.

The club's signature purple fluorescents throb like bruises overhead, their light bleeding into white and crimson accents that transform skin into living canvases of violet shadows.

Plush circular booths, each a velvet-lined confessional, line the walls, while intimate tables cluster around a dance floor that spread before the altar-like stage.

Tonight, three throne-like chairs wait in silent judgment at center stage, their emptiness a dare whispered to every masked face in the room.

Above, the second-story balcony opens to glimpses of starlight through retractable panels, its railings lined with watchers who lean like gargoyles over the spectacle below.

The VIP lounges nestle in shadowed alcoves along the upper tier, their walls containing whispers that would make diplomats blush and royalty squirm.

I designed these rooms with calculated cruelty; visibility comes at the price of exhibition, the wealthy paying dearly for the privilege of privacy that isn't quite private.

Obsidian shifts its skin nightly, sometimes housing writhing bodies on the main floor while whispered auctions occur above, sometimes reversing the hierarchy entirely.

Musicians who grace my stage often linger afterward, their fame temporarily suspended behind masks as they pursue pleasures unavailable in the outside world.

Their signatures on my contracts are worth more than platinum records, NDAs scrawled in desperation that seal my empire in secrecy.

Bodies press against each other in the already packed space, the air thick with perfume and anticipation.

Jaxon's gaze darts like a predator across the room as we navigate the floor.

"This place is incredible," August breathes, his lips grazing my ear, sending electricity down my spine.

I press my palm against August's chest, feeling his heart hammer beneath my touch.

"Why are there three chairs on that stage?" he whispers, his eyes never leaving the velvet thrones as he slides into the booth beside me.

Jaxon remains standing, his shadow falling across our table like a possessive claim.

"That's where the initiates sit," I murmur, leaning forward to rest my elbows on the obsidian tabletop, the cool surface a stark contrast to the heat building between us.

"Where you'll sit, between two strangers, while hungry eyes devour you from the darkness. When the bidding ends, you'll leave with whoever owns your card."

August's jaw tightens, a muscle pulsing beneath his skin as he locks eyes with Jaxon.

"You will not let her accept any fucking card," he growls, each word dripping with territorial rage. "She's not some trophy to be passed around."

A dark laugh escapes my throat as I lean back against the plush leather.

"Oh, my love," I purr, sliding my fingertips up his thigh, feeling the muscle tense beneath expensive fabric. "Only I decide if I withdraw, and only then if I receive a black card. No one controls this game but me."

My fingers drift higher, finding the rigid outline of his arousal.

"Besides," I whisper against his ear, "did you think I'd just sit here all night watching?"

"Christ..." he chokes out as my thumb circles his tip through his pants.

Across the table, Jaxon's smirk gleams in the purple light. Bastard. Let's see how composed he stays when it's his turn under my merciless touch.

August's breath warms my neck as he leans in.

"That woman in red keeps staring at you," he whispers, his lips brushing my ear.

Jaxon's hand tightens possessively on my thigh.

She stands in the corner near the stairs leading to the second floor. A glass of wine in her hand, talking to a woman with raven hair. Both are beautiful, from what I can see of their half-faces.

My eyes drift up, the second floor crowded with men in masks, the ones who come to collect their prizes for the evening.

"Look up," I murmur, tilting my chin toward the shadowed balcony where silhouettes hover like predators above water. "The real players never show their faces. They watch from above, bidding from darkness."

"You never mentioned that," Jaxon hisses, his fingers digging into my flesh. "If you think I'll let you..."

"You'll let me do exactly what I want," I cut him off, pressing my whiskey-cooled lips against his jaw.

The liquor burns a path down my throat, igniting something primal.

Through the haze of bodies, I spot her, copper hair cascading over bare shoulders, a midnight-blue gown clinging to her curves like water.

Three men surround her, their matching azure masks catching the light as they lean in, whispering secrets against her skin.

Her laugh carries across the room like broken glass. She is wearing a silver bracelet while the men pinning over her wear black.

"She belongs to all of them," I say, feeling August stiffen beside me. "And they to her."

It's not all that uncommon for women to flaunt their many companions. They come to feel safe, to donate, and to bid on their woman. To some, it is an ego thing. To others, to collect another invitee into their world.

In the center of the club, couples prowl like predators, positioning their bodies with calculated precision, shoulders back, necks exposed, fingertips trailing possessively across each other's skin. Their hunger is palpable.

Beyond them, exquisite masks catch the light, feathers and jewels adorning faces flushed with anticipation, while gowns cling to curves like liquid sin.

Men with razor-sharp jawlines hover in shadowed corners, their eyes gleaming behind ornate disguises as they track movement across the floor.

Some press their lips to strangers' ears, whispering promises they may or may not keep, while others nurse amber liquids that catch the light like trapped fire.

Black bracelets flash like status symbols on wrists throughout the room, while silver ones peek from beneath sleeves or behind backs.

The hierarchy is clear—black for privilege, silver for those kept waiting. I never considered this when choosing my tattoo artist's bracelets, though I understand the appeal of temporary freedom at black-only events.

"Round one will begin in fifteen minutes," the auctioneer announces, their voice slicing through the heavy air. "Please mingle before the round starts."

The pause in their words carries weight, an invitation to indulge in darker appetites.

I slide against the velvet booth, pressing into August as I rise. His breath catches at the friction between us. Jaxon grips my wrist hard enough to bruise.

"Where do you think you're going?" he whispers, pupils wide in the purple light.

"To walk around," I reply, my smile slow and venomous. The tip of my tongue touches my upper lip, leaving it glistening.

"There was nothing about walking around," Jaxon hisses through clenched teeth, his jawline sharp enough to cut glass.

"You're staying close to us." His thumb traces threatening circles on my pulse point.

I lean close to Jaxon's ear. "Fine, but silence on the floor."

My tone makes him flinch. His nostrils flare, uncertain what I've become tonight. I extend my hand to August.

"Come."

August and Jaxon exchange glances, a wordless conversation flowing between them like an invisible current. I catch the subtle lift of Jaxon's eyebrow, the almost imperceptible tightening at the corner of August's mouth.

They think I don't notice their silent brotherhood, their private code. I could decode it if I wanted to, I usually know exactly what passes between them, but I let them keep this small secret.

A smile plays at my lips as I watch their little performance.

His hand engulfs mine, warm and damp with anticipation, his grip tightening until our bones press together.

Another smile unfurls across my face as I feel the tremor in his fingers, the barely contained storm beneath his composed exterior. I catalog the tension coiled in his shoulders, the rigid line of his spine, promising myself I'll unravel him thread by exquisite thread before dawn breaks.

The bass of "Inhale Me" by 88DS pulses beneath my stilettos, each thud reverberating up through my legs as we weave between masked figures. The crowd parts and closes around us like dark water.

A flash of black cuts between August and me, severing our linked hands. The woman, with honey-streaked hair swept into an elegant chignon, lets her gaze crawl over him, unhurried and appraising.

My eyes dart to her wrists, finding silver.

My throat constricts, a metallic taste flooding my mouth as her manicured fingers brush his sleeve, deliberately, possessively.

The rage that surges through me is visceral, primal even, a dark, oily thing that coats my insides.

A flash of crimson catches my peripheral vision. She stands motionless amid the writhing bodies, blonde hair coiled in a severe bun, her mask studded with blood-red rhinestones that glitter like fresh wounds under the pulsing lights.

Her eyes, obsidian behind that mask, haven't left me since we entered.

When she passes, her scent hits me, jasmine, and something metallic, hauntingly familiar, raising goosebumps along my arms.

Her gaze shifts to August just as another woman, petite, dangerous in green silk that clings to her like a second skin, grazes her fingertips across his shoulder.

I watch her melt into the shadows, memorizing the curve of her neck, the exact shade of her chestnut hair.

From my right, a man in a black tuxedo approaches. His blonde hair catches the fluorescent lights, almost glowing.

I tilt my head up as he nears. Blue eyes lock onto mine, something in them strangely familiar.

He slides between August and me, hand extended toward me. I step back slightly, a silent refusal, and August appears at my side as if conjured, his breath hot against my ear, lips grazing sensitive skin.

"It's me and you, baby girl," he whispers, voice rough with possession as he claims the corner of my mouth.

His fingers press into my hip, five distinct points of exquisite pressure, while his gaze never leaves the mystery man retreating into the shadows.

As his eyes lock with Jaxon's across the floor, where the same elegant woman with raven hair circles him like a shark scenting blood.

Jaxon extricates himself with practiced ease, stalking toward us with predatory grace.

As August guides me through the crowd, the weight of unseen eyes presses against my skin like cold, wet hands.

I try to dismiss it, but the sensation crawls up my spine like a warning. I remind myself: this is an auction. Everyone is watching. Everyone is hungry.

I curve my lips into a calculated smile as August's hand presses into the small of my back, guiding me to our table.

The heat of his palm burns through the thin fabric of my dress.

A server materializes beside us, voice low and deferential, but Jaxon cuts him off with a sharp "No" that slices through the air. His jaw clenches, a muscle twitching beneath taut skin.

"Maybe after the first few rounds," Jaxon murmurs, his thigh pressing against mine beneath the table.

The friction ignites a current between us, hot and dangerous.

"By the way, how many rounds are there?" His breath caresses my neck, sending goosebumps cascading down my spine.

"Depends on the participants," I whisper, deliberately letting my lips graze the shell of his ear.

His response is ravenous, a growl that vibrates from deep in his chest, the sound traveling directly to my core. My thighs clench involuntarily, the absence of underwear suddenly acute, the cool air kissing my bare skin with each subtle movement.

August's fingers find my exposed thigh, his touch scorching as he traces the high slit of my dress. I guide his hand deeper, beneath the fabric, until his fingertips brush against my naked flesh.

The contact sends liquid fire through my veins, my pulse hammering in my throat as his pupils dilate to black pools.

His gaze drops to where our hands disappear beneath silk just as a staff member approaches, placing three auction paddles before us with practiced discretion.

Numbers 33, 13, and 53 gleam under the purple lights. The high count suggests a crowd larger than anticipated, bodies pressed together in darkened corners, watching, waiting, hungry.

I lift the auction paddle, its weight substantial against my trembling fingers. Anticipation courses through me like electricity, a delicious dread pooling low in my belly.

Around us, the crowd settles into its seats with predatory grace.

Above, silhouettes line the mezzanine railing—mostly men, their hungry gazes cutting through the haze like searchlights, with one or two women whose red-painted lips curve into knowing smiles.

The staff glides between tables, distributing black cards that gleam like obsidian under the pulsing lights. Jaxon's fingers dig into my inner thigh, each fingertip a brand against my flesh.

August's hand has barely moved, his middle finger making lazy, torturous circles against my swollen clit, sending shockwaves of pleasure up my spine while his eyes track the staff's movements with calculated intensity.

A staff member delivers a card to the woman draped in midnight blue satin. She stands encircled by her three men in tailored suits, their bodies forming a wall of expensive fabric around her as she tilts her head back, cheeks flushed beneath their collective gaze.

Another card passes to a man whose towering frame mirrors August's imposing height, his companion's stiletto nails raking possessively down his arm.

My eyes search for the final card until a staff member materializes before us, extending a silver tray toward Jaxon.

The blood in my veins crystallizes, turning to ice shards that pierce my lungs with each shallow breath. I had considered the possibility of my men being auctioned, but the reality slices through me like a serrated blade.

My fingers clamp around Jaxon's wrist with desperate strength, nails leaving crescent moons in his skin.

He feels my panic, his eyes boring into mine, seeking permission while something dangerous flickers behind his gaze.

Without breaking eye contact with the waiting tray, I incline my head slightly, my voice emerging as a strangled whisper.

"It's for charity," I manage, the words scraping past the knot of dread lodged in my throat.

He hesitates for a beat before picking up the card.

The lights shift to blood-red, staining every face.

I grip the two men beside me as conversation dies, replaced by shallow breathing and wet clicks of parted lips.

A white light slices the platform. The auctioneer appears, leather gloves creaking as they flex their hands, with his bone-white mask gleaming, his voice a velvet razor.

"Good evening," he whispers, the sound somehow penetrating flesh.

The auctioneer's voice slithers through the room.

"Welcome to Curiosity Killed the Cat." His gloved fingers spread wide in theatrical welcome. "Tonight's proceeds benefit survivors of sexual trauma."

He pauses, letting the irony hang in the air.

"Remember, at Obsidian, invitation supersedes nomination."

My gaze darts across the sea of masks. The woman in crimson has vanished into the crowd, but center stage sits the tall blonde stranger, his azure eyes drilling into mine from behind obsidian leather.

The silence pulses.

"This is where curiosity doesn't just kill; it devours. It consumes. It leaves nothing behind."

Then my eyes drift to the stage. His tongue darts out, moistening invisible lips beneath the mask.

"Anonymity isn't just enforced, it's sacred. Names are chains we've shed. Questions are weaknesses we've abandoned."

"Tonight is about surrender. But" he pauses with his finger to the sky.

One gloved finger extends, pointing nowhere and everywhere. "Remember: you came willingly. Your acceptance is written in blood. Those who decline... cease to exist."

The crowd's collective inhale sounds like a death rattle.

"Our first three offerings have submitted to the house's hunger. Bring them."

The spotlight becomes a predator, hunting new prey.

"$10 thousand marked your victim. $20 thousand draws first blood."

The auctioneer's eyes burn through their mask, scorching whoever they touch.

"This isn't ownership, this is a surrender of boundaries. This is breathing their air. This is feeling their heat. This is standing close enough to taste their fear."

Jaxon brings my hand to his lips, teeth grazing my knuckles. "I trust you," he breathes, the words a sacred vow between predators.

He slides from the booth with lethal grace; each button of his jacket fastened like armor before battle.

White-hot rage floods my veins as they position him in the center velvet chair, a king on a sacrificial throne.

The woman in blue trembles at his right while the third chair yawns empty, waiting.

Across the room, his companion's face fractures, tears threatening to shatter her composure. He brands her cheek with a kiss, then stalks to the stage like a wolf entering the kill zone.

Jaxon's eyes lock onto mine, burning with possession and promised violence. August's grip bruises my hip as I lean into him, coconspirator rather than conquest.

Between us, a silent pact forms in this den of predators.

The gavel rises. Their gaze impales the crowd.

"Shall we begin the feeding?"

The gavel falls like a gunshot in the dark. "Twenty."

The crowd descends into a feeding frenzy over the lady in blue, numbers slashing through the air like knives. Her sapphire eyes, cold as winter behind her feathered mask, never waver from her men, even as strangers bid to possess her body for the night.

A drop of sweat traces the elegant column of her throat, disappearing between her breasts.

Her men turn predatory, voices cutting sharper with each escalating bid. "$2 million."

"Two-point-five."

The vultures from upstairs lean forward over the railings, their hungry gazes dissecting her like surgeons.

When her trembling subsides, she bares her teeth, tongue darting across crimson lips like she's tasting blood in the water.

The auctioneer's voice slices through my skull: "$3 million?"

His eyes rake the crowd with surgical precision before tilting upward to the shadows. "Last call."

The silence crushes the air from my lungs. Even the music seems to hold its breath.

"Sold. $2.75 The gavel cracks like a gunshot.

I press back against August's chest, his heartbeat thundering against my spine. A savage smile spreads across my face. $3 million?

For Jaxon, I'd drain bank accounts dry. I'd burn empires to ash. $3 million is nothing but kindling for the inferno I'm prepared to ignite.

The lady in blue melts back into her seat, victory etched in her smile. The auctioneer's voice slashes through the perfumed air like a serrated blade.

"Moving along," he purrs, slamming the gavel with enough force to make my pulse stutter. "$20 thousand?"

I let someone else draw first blood. My eyes hunt for the raven-haired predator from earlier, but she's vanished into the shadows.

"$10 million." The voice floats down from above; feminine, hungry, dripping with intention.

My lungs constrict. My fingernails dig crescents into my palms until I taste copper on my tongue. Charity be damned.

"$11 million?" The auctioneer's gavel points like an accusation.

I thrust my paddle upward, marking my territory. "Eleven from the corner booth."

"$20 million." The same disembodied voice.

My head whips toward August, rage burning my throat raw. His jaw clenches, a muscle pulsing beneath his skin.

"$30 million," he growls, paddle rising like a weapon.

Jaxon's eyes, obsidian behind his mask, never leave mine. His shoulders roll once, twice, the only betrayal of the tension coiling inside him like a viper.

His gaze suddenly locks onto something above, and his entire body goes rigid. His lips press into a bloodless line.

"$40 million?" The auctioneer's voice caresses the hidden bidder upstairs, and something predatory erupts inside me, tearing through flesh and bone.

“$45 million,” the same hungry voice.

Something snaps inside me like a feral, ancient thing breaking free of its cage.

I rise to my feet, blood roaring in my ears.

“75 million dollars," I snarl, each word dripping venom.

My eyes never leave Jaxon's, claiming him, marking him as mine before this den of wolves.

The auctioneer chokes.

The crowd's collective gasp sucks oxygen from the room.

Whispers erupt like hissing flames, scorching the surrounding air.

In the many years of these auctions, no one has ever offered such a sum. The previous record of forty million is now shattered beneath my heel.

“Do I hear one hundred?” The auctioneer says.

Impatiently waiting for the mystery woman to counter my bid

The auctioneer's eyes flash with unholy hunger.

"$100 million?" His gavel hovers in the air like a guillotine blade, pointing toward the shadows above.

The silence stretches, taut as a garrote wire. My heart hammers against my ribcage, each beat a war drum.

"Going once..." His voice drops to a whisper that somehow cuts through the room. "Going twice..."

The crowd's collective breath catches, a hundred predators frozen mid-hunt.

Then: "SOLD!"

The gavel crashes down with such violence that the sound reverberates through my bones like a gunshot wound.

CHAPTER 57

JAXON

The auctioneer's voice fades to white noise as my gaze locks onto her, the woman on the second floor with raven hair. She's watching me like I'm already carrion.

My pulse quickens when she leans to whisper to the lady in red, whose blood-red nails tap against her champagne flute. Something in her platinum blonde hair, the sharp angle of her jaw, mirrors my bidder's face. A relative? An accomplice?

The overhead lights flicker, casting her features in grotesque shadows before she slips away.

"$6 million?" The auctioneer's voice slices through the room. "Going once."

August pulls Ellia against him, his fingers digging possessively into her waist. She whispers something, and his gaze darts to a tall blond man in the corner whose eyes devour her like she's already his property.

"Like hell," I mutter, jaw clenched so tight my teeth might crack. "I'll kill him first."

The lady in blue beside me cuts her eyes at me. I must have said that too loudly.

"Going twice!"

The crowd's hungry stares crawl over my skin like insects. I can't breathe. Can't move.

"SOLD!" The gavel crashes down with finality. "$5.5 million."

A woman's sob pierces the silence, mascara bleeding into her cocktail napkin as we're led from the stage like prized cattle to slaughter.

I can barely swallow as white-gloved attendants weave through the crowd; silver trays balanced on their fingertips.

The woman in the emerald silk gown with her honey hair twisted into a severe knot places a card with blood-red nails.

Light fractures across her jeweled mask as she pivots toward August, and I flash back to earlier: her fingers lingering on his arm while Ellia stood frozen beside them, knuckles white with silent rage.

"Quite the selection tonight," the auctioneer purrs to the circle of vultures, their laughter cutting through the murmur of the crowd. Cheering each other for their friend's selection.

A server weaves toward our table, and the room blurs at the edges, narrowing to a tunnel where only August, Ellia, and that goddamn tray exists.

Ellia presses herself against August's side, trembling. Her eyes wide with terror, she fixated on the approaching try.

Slipping into the booth on Ellia's side, "Don't touch it," I whisper, but my voice drowns in the clamor.

God, please don't fucking touch it, I repeat to myself.

The server bows, extending two black cards. "Your invitations, sir, madam."

August's fingers hover above the invitation. My heart slams against my ribcage like it's trying to escape.

I dig my fingers into Ellia's thigh, feeling her muscle tense beneath the thin fabric. She stifles a gasp, her skin warming under my possessive grip.

Ellia shakes her head, her fingers finding mine beneath the table. I exhale slowly as August hovers above the black card, without touching it.

"I can't do this," she whispers, and August withdraws his hand completely, leaving both invitations remain untouched.

Across the room, Emerald dress narrows her eyes at August's rejection, lips curling into something feral.

Good.

She marked him as her prey, but these two are mine to protect, not merchandise for tonight's auction block.

I settle back against the velvet booth. Ellia's grip tightens on both August and me, her pulse racing beneath my fingertips.

The white-gloved staff retreat, dispersing through the glittering crowd with their silver trays of fate.

"Jaxon!" Ellia's whispered voice cracks as her gaze locks onto a tall blond man across the room. "I need to leave."

Her hand trembles violently in mine, like a bird trying to escape a cage.

I lean in close while August presses against her other side, sheltering her between us.

"Let's go, then."

She shakes her head, eyes wide. "We have to wait for the next walkthrough."

I nod, tracking the blond man as he sips amber liquid from a crystal tumbler. Something in his jawline triggers recognition. His gaze meets mine before he slips into the shadows near the staircase.

Above us, men lean over the balcony railing, auction paddles hovering like vultures' wings.

Tonight, though, I'll ensure Ellia and August remain anchored beside me.

The auctioneer's gavel cracks against wood, pulling my attention to the stage.

Three women occupy the black velvet chairs: one draped in blue and silver, auburn hair cascading over bare shoulders; another poured into black silk that accentuates every curve; the third adorned in red and black lace, silver hair gleaming under the chandeliers.

Bidding commences, $3 million for the first, $5.5 million for the second. For the third, a frenzy erupts. As the numbers climb, Ellia's death grip on my hand finally loosens, blood rushing back into my numbed fingers.

Her eyes dart nervously around the room, and I follow her gaze, person by person.

Emerald Dress still watches August; her lips curled in silent fury at Ellia for keeping him from the auction block.

The gavel crashes down.

"Sold for $25 million," the auctioneer announces with practiced finality.

The women are escorted from the stage, disappearing into the crowd like smoke. Another crack of the gavel.

"Fifteen minutes until the next round begins."

Music swells as the crowd falls into an eerie choreography, bodies gliding across the dance floor in predatory silence.

I grasp Ellia's trembling hand and ease her from the table. August flanks her other side, our bodies forming a protective barrier around her as we navigate toward the hidden hallway.

I catch Victoria's eye across the room and signal with a subtle nod that we're making our exit. But before we can reach safety, a manicured hand shoots out, stopping August cold.

"You could have been mine," Emerald Dress hisses, her words carrying just far enough to serve as both threat and public humiliation.

August exhales softly, almost amused.

"You're confusing opportunity with delusion," he says, gently prying the emerald lady's hand off his arm.

Ellia laughs, and the woman whips her head toward Ellia.

"Do you know who I am?" she snarls, baring her teeth.

Ellia glances at the two of us before stepping forward. Her posture tells me this won't end well.

"Touch what's mine again, and I'll break every one of your fucking fingers," Ellia warns.

The emerald lady fixes all her attention on Ellia.

When she raises her hand toward August's chest again, Ellia recoils and punches her square in the nose.

The impact shatters bone with a sickening crack. Blood splatters across her face, and her mask flies off, revealing a woman in her fifties.

I tilt my head. August bursts into laughter. The club falls silent, save for the music, every eye on us.

Victoria materializes at my side, flanked by two staffers.

"Ma'am, you need to leave," one says, but Victoria waves him off.

"I'll handle this," she replies.

I nod and follow as we slip into the "Staff Only" hallway, like we're headed to the principal's office after a fight. The crowd resumes its wanderings once we're inside.

"Ellia, even if this is your club, you can't do that. Not tonight. You know the rules," Victoria tells her.

"Yeah, yeah. Get me the guest list, who's in and who's waiting," Ellia says, pressing the elevator button.

"Ellia?" I ask, tilting my head.

She doesn't answer. She steps into the elevator and turns to Victoria, while August and I pile in behind her.

Victoria nods, the doors close, and Ellia exhales a long, shaky breath, sliding down to lean against the sleek wall.

"Someone here doesn't belong," she murmurs.

The elevator opens onto the loft. Ellia stumbles in, struggling with her stilettos.

"Let me," August says, crouching to help and lifting her dress just enough to free the straps.

"Talk to me," I urge, my own mask dropping onto the oak table with a soft thud.

August takes his time slipping off her shoes and begins to massage her feet as they land on the floor.

God, she's gorgeous when she's being pampered.

"Something about that blond man and the raven-haired woman who had her eye on us," Ellia says as August carries her to the couch.

He sets her down, places her feet in his lap, and resumes the massage.

She gently removes his mask, and my heart skips a beat at the tenderness in her eyes. Then she reaches for her own mask, hesitates for a second, tears welling, and finally places it aside.

"That green lady had it coming," she says.

We all burst out laughing because she is not wrong.

"They're here," she whispers, voice like shattered glass.

The color drains from her face, leaving nothing but hollow terror in its wake. August wraps his arms around her trembling shoulders while I press my finger to my earpiece.

"Jenkins," I murmur, "we have a breach."

CHAPTER 58

ELLIA

Days have passed since the incident at Obsidian. Jaxon and Jenkins meticulously analyze security footage, comparing faces to registered bracelets.

A few discrepancies emerge, a testament to my security protocols.

The registration process requires each patron to upload a clear photograph and comprehensive personal details.

This verification ensures staff can confirm the bracelet's rightful owner. Unlike transferable fair tickets, these are strictly non-transferable once registered.

I designed this system with dual purposes: accountability for any misconduct and prevention of unauthorized access.

My exclusive clientele demands discretion alongside social opportunity, safety without isolation.

Here, celebrities, tech billionaires, and business magnates converge, escaping the vulnerabilities of conventional nightlife.

Our private rooms provide sanctuary for those who wish to shed public personas without sacrificing security.

Jenkins identified the woman in green, the one who received my impromptu fist, as a fifty-something Silicon Valley executive. Despite her year-long membership, her file revealed a pattern: young companions during her husband's absences and recreational substances that dissolved her inhibitions.

Perhaps excessively so on the night of "Curiosity Killed the Cat."

Michael's tall, blonde disguise remains unaccounted for, though we've flagged two Silver Tier members with similar features.

The resemblance between all three becomes uncanny after staring at their profiles long enough. How did he pinpoint someone whose appearance he could appropriate so effectively?

I massage my temples, but the puzzle pieces refuse to align.

Jaxon's warnings echo in my mind, warnings I dismissed, overconfident in my security protocols. Yet the evidence mocks my hubris. After all, Michael and Robyn tracked me across continents to Australia.

I sink deeper into the sectional, wishing the fabric would consume me whole while Jenkins and Jaxon's fingers dance across screens, projecting their findings onto the screens.

Words have abandoned me since that night. My failure weighs heavily, a perfect system compromised, and my people endangered because of my oversight.

"Got you something strong," August murmurs, appearing at my side with steaming coffee.

I manage a weak smile in return. He respects my silence, understanding how I retreat inward when faced with my own mistakes.

Each night since, he's wrapped himself around me like a human shield, an anchor I never knew I desperately needed.

From that first night in their embrace, I recognized something essential. Their touch quiets the chaos in my mind, a remedy I crave now more than ever, without having to voice it.

"Recognize her?" Jenkins interrupts my thoughts, holding up a profile.

I shake my head despite a flicker of recognition. She could be any member I've chatted with during my appearances, faces blurring together now in my uncertainty.

"All clear," Peter's voice crackles through the comms, his hourly report like clockwork.

Security teams circle the perimeter three blocks deep, watching every shadow and corner.

Jaxon's called in reinforcements for this operation. I should feel grateful for this protection, but the irony isn't lost on me; the one moment I let my guard down became the moment they breached my impenetrable fortress.

I stand, abandoning the coffee for a crystal tumbler of Macallan, something that might actually quiet my thoughts.

August's expression shifts from hurt to understanding as I take a conciliatory sip from his abandoned brew before setting it aside.

With a press of my fingertip against the concealed panel in the brick wall, the stained-glass window behind the bed rotates silently outward.

Every man in the room tenses, their eyes tracking my movement. Jaxon's disapproving glare reminds me how many times he's dragged me back inside from this vulnerable perch.

I arch an eyebrow at August like a silent command he responds to instantly.

Outside, he settles into one of the wrought iron chairs. I claim his lap instead of the empty seat, melting back against his chest as his arms encircle me like a fortress.

"Tell me a story," I whisper, already feeling the static in my brain beginning to recede at the prospect of his voice.

A low chuckle rumbles from his chest.

August's voice drops to a conspiratorial whisper. "When I was nine, I convinced myself our refrigerator was a portal to another dimension."

His chest vibrates against my back as he continues. "Every night after Mum went to bed, I'd sneak downstairs with a torch and my dad's old camera. I'd open the fridge door slowly, just a crack, and snap photos of whatever might be trying to come through."

I feel his smile against my hair.

"After two weeks, Dad caught me. Instead of getting cross, he helped me develop the film." August's fingers trace idle patterns on my arm. "We spent hours analyzing blurry shots of butter and milk bottles. Dad even made-up elaborate stories about the 'creatures' we'd captured."

He chuckles softly. "I kept a journal of 'interdimensional visitors' until I was eleven. Still have it somewhere, complete with Dad's ridiculous scientific notes in the margins about 'yogurt beings' and their 'pudding civilization.'"

His voice warms with memory. "Sometimes I think he enjoyed our midnight investigations more than I did."

We both laugh. August seems to make it his mission to soothe my frantic thoughts with these silly stories from his New Zealand childhood.

Jaxon always laughs when we're in bed listening to his stories, like he's right there with us. I tap August's chest three times, then snuggle into the crook of his arm, one arm around his back and the other resting over his heart.

For a while, we just sit there, listening to the world outside.

"It won't be like this forever," he murmurs.

"Yeah, but when it's over, will nights like this disappear too?" I ask.

He presses a soft kiss to the top of my head, lost in thought. Maybe he's wondering the same thing: once the people hunting me are dead, once I return to the public eye and he heads back to rugby, will these quiet moments vanish too?

Rising to my feet, my fingers grip the rough concrete railing as I lean out, surveying the street below.

Public nights always set Jaxon's nerves on edge, especially now that we know Michael slipped through our security at the club and vanished like smoke after we spotted him.

The neon sign of Ink Link casts purple shadows across the faces of patrons, spilling onto the sidewalk.

Even on a Tuesday, this city pulses with insomnia. Dakota and Arik huddle near the entrance, cigarette smoke curling around their laughter, while Riley gestures emphatically at Cedar under the streetlight at the corner.

When I step back from the edge, I catch August watching me, his eyes darkening as they trace my silhouette.

My throat tightens. "If something happens to me..." I whisper, the words like broken glass in my mouth.

He's across the space in an instant, his warmth enveloping me before I can finish. His fingers thread through my hair, cradling my head with a gentleness that contradicts the fierce tremor in his voice.

"Don't," he breathes against my temple. "Where you go, I follow. Always."

I look up at him, my vision blurring. The raw devotion etched across his face makes my chest ache.

"August..."

I lean into his touch.

"If I'm gone..." My voice breaks. "Promise you'll find someone else to love."

August's fingers dig into the nape of my neck; his exhale is ragged against my skin.

"Don't you understand?" His voice cracks with raw desperation. "There's no replacing you."

His thumb catches a tear I didn't know had fallen. "You've carved yourself into every part of me."

His forehead presses against mine, our breath mingling. "If you're gone, I'll be nothing but the hollow space where you used to exist."

He kisses my forehead, his lips burning against my skin like a brand, a promise. When he pulls me against him, I feel my heart crack open.

The truth hits me with devastating clarity. Without him, I'd be a ghost walking through the ruins of my own life.

August fills the jagged spaces inside me that even Jaxon's love can't reach.

Between them, I exist fully. Without either, I'd shatter into something unrecognizable, something less than human.

CHAPTER 59

ELLIA

What was once my sanctuary has transformed into a prison of luxury. I ought to feel grateful for their protection, but these men, these men I adore, are suffocating me slowly.

From my perch, I observe life continuing without me. Lovers stroll hand-in-hand, tourists fumble with maps, shopkeepers exhale smoke into the afternoon air.

This stone railing has become my theater seat to a world I can no longer touch.

Hour after hour, day after day, I sit with my back against cold stone, legs dangling over the edge, dreaming of another existence. I would sacrifice anything; a vital organ, even, for this deadly game to end.

The two men who hold my heart keep me hidden away, forbidding me from events at Obsidian. Not even disguising myself with a mask and concealing my telltale white streak would convince them to risk it again.

The Curiosity Killed the Cat Masquerade at Obsidian was my one taste of freedom they permitted. I saw it in their eyes, both of them captivated by the spectacle, despite such elaborate affairs being standard fare at the club. But for them, it was extraordinary. For me, it was merely a fleeting moment of normalcy.

I was sore for days after that night, both were so sexually charged I barely had time to breathe before I was swallowing more cum or in positions I didn't think I could get into. But all good things come to an end.

My music comes in sporadic bursts now.

Some days, I can't even look at my instruments without tears threatening. I take responsibility for redirecting the plane here instead of Idaho.

How could I have known? That motorcycle ride, the only time Jaxon ever left me alone, was my desperate gasp for air, for the scent of trees, for a moment's peace in my racing mind.

"Triggered" by Chased Atlantic drifts from the loft, melting into the night air while I remain frozen, watching the world pass by.

The guys want me to heal, to move forward, but I can't seem to leave this spot.

Since eliminating our pilot, finding a replacement has become impossible. Jaxon has interviewed countless candidates, but he and Jenkins can never reach an agreement. My wings have been clipped.

"Baby girl, can I get you anything?" August's voice floats from the doorway of the floor-to-ceiling stained glass window.

He keeps his distance, afraid to approach, and I don't blame him. I'm a hollow version of myself, suffocating in plain sight.

"No," I whisper without turning.

Meeting his eyes would shatter the fragile dam holding back my tears. Isolation has become my shield, my crutch against the overwhelming tide of emotions.

From my perch, I watch the tattoo shop's revolving door of clients.

Arik and Dakota lounge on the sidewalk, cigarette smoke curling between their laughter. Lyric has barely left Dakota's side all day, hovering whenever he's between appointments.

Riley emerges periodically, phone pressed to her ear, trailing smoke signals into the afternoon.

The neighborhood has come alive with music spilling from bars that have thrown their doors open to embrace the weather.

Whenever I look down, Arik's eyes find mine. He exhales skyward, a deliberate performance I answer with a small headshake each time.

In this gilded cage, Arik has become my only connection to normalcy.

When Jaxon and August discovered our conversations, their possessiveness manifested physically, their bodies reclaiming mine with an intensity that left me breathless, reminded of who holds my heart.

If only they understood I've been theirs completely since the beginning, and no friendship could change that.

Even through my melancholy, my body still craves their touch, awakening hungry each morning.

This newfound appetite for pleasure surprises me. I never considered myself someone ruled by desire, yet with them, I surrender willingly to this sweet addiction.

August slices through my thoughts.

"It's not going to be like this forever, love. Only until..." He stops, the unfinished sentence hanging between us like a noose.

I stare at the night sky, each star a mocking pinprick of freedom I can't reach. My lungs feel concrete-filled.

"I am so tired, August." The words scrape my throat raw.

"Talk to me, baby girl. We can fix this."

I twist to face him. August's silhouette cuts against the stained glass, muscles tensed beneath his crossed arms.

His chestnut eyes, God, those eyes, drown in concern I don't deserve.

"It can't be fixed, at least not right..."

The world explodes.

CRACK!

My brain registers a gunshot before my body feels anything.

Screams erupt below. People scatter like marbles on concrete. I look down, my gray shirt blooms crimson, spreading fast, too fast. My mouth forms words my voice can't find.

"ELLI, NO!" August's scream tears through the chaos.

Another CRACK! White-hot fire rips through me. My body pitches forward, I'm falling, falling...the railing no longer beneath me.

Time stretches like taffy. I should be terrified, but there's a sick relief in the surrender. Maybe this is how I die, and I'm not scared.

My descent jerks to a violent halt. Blood rushes to my head, the world inverted.

August has my ankle, his fingers digging through the railing gap, his face contorted in a primal scream I can barely hear.

"ELLIA! HOLD ON!"

My stomach burns like I've swallowed molten metal. Blood streams between my fingers, dripping upward in this upside-down nightmare.

Was I the target? No—yes—maybe, my thoughts splinter like broken glass.

Voices below clash and collide: "DROP HER!" "WE'LL CATCH HER!" "LET GO!"

Would August drop me? Would I want him to? Death below or death above, what's the difference? The choice paralyzes me.

"REACH UP!" August roars, arm straining through the railing.

Move, Ellia! Just fucking MOVE! My body betrays me, heavy as stone.

I press my hand to my stomach; hot, wet, wrong, and force my muscles to obey. I reach up, fingertips stretching toward salvation...CRACK!

Silence swallows everything. Pain becomes a universe I inhabit alone. Voices drift like smoke: "Ellia, we got you."

The world spins, neon lights bleeding into darkness. Is that the tattoo shop sign, or am I already seeing hell?

"Get her on the table, lock the fucking door!" The voice ricochets through my skull.

Fluorescent lights stab my retinas. Blood, my blood, everywhere. Heartbeat in my ears like war drums.

I shouldn't fear death. I've mocked it before and danced with it. But now? Terror claws up my throat.

"Tiger Lily, look at me!" Arik's voice breaks through the static.

I can't. I won't.

My world fractures into shards. Faces hover, distort, multiply.

"Jaxon," I whisper, needing him like oxygen.

Where is he? My lungs won't expand. My body's betraying me.

Someone screams for space. Bodies press against me, faces blurring into a grotesque carousel of horror.

The pressure on my stomach isn't just concrete, it's a fucking building collapsing inward, crushing organs, shattering bone.

My blood sprays with each heartbeat, painting everyone crimson. One bullet? Three? Five? I can't tell where one wound ends, and another begins.

"Don't you dare fade on me!" Arik's voice cracks like thunder, his fingers digging into my wounds.

My tongue swells to fill my mouth, choking me.

"Need... Jaxon." Copper floods my throat, drowning me from within.

The door doesn't just open—it EXPLODES inward, glass splinters flying like shrapnel. Jaxon's silhouette fills the frame, feral, monstrous.

"ELLIA!" His scream rips through the room like a physical force, making everyone flinch.

Voices clash violently like accusations, defenses, curses. Someone shoves someone else. Glass shatters.

I wrench my eyelids open to see Jaxon's face, a nightmare mask of rage and terror, veins bulging at his temples.

Arik's hands disappear beneath scarlet pools that were once my flesh.

"Jaxon," I sob, blood bubbling between my lips.

My heartbeat stutters, feel it skip, falter, race to catch up.

"I know, baby, I know, I know," he chokes out, hands trembling as they grip my face too hard, fingertips bruising.

"HELP ME, GODDAMMIT!"

Hands everywhere—pulling, pushing, pressing. Someone's crying hysterically. Someone else is praying. The fluorescent lights above strobe in my vision, each pulse bringing fresh agony.

"I have to turn you," Jaxon snarls, teeth bared, something inhuman in his eyes.

Bodies pin me down like a crucifixion.

"NO!" The scream tears my throat raw.

My back arches off the table.

"NO NO NO!"

I've been here before: violated, helpless, bleeding out. Tears burn like acid.

"Jax... please..." My voice fractures into glass shards. My lungs seize, refusing air.

Arik wrenches me upward against his chest. The movement sends lightning through my nerves, and I SCREAM, a murderous, animal sound I don't recognize.

His hand crushes my skull against his shoulder, blood from my mouth soaking his shirt.

"You promised," I sob, blood and snot and tears mixing on my face. "You promised never to hurt me!"

My body convulses, betraying me. I can't feel my legs anymore.

"Please," I beg, the word disintegrating into a gurgling wail as darkness closes in from all sides.

"I know, baby," Jaxon's eyes glisten. "I'm sorry, I'm so fucking sorry. But I have to do this."

His hands move with terrible purpose.

"Three entry wounds, two exit."

He said three. I cannot escape that number, and maybe I don't want to. I knew I would die by three. This is what my guardian implied while I lay motionless on that mountain.

When Jenkins materializes like a nightmare, his face twisted with rage.

My vision collapses to pinpricks of light in a sea of darkness. The pain claws through me, a rabid animal devouring my insides.

Surrender beckons, sweet oblivion just a breath away, but something feral inside me digs its heels in, refusing to let go.

"YOU'RE FUCKING KILLING HER!" August's roar shatters the air as he lunges forward, colliding with Jaxon's shoulder. More bodies tangle above me.

Copper floods my mouth, drowning my words. I choke, spitting crimson onto my chin.

"Aug...stop...please, " Each syllable costs me, payment in agony.

"Tiger Lily, stay with me!" Arik's voice fractures against my ear as hands wrestle for position on my wounds.

Through the chaos, faces swim in and out of focus, strangers gawking, mouths agape in horror.

Then I see her, Lyric, frozen in the doorway, tears carving silent paths down her ashen cheeks, her image of me shattering before my eyes.

CHAPTER 60

AUGUST

"Jaxon! She's been shot!" I scream into the phone, my voice raw.

Pain sears through me like acid. He's not here; he's with Jenkins, revising protocols.

"I tried to save her. But that last bullet, my grip slipped."

Jaxon will never forgive me.

"What?!" His roar cracks the line. I hear him bellowing at Jenkins behind me. "I'll be right there," he growls.

"She fell, she's at the tattoo shop. Jaxon, I'm so sorry."

I pace the balcony, breath coming in ragged bursts. The call cuts off before I can add that the artists caught her.

Below, her blood pools everywhere. Christ, I let the woman I swore to protect get shot, sending her tumbling three stories. If she lives, I'm done for. Jaxon will kill me for letting her perch on that railing.

My legs won't stop moving. I should stay and hold my position. But I have to see her. She needs me. The elevator is an eternity. What if I'm too late? Tears blur my vision. My heart thunders: if she dies, I die.

The doors finally slide open. I sprint into the garage, skidding around the SUV and colliding with Jenkins. He goes flying backward.

"Fuck, man!" he yells, scrambling up.

"Follow me."

He darts through the back alley. Briggs waits at the corner, gun at the low ready, eyes scanning shadows. I shove him out of my path. He stumbles but steadies, covering me.

We sprint across the street. Jaxon's silhouette appears at the tattoo shop door. One furious glance, then he blasts the glass into shards.

"ELLIA!" he bellows, shards raining.

Inside, chaos. Ellia lies on a vinyl table, blood fountains from her abdomen, dripping in slow, crimson arcs onto the floor.

Arik presses down on the wound, his arms shaking. The world feels distant, like I'm watching from underwater.

"Jenkins! Smash every camera!" Jaxon snarls.

Tattoo artists stand frozen, gloves still on. A pair of girls in the corner weep openly, mascara black streaks running down their cheeks. Jenkins takes every phone he sees and smashes it to the ground.

"I suggest you all keep your phones away before I smash them too," he says, loud and direct, looking at everyone in the shop.

"Jaxon, please...stop," Ellia sobs, voice fractured. "You said you'd never hurt me.

My chest rips open. It's the same nightmare from the mountain, only this time she's conscious and terrified.

"Get the doctor en route," Jenkins hisses into his radio. "How long?"

A sharp pause.

"We don't have that long."

I slam into Jaxon's back with my shoulder.

"YOU'RE KILLING HER!" my voice breaks into a feral howl.

He doesn't even sway.

"August...make him stop," she chokes, each word gargled through crimson froth.

Her eyes roll wildly, seeking mine but finding nothing. Cedar's fingers dig into her scalp, desperately trying to stabilize her convulsing head. Blood pulses between Arik's fingers with each of her failing heartbeats.

Jaxon rips open his black med-kit, instruments clattering.

"Two fucking exit wounds. August, GET YOUR ASS HERE NOW!"

His eyes bore into mine, not a gaze but a weapon.

Arik's shirt is soaked through, her blood spreading across his chest like a blooming rose. Cedar's knuckles go white as he pins her thrashing wrists. Her back arches unnaturally as a scream tears from her throat; primal, animalistic.

My fault. Every one of her screams, hammer, and railroad spike through my skull.

Blood sprays with each cough, speckling the floor, my face, everywhere. It drips from her chin in thick, viscous ropes.

“Her lung,” Jenkins mutters over my shoulder. “It’s collapsed. ETA ten minutes, Jax,” he adds.

They shove overturned chairs and tables in front of the shattered door.

“Get Peters in the back, await the doc!”

My hands convulse like dying spiders, Ellia's blood saturating my shirt until it sticks to my skin like a second hide.

I slam my knees against the table, crushing her thrashing legs down as Jaxon barks commands.

Her flesh, fuck, it's turning to ice beneath my palms.

Tears scorch trails down my face, blinding me.

"Please, Arik..." Her voice gurgles through the blood filling her throat. "Make him stop. He promised."

Her sobbing fractures into raw animal sounds.

"Tell me about the lilies," Arik whispers, voice cracking. "The purple ones."

His trembling fingers smear crimson across her forehead as he pushes matted hair from her face.

"They..." A violent spasm wracks her body. "Black."

Arik's face twists like he's been gutted. What the fuck about lilies?

Jaxon plunges gauze into the crater in her back. Ellia's scream—a sound that will haunt my nightmares forever—rips through the room, shattering something fundamental inside me.

On the mountain, she was at least unconscious. Now she's drowning in her own blood, fighting with diminishing strength against the inevitable.

The floor beneath us has become a lake of red. I'm watching her die in real time.

“One more time,” Jaxon whispers, voice eerily calm.

Her mouth gapes like a drowning victim. Nothing comes out.

Then, "Don't," she sobs, the word tearing from her throat. "Don't."

Ellia convulses violently, spine arching away from his grip as if electrocuted.

"Please," she chokes, arterial blood spraying with each syllable, hot droplets peppering my face.

My stomach heaves. Every scream flays me alive. Jaxon's hands disappear into her wounds, crimson to the wrists.

If he doesn't stop this hemorrhage in seconds, she dies. My tears burn like acid, vision blurring as I struggle not to shatter along with her.

She goes limp without warning. Her head lolls obscenely, neck muscles surrendering.

"FUCK!" Someone says behind me.

"Cedar, August, LET GO NOW! Lay her flat!" Jaxon's voice cracks like a whip.

He staggers back, arms dripping scarlet ropes onto the floor. I scramble away, choking on bile, then lunge to her right side.

Arik's knuckles go bone-white as he bears down on the wounds, blood still pulsing between his fingers with each weakening heartbeat.

"Baby, I'm so sorry," I rasp, cradling her face between trembling hands.

Her skin is death-cold, her matted hair soaked through. The white streak I once traced with my fingertips now glistens dark red in the harsh light.

I'll die before I forgive myself for letting her slip.

"Look at me," I beg as her eyelids flutter weakly, pupils blown wide with shock.

Her head drops sideways like a broken doll's. Her eyelids struggle to rise.

"It was... three," she gasps, each word bubbling through the blood filling her lungs.

Her voice is barely audible yet somehow deafening, slicing through my soul.

"Thank you for being here this time."

Jaxon lunges like a predator, fists knotting in my shirt. My spine cracks against the wall, head whip lashing, his face, contorted, and feral, fills my vision.

Blood vessels explode across the whites of his eyes like crimson lightning as he slams me against the wall again.

"WHAT. THE. FUCK. HAPPENED?" Each word hits like a sledgehammer, his spittle spraying my face, burning where it lands on my raw skin.

"She was." My windpipe crushes inward. I can't breathe.

Five feet away, Ellia's blood hits the floor in fat, rhythmic drops. Tick. Tick. TICK. Each one a goddamn countdown.

"Railing, when the shots..." Something tears at my throat. "I HAD HER LEG, JAXON! I SWEAR TO CHRIST I HAD HER!"

My voice shatters.

"But that last bullet," My fingers convulse, still feeling her ankle sliding through them like smoke. "I'm sorry."

"SORRY?" He slams me again, my skull bouncing off drywall. "SORRY WON'T STOP HER FROM FUCKING BLEEDING OUT!"

His forearm crushes my windpipe. Black spots dance at the edges of my vision.

Jenkins materializes, yanking Jaxon backward.

"Not here." His voice cuts like steel as he jerks his chin toward the terrified onlookers pressing themselves against the walls. "Too many civilians. Too many phones."

Jenkins grips Jaxon's shoulders, but Jaxon shakes him off like a rabid animal.

The veins in his neck bulge as he stalks the perimeter of the room, his boots leaving bloody footprints on the linoleum.

The onlookers press themselves against the walls, eyes wide with terror.

Arik's knuckles turn white around Ellia's limp fingers.

Cedar hovers at her head, whispering desperately into her ear, his lips almost touching her blood-spattered skin.

"Look, man," Cedar's voice cracks as he straightens, Ellia's blood soaking his shirt front like a butcher's apron. "Arik and Dakota were smoking when the shots rang. They caught her when the last bullet tore through her."

Jaxon crosses the space in two violent strides; his face contorted with rage.

"Where did the shots come from? " Each word drips with venom.

Cedar's whole body trembles, Jaxon's hot breath on his face.

"Over there." His shaking finger points down the street. "Left of us. Right of Ellia's loft."

"I'm on it." Jenkins bolts through the back door, gun already drawn.

I crash to my knees beside Ellia, bone cracking against linoleum. Her moans, those animal sounds that kept her alive, have withered to whispers.

Each breath tears through her punctured lung with a wet, guttural rattle that freezes my blood. Crimson froth bubbles at the corner of her mouth, overflowing in a thin scarlet ribbon down her jaw.

"I'm so tired," she exhales, the sound like sandpaper scraping bone. "I was so alone on the mount..."

I lean in, ear hovering above her blood-flecked lips, waiting for another breath, my heart jackhammering against my ribs so violently I taste copper. But nothing comes.

Arik's tears splash onto their joined hands; hot, useless things. Her last words evaporate like mist, the silence that follows more deafening than any scream.

"Jaxon!" My voice breaks. "She isn't breathing." The words come out strangled, unrecognizable.

"FUCK!" His roar fills the room as he lunges forward, pressing his fingers against her throat. "Where is the FUCKING doctor? She needs blood!"

Jaxon starts CPR. "No, you broke her rib last time!" I grab his wrist, remembering the sickening snap, the way her body had jerked like a marionette.

"The sound..." I begin pacing.

His eyes lock on mine, feral and desperate.

"Would you rather she fucking die?"

The question slams into me like a physical blow. I back away, defeated.

"Docs here!" Peters' shouts from the rear hallway.

Jaxon snatches her limp body off the table, her head snapping back like a broken doll's as he bolts through the back door.

Doc Kirkland's waiting van floods the alley with harsh fluorescent light, gurney already deployed.

Cedar and Arik surge forward behind me, but I whirl on them, blood-slick hands shoving their chests.

"Control those fucking people!" I snarl, teeth bared.

"Every name, every address. Anyone breathes a WORD about this..." My voice drops to something feral, unrecognizable.

I don't wait for an answer, already spinning back toward where Ellia lies motionless, her skin gray-blue under the merciless lights as Doc rams a tube down her throat, in her arms, and Jaxon hammers her chest with desperate, violent compressions.

After an eternity of death-silence, Ellia's chest spasms; a single, ragged gasp that tears through her throat like barbed wire. Her eyes remain sealed shut, face still death-mask pale.

"She's crashing! Move or lose her!" Doc barks, already slamming equipment into the van.

Jaxon seizes my shoulder, fingers digging deep enough to bruise bone, and hurls me inside beside her still form.

"Don't you fucking let her slip away again," he hisses, face inches from mine, pupils contracted to pinpoints. "The team and I are going hunting."

He slams the door with such force that the entire van rocks on its chassis, metal screaming against metal like a wounded thing. Through the window, I watch him stalk back toward the tattoo shop, shoulders hunched, spine curved like something prehistoric and vengeful.

His hand reaches for the gun at his hip, fingers steady with a murderous hunger that promises to paint these streets crimson before dawn breaks.

I turn my attention back to Ellia, her fingers like frozen twigs between mine. The woman I promised to protect. The woman whose blood is cooling on my skin.

Doc's face is carved from granite, eyes hollow with the knowledge he won't voice. Her chest barely moves. Each breath is a battle she's losing as we begin moving.

My throat closes, something feral and wounded clawing up from my chest.

I press her limp hand against my stubbled cheek, tasting salt and copper as I whisper, "Fight, baby. Please. I can't..." My voice shatters. "I can't exist without you."

THE SCATTERED SOULS TRILOGY

Book One: Die Alive

Book Two: Kill to Breathe

Book Three: Scars of Our Souls

www.ingramcontent.com/pod-product-compliance
Lightning Source LLC
LaVergne TN
LVHW100505110826
845146LV00002B/524

* 9 7 9 8 9 0 4 1 7 7 9 6 6 *